THE WOMAN IN THE CASTELLO

"Like Jess Walters's *Beautiful Ruins*, the glamour and heady indulgence of the era take center stage in this captivating, multilayered story that will keep you guessing to the end."
—Susan Wiggs, # 1 *New York Times* bestselling author

KELSEY JAMES

More praise for *The Woman in the Castello*!

"An impromptu movie set in a medieval castle in 1960s Italy
provides a fascinating backdrop for this fresh Gothic tale
filled with mystery, family secrets, and unexpected romance."
—Lorena Hughes, author of *The Spanish Daughter*

"You'll get lost in the pages of this lush, entertaining story
as you follow aspiring actress Silvia Whitford through the
dark towers and crumbling staircases of a remote Italian castle,
where she uncovers twists and turns around every corner,
including shocking family secrets you'll never see coming."
—Ellen Marie Wiseman, *New York Times* bestselling author

"*The Woman in the Castello* has it all—mystery, romance,
and an enchanting cast of characters with a plucky heroine
at its heart. Against the richly drawn backdrop of postwar
Italy, in a castle brimming with secrets, Kelsey James
explores the enduring and sometimes destructive power of
love, family, and ambition. A page-turner from start to
finish, *The Woman in the Castello* is a marvelous debut!"
—Amanda Skenandore, author of *The Nurse's Secret*

"A young actress desperate for stardom agrees to film a horror
movie in her aunt's crumbling Italian castle. Then the aunt
disappears. What secrets lurk in her past—and in the mysterious
lake behind the castle? *The Woman in the Castello* is a
thoroughly original blend of mystery, family drama, and sultry
romance, all unfolding in the fast-paced world of a Swinging
Sixties movie set. A riveting debut from author Kelsey James!"
—Elizabeth Blackwell, bestselling author of *Red Mistress*

THE WOMAN IN THE CASTELLO

KELSEY JAMES

JOHN SCOGNAMIGLIO BOOKS
Kensington Publishing Corp.
www.kensingtonbooks.com

JOHN SCOGNAMIGLIO BOOKS are published by

Kensington Publishing Corp.
119 West 40th Street
New York, NY 10018

All Kensington titles, imprints, and distributed lines are available at special quantity discounts for bulk purchases for sales promotion, premiums, fund-raising, and educational or institutional use.

Special book excerpts or customized printings can also be created to fit specific needs. For details, write or phone the office of the Kensington Sales Manager: Kensington Publishing Corp., 119 West 40th Street, New York, NY 10018. Attn. Sales Department. Phone: 1-800-221-2647.

The JS and John Scognamiglio Books logo is a trademark of Kensington Publishing Corp.

ISBN: 978-1-4967-4291-9

ISBN: 978-1-4967-4292-6 (ebook)

First Kensington Trade Paperback Edition: August 2023

10 9 8 7 6 5 4 3 2 1

Printed in the United States of America

To my parents, who always put us first

THE
WOMAN
IN THE
CASTELLO

CHAPTER 1

By the time I reached Cinecittà Studios, I was footsore and dry-throated. I squeezed my purse tightly between my fingers, keenly aware that the small wad of wrinkled lira notes it contained was the very last money I had in the world. But I'd made it here, finally. Cinecittà beckoned me cheerfully, its stucco exterior the color of Roman sunshine, the chrome letters of its name glinting.

A uniformed guard gave me general directions of where to go, and I stepped through the open gate with my heart skipping. The lot was more peaceful than I expected, with green grass and tall umbrella pines dotting the grounds. It was a relief, after the crowded bus ride alongside white-socked children and kerchiefed Italian grandmothers and a blotchy-faced man who'd made sucking noises at me. I got the tingling sensation I always got in proximity to greatness—just over there was the famous Stage 5, where *Cleopatra* had filmed a few years ago with Elizabeth Taylor and Richard Burton.

Eventually I found the building where I'd be filming *Five Days in Roma*. Only four lines, but plenty of background scenes, too, and the studio had flown me here all the way from Los Angeles and put me up in a hotel. It was a third-class establishment, with a shared bathroom where you had to pull a cord to activate the hot water, but even so. My mother and Lulu—short for Lucy, but we almost always called her Lulu—were there now, not that the studio needed to know that. I pictured them when

I'd left that morning, still curled up together in the bed we all shared, a half-smile on Lulu's sweet little face and her eyelashes curling against her cheeks.

I'd received instructions to report to the director's office today, even though production wasn't officially starting for a few more days. Perhaps Roger Albertson wanted to give me a little pep talk before we began. I walked through the antiseptic hallway lined with offices and knocked on his door, smoothing the skirt of my white cotton dress, scoop-necked, belted, and patterned with bouquets of flowers. It was the best dress I owned and had cost fifteen dollars at Hudson's, an extravagance I couldn't afford, but my mother had insisted, determined I should look the part of the blossoming Hollywood starlet. It was a little more prim and feminine than my usual style—I wasn't big on dainty florals, preferring a younger mod look—but I couldn't deny her anything, not in her condition.

"Come in."

The man sitting behind the desk wasn't Mr. Albertson. He looked like another one of the actors. He was blond and sun-beaten and square-jawed, with the sort of roguish good looks that would make him perfect to cast in one of the Westerns that were so popular right now. I could easily picture him as the gunslinging cowboy riding a horse.

"I'm looking for Mr. Albertson?" I made my voice soft and girlish, my consonants feathery light, the way the casting directors seemed to like. It hadn't quite become a habit yet, and I still forgot to do it sometimes.

"Yes. He's gone already, I'm afraid. Slunk off like a coward." The man who wasn't Mr. Albertson lit a cigarette and came around to lean back against the front of the desk. He acted as if the office were his, and I frowned.

"Do you know when he'll be back?" My consonants hardened, and my voice deepened. There was no point pretending for a stranger, and an impertinent one at that.

"Oh, that's much better. You shouldn't try to be a Marilyn. You have more of a Natalie Wood thing going on." I stared at him blankly before I realized he was talking about my voice.

And then I winced at the reference; I'd adored Marilyn and been devastated by her death. His rudeness shocked me into silence. "One of the actresses, I suppose?"

"Silvia Whitford. I'm playing the secretary."

"You better sit down." He gestured toward a chair. I considered refusing him, but he spoke with such authority that it occurred to me he might actually be in possession of some, so I sat. I'd stay only as long as it took to learn who the hell he was and what had happened to Mr. Albertson. He let out a billow of smoke and crossed his feet at the ankles. "I won't beat around the bush. The picture's over. The producer and his investors, well, had a falling out, I suppose. There's not enough money left to shoot a single foot of film."

I swallowed around something sharp that seemed to have stuck in my windpipe. I tightened my grasp around my ivory patent leather purse. It couldn't be true. Perhaps this was an elaborate joke, a prank to play on the new arrivals. After all, I didn't know this man from Adam.

"Who are you?"

"Oh, right. Sorry. Paul Rudderman. Assistant director. Or I was supposed to be, at any rate."

My throat constricted further, and my head grew light. It was a hot July day, but the air-conditioning in the room didn't seem to be working, and a fan rattled uselessly in the corner. My thighs stuck to the vinyl, and a bead of sweat trickled down my neck. I thought I might faint, but I didn't want to do it in front of him.

"If you phone Sam, he can get your return airfare sorted out for you. Your room is booked through the end of the week." He bumped his cigarette against an ashtray and recrossed his ankles. His insouciance infuriated me. He'd just delivered the most devastating news imaginable—he couldn't begin to fathom how devastating. "That's all. You can send in the next one, if someone else is lurking out there."

I didn't move. I couldn't; my muscles had atrophied in the stuffy little office. My stomach had bottomed out after growing heavy with fear.

"What about money? I was promised a hundred dollars a week." It wasn't a fortune, but it was the best paycheck I'd had in a while and had felt like a windfall, given they had also promised to pay for my room. Three weeks of shooting, they'd said.

"Yes, well. Not if there's no film, I'm afraid. You can check your contract."

And suddenly it was all too much. I burst into tears. Through my sobs, I could see that Mr. Rudderman had grown positively alarmed. His rough-and-ready exterior softened a touch.

"Hey there, it's not as bad as all that. You'll find work on another picture. It's what I'm going to try to do. We're in the same boat, you know."

I hiccupped into my hands. "No, you don't understand. I needed that money." It was more honest than I'd intended, but it was the truth. I was near to broke. My mother wanted to be buried in Italy, where she'd grown up, and had spent the last of her savings on airline tickets for herself and Lucy. She'd sold her little house in San Diego years ago so she could be with me in Los Angeles, and our apartment had been a month-to-month rental. We'd packed everything we needed into suitcases, and we weren't planning to go back. This picture had seemed like a miracle; my big break. And in Rome, with free accommodations for three weeks. It would have been enough to get us settled here and get me on my feet.

Now I had until the end of the week before we were out on the streets. I pictured my darling Lulu, probably at the breakfast table right now, singing half-pronounced nursery rhymes for her *nonna* and littering the floor with crumbs.

Mr. Rudderman looked sorry for me, which only made me angrier. "Hey, if I hear of anything, I'll keep you in mind. Miss Whitman, right?"

"No. Silvia Whitford." My words were acid. I finally found my strength and got to my feet. "No wonder this lousy picture is over, when you couldn't even bother to learn the names of the cast. I suppose you figured since you were firing everyone, you didn't need to remember who any of us *are*. That we're real people. That would have been too much courtesy to expect."

My face grew hot, and I turned to go.

"Hey, hey, hey. I'm sorry, all right? This isn't my fault."

I walked out of the office and slammed the door. Then I put my face in my hands and cried some more, and wondered how I'd ever be able to tell my mother the news.

I finally made my way back to the hotel, after another bumpy, crowded bus ride. I was nauseated at the end of it, but I didn't know whether that was due to the journey or my anxiety. I found my mother and Lulu playing with her toy cars in the hotel lobby, while the lone receptionist snoozed behind the counter. The terrazzo floor wasn't the cleanest, and I pursed my lips. But poor Lucy needed to play somewhere. My mother was crouched next to her and laughing. She was having one of her good days. They were still mostly good days.

"Mommy!" Lulu ran over and hugged my legs. I bent down and kissed the top of her silky dark curls, breathing in her sweet toddler scent.

"Back already?" my mother asked. I adored my mother, but we were opposites in every way—fire and ice, my father had called us. Where I could never hide what I was feeling, my mother was always calm and collected. She placed great importance on her ability to *fare la bella figura*—litcrally, to make a good figure, but really meaning to put up a good front and make a good impression.

"Yes. Just a quick check-in before we start." I didn't like lying. But I couldn't tell her, not yet. Not until I had a plan. I refused to put this weight on her shoulders, on top of everything else.

"I was thinking of taking Lucy to the park."

I knelt to hug Lulu properly, and she wrapped her chubby little arms around my neck. And then yanked on one of my earrings.

"No, no, sweet pea. We don't yank." I looked toward my mother. "Oh, let's. She needs to run around."

And so we toddled over to the Villa Borghese gardens, Lulu between us holding each of our hands and punctuating our journey by pointing out the cars and naming their colors, with mixed accuracy. The gardens were only a few blocks, really, but with Lulu, we went nowhere quickly.

When we finally reached the rolling green lawns and cypress trees, some of the tension left my body. I found Rome's frenetic pace exciting, the Vespas and the horns blaring and the shouted Italian, but it was very different than Los Angeles, with its low-slung sprawl and laid-back California vibe. The humiliation of the morning and the terror about the future dissipated the tiniest fraction. I saw it in my mother's face, too, the worry creases in her forehead smoothing a little. My mother was pale and fair, with clear blue eyes—again, the opposite of me, with my dark hair and big brown eyes—although there was similarity in the shape of our faces, our high cheekbones and classic Roman noses. My lips were fuller than hers, and I had straight hair with flipped ends that I teased into a bouffant, whereas hers was almost always up. I was supposed to favor an aunt I'd never met, who still lived in Italy, and I balanced the topic on the tip of my tongue.

"Did you plan to see your sister?"

My mother gasped. Her sister was a taboo topic, and only my current desperation had made me broach it. "No. Why would you ask this?"

They had had some kind of falling out during the war and never spoken again after my mother moved to America. My father had been one of the soldiers who helped drive the Germans out of Italy, and somehow found time to fall in love with and marry my mother when they marched through. I'd been conceived during their whirlwind romance, and after the war, my mother and I had journeyed to join him in California. I'd always found it terribly romantic.

Lulu tugged her hand out of mine and darted across the grass to investigate a squirrel, then watched in awe as it scampered up a tree. "Squirrel! Squirrel, Mommy!"

"Yes, darling. The squirrel is in the tree now."

I adjusted my sunglasses. I couldn't tell my mother the real reason. That when she was gone, it would just be me and Lulu, and I was scared. One of my neighbors in our Los Angeles apartment building was a single mother, and I'd seen the social workers arrive unexpectedly to harass her, and I could still hear her screams the morning they took her sweet baby away. I didn't know if I'd be able to provide for Lulu by myself. I needed help. I swallowed around that sharp thing in my throat again. "I just thought I'd like to meet her. We are here in Italy, after all."

"She won't give you any money for Lucy. I know that's what you're thinking. Why don't you ask her father?"

Now it was my turn to be shocked. Lulu's father didn't know she existed, and I'd make sure he never would. He was a struggling musician whom I'd moved in with impulsively, whose moods ricocheted between charming and cruel. He'd hit me when he'd been drinking, more than once, his dry, guitar-player's hands lean and calloused. Aside from Lulu, my improved skills with makeup were the only thing of value I took away from that relationship.

"How dare you suggest such a thing." I studied my mother, who retied her chic white-and-blue floral headscarf around her chin and smirked at me. She favored ladylike swing dresses that accentuated her wasp waist, one feature we both shared. I was partial to shift dresses with contrasting colors, especially black and white, big button accents, and big sunglasses. Soon, we might have to sell off our nicest items. The headscarf was real silk, and I wondered what price it might fetch.

"You see? Now you understand. Some people we cut out of our lives for a reason, Silvia. We won't speak any more about this."

I nodded, but it was another lie. Because I'd seen the letter my mother received from Italy three months ago, the one she'd tried to keep hidden. She'd saved it, packing it in her worn leather suitcase for our journey, the envelope creased and the ink smeared. I'd found it when going through her things looking for something of Lulu's, and I hadn't read it—I wouldn't invade her privacy so deliberately—but I had noted the return address.

Gabriella Conti, Castello del Lago. I'd looked on a map and found that it wasn't so far from Rome: a little town about forty miles outside of the city.

I didn't want to go against my mother's wishes, but just knowing there was another person in the world who might help, whatever my mother said, made our circumstances slightly more bearable. Even the name of the town sounded alluring, and it seemed to beckon me.

If my mother wouldn't go see her sister, perhaps I would.

CHAPTER 2

On what would have been the first day of the movie's production, I kissed my mother's sallow cheek and squeezed Lulu before leaving our charmingly worn hotel room, with its wrought-iron bed and old wooden armoire and big windows facing the street. My mother wished me good luck as I left, and the bitterness of the lie nearly made me confess. Instead, I smiled at her and reminded her I'd probably be back quite late.

Then I headed to the nearby Via Veneto, the most fashionable street in Rome, its sidewalk crammed with cafés where Americans smoked and laughed and drank in the open air. I passed the Excelsior, the city's best hotel, and caught a blast of air-conditioning and expensive scent as a rich American woman pushed through the elegant revolving door. The movie stars sometimes stayed here when they came to town to film, and I'd glimpsed someone last night, although I couldn't have said who. All I'd really seen was the insect-like swarm of aggressive photographers they called *paparazzi* waiting outside for her, camera bulbs flashing in the dark.

I had imagined they might be waiting for me, someday. But I hadn't come here to daydream. Instead, I entered one of the cafés and asked a harried, skinny male waiter in my sweetest Italian if I could speak to the manager. Luckily, I spoke fluent Italian, thanks to my mother.

I'd spent the last few days pursuing acting and modeling opportunities, to no avail. So now it was time for plan B. I needed money, and I wasn't above waiting tables to get it. I'd waited plenty of tables in Los Angeles. When I'd been heavily pregnant with Lulu, I'd had to trade my modeling work for a steady waitressing job, and I'd never forget my swollen ankles at the end of the day, the body-deep exhaustion that made me fall asleep the moment my head hit the pillow.

"*Mi scusi*," I tried again, but the man just shrugged me off and continued serving customers, delivering a tray of Pellegrinos and caffè Americanos to a large and boisterous group. At another table, an Italian man read a newspaper attached to a wooden pole and asked the waiter to bring him stamps.

"You look like you could use help," I offered as the waiter passed. "I'm looking for a job."

He just laughed derisively. "There are no jobs here, little girl."

I bristled. I was twenty, but looked older; I was hardly a little girl. My throat constricted. It was a popular café, maybe too popular. I hadn't necessarily expected to find an opening on my first try, but I thought I'd at least get a nicer rejection.

"I speak perfect English. Like an American."

The waiter kept walking into the interior of the café and ignored me.

I sighed and decided to try the café next door. Surely with so many American customers jamming themselves elbow to elbow, filling up the ashtrays and tipping more than was expected, someone would find use for another pair of hands.

Maybe hiding I was an American was a mistake. I'd been told the Italians were wild for our magazines and our movies; perhaps being an American model would carry some weight. I'd even seen a peeling old poster on a brick wall of John F. Kennedy, the sad sight of his ripped paper cheek giving me a little pang of sadness at the memory of his assassination two years before. Our country's first Catholic president had been very popular among the Italians, according to my guidebook.

I tried several more spots on the Via Veneto and made it clear, this time, that I was an American expat, but that went over even worse. Maybe it had been foolish to think I could just waltz in

and get a job. It had always worked back home; managers usually liked a pretty face. I couldn't think about what would happen if I failed. Being penniless in a strange city was too awful
to imagine.

I'd probably aimed too high, going to the Via Veneto. I moved
on to the side streets, consulting the little map in my purse as I
made my way toward the Piazza del Popolo, and tried all kinds
of places—cafés, boutiques, a grocery store. I paused out on
the sidewalk after my twentieth inquiry, my mouth tasting of
failure and my cotton dress damp with sweat. Cars and Vespas
zoomed by, and two nuns passed around me as if I were a stone
in their path. Just beyond them was a young Italian woman
wearing a miniskirt with a daring hemline and red lipstick; the
contrast of her against the nuns distracted me a little from my
concerns. If I'd been in a better mood, it might have made me
smile. Rome seemed to be like that, the modern and the ancient,
the carnal and the godly all mashed up together.

By the time I reached the Piazza del Popolo, I was hot, and
tired, and depressed. There was a large church on one side of the
square, its facade weathered and pockmarked travertine, a set
of grand shallow steps leading to its door. Despite my worries,
I marveled at it for a moment. Rome wore its history carelessly,
its ancient churches and Roman temples and fountains as com-
monplace as the cats who wandered them. But I was astonished
by it all. There was nothing even close to this old in Los Angeles, where everyone seemed obsessed only with what was new.
I hadn't been inside a church in about a year, and the idea of its
cool dark interior tempted me to enter.

I sat in one of the pews for a while, resting my feet, gazing
reverently at the vaulted ceilings and stone pillars. I offered up a
quick prayer for guidance, inspired by the setting and guessing
it couldn't hurt, even if I was hardly the most attentive Catholic.

After I'd regained some energy, I took a moment to walk
around the church, and in one of the side chapels, a couple of
tourists were pointing at the paintings and consulting a guidebook. I peeked and was struck by the dark moodiness of them,

the dramatic lighting of the figures. In one, a man was about to be crucified. Not Jesus—Saint Peter, maybe. The startling violence of the scene sent a chill down my spine.

I emerged again into the bright sunshine, unsure what to do next. I felt the full force of my foreignness, and ignorance, and wished my mother still had friends here who could help us.

I heaved a breath. She may not have friends, but she did have a relative. Maybe the church had given me some clarity after all, because I could see only one path left open to me. It would mean another long walk, since I didn't want to waste any money on the tram, but it was still morning. I had time.

My path to the railroad station took me past the Trevi Fountain, and I paused in awe of its baroque beauty, admiring the grotto-like rock formations and cascading water. A group of laughing young girls sat on its stone edge, eating gelato, letting it melt onto their fingers, and I envied them. It was a hot day, and my dress stuck to my skin. Tourists milled about, and for a brief moment I almost felt like one of them. This was a sight I'd longed to see: the very water Anita Ekberg had waded into wearing her busty evening dress in *La Dolce Vita,* a moment that had made her an international icon. The right movie, and the right scene, could do that for you, and it made this spot magic for me. I watched as a happy couple tossed coins over their shoulders, making wishes, and the illusion shattered. I had a lot I'd wish for, but I couldn't spare the money.

I kept walking.

The local side streets interested me, too. Electrical wires overhead crisscrossed between weather-worn stone buildings, and I wrinkled my nose as I passed a fish stand, where silvery bellies flashed in the sun. Another vendor hawked luscious piles of shiny eggplants, bright-red tomatoes, and velvety apricots, which were carefully assessed by a stout matron in sensible square-heeled shoes. I jumped out of the way as a man on a Vespa sped through the alley, heedless of the foot traffic.

The railroad station was a stark contrast to the rest of Rome: a modernist glass and concrete structure. I didn't like to go behind my mother's back, and guilt sliced into me. But I didn't see what choice I had. I pressed through the crowds, overwhelmed and a little lost, until I located a ticket counter. A helpful agent explained the timetables to me and booked me a second-class ticket on the local train to Castello del Lago. He told me conversationally that the town had a castle, one of a number in the region that had become popular filming locations for *gialli*, a type of Italian thriller.

I headed toward the track he'd pointed out and tucked away the tidbit as interesting. Maybe I could ask around up there to try and find some work. Mostly I was preoccupied with the ticket price: I did the lira conversion in my head and figured out that the roundtrip fare had cost me less than two dollars. Even two dollars was precious now, when every cent counted. After the hotel reservation ended, we only had enough money for a few nights at a hostel.

But this was a chance I had to take.

The crowded train journey took about an hour, and then I found myself slightly disoriented on a lonely platform without a station house. I walked toward the road and considered my options: the steep downward slope to a strange green-blue lake, perfectly round and still, at the bottom of a bowl of trees. Or up to a little medieval town crested by the castle. The uphill road forked toward the surrounding countryside, and a lonesome donkey made the return journey, its saddlebags stuffed with wilting vegetables. It must have known where to go, since no one attended it. It looked hot, and flicked its tail.

I followed it toward the town, and soon my calf muscles burned from the steep climb. Thankfully my shoes were flat, but the Mary Jane straps dug into my skin.

The moment I entered the town itself, the air seemed to shift, growing weightier and more silent. Even the clacking of my soles on the cobblestones grew muffled. It was more humid than in Rome, and I could almost taste the warm moisture, tinged with earth and must. The contrast to the city was jarring.

I lost track of the donkey, who certainly knew its way better than I did. There hadn't been a street address on the envelope, just the name of the town, but I was sure that a local resident could help direct me. In a tiny community like this, someone was sure to know who my aunt was and exactly where she lived. So I crept through the warren of narrow streets and tried to shake off my growing sense of claustrophobia. My mother called these little alleys *vicoli,* and there's no perfect English translation for the word, for the skinny, twisting slices of cobblestone path, the arches above keeping the walls from leaning in and collapsing into one another. Most tourists would find them charming, but the deeper into the town I climbed, the more my skin prickled from the eerie quiet. The sky was gray, threatening a summer thunderstorm, and little light filtered into the maze. The yellow lanterns hanging by the doorways blazed even in the middle of the day.

At last one of the *vicoli* deposited me into a small piazza, with an empty fountain at its center and a tiny café. The fountain had green mold along its bottom, and some of the stone was cracked and falling away. Three old men sat outside at the only table, listening to a soccer match on the radio and slapping down well-worn cards. The wine they were drinking stained their lips red. I approached tentatively, and the cards stopped thwacking as all of the men turned to stare at me. I smiled wanly.

"Excuse me, do any of you know where I could find Gabriella Conti?" I asked in Italian. Now their surprise—already great from seeing a stranger—increased. Bushy eyebrows shot into foreheads, and one man let the cigarette dangling from his lip drop onto the table. Then they broke into uncomfortable laughter.

"You don't want to see her, sweetheart," one man said. He tipped the remainder of a carafe of wine into his cup and swallowed it thirstily.

"She doesn't like visitors. She'll toss you out on your rump."

"Remember what happened to Matteo?" At this, all three men laughed more genuinely.

I frowned, my determination wavering. *Some people we cut out of our lives for a reason,* my mother had said. I hadn't paid her words much heed; my desperation on behalf of Lulu had made them easy to ignore. Now I wished I'd pressed my mother for more information.

Not that she'd have given it.

"Please. Can you provide directions?"

One of the men shrugged and pointed a crooked finger toward the top of the hill. "Not hard to find. She lives in the castle."

I opened my mouth in astonishment and shifted my gaze upward. When I'd discovered she lived in the town of Castello del Lago, it never occurred to me that she might reside in the actual castle it was named for. Perhaps they were only teasing me, and would laugh when I climbed all the way up there only to find sheep grazing beside a ruin of stone. But the man's voice contained no trace of hidden amusement. I couldn't see the castle well from the piazza, just a glimpse of crenellated towers. I didn't know anyone still lived in castles: I suppose I'd assumed that they were all museums or religious institutions or something of that sort. That my aunt lived in one seemed impossible, but hope flared up inside of me. If it were true, surely she'd be able to help us.

I nodded at the men and continued my climb. The *vicoli* beyond the square seemed as if they'd been carved into the rock of the hillside, and the buildings crouched gloomily over them. My legs grew sore as I ascended the hundreds of steep stone steps. They explained the donkey: even Vespas would be useless here, and a car was entirely out of the question. Here and there, laundry lines crisscrossing above reminded me that real people lived here, but I spotted so few faces flashing in the windows that it was hard to believe. It almost seemed like they were hiding from me.

I did see one woman appear suddenly in the mouth of a *vicolo*, as if she'd materialized out of the sunless air, and the sight of her startled me so much, I paused to stare at her. She wore a black dress down to the ground, and I wondered if she was still mourning someone from the war. I'd seen bullet holes scarring some of the buildings and got the sense that while Rome had moved on, Castello del Lago was stuck in another time. She shouted something unintelligible at me, her mouth gummy.

Finally, I climbed the last set of stairs and ended up in another square, this one empty of people and with only one tiny *bar-tabacchi,* its door firmly shut. I was thoroughly sick of the cobblestones at this point, uneven under my feet, leaving me off balance. The shutters on the buildings here were all closed tight. There were a few deserted wooden stalls from a long-over vegetable market, their counters strewn with leftover shriveled carrots and zucchini, buzzing with flies.

On the opposite side of the square was a giant stone archway, and I passed through it onto a straight cobblestone path lined with cypress trees that led to the castle. It was slightly cooler above the town, and the trees shivered in a soft wind.

During my climb, I'd imagined a number of ways my aunt might react to my arrival, but now that I'd reached the castle walls, a new problem presented itself: how to get inside. In front of me, a bridge stretched across a ravine, and the plunging elevation as I glanced down the sides made me dizzy. The castle in front of me was imposing, featuring four large round towers, one choked with ivy, and sand-colored stone walls patched up in places with red brick. Most of the windows were small and narrow, with rivulets of green algae staining the rock beneath them.

I crept forward tentatively, and on the other side of the bridge found that a studded metal door hung open, almost as if my aunt had been expecting me. I stepped through into a large stone courtyard populated by no fewer than six scraggly, feral cats. On one wall was a fountain of a lion, ugly mouth gawping, the marble blackened with age, and a gray striped kitten curled in its empty basin. Nearby, an ancient-looking red porphyry column lay on its side, cracked across the middle. On the farthest wall was a two-story arched colonnade, with a wide set of stairs leading to one of the four towers and what I guessed was the front door.

I climbed to the top—God, I longed to sit down—and my nerves kicked in, my heart galumphing in my chest as I stretched out a hand to knock.

I never got the chance. A fortysomething woman wearing

a burgundy velvet housecoat opened the door and exhaled a stream of cigarette smoke into my face.

"Are you with the studio?" she demanded, in Italian.

I coughed and wiped a watering eye. "Excuse me?"

"The movie studio." As if this explained everything.

"Um, no." I took a deep breath. It was now or never. "I'm Silvia Whitford. Are you Gabriella Conti?"

The woman slowly removed the cigarette from her mouth and widened her dark brown eyes. I knew it was her, without her having to say a word, because those eyes and those cheekbones and that mouth were all twins of my own. "*Dio santo.* You better come inside."

CHAPTER 3

The inside of the castle wasn't as gloomy as I expected. It was undeniably dilapidated, but it was a gorgeous sort of decay, the look of riches turning to ruins but making no particular hurry about it. I took in the worn terra-cotta floors, plaster walls, and intricately painted wood-beam ceilings silently as my aunt narrated it all.

I was relieved my aunt had let me inside. I hadn't been entirely sure she would. But she seemed extremely interested in me, and I reveled in the intensity of her attention. She had the sort of presence one rarely encounters and always remembers— that star quality that makes someone the center of attention in any room. I was mesmerized by her. Even in a housecoat, she exuded refinement, and her face had an arresting quality that mine lacked. She wore heavy makeup, and her dramatically arched black-penciled eyebrows made her face even more expressive.

"This is the gallery. Those paintings are from the Renaissance, but they're ruined, now," she said, waving her cigarette toward a frieze of waterlogged fat cherubs and what may have been hunters on horseback. There were only a few actual picture frames still hanging, and square patches in a darker shade of beige showed where the rest had once been. The damp walls blistered and peeled, littering the floor with flakes of plaster. A massive patch of horrible-looking mold marred one wall, and there were enough spiderwebs in the corners to keep a small army of arachnids happy.

We'd begun the tour in the northwest tower, where the entrance to the castle was located, and had already passed through the armory. I was glad to leave it behind; the wickedly sharp swords and spears ornamenting the walls belonged in a museum, not someone's home. It wasn't the most welcoming beginning.

She hurried me through the first floor, or the *piano nobile*, as they called it here, barely pausing. The long, large rooms connecting the four towers still harbored traces of grandeur but had an abandoned air, and looked as if they'd been picked over by vandals. Pieces of green marble had been chipped off the walls. Sconces had been removed, and bare wires poked out like insect legs. An iron chandelier decorated with elaborate metal roses was missing its lightbulbs. She didn't bother to turn on the lights, perhaps because of all the missing fixtures, and the spaces were full of shadows.

The rooms in the towers, in contrast, were smaller and more medieval, with lower ceilings and less adornment. They were also stuffed with junk. In one, I observed piles of yellowed newspapers, a broken umbrella, a giant wardrobe full of moth-eaten men's suits, a battered trunk. Another was crowded with broken furniture: three-legged chairs with disintegrating embroidery, a half-rotted table, a harp with no strings. That distinctive smell of ancient wood permeated the air.

"This is the great hall," she declared, as we entered what was easily the biggest room of the tour. "Across it, there, is the northwest tower, where we began. You can't get lost if you remember that the layout of the castle is a square. The courtyard you entered is its heart. If you keep walking, eventually you will end up right back where you started."

I frowned. The castle air was cool and damp, like being in a cave, and I rubbed at the goosebumps that had erupted on my skin. Her description made me feel trapped.

The great hall was almost entirely empty of furniture, aside from a faded green fringe-bottomed sofa and a suit of armor missing a gauntlet standing forlornly by the giant marble fireplace. It was on the side of the castle farthest from the bridge at the entrance, and through the narrow windows I caught flashes of a lake. There was also a grand split staircase with wrought-iron railings and marble steps, dulled and worn by time.

"My husband's family were Italian nobility. They owned this castle for hundreds of years. It's mine, now. Do you like it?" Her manner was abrupt and direct, but I found it refreshing. She was so different from my mother, with her polite smiles and gentle manners. And her secrets.

"It's very impressive," I said, carefully. It made sense one family had owned it for so long; I had the impression that there'd been hodgepodge renovations over the years. The castle had a jumbled-together feel of different eras of history colliding.

"I despise it. This cursed pile of stone is my albatross." She exhaled another mouthful of smoke, which evaporated into the enormous room, and studied me. "Your mother told me you looked like me. That you are an actress, too. She only wrote to me once, a few years ago. She never answers my letters."

I digested this information, and the questions I wanted to ask filled my mouth. I didn't know where to begin.

"Did your mother tell you about me?" Now her eyes beneath those dramatic eyebrows turned sharp and incisive. She sucked in a lungful of smoke and held it as she waited for my response.

"No. She won't talk about you. She doesn't know I'm here."

Gabriella turned away from me, and I couldn't see her expression. When she did speak, she sounded hoarse. "I suspected as much. Come, let's have something to drink."

She doubled back, and I followed her down a narrow, spiral stone staircase in the northeast tower, which led to the kitchen on the ground floor. The kitchen clearly wasn't the original, and I was relieved by the touches of modernity—although the appliances were only modern in comparison with the rest of the castle. There was an icebox with a noisy coil on top and cabriole legs that could have dated to before the war, as well as a small mint-green oven. Brown and yellow linoleum covered the floor. An enormous hearth with soot-blackened bricks looked like it hadn't been used for a long time, judging by the spiderwebs—

truly, there must be *thousands* of happy spiders. Gabriella spooned coffee grounds into a silver moka pot and filled the base with water before putting it onto the stove.

"If you want something stronger, I have grappa."

"Coffee is fine, thank you." *It's barely afternoon,* I almost added, but stopped myself just in time.

Gabriella gestured to a large wooden table in the center of the room, and we both sat while we waited for the moka pot to boil.

I considered what to say. Gabriella struck me as the sort that perhaps wouldn't have minded me not beating around the bush. But mentioning money troubles too soon felt tacky, even exploitative. I finally settled on: "You were an actress?" It seemed a safe place to begin.

Gabriella raised one of those extravagant eyebrows, and her eyes took on a dreamy quality. "Oh, yes. I was a very great actress. I was the courtesan in *Giovanni of the Black Bands.* A starring role."

"Oh?" I stretched my memory to recall what little I knew about Italian film. I hadn't the faintest idea who Giovanni of the Black Bands might be, but she spoke the name authoritatively, as if it should be obvious.

"He was a Medici," she said, noting my confusion. I'd never been able to hide what I was feeling or thinking. "A great military leader who helped unite Italy. Like *Il Duce.*"

The words *Il Duce* hit me like a punch to the gut. Even I wasn't *that* ignorant. And suddenly I understood all too clearly just the sort of acting work my aunt, twenty years ago, would have been able to find.

"You were in a Mussolini propaganda film?"

I hadn't meant to say the words and certainly hadn't intended the sharp accusation behind them. But I usually couldn't stop myself from saying things any better than I could stop my face from showing them. I was *outspoken*, my mother often bemoaned, as if this were a terrible flaw.

"Oh, yes. That's why your mother shuns me now. I'm a dirty *fascista.*"

Her declaration stunned me into silence. After all, it's not every day a person meets a long-lost fascist aunt who lives in a castle.

She continued: "And that's not even the best part. The movie was a co-production with Germany. There was a version dubbed in German. So it was a Nazi propaganda film, as well." Her features twisted into a wry grimace.

"Oh my God." I couldn't believe what I was hearing.

"I suppose you'll leave now." My revulsion must have been obvious. She sounded wounded, and got up to attend to the bubbling moka pot. I tried to overcome a sudden wave of nausea. She assumed correctly, and I stood up. I wasn't quite sure I could retrace my steps to find my way out, but I could try.

I left the kitchen without another word.

My mother had been right about her. I understood now why she had cut ties with her sister and why she never wanted to speak about her. My own grandparents had been killed by Nazis in the war, a topic my mother never discussed, and she'd been left to fend for herself. She had welcomed the American soldiers with open arms: my father, especially. For his part, he'd risked his life to fight the Nazis, and seen friends die. I'd betrayed my mother by coming here, and shame washed over me.

I stumbled back up the stairs. I must have turned the wrong way, because I found myself in the decrepit dining room, the plaster walls mottled black in places, as if the castle were diseased. Spiderwebs coated a giant candelabra on a long dark wood dining table, and decorative metal studded the leather backs of the elaborate chairs. Fraying oriental rugs and tapestries softened the room's spookiness a little. The space was a lot like my aunt: theatrical, elegant, and perhaps beneath it all a little sinister.

The windows in this room faced not the lake, but the precipitous ravine around the castle, and beyond, the countryside around the town. I wondered how anyone could eat in here, with that dizzying view. I jumped as a cat slunk out from under the table and rubbed against my leg. It stared at me with its only eye, the green orb flashing.

I couldn't find the front door. I knew it was in the northwest tower, across the great hall—but which way was the great hall?

My shock over my aunt's confession dissipated as I wandered. It wasn't as if she was the only fascist in Italy, after all. The country was full of people who had supported Mussolini. It wasn't until after the Allied invasion that Italy had switched sides in the war. And the American tourists who had flocked here in recent years didn't seem to dwell on it much.

When I finally found my way back at the top of the kitchen stairs, I hesitated.

I didn't have to like her, or forgive her, to accept help from her. Did I? If you looked at it from the right angle, maybe it could even be viewed as a type of justice. She'd wronged my family, and this could help her atone for her sins.

That is, if she were even sorry.

I supposed there was only one way to find out. I went back down the stairs.

Gabriella looked surprised that I'd returned. I wasn't sure how much she cared about ever seeing me again, but her joy and relief were palpable.

"You would have found out this about me sooner or later. I figured it was better I tell you straightaway," she explained.

My mother would never have confessed something as easily as Gabriella had, and I appreciated her candor, even if what she'd told me churned my stomach.

"Did you mind? That your movie was being shown to the Nazis?" I jumped right back in where we'd left off, not wasting breath on formalities.

"I didn't think much about it one way or the other. I was just excited to be in the movie."

It wasn't a completely satisfactory answer. She could probably see what I was thinking, because she kept talking. "I ignored what it was convenient to ignore, so that I could take what it was convenient to take. Don't pretend to me you've never done the same."

Her words stilled me. She had a point. After all, wasn't that why I'd come back downstairs? I'd decided to overlook what she'd done in order to get help for Lulu. The level of transgression wasn't nearly the same, of course, but it made me more willing to hear her out. So instead of leaving again, I crossed toward her to take the little espresso cup she offered and carry it back to the table.

"A movie studio had held a postal contest where you mailed in your picture. The winner got a studio contract. I won."

"I see."

I had surmised from the scraps of information my mother had provided that her sister hadn't been with her during much of the war. Now I had a clearer idea of how that had come about. My grandparents had fiercely opposed the German occupation. Meanwhile, my aunt had been acting in propaganda films for the enemy.

"And then there was a man, too, of course. A Nazi, actually. Does that disgust you?"

I stared into the dark espresso to avoid looking at her. In point of fact, it did. I couldn't even imagine how my mother must have felt.

"Didn't you know? What the Nazis were doing?"

"I knew some. But he was just a man, Silvia, and handsome. I was young. A man like him had never paid me attention before. Powerful, sophisticated. Love is blind, you know." My aunt took a final luxurious drag of her cigarette and stubbed it out into her saucer. "Maybe you would like that grappa now, after all."

She didn't wait for me to respond before locating a bottle and tipping some of it into each of our espresso cups. "*Caffè corretto*, we call this here."

And I drank it, never mind the hour. Some situations simply call for a stiff drink, and this was one of them. Even as forthright as I usually was, I hadn't the faintest idea how to respond to any of this. I did know something about love being blind, or I never would have taken up with Lulu's father, and I related to what she was saying about being young and overcome. I'd been insecure when he first took an interest in me, and wanted his approval; I'd mistaken my own anxiety around him for passion.

But a Nazi. That was something different. I had to think that I'd have known better, in her shoes.

Luckily, a distant booming spared me from further reply.

"The movie people. *Dio santo*, I'm not even dressed."

"I'll show them in. To give you a moment."

The truth was, *I* was the one who needed a moment to get away from her again and grapple with everything I'd learned. I didn't wait for her reply and half ran out of the kitchen, following the booming until I located the door. I still didn't know why there were movie people here, but after the dual disaster of losing my job and then finding out my aunt was a Nazi lover—quite literally, from the sound of it—it seemed like fate itself had come knocking.

I swung open the studded slab of metal with a dramatic creak and found three men standing before me, looking a bit short-breathed and windblown from the climb.

One of them was Paul Rudderman.

CHAPTER 4

I quite enjoyed the spectacle of opening a castle door to visitors. But I enjoyed even more the look of confusion and astonishment on Paul's face.

"May I help you?" I asked them all, just as polite as you please. One of the men with Paul was auburn-haired and wearing a bright paisley scarf around his neck. The other had a dark brown mop-top, probably an attempt to emulate the Beatles, and ice-blue eyes behind big thick-rimmed black glasses. The paisley scarf man gave a polite and disinterested smile, and the glasses man barely nodded. He looked impatient.

"This is a surprise. Silvia Whitman, right?"

I scowled. But Paul held up his hands in mock surrender. "Only teasing. I'm not likely to get it wrong again, after that dressing down. Which I fully deserved, I might add. Gentlemen, this is Silvia Whitford, who I almost worked with on *Five Days in Roma*. Miss Whitford, Richard Gunner and Claude Lynell, production manager and art director for *The Revenge of the Lake Witch*."

I thought about playing like I didn't remember him, just to bruise his ego a little, and then thought better of it. "Well, you found new work awfully fast. Why don't you all come inside."

Playing lady of the castle was a completely novel experience, and far superior to playing lady of the dingbat. But my aunt swept in just then, dispelling the illusion that this castle could be anyone's but hers. She had traded her velvet housecoat for a vivid green sheath dress and chunky gold earrings that dangled almost to her shoulders. Her shoes were leopard print, and her lips had been repainted a bright fuchsia. Five minutes away from her had done nothing to resolve my complicated mix of emotions. Fascist or not, she certainly had style. And she knew how to make an entrance. Every eye turned toward her.

"This is my aunt, Gabriella Conti." It felt odd to introduce her that way, as family, considering she was practically a stranger. And after what she'd confessed, I wasn't exactly pleased to be claiming her as a relative. But I wasn't sure what else to say.

Richard, the thick-glasses one, checked his wristwatch. "We have two more castles today, so we'll get out of your hair quickly, ma'am. We already took the exterior photos, so we just need to see the terrace and the gardens, and we'll be on our way."

Gabriella just looked at him blankly. Whatever her capacity for English might be, his fast-talking had gone right over her head. I quickly translated for her, and she frowned. "Other castles? *Non capisco.* You shoot the movie here, yes? You pay me?" She said this in English to the men, and Claude shuffled uncomfortably. Richard gave an exasperated sigh. He was clearly more tightly wound than Paul, and his clothes reflected it: his brown-and-orange-striped polo shirt was tucked tightly into his high-waisted pants. Paul had a more relaxed look: low-slung khakis, loafers, a blue button-down, sleeves rolled up, fine blond chest hair peeking out at the top. He smiled soothingly at Gabriella, like a cowboy coaxing a saddle onto a horse.

"We're evaluating it as an option. I'm sorry if that was unclear."

"We don't have time for this. We already know we can rule this one out. Thinking about getting the equipment up here is giving me hives. I say we just go."

"Richard, we can spare ten minutes."

Gabriella looked thoroughly baffled, and Claude was ignoring the squabbling entirely and taking pictures of the foyer, seemingly captivated.

"I say we go with Castello Orsini-Odeschalchi and call it a day. There's not even a hotel in town here. Figuring out the accommodations would be a nightmare." Richard wasn't concerned about offending my aunt, apparently, now that it was apparent her English wasn't exactly fluent.

"The terrace is this way," she said, icily. She'd understood enough. She walked forward officiously, and the little group followed her through the great hall.

"That castle in Arsoli could work, in a pinch. No lake, but at least it's tried and true." Richard followed Gabriella reluctantly and checked his wristwatch again. "This place is a wreck."

"It has atmosphere, though, don't you think?" This was the first time I'd heard Claude speak, and his voice was gentle and lilting.

"It really does." The ceiling in here was elaborately coffered and frescoed, as well as water-stained, and Paul surveyed the sad, soggy angels with his hands in his pockets. The stone beneath the plaster walls was exposed in places, as if the castle had sloughed off its skin. "The production management challenges aren't the only consideration, you know, Richard." Paul said it genially enough, but I detected a hint of annoyance.

When we reached the northeast tower, we went down the set of stone steps that led to the kitchen. We passed through it and into a dark room being used for storage, containing empty potato sacks strewn across the floor, and old vegetable and fruit crates stacked into precarious towers. The air was close, and my skin turned clammy.

We exited a doorway onto a vast stone terrace at the base of the castle, and the view stretching before me made my stomach drop.

A ridge of trees had blocked the view of the lake on my approach, but now it stretched out before us in all its glory.

"A volcanic crater lake. Very deep and very cold," my aunt told me in Italian, as I took it in. I walked toward the stone wall at the edge of the flagstones and looked down to tiers of hanging gardens that descended all the way to the water's edge. The same sense of vertigo I'd had upon arrival overcame me again, and I stepped back. But there was no escaping the strange, vivid turquoise water around us. One got the sense that if it weren't for the severe stone walls of the gardens and the dense mass of trees that spilled down the slope of the caldera, trapping the lake in its perfect sphere, it might rise up and swallow us.

I looked at the faces of the three visitors, and all three were dumbstruck. Claude's mouth hung open, and his camera dangled limply around his neck, forgotten. After a moment, though, the spell broke, and he picked it up and focused the lens. The whirring of the shutter snapped Richard and Paul back to their senses.

"It's unsettling. That color. Almost unnatural." Richard stepped forward and placed his hands on the wall. He leaned forward to get a better look, and I hugged myself and held my breath. If he lost his balance, he'd break his neck.

"Must be the minerals or the algae or something," Claude said, from behind his camera.

"This place gives me the creeps."

"Well, that is sort of what we're going for, in a horror film," Paul said, dryly.

My aunt just stared at them all with daggers in her eyes, still fuming about the other castles, I guessed. "They better not be wasting my time. I can't pay to maintain this place for another year, I really can't," she said to me, in Italian. "I've had movie people come here before, you know, and it never went anywhere. They're all flakes." I sucked my lips. I'd hoped she was rich, since she lived in a castle, but apparently not. Given the state of the interior, it wasn't a complete surprise. My motives for visiting her hadn't been entirely pecuniary—I'd wondered about her for my whole life. But I had to admit that they primarily were. We were in a really tight spot.

"Say, how'd you find another gig so fast, anyway?" I asked Paul, as he continued to survey the lake.

"The first assistant director just got fired. Artistic differences with the director. Lucky for me."

"Is casting finished yet?" I smiled the way a person does when they are acknowledging their forwardness and trying to temper it with charm. If I could get another job, I wouldn't have to beg for a handout from Gabriella.

"Not yet. But there aren't any small parts. Just a handful of roles, really."

"Who said I wanted a small part?" Now I really turned that smile on, a provocative, good-natured smirk. Plus, I had sex appeal. Paul was a red-blooded, toothy American male, and sex appeal never hurt when you were trying to get a part. But Paul didn't seem to notice my charms. He just surveyed me the way he had the lake, a thorough and professional evaluation.

"Paul, Claude has all the pictures he needs. We gotta split." Richard straightened his bangs.

"Let me do a screen test. You do sort of owe me, you know."

Paul looked amused. "I guess I sort of do. I'll try, okay? No guarantees."

And with that, the three of them departed the way they came. My aunt didn't bother to show them out. We stayed on the terrace, gazing at the lake and avoiding conversation. I still didn't know what to say, but when it came down to it, I was too poor to be a very good moralist.

"You know, I wouldn't mind some more coffee," I said, and Gabriella's fuchsia mouth lost its tight little frown.

"They left quickly enough. The pot is probably still warm."

I'd gained enough presence of mind to be able to press my aunt a bit further about her politics. Over a cup of *caffè corretto*, I delved in.

"How could you?" I began, without preamble. "How could you have not cared what was happening?" I may have been born in Italy, but I'd grown up an American. I knew about the millions of Jews who had been murdered, and I'd seen photos of the concentration camps.

She paused, her espresso cup suspended in midair, and fixed me with a hard stare. Then she sighed and set the cup down.

"I was very selfish back then, Silvia, and very focused on my own immediate concerns. To get to be a movie star, for a girl who grew up on a farm in the country, was no small thing. And when I came to Rome, there were people—much finer, richer people than I'd ever encountered before—who filled my head with all kinds of new ideas, about Italy's greatness and glory. It was exciting."

"So you did know."

"I knew enough, I suppose. I didn't understand the scope of it. It's no excuse. But it all felt very distant from me."

The caffeine and grappa had made me jumpy, and my blood raced through my veins. I debated again whether I should just leave, and felt the sting of my disloyalty. I wondered what my mother would think, if she could see us now.

I told myself that if she could help my mother and Lulu, then it would make it all right.

"Can we talk about you, instead? I want to hear everything." Her moment of vulnerability vanished, replaced by her earlier brusqueness, and something else, too—an increased intensity in her expression as she waited for my reply.

And so I told my aunt all about myself, over three cups of *caffè corretto*. I told her about trying to break into the movie business, about how good of a mother her sister had been to me, about darling Lulu. Gabriella drank it all in, riveted by every word. An actress always enjoys an attentive audience, and by the end of the third cup, I wasn't thinking as much about her past misdeeds.

"So your mother is in Italy with you and still does not want to see me?" Gabriella leaned back in her chair. "You know, I'm still angry at her. So deeply angry. But I want to see her. No one holds a grudge like your mother, Silvia. Absolutely no one, and we Italians are famous for it."

"I'm sorry. I'm going to try to change her mind."

Gabriella lifted one of her fabulous eyebrows, quite independently of the other, and I thought it was only fitting that she possessed that particular skill. "Have you ever succeeded? At changing her mind?" Her tone was one of frank curiosity.

I considered the question. "No, I guess I haven't."

She pulled a cigarette out of a little gold case—her third—and smoked it. "So. Have we reached the point in the conversation where you're going to tell me why you've really come?" Her words sharpened, and the corners of her mouth creased in disapproval.

"Excuse me?"

"You've told me all about little Lucy. You didn't take a train here and climb up all those damned stairs just because you wanted to meet me. I'm not a fool."

She sounded hurt. I was embarrassed at how transparent I'd been, and, of course, by the fact that she was right. I put my head into my hands and moaned. "We're going to be homeless soon. I came here for help." Just saying the word *homeless* felt unreal. We'd never teetered this close to the brink before. We'd always had the security of my mother's slim savings. Gone now.

"Save your tears, Silvia. I haven't got any money. This place is falling down around my ears, can't you see that?" She slammed her little white cup down into her ash-covered saucer. "Look, if you need a roof over your head, you are welcome to it. You can share it with me and the mice."

My head snapped up. "Do you mean it?" I wiped a palm against my cheek.

"You would really want that? You didn't just want money, and *poof*, you'd never see me again?"

"I wasn't exaggerating. We're flat broke. I'd love to stay here." It was full of dangers for Lulu, of course—there was a suit of armor, for God's sake, and the *stairs*—but it was shelter. A castle, no less. Choosing between a Roman sidewalk and a castle wasn't exactly a tough decision.

Now my aunt smiled broadly, the first genuine smile I'd seen from her since I'd arrived. Fuchsia lipstick smeared her front teeth. "Well, then. You have the unenviable task ahead of you of changing your mother's mind, for the first time in your life. I wish you luck, Silvia. I really do."

CHAPTER 5

When I arrived back at the hotel room, I found Lulu sprawled sideways in the middle of the bed, her breaths deep and even. The lights were off, and my mother sat in a chair by the window, her face illuminated by the glow from the street outside. She looked tired. She was only forty-two, but the last year had aged her. Her hair was mostly gray now, and her gentle prettiness had turned from delicate to brittle.

"How was your day?"

"Good." I was grateful for the dark, so she couldn't see how guilty I looked. I'd have to tell her what I'd done soon, and I couldn't bear it. "I didn't have any of my lines yet, but I had a scene where I make eyes at the leading man."

I could hear how high and false my voice sounded and knew my mother did, too. She had turned her face toward me, away from the window into the dark, so I couldn't see her expression as she responded. "What aren't you telling me, Silvia?"

She could usually tell when I lied. Despite being an actress, I'd never been great at lying to her. On top of that, she was eerily perceptive.

"Nothing, Mama." I came and sat next to her by the window. As good as she was at keeping her own secrets, she was even better at ferreting out those of others. She'd known, too, when the doctor hid behind his scarred wooden desk and told her that she was merely experiencing fatigue. That the bruises were just the result of getting older. She'd made him tell her the truth. She'd try her best to make me do the same, and I steeled myself.

"You're keeping something from me. Tell me what it is." The rest of her body may have grown frailer, but her voice was as clear and robust as ever. It was so different from her sister's husky register, full of gravel and smoke.

It was so unfair of her to always demand the answers that she herself never gave, and I snapped. "You first." The anger in my tone surprised even me. But there had been so many lies over the years. When my father died in a car accident when I was eight, she had blamed the rain. I didn't know until years later that he'd been drunk.

She sat back in her chair as if slapped. I was immediately ashamed. "I'm so sorry. It's just—you grew up here, and there's not a single person that you want to see. You never talk about your childhood. It's like there's a whole part of you I know nothing about."

She considered me, her fair skin almost translucent in the light from the streetlamps. I could see her blue veins, and on her arm, a dark purple bruise that made me flinch.

"Everyone from that time of my life who I loved is dead, Silvia. And everyone else will have forgotten me by now."

"Almost everyone." I swallowed. Tonight was the second-to-last night on the hotel reservation, and I couldn't put off telling her much longer. "I went to see her."

"*What?*" she yelled. She never yelled. My mother, who never lost her composure, looked at me with such raw heartbreak that I flinched again, her expression more gut-wrenching than the bruise. She stood up and paced the room. I'd expected her to be upset, but I hadn't been prepared for her explosive fury. "How could you betray me like this?"

"Shh. Lulu." I nodded toward the bed. My little angel rolled over and rubbed an eye, but blessedly, stayed asleep. But my mother didn't show any signs of calming down. Tears streamed down her face, and I panicked now, because I'd never seen my mother cry. Not even when she'd pushed the doctor into giving her his real diagnosis.

"I *need* you right now, Silvia."

"I know. I know you do." Even before her illness, our little family was our whole world. For both of us. Neither of us had anyone but each other, and Lulu. I'd never threatened that before. I'd been on a couple of dates, which my mother had objected to, but I hadn't even had a real boyfriend since Lulu's father.

"Then why?"

I took a deep breath. I hadn't wanted to burden her with this, but I could see there was no other choice. "I lost my job." I said it quickly, as if by getting it over with, I could make the news any easier. "We're almost broke."

I watched her shoulders sag. She slunk back into her chair. This reaction shook me, too. Because my mother was so brave. I'd never seen her seem so defeated.

"She told you, I suppose."

"That she was a fascist? Yes."

For a moment, she grew completely still. Then she turned her face away from me and wiped her tears.

"She always wanted to be famous. When she finally got her chance, nothing could stop her. She cared about it more than anything. More than her own family."

She stopped speaking, but I understood the rest. When I had decided to become an actress, my mother had despaired. It made more sense now.

"I'll always put you first, Mama. You and Lulu. I'm doing this for both of you. It's my only shot at real money."

She patted my hand and then left hers there, gently covering mine. "You're not like her. I thank God for that every day."

I wondered if this were entirely true, and chewed on it for a moment. I had to admit I'd been impressed by my aunt's personality and style. She had a theatrical heart, like me, and that was a part of me my mother had never understood. I wouldn't mind getting to know her better.

I knew I had to push my mother just a little bit further.

"She said we could stay with her. I don't think we have a choice."

"*No.*" The vehemence of that word startled me as much as her tears. "We will find another way."

And then my mother removed her hand from mine. All the naked emotion she'd shown me disappeared, as if a door on it had closed. I sighed, mourning the loss. It was the most honest she'd ever been with me. But I knew the conversation was over, as far as she was concerned.

Still, she'd shared more of herself with me than she ever had before. And just before she'd shut me out again, I'd caught a flicker of something like relief.

I sat in the dark, watching Lulu's chest rise and fall, as I tried to understand it. There was nothing to be relieved about. We were in a terrible predicament. I ran over the entire conversation again in my mind. It didn't make sense.

And then, suddenly, it did.

I realized that whatever she'd been worried my aunt had told me, it had been something else entirely.

The front desk clerk scowled at me when I came downstairs the next morning. He was a rather handsome doe-eyed man in his thirties, but he was always grouchy, surprising for someone who napped as much as he did. Today he looked especially put out.

"Ciao!" Lulu bellowed at him. It had become her favorite new word since we arrived. My mother beamed at her with so much love that seeing it made me ache.

"Message for you," the clerk said to me, and sighed exuberantly.

"Oh?"

"You are to report to the studio at thirteen o'clock. A messenger will have a delivery for you soon."

The studio, I assumed, could only be Cinecittà. "Who left the message? What kind of delivery?"

He shrugged. The effort of taking a message and relaying it at all, he clearly felt, was above his call of duty. Getting all the details would have been too much to expect.

Luckily, a messenger did arrive while we were at the hotel breakfast (included, thankfully, and I didn't even blink when my mother stuffed her purse with rolls). A quick glance showed me that it was pages from a script. Specifically, *The Revenge of the Lake Witch.*

"He came through." I stared at the pages in wonder. It wasn't often that men in Hollywood held up their end of a bargain. I'd learned that lesson before. But Paul had made good on his word.

"Who did, dear?"

"I got an audition. It's for today." And a little ecru card on top of the script had a message scrawled: *Callback auditions at 1. Be off-book. Paul.*

"You said your agent dropped you." This was true. When I told him I was moving to Rome, that was it. He said he didn't know the scene here well enough to get me anything good—not that he'd ever gotten me anything good in Los Angeles. When he'd first signed me, he'd deemed me "both sexy and sweet, a dynamite combo that will make you a star." A year later, he'd downgraded his assessment to "not adorable enough to be the girl next door, not seductive enough to be a bombshell." He'd decided my ultimate career goal should be to play the role of the best friend, or maybe even the heroine's unworthy rival. I hadn't protested much. I mostly just cared about getting steady work to provide for Lulu.

"It was someone else. The assistant director from the movie that fell through."

My mother looked at me sharply over her espresso. "And what does he want in *exchange* for this grand favor?"

"Mama, not *every* man in Hollywood is a pig."

"Just most of them."

I couldn't dispute that.

I turned back to the pages. Paul must have pulled strings to get me in for the callback round if first auditions were already over. I was flattered.

But my nervousness soon overwhelmed my gratitude. I had only hours to prepare and to memorize my sides. A perusal of the pages revealed that I was to audition for the part of Bianca, the young heiress.

A starring role.

I put a hand to my mouth. I'd never auditioned for a part this big before. I'd barely allowed myself to dream of such a thing. Immediately, I wanted it so bad, it physically hurt. My stomach cramped up from the nerves, sudden and urgent. I needed this part the way I loved Lulu, desperately and intensely, and I knew I'd do just about anything for it.

"Mommy, read book!" Lulu pointed at the script before me.

"I'd love to read you the book, sweet pea."

And so I did. Right there at the breakfast table, unconcerned about the other patrons, I read my lines, rolling them around in my mouth, getting the feel for them.

It was horror, but it wasn't just cheap thrills. Even from the few pages I had, I could tell the script was good.

"Different book, Mommy!" Lulu demanded, and my mother and I laughed.

"I'll watch her. You go prepare."

"I'll go bring some of her books down first."

I was grateful my mother was still well enough to help with watching Lulu. Otherwise, I'd really be sunk. I felt bad about it, of course, but my mother always insisted she wanted to do it—and we didn't have a lot of alternatives at the moment. Or at least, the one alternative we had was one my mother wouldn't consider.

After bringing Lulu some of her toys and books to play with in the lobby, I went to the Villa Borghese gardens to sit on a bench and memorize my lines. Luckily, I'd never had trouble with memorization, not even with short notice. But I was intimidated by the size of the role and wasn't sure I was a good enough actress to pull it off. My biggest movie role to date had been the part of a secretary who had poured a glass of water on the boss's head, in revenge for him getting fresh. Sassy secretaries were my specialty.

In one of the scenes I'd been given, Bianca—who had just inherited a forbidding castle—happened upon an American tourist stumbling through her gardens. In another, she confronted the spirit of her ancestor, a witch who was burned at the stake in the fifteen-hundreds, and whom the tourist had accidentally revived. My last major part had been as Bianca in a high school production of *The Taming of the Shrew*—another Bianca, which felt like a good omen. Shakespeare's Bianca had also been a young ingenue. I hadn't been particularly convincing in the part, but I was a better actress now. Probably.

Once I had the lines down, I took a bus to the studio. I'd be over an hour early, but I'd rather wait there and scope out the competition than risk being late.

It was almost funny how familiar Cinecittà Studios felt. I could have been on the Fox lot back in Los Angeles. And the waiting areas before auditions were the same everywhere: full of gorgeous girls eyeing each other. Some with venom, some with envy, some with a sense of nervous camaraderie. I arrived first, so there was no one to evaluate myself against yet.

But then I found myself staring at an apparition in the hallway. Quite possibly the most beautiful woman I'd ever seen sauntered into the waiting area and took a seat. She had black hair, olive skin, and a chest and hips that could stop traffic. My own curves were speed bumps in comparison. I had quite a nice figure, and my chest usually got plenty of male attention, but I was skinnier and a bit leggier than her. Her daringly short dress with bold orange and pink swirls only made her more eye-catching and did nothing to disguise the fact that she had the type of silhouette to make Anita Ekberg jealous. In some ways, we did look a little alike, but my hair and eyes weren't as dark, and my features had once been described as elegant, whereas hers were sensuous. Everything about her was more exaggerated, like I was looking at myself in a funhouse mirror.

Her full lips were wet and glossy, and she studied me curiously. If she were auditioning for Bianca, I didn't have a chance.

It had been a mistake to come early.

"Are you here for the audition?" I asked, weakly.

She shook her glossy black hair over her shoulders. "No. I've already been cast."

My disappointment was so intense I couldn't breathe. The front desk clerk must have gotten the message wrong. Or maybe Paul had set this whole thing up as a prank to pay me back for telling him off. He hadn't seemed like the cruel type, but you never knew.

But then she continued: "Yes, I'm going to play the witch. I'm here to read with the girls auditioning for Bianca. That's you, I'm guessing?" She spoke English fluently but with an Italian accent. My relief was so palpable it must have shown in my face, because she laughed. Not unkindly. And then the relief gave way to confusion, because *she* was the witch? I'd been imagining an old crone.

"If you want to practice beforehand, I can read with you now." She sounded sincere.

"You wouldn't mind?"

"No. I had to come early to sort out some paperwork, but it didn't take as long as I thought, so I'm just waiting around until the Biancas all get here. And it's good practice for me, too. I'm Lucrezia Fileppi, by the way."

"Silvia Whitford."

I scanned the lines again, and suddenly, something clicked. With Lucrezia sitting before me, every inch of her exotic and glamorous, a different Bianca materialized. She wasn't a young ingenue. The innuendo in her lines jumped out now so clearly that I felt foolish for not seeing it before. Bianca wasn't the usual damsel in distress; she was darkly comic and sensual.

It's a crass metaphor, but I always think of a new script like a new lover: sometimes the connection is immediate and easy. More often it takes some time, some gentle breaking in, until it's comfortable.

This script was the type that surprised you, then knocked you against the wall and left your legs shaking.

I went over the scene with Lucrezia, and afterward, she smiled at me.

"Hey, you're really good. Break a leg in there, okay?" She winked at me.

Her praise buoyed my spirits so much that I didn't even notice as the other aspiring Biancas filtered in. And when the casting associate called my name, I stepped forward with confidence.

This was a part I knew how to play.

CHAPTER 6

The screen test took place on one of the soundstages, and in some ways, it felt like any other audition: a cluster of men watching, a camera whirring, bright lights. My heartbeat kicked up a notch, and I knew I had to channel the excitement rather than let it overwhelm me; otherwise, I'd stutter or muddle my words. It had happened before. Not often, but it was always mortifying.

I surveyed the men assembled behind the camera, guessing their roles, sussing out whom I had to impress. There were five in total, and it didn't take me long to discern who was who: there was an older Italian man with thinning hair, standing while everyone else was seated, whose eyes raked over me almost proprietarily. The producer, almost certainly. It seemed as if producers in Italy weren't any different than producers in Hollywood, and the way he was looking at me made my skin crawl. But I forced myself to flash a smile at him.

Then there was a man in his fifties with silver hair and just the slightest thickening around his belly, who exuded calm confidence and authority. The director, if I had to guess, and maybe the writer, too. It was easy to tell these were the two most important men in the room because of the deferential body language of everyone else—the sideways glances, the slight leaning toward their orbit. Then there were Paul and two other men, probably the casting director and the casting associate. The one I guessed was the associate operated the camera.

I stepped in front of it. My hands trembled slightly, but my voice, when I introduced myself, was strong and even. It amazed me how I could be such a bundle of nerves on the inside and so composed on the outside, and it often transpired that the more nervous I was, the better I did, the adrenaline zipping through me and carrying me through an audition without a hiccup.

But not always.

I was the most nervous I'd ever been, which meant either I was about to have the best audition of my life, or I was about to fail spectacularly.

"I'll be reading the part of Bernard. Ready whenever you are, Miss Whitford." Paul straightened the script in front of him. He gave me a nod of encouragement, but I thought he looked a bit apprehensive. When I'd met him before, he'd seemed so self-assured, ready with a square-jawed smile, his sandy hair spilling carelessly onto his forehead. But the smile was absent, his mouth closed tight, and the angle of that memorable jawbone appeared sharper than usual. He probably didn't want me to embarrass myself, since he'd stuck his neck out for me.

He couldn't possibly want that any more than I did. But it made me more nervous still, and I wiped my sweaty palms on the sides of my dress. It was the same white cotton number I'd worn when Paul fired me, but it was my best dress. I couldn't afford to be superstitious.

I closed my eyes for just a moment and breathed in: one, two, three.

Then I opened them and turned my attention toward Paul. And the director, sitting to his right.

In the scene, Bianca had just found the men roaming through the castle gardens. The first time I'd read it, I pictured her being startled and confrontational, but my session with Lucrezia had given me a different idea.

"Excuse me, gentlemen, but I don't believe you were invited." I spoke the lines playfully and flirtatiously.

"Sorry, we got a little lost. Your garden could use some tend-ing. You should get someone to help." Paul spoke the lines flatly, so that he wouldn't influence my performance.

I reacted not to his words but the insinuation behind them, so that no one could miss the fact we weren't really talking about a garden. I drew on my experience as the affronted sassy secretary—after all, I'd played four—gasping in mock affront and raising both eyebrows. I would have done just one if I could, but I didn't have my aunt's skill in that department. "I can tend my garden just fine on my own, thank you," I said, archly. The producer chuckled and grinned at me. I suppressed a shudder and continued. "I don't suppose you're offering?" I eyed Paul skeptically, as if he couldn't possibly be up for the job. I landed the line perfectly, and this time the whole room laughed. Even Paul, who wasn't supposed to react at all, cracked a smile. He slouched comfortably in his chair and stretched his legs out, long and lean.

"I'm at your service."

I mimed handing him a pair of shears. "Let's see how you do."

I knew from the script that Bernard proceeded to promptly cut his hand, inadvertently dripping blood onto an ancient stone slab that had once been the witch's sacrificial altar. His accidental offering would revive her spirit.

"Ouch."

"Oh, dear. Not much of a gardener, are you?" I smirked at him but kept my eyes soft and appraising.

"You've hardly given me a chance."

I considered him, letting the pause draw on almost uncomfortably long.

"Why don't you come up, and I'll help you with your hand." The line was supposed to be "why don't you come up to the castle," but on an impulse, I tweaked it, adding just the right emphasis to "why don't you come up."

It was the last line of the scene, and I exhaled in relief. The producer widened his stance and placed his thumbs in his belt loops. He leered. Paul looked at me thoughtfully, the way he had at the castle when I'd first asked him to get me a screen test.

The casting director and director were inscrutable. I thought I'd done pretty well, but it was always hard to know for sure.

Then the casting associate, pale, young, and skinny as a string bean, hopped up. "I'll go grab Lucrezia."

He returned with her seconds later, and I was once again stunned by her, sleek and glossy as if she'd stepped straight out of a magazine. In our scene, Bianca encountered the ghost of the witch, and learned her sad story—how she'd been shunned and then burned at the stake by the townspeople, though she'd only ever used her powers to help them. She winked at me, and we glided through the lines, natural as dancing. I looked at her with awe and jealousy, rather than terror. My version of Bianca was a little afraid of her, but mostly, she was tempted by her. The feelings came so naturally, I barely had to act at all.

When we finished, no one spoke for a couple of minutes. The director stared at me so intently that I squirmed. It occurred to me that maybe I was supposed to leave, and I opened my mouth to ask. But then he spoke.

"Why have I never seen her before?" He spoke with a deep voice and hard consonants from an accent I couldn't quite place.

"She wasn't in the first auditions. We discovered her when we were scouting locations. Her aunt owns one of the castles," Paul said.

"Which one?"

"Castello del Lago. Jerry, if you run and find Claude, you can ask him if he's finished developing the pictures."

The young man called Jerry sprung out from behind the camera, a flush spreading across his pale cheeks and his glasses sliding down his nose. The man I guessed was the casting director was his opposite: heavyset, olive-skinned, and sour. He frowned at me. I suppose Paul had horned in on his territory by getting me a spot, and maybe he resented it.

"She's utterly charming," the director said, and the casting director's frown deepened. Hope surged through me. I'd experienced this before, where the creative team discussed me as if I weren't standing right in front of them, and knew it was best not to interrupt. The director, I could already sense, had a stubbornness and contrariness to him. He reminded me a bit of my grandfather, who'd reveled in pushing people's buttons and valued no opinion besides his own. It was easy to imagine him firing the prior assistant director over a disagreement, and just as easy to picture Paul adeptly smoothing his ruffled feathers whenever the need arose.

"She's not Italian," the casting director said. "We will have to find a different voice actress for the Italian version. And she should speak English with an Italian accent."

"Bianca is a rich young girl who could have been educated abroad. The accent is not important."

"*Mi scusi, ma parlo italiano come un madrelingua.*" I couldn't help but butt in, and everyone stared at me as if a rock had spoken. Except for Paul, who'd never stopped watching me.

"There you go," the director said. "Less work for you."

The casting director harrumphed. Lucrezia beamed at me, and the producer sucked his lips.

Then Jerry reappeared, holding a stack of photographs. The director glanced at them. "Her aunt's castle, you said? It would lend a nice sense of neorealism." He threw the photos down. "She's perfect, and the castle is perfect. Jerry, you can tell the other Biancas to go home."

I gaped at him. My vision warped, and I didn't know if it was because I'd grown light-headed or because tears had sprung to my eyes. I had no way of telling, because I was numb from shock. And then I burst out laughing. I was going to be a *lead*. I was so giddy, I half-expected my laughter might buoy me up and float me across the room.

I'd dreamed of an audition ending this way, but I never thought it would really happen. When my mother decided we should move to Rome, she'd called it a city of miracles, and in that moment, I believed she just might be right.

"Thank you. Thank you so much. I won't let you down." I wiped a cheek. So I was crying, then.

"You won't. I'm sure of it." The director approached me, hand outstretched. "I look forward to working with you, Miss Whitford." He pronounced the T sharply, as if it speared my surname into two unconnected syllables. *Whit-ford*. His skin was dry and rough.

"Richard's going to have kittens when he hears about the castle," Paul said, but he was smiling, his teeth white and square. "Congratulations, Silvia."

CHAPTER 7

Officially booking Gabriella's castle for the movie had to be handled in person. There was paperwork, and then countless details to go over. The producer suggested that I accompany Richard for the errand, to help everything go as smoothly as possible. And then I had gently suggested that if Richard wouldn't object, my aunt might be more amenable to a visit from Paul, whom she'd taken a liking to on the first visit. This wasn't strictly true, but she'd taken a strong disliking to Richard when he'd disparaged her home. The producer had easily agreed.

And that's how Paul and I ended up together in a minuscule red Fiat, puttering along the *autostrada* leading out of Rome. The car didn't suit Paul at all; he was altogether too large for it, and its engine whined pitifully as we turned off onto smaller roads and started to gain elevation. My stomach dropped away along with the roadside; suddenly, only flimsy guardrails protected us from the steep slope, and hills bunched up around us. At least the countryside was pretty: we passed vineyards, green farmland, olive groves, a field of bright yellow sunflowers. It was hot, so we had the fabric roof rolled back, and the wind whipped the strands of hair that had escaped from my polka-dot headscarf.

"What did Richard say when he heard the news?"

Paul grimaced. He swerved too fast around a curve, the steering wheel looking like a toy in his hands and his thighs almost bumping up against it. "Well, that's part of why this is a particularly delicate mission today. We have to convince your aunt to house the cast and crew. There's no other practical solution."

I let out a breathy laugh. "What, you mean everyone would stay in the castle together?"

He shrugged a shoulder.

"They did the same thing for the production of *Castle of the Living Dead* last year. And Claude thinks we can do some of the interior shooting on location, which would save us a bundle. It would mean we might be able to afford Terrence Leopold for the part of Bernard."

My heart skittered along my rib cage. "Are you serious?" I gripped the side of my seat, and I couldn't tell if I was more afraid of Paul's driving or of the prospect of acting alongside one of America's most famous leading men. I'd grown up making googly eyes at Terrence Leopold. I hadn't seen him in much lately, though.

"Don't get too excited. It may come to nothing."

"Too late." My pulse pounded. I might get to play the love interest for *Terrence Leopold*. Terrence Leopold of the cleft chin and devilish smile and suave British accent and string of ex-wives. He had perfect comedic timing but had done darker, more serious roles, too, including suspense. He'd be perfect for the part. I was suddenly sure that no one else could do it justice. Something bubbled up inside me that might have been laughter or nausea; to be on the safe side, I kept my mouth shut.

"Yeah, Richard came around to this location pretty quickly once he realized the budget implications. Also, our second-choice castle isn't even available anymore."

"You're sure good at handling people." The words came out sounding like an insult, and I bit my tongue. I should have been nothing but grateful after Paul's help, but I still couldn't shake my initial perception of him as inconsiderate. He struck me as the fixer of a production—every picture had one—the one who buried the story of cheating costars, or planted it for publicity, depending on the producer's whim. The one who got grass for the cast parties. The one who made everything run smoothly, never mind who got bruised in the process, as long as the bosses were happy.

"I like to think I'm good at my job." He said it mildly enough, but there was a touch of acid behind it. He'd known I hadn't been paying him a compliment. "And how about you, what's your story? Small-town prom queen who dreamed of being an actress since she was a little girl?"

He directed a teasing smirk at me. I rolled my eyes behind my big white sunglasses, but without real annoyance, because he was wide off the mark. In truth, I'd been a homely, scrawny kid until, quite suddenly, I wasn't. No one had been more surprised than me. I'd never dreamed of being an actress as a child, because it hadn't seemed possible. I'd just loved movies. After my dad died, I'd sneaked into the Roxy just about every day, enjoying the air-conditioning and the smell of buttered popcorn and pictures that took me far away from school and tragedy and my run-down little bungalow. My mom was busy with work, and lost in her own grief; she hadn't missed me.

"Not quite. I dropped out of high school." I looked out the window. I'd been a decent student, in English especially, but my junior year, after I'd grown a foot and sprouted breasts, I was offered a local modeling job. "My mom raised me alone after my dad died, and I wanted to help her out with money." My mom had argued with me, of course, and I'd assured her I was just taking a year off. By the time the year had passed, I'd moved to Los Angeles and gotten pregnant.

Paul rounded another curve, and my stomach careened sideways. The engine grew even noisier, so we had to half-shout over it. The smell of car exhaust filled my nostrils, and my legs stuck to the white vinyl seat. "I'm sorry about your dad."

I thanked him with a tight-lipped smile. "It was a long time ago." I remembered my father as affectionate, silly, and boisterous, and I'd adored him. But I'd been young, and my memories of him had grown hazier over the years. "So what do you know about the director?" I asked, shifting the conversation away from personal matters.

Paul kept his eyes on the road, which I appreciated, but I could feel his attention focused carefully on me, an awareness that was almost tangible. We sat so close in the teensy Italian car that we were almost touching. "He's Swiss by birth and has lived in Italy for a decade or so. He's written and directed several horror films before this one, all well-reviewed by the Italian critics but underappreciated in America. He's really hitting his stride, though. He could be the next Hitchcock."

I raised my eyebrows. I still remembered the white-knuckled terror I'd experienced when I saw *Psycho* five years ago; how I'd gripped the movie theater chair with all my strength. I doubted he could be that good. I was by no means sure *I* could be anywhere near as good as Janet Leigh.

"I really hope so," I said.

Finally we reached the base of the town and Paul found a spot to park on the side of the road. The streets were too narrow to accommodate even the tiny Fiat, so we'd go the rest of the way on foot.

The town was as eerily quiet as before, and an entirely different world from the *autostrada*, where the Italian sun beat down on asphalt. Here, a morning haze radiated off of the cobblestones, and soggy laundry flapped above, raining droplets of water. It probably would take forever to dry in the thick, muggy air. A strange creaking echoed as we moved forward, and we entered a tiny piazza I hadn't seen last time, empty except for an old stone olive press. In the fall, they'd probably have a blindfolded donkey attached to its wooden handle walking in circles around it, wheezing and braying. Its current disuse meant it couldn't have caused the creaking I'd just heard, though, and my skin prickled.

On the next street, we did see an actual donkey, hitched outside of a dirty, faded pink stucco house. Shallow steps led up to the front doors of the houses, while the doors at street level, I ascertained, contained furrier inhabitants. I supposed the villagers would need some way to transport goods up the steep streets without cars. Or transport themselves, I thought wearily, shifting my weight from one leg to the other to relieve the soles of my feet.

In one of the wider streets, we passed a little stone church, and I was surprised to see its doors closed, as if visitors weren't welcome. A small arched shrine cut into a stucco wall across from it was empty, spiderwebs coating the bottom. The church bell clanged just then, surprising me so much that I nearly tripped on the cobblestones. Its noise seemed to vibrate through me.

"There's something about this town that's a little odd," Paul said.

"I've noticed, too."

When we reached the main piazza, the same three men I saw last time were there again, thwacking their cards. They glanced up at us and then glanced back down. One grunted.

Two different men entered the piazza on the other side, about the same age as the card players, their skin browned and creased, but their arms ropy and muscled in their short-sleeved shirts. The largest of the card players jumped up at the sight of them and gesticulated rudely, and all of them shouted. The reaction was so swift and alarming that Paul and I paused, hanging back so as not to attract attention.

Then a window from one of the houses burst open and a woman wearing a modest headscarf leaned out of it, shouting too, and the sudden volley of insults in the recently silent square was shocking. It was as if the still portrait of the town had been torn apart, revealing violence beneath.

Then one of the two men ran at the card player who'd jumped up, grabbing his shirt and swinging at him. I heard a crunch as knuckle and nose connected. Paul and I slowly backed up, not wanting to become involved. We turned and walked away, then chose another *vicolo* and continued onward toward the castle. I was breathing hard.

"That was weird."

"Not really." Paul had his hands in his pockets. He didn't look shaken at all. "I've been living in Rome for about a year now and I see brawls like that all the time. Usually the communists and the fascists. Or whatever the fascists here are calling themselves now, I forget."

I thought instantly of my aunt, rasping *dirty fascista*. Apparently, she was hardly the only one.

"Seems like there's unrest everywhere right now." Back home, the headlines had all screamed about Vietnam, and I'd heard Lulu's father had applied for conscientious objector status to try and avoid the draft. I hugged myself, rubbing the ribs he'd once bruised. The irony wasn't lost on me. "It's funny everyone's so crazy about horror movies. Seems like the world is horrific enough." I winced. I hadn't meant to say what I'd been thinking—but then I never did, and I could never seem to stop myself. "I mean, I adore the genre of course, and I'm so excited about this part . . ." I was babbling, trying to undo my faux pas. Paul didn't seem offended by the comment, though. He just looked pensive.

"I know what you mean. But I think maybe that's why. It's cathartic."

The *vicoli* got steeper, and as I climbed the shallow stairs, I pressed my palms against the clammy stone buildings to keep my balance. Paul shuffled in front of me; the next alley was so narrow that we would have to walk single file.

"Before we get there, I should tell you. I only just met my aunt. So I don't know how big of a help I'll be." It was awkward, too, to be assisting Paul with his negotiation. I remembered how desperate my aunt seemed for the money.

"Don't worry about it. I'm just happy to have a translator."

I paused, catching my breath. Paul slowed his pace. "Also, my mom is in Italy with me. I know there's no hotel in town, but did Richard mention if there was a *pensione* or anything like that?"

Paul looked back over his shoulder. He didn't even seem winded. "There are a couple. Only a few rooms each. We can stop by them on the way back to the car."

I breathed a little easier.

"Thank you."

My mother would still refuse to stay in the castle, I was sure, and I didn't plan to tell anyone about Lulu if I could help it. Being a mother "hurt my marketability," as my agent had put it. Also, once men knew I had an illegitimate child, they treated me differently. Like a whore, most of the time. They acted like there was suddenly an open invitation to get in my pants.

We crossed the final piazza with the *bar-tabacchi* and into the tunnel of cypress trees that led to the castle. The path leveled, and my calves stopped burning. The castle emerged before us, even more formidable than I remembered it.

We both stopped before the bridge, marveling at it.

"It really is perfect," Paul said. His face was almost worshipful.

It would be perfect, as long as my aunt agreed to put up a couple dozen movie people in her home. The importance of the task before us struck me afresh. The stakes couldn't be higher. My career, Lulu's future, and *Terrence Leopold* all hung in the balance.

My aunt, when she opened the door for us, looked both more glamorous and more eccentric than when we'd first met. The sharp-edged beauty of her face startled me anew; I hadn't quite remembered the dramatic cut of her jaw or the size of her dark eyes. She answered the door wearing a lurid pink and green kimono, a feather boa, and a gold velvet turban.

"So you're here," was all she said before disappearing, leaving the door hanging open. She didn't invite us in, but we stepped carefully over the threshold anyway. The contrast of the dank castle air to the sticky July heat in town left me feeling almost feverish. The foyer, I knew, was deceiving. Ornate gothic chairs sat imposingly against the walls, which were decorated with particularly fine oil paintings of classical scenes. You wouldn't guess that the rest of the rooms were mostly empty of furniture, the plaster walls naked and crumbling.

My aunt strode through the great hall and we followed her, about ten feet behind and trying to keep up, and then continued down the spiral stone steps to the kitchen. She whirled around abruptly to face us.

"My beautiful niece is here. I'm so glad." She patted my

cheek and then pinched it. "They tell me you're going to be a movie star."

She looked proud, and I was touched. "It runs in the family, I guess."

"We are so alike. Your mother was very wrong to keep you from me."

I had no reply to that, but luckily, she didn't seem to expect a response and busied herself with the moka pot. Paul took off the canvas satchel he'd been wearing that contained the paperwork and set it on the table.

"I have good news, Signora Conti. Not only has the director chosen your home as one of the shooting locations, he'd like it to be the primary shooting location. We will be here two weeks, and we'd pay you significantly more than what we'd first discussed." Paul took a seat and smiled dashingly at her. Even my heart pitter-pattered in response. He sure knew how to turn on the charm.

Gabriella sat across from him, suddenly very formal, and crossed her hands. "What aren't you telling me?"

I almost laughed. She was just as perceptive as my mother. Paul cleared his throat. "What do you mean?"

"You come here in person and bring my niece to make things nice. It is for a reason, no?"

Paul frowned a little. "Well, we thought you might be interested in going on vacation while we're shooting. A beach resort, all expenses paid, of course. That way, the cast and crew could stay here without getting in your hair. And we wouldn't have to disrupt your schedule for the interior shooting. You said before there are twenty-five bedrooms, is that right?"

I whistled. Luckily, the moka pot boiled just then, and Paul didn't hear. His manipulation was expertly done, and I decided I'd pegged him right. He was the fixer.

Gabriella pulled her kimono tighter around her waist. "You say everyone stays outside, no?"

Paul's smile grew even toothier, which I hadn't thought possible. He really was remarkably handsome, and his smile had a boyish roguishness to it. Now that I knew him better, I understood why he'd chosen to be behind the camera rather than in front of it; he probably preferred the greater level of control. But it must have been a deliberate choice, because with his face, tanned and angled in all the right places, he wouldn't have struggled to find work. His blond sideburns, I noted, came down exactly to the lobe of his ear, ending in a sharply shaved line, and that was him in a nutshell: his casual, slightly wind-blown exterior belied his careful precision. "Initially we were only interested in exterior shooting. But now we'd like to come inside, too."

My aunt let out a string of curses in Italian and walked over to the stove to get the pot. "Silvia, you must tell him this is impossible. I can't have the castle overrun. My husband would roll over in his grave."

I swallowed hard, hesitating. "If we can't shoot inside, they'll pick another castle," I told her. I didn't know if that were true, and it felt wrong to push her like this, but I did it anyway. I didn't feel great about it. "They might cast Terrence Leopold as the lead. You'd get to meet him."

Surely my aunt knew who he was, and I thought her love of movies and movie stars might help persuade her. But her forehead remained creased with worry, and there was a flash of fear in her eyes.

"The castle is haunted, you know. I've made my peace with the ghost, but other people don't like coming here."

I studied her expression to see if she was serious. Apparently she was. Or she truly was a great actress. It didn't shock me that she was the type to believe in ghosts, but I didn't believe that was her real objection to Paul's offer. I remembered the way the men in the piazza had talked about her, and it occurred to me that my aunt might be something of a recluse. I wondered when she'd last had real visitors, besides me and the movie people. Or when she'd last left the castle.

"What's she saying?" Paul had the papers spread out before him and was squinting at the type.

"She says the castle is haunted."

"Excellent. Herman will love that." The director, whose

name I'd learned was Herman Meyerson, had told Paul staying in the castle would help us all to absorb the right atmosphere and get into the minds of our characters.

"So who's the ghost? Maybe we can incorporate elements into the script."

I asked her, and she brought the moka pot and cups to the table, looking deadly serious. She switched to English and told us, "It is a very sad story."

She poured, and we all sipped the brew while she folded her hands and stared at each of us in turn, her gaze uncomfortably intense. I shifted my eyes away and grimaced as I watched a hairy spider scuttle into a crack in the brick hearth. I was glad we were sitting in the bright kitchen, at least, and not the cavernous great hall with its sad suit of armor.

"My husband's family began building this castle in the fourteen-hundreds," she told me, switching back to Italian, and I translated for Paul. "The noble families fought over it for more than a century."

She looked mournful. Her espresso steamed in front of her, untouched. "My husband's ancestor, Giovanni Conti, married a beautiful woman named Serena. But she was unfaithful. She had an affair with his rival and bore him a child. When Giovanni found out whose son he was, he was so enraged that he ordered the little boy to be drowned in the lake."

I shivered and sipped the hot espresso. I didn't like this story. Hearing about dead children always profoundly disturbed me, and I longed to go home and hug Lulu, and run her dark curls through my fingers.

My aunt continued: "Serena didn't want her son to die alone. So she filled her pockets with stones, and clutching him to her breast, jumped off the wall of the castle gardens. Now she roams his nursery in the northeast tower. It's the oldest and most protected part of the castle, but no one is safe when the enemy is within." She paused for effect. Her flair for drama made her an excellent storyteller, and she spoke slowly to enhance the impact of her words. "She's always wearing white. You can hear her wailing at night. When my husband lived, our houseguests reported that she visited their dreams, luring them to join her in the lake."

I translated it all for Paul, a little reluctantly. I didn't like repeating it. His eyes gleamed.

"That dream bit is good. We might use that."

I wanted to leave. The story chilled me.

"Signora Conti, the terms of the new agreement are detailed here, in Italian." Paul slid a page across the table to her, and she took it but only skimmed it perfunctorily. "Is this satisfactory?"

My aunt pushed the paper away. "I want to think about it."

"Of course. Take your time. If you don't mind, I'd like to take some pictures of the gardens. We didn't get a close look before."

He pushed out his chair and fished a camera out of his satchel.

"This way," Gabriella said, and we followed her out to the terrace and then down steep stone stairs to the hanging gardens' third and lowest level. It was completely overgrown with vines and shrubs; the shrubs might have been pruned into figures once, but it had been long ago. A few gnarled trees still produced lemons, and I smiled to see the pop of yellow. We walked alongside the waist-high wall, and thirty or so feet below, the lake lapped at its mossy stones.

The fall wouldn't kill you. But a woman with stones in her pockets could jump and drown. I shuddered.

As we explored, we stumbled upon a large statue of a woman, her face contorted in terror, her base choked by weeds and flowers.

"The nymph Daphne, who turned into a laurel tree to avoid being raped by Apollo," my aunt explained, in Italian.

"Oh, this is perfect for the garden scene," Paul said. He snapped several close-up pictures of her face. "After Bernard spills blood on the altar, we want to show an eerie statue changing its expression to a smile. Claude can get started on a clay version of this that's smiling."

I turned away to look at the lake instead. I'd been trying to avoid it after Gabriella's story, and its strange turquoise color seemed even more disconcerting than before. I couldn't help but picture a dead woman and her child, their white and bloated faces flashing beneath the surface.

Gabriella looked up at the gray sky, as if consulting the heavens. "Silvia, do you want me to let them all come stay inside the castle? I will do it for you, if it means you will stay here with me. But tell him I don't want to go to the beach resort."

My gut twisted. I hated being put in this position. Her reluctance pricked my conscience.

"Yes. Yes, I do want you to." I swallowed, as if I could remove the taste of shame from my mouth.

"Well, then. I'd better go sign the papers."

CHAPTER 8

I had to hand it to Richard: he may have been self-important and a little rude, but he was good at his job. Overnight, my aunt's castle became a hive of activity. It turned out it could be reached by vehicle, after all, via a gravel drive at the bottom of one of the towers that connected to the road encircling the lake, so getting the equipment delivered hadn't been as difficult as he'd feared. The principal restaurant in town was enlisted to provide craft services, and the bedrooms and bathrooms were made habitable—moldering mattresses were replaced and the closets stuffed with fresh linens and towels. Paul, Richard, and the director of photography spent a lot of time going over the locations and planning the shooting schedule. Claude readied the scenes for the first few shoots with his team of set decorators. The costume director, a sweet woman named Mrs. Leskowitz, with gray corkscrew curls and glasses that hung from her neck on a beaded gold chain, turned the old armory into her sewing room. My aunt watched it all with a withering glare and mumbled about her husband turning over in his grave.

It only took three days to get the castle ready for shooting, and I checked in periodically to watch the transformation. I stayed with my mother and Lulu at a *pensione* in town, where I'd rented a room after getting an advance on my first paycheck. Morning glory crawled up the facade of the little stone building, and inside it was even more basic than the hotel in Rome, but it was cheap and clean. The proprietress, Signora Ricci, had six children who could be playmates for Lulu, and I paid her extra to help watch her, since I knew how hard it was for my mother in her condition. Her husband was a farm laborer in the surrounding countryside, and Lulu squealed with delight when she got to pet his sweet donkey named Ruffina.

The day before filming began, I packed my suitcase and squeezed Lulu tight. The rest of the cast would be arriving soon, and I wanted to stay at the castle while everyone got acquainted and settled in. I might be able to sleep at the *pensione* here and there during the next two weeks, but I expected we would be working late most nights.

"Mommy has to go work now, baby. She'll be thinking about you every second she's away."

Lulu only briefly glanced up from playing with her doll. "Bye, Mommy!" she shouted, and I kissed her once more, my heart aching. I'd see her the next day, since I wasn't even in the first scene, but I knew our time together would be more limited until the movie wrapped. But I'd earn enough that we could rent an apartment afterward, and I clung to that fact. Then I'd manage to get a waitress job, just maybe not on the Via Veneto, and hopefully I'd get more movie parts. Things would be better.

"Go. It's fine," my mother said, and squeezed my hand. "You'll be great."

"Thanks." She must have been able to see that I was on edge. My mother didn't often offer praise where my acting was concerned, probably because she'd never fully forgiven me for leaving school. I picked up my suitcase and turned to go.

"You can't trust her, Silvia," my mother said, just before I closed the door—so quietly I wasn't sure she even meant for me to hear. I didn't have to ask who she meant. I paused only for a moment before continuing down the poky tile stairs, the hallway light flickering.

Unsurprisingly, I was the first actor to arrive at the castle. The bedrooms were all located on the second floors of the towers, and a production assistant with a clipboard assigned me one in the northeast wing. I gulped down any protest; I didn't believe in ghosts. I'd hardly be spending time in my room anyway, except to catch a few hours of sleep between shooting.

I was already familiar with the spiral stone staircase that led to the kitchen, so tight I could easily touch both walls as I climbed. This time, I took it up instead of down, and it deposited me into a hallway that bisected the entire tower, adorned with dusty oriental runners and disintegrating tapestries. Four wooden doors lined each side, and one had a paper sign with my name written in thick marker.

I hadn't expected special treatment, despite being a lead, and a quick survey of the room proved I'd been right not to. It was surprisingly tiny for a castle, with just a wrought-iron bed, a narrow window, and an old wooden dresser. The plaster walls were unadorned, although the wood-beam ceiling still bore an intricate red and green painted design, faded over the centuries.

After I dropped my suitcase, I headed to the kitchen, where I found my aunt in earnest conversation with Richard over espressos.

"The contract. It's in the contract," Richard said, jamming his finger on the table. Gabriella just shook her head.

"*Non capisco.*"

"I think you *capisco* just fine, is what I think." His voice rose. I paused awkwardly in the doorway, unsure whether to intrude.

"Silvia. Thank God. Can you please explain to your aunt that she can't stay here during production?"

Gabriella had her hands folded gracefully in front of her, but at his words, her eyes flashed with anger. He was right; she understood him perfectly.

"Well, I think Paul told her it was all right. He didn't think it would be a big deal."

"What?" Richard took off his big glasses and rubbed his eyes with his hand. "The producer never should have let him do the negotiation. It *is* a very big deal, actually. Whenever an owner is around, they always muck things up and complain. It can be a major complication. Did he amend the contract?"

I shrugged. I didn't actually know. Richard heaved an exasperated sigh. "Look, she has to go. Talk her into it, won't you?"

I opened my mouth to protest, but he pushed past me to the hallway before I'd uttered a word.

I knew better than to even try and convince her. My aunt seemed just as stubborn as my mother. Besides, I didn't want her to leave. I'd only just started to get to know her, but already she'd told me more about her past than my mother herself ever had. I wanted to learn more.

"When does Terrence Leopold get here?" she asked, her voice lilting in girlish excitement. They had managed to get him for the part, and I couldn't even pretend to be calm. I joined my aunt at the kitchen window; this one was wider than many of the others and directly overlooked the gravel driveway.

"I don't know. It could be anytime today."

"Do you think he really threw his cocktail at that poor waiter?"

Terrence Leopold made the tabloids regularly, not only for his tumultuous love life, but for general public misbehavior. He was known to be a heavy drinker.

"Probably."

As it happened, the next person to arrive was Lucrezia. She made a fittingly cinematic entrance in a green convertible, driven by a man with a mop of curly dark hair. He helped her unload a truly astounding amount of luggage—I didn't know how it had fit in the trunk—and dipped her low into a goodbye kiss before departing. Once he was out of sight, she immediately reapplied her lipstick.

I went outside to greet her.

"Silvia!" We kissed each other on both cheeks. "I'm so glad you're here already. God, I can't believe they're actually making us stay in this dreary place." She caught the attention of a production assistant and gestured at the luggage. He frowned at it, but one glance at her and his whole face changed into slack-jawed astonishment. He rushed to help her.

"It's not so bad. I think it could be fun." I felt a bit defensive.

"Oh, I forgot your aunt lives here. I've gone and, what's the phrase, 'put my foot in it,' haven't I? And I was so determined that we should be friends." She smiled apologetically at me, and it seemed genuine. She looked wonderfully chic, of course, in a shift dress patterned with bright yellow and orange daisies. "It's not the castle I mind, truly, it's just being away from Rome." She nodded toward the green convertible disappearing down the steep drive. The terrace and gardens were around the other side of the tower.

"I understand. I'm sure it will be hard to be away from your boyfriend."

For some reason, she laughed. "My boyfriend? No, Massimo is just a bit of fun. He is a dear, though. But I will admit I have a very"—she paused, touching a finger to her pointy chin—"active social life. I went on a date with Roy Samuels last week, you know."

I gasped. "Did you really?" He was a handsome American actor who had starred in a number of Spaghetti Westerns. I was impressed but not surprised, given her looks.

"I've made it a point to date almost exclusively American men. That's how I learned English so well. They've all been happy to help. They've tutored me very thoroughly." Her expression turned sly.

"I'm sure they did," I said, laughing.

"Is it okay if I speak English with you? I know you speak Italian, but if I'm going to make it big, I have to be completely fluent."

"Sure." I was relieved to hear this; speaking in Italian required a little more effort for me.

"Have you been to any nightclubs in Rome yet?" She patted her black hair, which was shinier, wavier, and longer than mine, the ends reaching the top of her breasts.

"Not yet." I couldn't remember the last time I'd been out drinking and dancing. It must have been before Lulu was born.

"Let me take you out when we're back in town."

"I'd love that." I didn't expect we'd ever actually go out, but it was the polite thing to say. We followed the production assistant hauling her luggage up to her room, which turned out to be down the hall from mine. "So it's one of your big scenes tomorrow."

We were beginning with the witch being burned at the stake in the fifteen-hundreds.

"Yes, and almost everybody gets at least part of the day off. They're going to clear the set when I show my breasts." She winked at me. "It's why I wanted this role. I didn't want Bianca, you know, so don't think I'm your rival or anything like that. My breasts are going to steal the show." She laughed, and I laughed with her, slightly shocked and also relieved. I had wondered if she'd considered auditioning for Bianca instead of the witch, and was glad she hadn't.

"I don't doubt it."

I offered to help her unpack, which she gratefully accepted, and I admired her assortment of stylish and expensive clothes. She filled me in on all sorts of gossip about the scene in Rome, and also the news that Terrence Leopold was most definitely single at the moment. I listened with keen interest.

By the time we finished, I was as determined as she was that we would become friends. Hopefully, good friends.

Lucrezia and I arrived in the kitchen arm in arm, already giggling together like schoolgirls. Her presence filled me with hope. I'd been scared that work would be hard and lonely, but already I had a confidante.

My aunt, when she saw us enter, didn't smile. Instead, her expression turned downright fierce, and her eyes flashed with something dark that might have been jealousy. She looked formidable, with her turban and her fuchsia lips contracting into a frown. Lucrezia stopped laughing and looked at me questioningly.

"This is my aunt, Gabriella Conti," I said, feeling suddenly uneasy. "Aunt, this is Lucrezia. She's playing the witch in the movie."

My aunt rapped her fingernails against her gold cigarette case. "She's too beautiful. She'll steal all the attention for herself. Don't befriend your rivals, Silvia."

Lucrezia burst out into shocked laughter. "Well, I never."

"*Aunt.*" I was too astonished to say anything else. I knew she was direct, but I hadn't expected her to be so impolite.

"I'm just looking out for you, dear. I know her type." She plucked a cigarette from her case delicately. "Please make sure everyone knows they're not to touch anything of mine. They need to know what are props and what aren't. I know exactly how many pieces of silver are in the sideboard." She looked straight at Lucrezia.

"She's not going to steal your silver! Lucrezia, I'm so sorry."

Lucrezia's initial amusement had evaporated, and her exquisite features turned hard. She stared my aunt down, her cold anger sublimating off of her. My aunt breezily lit a cigarette, unaffected, but never broke eye contact. Lucrezia looked away first.

"I'm going to step out and get some air," Lucrezia said, icily. She headed toward the storage room and door to the terrace, and a moment later, we saw her appear on the gravel driveway. She lit a cigarette and looked out at the lake.

"Why did you do that? I'm trying to make friends." I hadn't realized how angry I was until I choked out my words. It occurred to me Gabriella hadn't really been welcoming to anyone, aside from me. She'd been civil to Paul, but only barely, and she'd needed the contract to help pay her bills.

"She's not your friend."

I sighed in exasperation. Richard had been right. She couldn't stay here.

"Look, about the beach resort Richard mentioned—"

I never got a chance to finish my sentence, because my aunt suddenly cried out. She dropped her cigarette and clasped her throat, her fingers tangling in the beads of her necklace. "No. No, this cannot be."

I rushed over to the window and saw what had distressed her: it appeared as if almost the entire cast and crew had arrived at once. The drive was clogged with cars and vibrating with the noise of idling engines and greetings and shouted instructions. Over twenty people would be staying full-time in the castle, including two camera operators; a gaffer to oversee the lighting setups; the director of photography; a grip to assist him and the gaffer; two production assistants; a hair and makeup artist; the costume director and her assistant; a script supervisor; and a few set decorators. Of course, so would all of the cast, and the most senior crew: Mr. Meyerson; Claude, who oversaw the set decorators and the movie's visual style; Richard, who handled the budget, shooting schedule, and many of the day-to-day logistics; and Paul. A stripped-down crew compared to what we might have had at Cinecittà, but still a full house, to be sure.

I saw both Mr. Meyerson and Paul arrive with none other than Terrence Leopold; they must have personally escorted him from Rome. He looked exactly like what I'd pictured: dark sunglasses, white impish smile. Lucrezia quickly recovered from her spat with my aunt to go and say hello. The grip and camera operators unloaded additional equipment from trucks.

"I'm sorry. I know it must be strange having so many people here. Uncomfortable." I attempted to pat her arm and instead touched her pointy elbow. I withdrew my hand. "Maybe Richard was right. It might be easier to go away for a bit."

But she wasn't even listening to me. She'd gone pale as a sheet and muttered to herself, her hand still placed protectively around her neck. I couldn't catch anything she was saying.

"You don't look well. I'll get you a glass of water."

"You have to make them leave, Silvia." Her words were strangled. She truly looked distraught. It wasn't a bid for attention, a way to exercise her flair for drama; her sharp-boned face was pure anguish. "Please. Please do this for me."

I pitied her, of course, but I also couldn't suppress a twinge of annoyance. Everything had fallen into place so perfectly, I half-believed it must be destiny. Except here was the fly in the ointment, my own flesh and blood, the estranged aunt my mother had warned me not to trust.

"I don't know what I could possibly do." Perhaps it was heartless of me to not even try. But my own situation here still felt precarious. "I'll go get Richard, and you can talk it over."

"Good. Tell him I've changed my mind. They can't shoot the

movie here. This is my home." She took her hand off her neck and dabbed the corner of an eye. Had that been a tear?

"But—they paid you, didn't they?"

"I'll give it back."

I huffed, my irritation increasing, but also my worry. This could cause a major disruption, possibly even end the picture, and I couldn't afford to lose another job.

"I thought you wanted to spend time with me. I have to go where the picture goes."

"No, Silvia, you must stay here with me." Gabriella looked afraid again. I realized that her eccentricity might actually be true instability. "You have to make them all leave."

"I'll get Richard," I said again, and my legs shook from adrenaline as I exited the kitchen. I didn't know where he might be, but I quickly located a production assistant named Roberto, a lanky man a little younger than me.

"Can you find Richard for me? Tell him he's needed in the kitchen urgently. My aunt is saying she doesn't want them to film here after all. She's having a bit of a fit."

His eyes widened in astonishment—whether at the news or at the fact that I was entrusting him with such a task, I couldn't say—and he bounded off.

I waited until he returned obediently, an exasperated Richard in tow. I didn't accompany him into the kitchen. It was better if I stayed out of this fight. I didn't even stay to listen.

Instead, I went out the drive to meet Terrence Leopold.

CHAPTER 9

I'd met a handful of truly famous actors before, and it's often disappointing. They're usually smaller than you imagine, or less handsome. If you saw one on the street wearing sunglasses, you might look right past him.

Terrence Leopold wasn't like that. If anything, he was even more good-looking in person, and he exuded charisma. It wafted off of him like a strong cologne, knocking people back and stunning their senses. He stood in the driveway just outside his car door, where a ring of cast and crew had formed, unable to resist the pull into his orbit. He wore cream cotton chinos without a wrinkle on them—I haven't the slightest idea how he managed that after an hour's drive—a red knit mock turtle-neck, and brown loafers. He was as effortlessly stylish as Steve McQueen, only he was dark instead of fair. I had arrived too late to find a place in the circle and watched from the door as he shook everyone's hands. Lucrezia had lost no time in sidling up beside him, and I heard him greet her with British consonants as crisp as his pants, and saw him dazzle her with one of his wicked smiles. I could hear my own blood rushing, and my tongue suddenly seemed two sizes too large.

The idea of starring alongside him, of kissing him, had excited me. Confronting the reality of him in the flesh made me excruciatingly nervous.

Finally he broke away from his admirers. Then, to my utter

shock, he strode straight toward me. The rushing in my ears grew louder, and I stood still as a deer in the headlights.

I gawped at him, my mouth flapping open in search of oxygen or speech, but I was unable to breathe or utter a word.

"Excuse me." He gestured toward the door, which I realized I was blocking. "Are you from craft services? I'd just about murder someone for a glass of cold water and a sandwich. Can you have it brought to my room?" He winked at me and then pushed his way past me, not waiting for me to vacate the doorway.

I was too stunned to reply. My cheeks burned. He must have known who was cast to play opposite him, surely? Had he not seen a photo, or just not recognized me from it? Maybe it didn't matter to him one way or the other who played Bianca, since he was the only star who counted.

By the time I turned to correct him and introduce myself, he was already through the foyer and into the cavernous room beyond.

I was utterly mortified. I couldn't imagine facing him on set now, and have him look at me with a gorgeous puzzled face, wondering why the sandwich girl was standing beside him in the spotlight.

And I'd be damned if I was going to go get him a sandwich.

I released my breath in a whoosh and returned to the kitchen to see how Richard was faring. My aunt would serve as a distraction, at least, although I longed for someone to whom I could confess my embarrassment.

To my surprise, I found the kitchen empty. My aunt's espresso cup still sat on the table, apparently untouched. In my previous visits, she'd been conscientious about cleaning up the dishes, and the sight of it made me oddly uneasy.

"Silvia?"

I jumped. Richard appeared beside me, and I wondered why I hadn't heard his approach. I must have been too distracted.

"Where's Gabriella? Did you talk some sense into her?"

"I did. Wasn't as hard as I thought, actually. She's probably upstairs packing for the beach resort."

"Really?" I worried my bottom lip with my teeth. "Well done, I suppose. I didn't expect her to budge." Relief overcame me. She wouldn't ruin the picture, after all.

I studied Richard, but his face was oddly blank, aside from his startling blue eyes, which were full of an unreadable emotion. But maybe that was normal for him. He seemed like an intense guy.

"She was upset, don't get me wrong. But she said she couldn't bear to stay here." He shrugged.

"I better go tell her goodbye."

"I'd let her cool down a bit first."

"Fair enough."

So I left to find Lucrezia instead, and hear all about her first encounter with Terrence Leopold.

Still, the strangeness of my aunt's sudden acquiescence niggled at me. I wondered what exactly had changed her mind.

I surveyed the bedroom, tiny and bare as a monk's quarters, still dim except for a triangle of lemon sunshine filtering through the small window. I grabbed my wristwatch off the nightstand and squinted at it. I'd slept in, but then I'd been up late rehearsing my lines, and the mattress was new and soft. Above, the ceiling beams were riddled with holes—woodworms, probably—and I could make out a long-legged spider spinning its web. I fought to push the clean, soft blankets off me as I climbed out of bed onto the cold terra-cotta tile floor.

I was relieved for the lack of dreams. When I was younger, I used to suffer night terrors and sleepwalking, and I still remembered the fear that had seemed to sap the blood from my veins, the disorientation when I woke up down the hallway, or in the kitchen, or once on a neighbor's lawn. I mostly grew out of it, but after my aunt's ghost story, I had fretted a little about sleeping here.

I pulled on a robe and padded down the hall to the larger of the two shared bathrooms off the hallway, featuring a black-and-white mosaic tiled floor that was pitted and cracked in places, an old pedestal sink, and a clawfoot tub retrofitted with a rusted shower head. I splashed water on my face and brushed my teeth.

It was a rare leisurely morning; most days, I'd have to be up before the sun. But I was wired and anxious anyway, running my lines through my head as if someone might grill me on them at a moment's notice. I knew the entire script by heart, and if I kept going over it, I worried I'd end up stiff and over-rehearsed. So I decided to spend the day with Lulu instead, knowing it would calm me down and clear my head. Being around Lulu always grounded me. I got dressed quickly so that I could head straight to town and gather that sweet bundle into my arms.

Downstairs was already bustling. The great hall had been set up as unit base, with stations for makeup and costumes. The craft services table was equipped with three large silver coffee percolators and trays of fruit and pastries. Despite the activity, the room still felt oddly oppressive. Something about the turquoise lake peeking through the narrow windows gave me the chills. It was like you couldn't escape it.

I spotted Terrence Leopold in conversation with the costume director, Mrs. Leskowitz, jabbing a finger at the suit proffered in her hands in apparent disgust. My cheeks turned hot. His mistake yesterday had left me confused and off-kilter. I didn't want him to see me again, and I ducked back into the staircase, deciding to head down to the terrace, where they'd be readying for Lucrezia's first scene. It would be the most expensive and elaborate of the picture, and as eager as I was to see Lulu, curiosity about Lucrezia's performance made me linger. It would help my own acting to better understand her interpretation of the witch. And I was determined that Terrence should respect my skills after our first scene together. We weren't shooting in chronological order, and tomorrow would be the scene where he kissed me. There'd be no time for us to warm up to each other, and me to get over my nerves; I had to approach it like a seasoned veteran, detached and matter-of-fact. I imagined him tripping over his tongue apologizing afterward for not initially recognizing me as a fellow professional.

Mr. Meyerson was working on the blocking with Lucrezia

and some of the extras when I arrived. The crew had erected a massive stake surrounded by hay, where Lucrezia would be burned by the villagers. She stood on top of the bales stoically while Mr. Meyerson described something to her.

The villagers, I knew, had been recruited from the town: they wore black executioners' hoods, but I thought I spied the meaty hands of the card players from the piazza. It seemed fitting somehow. I'd witnessed how quickly their lethargy could erupt into violence, and I wouldn't be surprised if their ancestors *had* burned some witches a few hundred years ago. I could easily picture the town rising up with pitchforks and marching to the castle.

The cameras and big canister lights had been set up, and faced the tower, which loomed behind the stake. I admired the artistry of the staging. The scene took place at night, but modern filming techniques and special effects meant they could shoot it during the day. It looked creepy enough even without a black sky above; a dozen hooded men holding axes tended to have that effect.

Lucrezia looked completely at ease and utterly gorgeous in a medieval-style dress with a tight red bodice and a flowing skirt that clung to the shape of her legs. Someone tied her to the stake with a thick rope, and she didn't even bat an eye. Mr. Meyerson gestured to the piles of wood in front of the hay that would light on fire, and she nodded, sanguine.

Then Mr. Meyerson returned to his chair beside one of the camera operators. There was another camera attached to a crane, and I'd bet my next paycheck they'd use that footage for the final shot, showing the whole terrifying scene from above, the witch at the center, encircled by her executioners and about to burn. It would be jaw-droppingly poignant and dramatic. It began to dawn on me that perhaps Paul was right: perhaps Mr. Meyerson really was going to be the next Hitchcock. Tension, mingled with a sense of awe, seemed to settle over the whole set. We could all feel that we were about to be part of something special.

Paul shouted orders from a megaphone. The cameras started rolling.

The sound, unlike American films, wasn't recorded. We would do the studio syncing later. But even so, the set fell quiet as everyone stopped what they were doing to watch her. She lowered her chin to her neck, as if in gentle despair, and when she raised her head again, she was transformed. Her eyes seemed to glow with their own fire as the flame flared to life around her. It leaped high up from the piles of wood, arranged alarmingly close to the hay. If a spark leaped to the bales, how quickly would it spread? I knew we were on a tight budget and that some corners would need to be cut, but I hadn't processed exactly what that might mean before. I already knew they were only doing one take of this scene, and now I understood it was probably because of the danger as well as the expense.

Smoke filled my nostrils, and I held my breath, but Lucrezia didn't look afraid. Her face was full of righteous fury as she gave her speech cursing the villagers, swearing that she would rise up again to enact her revenge.

She was magnificent.

I've never been the jealous type, and her talent didn't make me jealous now. Instead, I was proud: proud that I was becoming friends with such a rising star, proud that I was acting alongside her. But I admit I felt the pressure of expectation for my own performance weigh down more heavily upon me.

Perhaps it had been a mistake to watch her. Now I was more nervous than ever.

I quietly slipped back into the castle, perspiration dampening my dress. My limbs seemed to operate of their own accord as they carried me through the great hall, down the stairs into the courtyard, and all the way to the little *pensione,* where Lulu was busy scrabbling about with her new playmates. Signora Ricci was keeping a careful eye on them, and my mother sat in a chair nearby, watching, looking tired but happy.

My mind had gone perfectly blank, stunned by the terrible beauty of Lucrezia's performance, but my arms scooped up Lulu and pulled her close to me until her little head was nuzzled in the crook of my neck.

Only then did my pulse stop racing. With Lulu nestled close, my lungs expanded, and my heart swelled with love.

Intimidated as I was, I told myself I could make it through this movie. I'd be *good*, damn it. I had to be.

For Lulu, I'd do absolutely anything.

CHAPTER 10

Mrs. Leskowitz, it transpired, was a miracle worker. It was still black outside when I arrived at her station in the great hall, and the weak small bulbs on the chandeliers and wall sconces cast dim and shadowy light. But her little area was a vibrant burst of color. The clothing racks had been arranged in a square to form a little room of sorts, and she sat on a shabby velvet chair—an original from the castle, I guessed—at the center of it, pins in her mouth and a costume on her lap. Her assistant, a Black woman named Sarah with a petite frame, short natural hair, and big eyes, was busy sorting clothes on the racks. There were changing rooms with cloth privacy curtains erected on metal poles. Mrs. Leskowitz rose and nodded a good morning at me when she saw me arrive, and Sarah brought over my first costume: a stunning iridescent evening dress of silk chiffon and sequins that looked like it had been poured straight from a bottle of champagne. It had a deep V neck to show off my cleavage and a long, flowing skirt. I'd seen it before during the costume fittings, but even so, I gasped when Sarah handed it over to me.

After I slipped it on, Mrs. Leskowitz zipped the back for me and studied me with satisfaction. I took in my appearance in the cheval mirror, and the blood rushing in my ears quieted to a dull roar. I was still keyed up, but in this dress at least I looked like Bianca, rich and confident and flirty.

"Thank you. It's marvelous," I said, as soon as I found my voice. Mrs. Leskowitz and Sarah beamed at me.

"You knock 'em dead, sweetie," Mrs. Leskowitz said, in a thick New York accent. "Especially that puffed-up peacock you're starring alongside."

I laughed in surprise. No one else had spoken a word against Terrence, so far as I had heard. "I admit I did see him get upset at you yesterday. I hope everything's all right."

"He thought the suit I chose for him made him look too old. The man's nearly forty, for God's sake. He should look *sophisticated*." She shrugged. "Stress makes people unpleasant."

"Stress?" I wondered what Terrence Leopold could possibly be stressed about. He was famous, and handsome, and a wonderful actor. I doubted *he* would be nervous this morning.

"Well, money troubles, from all the divorces, but also"—she leaned in close, and I could smell sugared coffee on her breath—"he's desperate for this picture to be a hit. No one films in Italy unless their star is either rising or falling. His is falling. Yours is rising, sweetie." She squeezed my arm.

"I hope so." I studied my reflection again and chewed my lip. It hadn't occurred to me that Terrence was on the downswing, although now that she'd said it, I saw the truth in it.

"You have some time before hair and makeup. I can run lines with you if you'd like."

"Would you really?"

Mrs. Leskowitz's eyes gleamed, and Sarah winked at me. "She used to be a vaudeville actress back in the day. Sewed all her own costumes." Sarah had a sweet, girlish voice. She motioned for me to spin around so she could inspect the back of my dress, and I felt a slight pinch as she pinned something.

"And what costumes. Those were the days."

So for the next fifteen minutes, I ran lines with Mrs. Leskowitz, who did have a vaudevillian flair for drama, and then I scurried over to hair and makeup. By the time they'd finished with me, I looked like I deserved to be starring in this picture. Maybe I wasn't as glamorous as Lucrezia, but I was beautiful. My lips were a deep pink; my eyebrows had been plucked and thickened and darkened so that they were almost as impressive as my aunt's. My figure in the champagne dress was something to behold.

At the very least, there'd be no more confusing me for the sandwich girl.

Still, the roar of blood in my ears grew louder again as I headed to the terrace to get ready for rehearsal. I hadn't spied Terrence yet, but then, his call time was a bit later than mine, since I had to do several solo shots before he arrived.

Unlike the stake scene, which had shot at the base of the northwest tower, this scene would be on the terrace in the middle of the castle, overlooking the gardens. My evening dress provided almost no protection against the chilly morning, and I was wide awake now, despite the hour. The scene took place in the early evening, but we'd be shooting it after dawn, when the sun was similar. The sky had lightened just enough that I could make out the dark shape of the lake. The water appeared inky-black now instead of turquoise, and I thought again of the dead woman and her child, their pale bodies sagging limply toward the muddy bottom.

It was just a story, and likely it wasn't even true. Still, I glanced away, focusing instead on the movie cameras that had been set up. I introduced myself to the camera operators and the grip, hoping my voice wouldn't crack from nerves, and then Herman Meyerson arrived, holding a cup of coffee and two pastries on a paper plate.

My stomach growled. I had completely forgotten to eat.

"I brought an extra," Mr. Meyerson said amicably, and I blushed. I must have been staring. He held out the paper plate, and I gratefully plucked up a cornetto, which was similar to a croissant. "Actresses always forget to eat before their first scene of the picture. I come prepared."

I laughed. "I don't want to mess up my face."

"We have Aurelia on standby."

That was true. Aurelia, a twentysomething Italian woman with a short bob and coral lipstick who had attended to me earlier, joined us outside. She wore an apron full of the tools of her trade and wielded a makeup brush in one fist like a spear. So I accepted the cornetto gratefully, and when I finished, Aurelia fixed my lips.

"So I'm not the first actress to be preoccupied before her first take, then?" I asked, lightly.

Mr. Meyerson smiled fondly at me. "Don't worry. Right now, all you need to do is stare out at the lake and look thoughtful and beautiful. It won't be hard. Look how gorgeous you are."

There was nothing remotely lecherous about the way he said it; it was more fatherly, and I was flattered. "Thank you."

"Follow me, and I'll show you just where to stand."

I placed my hands on the stone wall where he showed me, and forced myself to look back out at the lake. The sun had risen and painted the sky orange. We were above the fog line at the castle, but mist rose off the water below. I tried to look dreamy and romantic. Yet the thought of those waterlogged corpses pushed its way forward in my mind once again.

"Not quite like that. You look frightened. There will be plenty of time for that later." Mr. Meyerson chuckled. "You are thinking of the handsome American man who you've only known for a few short days, but who has already found his way into your heart. You're envisioning a future with him."

I allowed my muscles to relax. On the edge of my vision, I saw Paul arrive.

"There. Just like that. That's perfect. Hold still."

Mr. Meyerson retreated, and one of the camera operators moved nearer to me to capture my profile.

And then everything seemed to happen in quick succession: Paul calling out "last looks," Aurelia coming forward to fix a strand of hair that had blown into my face, Paul yelling "lock it down" and "roll camera." Finally, Mr. Meyerson's authoritative rumble declared "action."

I stared at the lake. I pictured Terrence Leopold wooing me, but for some reason, what I heard in my mind was Paul's calm voice as he called the roll. I stood there for at least a full minute, holding my expression, studying the flat turquoise water.

"Cut!"

Mr. Meyerson walked over and touched my elbow. "That was marvelous. Now let's do it again."

*   *   *

When Terrence Leopold arrived on set, my first thought was that he should have listened to Mrs. Leskowitz's advice on the suit. I supposed a more classic American style of the type you might see on Madison Avenue wasn't avant-garde enough for a fashion icon like Terrence. He still looked splendid, in a slim-fit three-buttoned gray number and skinny tie, but it was much more of a British mod look and not as fitting for his character.

"All right, I'm here," he said. He was fifteen minutes late for his call time, but no one commented on it.

"Good." Mr. Meyerson rubbed his hands together. "You're going to walk to here and stop short when you see Bianca. You're going to look at her like you've never seen a vision so beautiful. It shouldn't be hard. After we get that shot, Silvia, you're going to turn around slowly, very slowly, elegant and sensuous. And you'll look happy to see him, but also a bit anxious. You have a lot on your mind."

Well, that should all come easily enough, I thought.

But Terrence surprised me. "Look, before we start. Are we sure you've cast her right? I mean you're saying she's supposed to be this goddess, but let's be honest here, she's not exactly Lucrezia Fileppi."

A flush crept up my neck. He'd only said exactly what I'd thought myself, but hearing my deepest insecurities confirmed by one of my icons mortified me more than I could describe. I wished the lake would flood and swallow me up. His brazenness in insulting me so openly astounded me.

"I'm quite sure." Mr. Meyerson's words were clipped and hard, his Swiss-German accent more pronounced than before. "Stand there."

Mr. Meyerson's defense of me mollified me the tiniest degree. Terrence was a big enough star that it wasn't out of the question for them to recast me at his request. I couldn't bear to look at him after his comment, so instead I took in the dizzying view of the gardens tumbling into the lake. Standing so close to the edge only unsettled me further, reminding me of the precariousness of my position, and I inched away from it.

My eyes drifted toward Paul, who was staring at Terrence

in open disgust. As the fixer, I would have expected him to be willing to do whatever it took to keep Terrence happy, but his amicable cowboy smile was nowhere in sight, and he was gripping his megaphone like he meant to throw it. He'd helped cast me, so perhaps Terrence's criticism felt personal.

"Final checks," Paul said, and I went back to contemplating the gardens and the lake and my uncertain future. Just like Bianca. When I turned to face Terrence, I didn't have to try to act like I had a lot on my mind. And I had to give Terrence credit: he must truly be a terrific performer, because he looked at me exactly like the goddess he thought I wasn't.

His casual cruelty had rattled me. I'd spent my entire childhood scabby-kneed and awkward, and his words had reduced me in an instant to that lonely, sad girl sneaking into the movie theater in San Diego. But that wasn't what bothered me. I wasn't even particularly vain, for an actress. It was that he'd meant to hurt me, to put me down. But I couldn't let it get to me. I was a professional, damn it.

It only took a few takes to get through the first shot. The next shot would require dialogue, and even worse, kissing. Despite my best efforts, I was still so upset that I didn't trust myself to speak. So I did what I always did when my emotions got the better of me: I closed my eyes and thought of Lulu's rosebud mouth and her chubby little hands, and remembered how it made me feel when she buried her face in my shoulder.

By the time Mr. Meyerson took us through the blocking, I'd calmed down. In the next shot, Bernard would confess his feelings for Bianca, and I relished the idea of Terrence groveling before me.

Mr. Meyerson called "action," and Terrence sidled up beside me at the terrace wall, so close I could feel the heat of his body beside mine.

"I thought I might find you here. It's a favorite place of yours, isn't it? Thinking about her again, aren't you?"

Terrence's American accent was still Mid-Atlantic posh, his words precise and cultivated. Funny to think how I'd been fantasizing about a real-life romance with him, about how I'd kiss him and touch my finger to the cleft in his chin in the crepuscular light. It was a relief there'd be no on-set shenanigans between us, now. It was true I hadn't been with a man since Lulu's father, but if Terrence hadn't been rude, I might have been at risk of tumbling into an ill-considered affair.

That was the last thing I needed. I didn't know why I was drawn to unkind men.

"I've been having nightmares about her every night. Awful nightmares. Even now, I can sense her, like she's lurking inside me. I'm frightened, Bernard." I met Terrence's warm brown eyes and allowed him to take my hand in his.

"I won't let anything happen to you. I'm crazy about you, Bianca. Head over heels. So long as I'm here, the witch won't touch a hair on your head."

I pulled my hand away. "But you're not going to be here much longer. Oh, Bernard. I need to get away from this awful place."

"Then come with me." He cupped my face with his palm. His skin was soft.

"What are you saying?"

"I'm saying I want you to marry me, and leave this haunted pile of rocks behind once and for all."

And then, before I had a moment to catch my breath, he wrapped his arms tight around me and kissed me, long and slow. He was a fantastic kisser, the best I'd ever encountered.

Thank God he'd insulted me.

"Cut. Let's do it again."

"Hang on a moment." Terrence released me so suddenly I stumbled backward. I reached out to catch myself on the stone wall and scraped my fingers. Terrence rubbed a sleeve across his mouth. "Can't you get her to show a bit more expression this time? Her face is so blank. When she does her lines, it reminds me of a dying fish flapping its mouth."

I gasped. "What the hell is your problem?"

"There. That's more like it. Try to show that kind of passion in the next take. But love and not hate, of course."

Hot blood rushed into my cheeks. "There's no reason to treat me this way. What do you have against me, exactly?"

"Look, love. I really want this picture to do well. I have an ex-wife in Kensington who's counting on it. And I'm not sure you're good enough. So try to be better. For both our sakes."

Aurelia came over just then to touch me up. "He's a pig. Most of the famous ones are," she whispered as she sponged something over my skin.

"Thank you."

She winked at me before heading back to her spot.

Mr. Meyerson walked over and stood between us, like a father mediating a fight between squabbling children. "Silvia, that was an excellent first take. On the next one, make your features even more exaggerated. Everything must be more exaggerated on camera. Terrence, leave the directing to me. I don't expect to have to say it again."

Just then, one of the big canister movie lights popped loudly, its bulbs sparking and dying. The light itself teetered forward on its spindly stand, and I barely had the presence of mind to jump out of the way before it came to a dramatic crash beside me, shards of glass littering the stone. I screeched. It was a big, hulking thing, and if it had hit me, I'd have been seriously injured. Maybe even killed.

"What the hell, Carlo?" Paul shouted. Carlo was the gaffer, responsible for everything to do with lighting on the picture, a jovial mustached man who had struck me as a consummate professional. He looked shaken, his usual cheer gone.

"The sandbags were all in place around the base when I checked last night. I checked, I swear I checked. It shouldn't have fallen. I'm so sorry, Paul. Silvia."

"So what do you think happened?" Paul spoke more sharply than I'd ever heard before. His eyes sparked like the lights.

"Maybe someone bumped the sandbags out of position. And the stones on the terrace are uneven." He didn't sound convinced. The idea flashed across my mind briefly that perhaps someone moved the sandbags on purpose. After Terrence's cutting remarks, what happened felt personal, as if someone didn't want me on this picture. But of course that was absurd—paranoid. The timing couldn't have been planned so precisely. The light could have fallen near any one of us.

Everyone stared at the canister in shock, and no one spoke for a minute as we all processed the danger we'd just escaped. Finally Mr. Meyerson called out, "Everyone break for thirty," before walking over to me and placing a hand protectively on my arm. "Are you all right, dear?"

I nodded, not able to find my voice. I knew it was probably just a freak accident. But I couldn't help but think that the castle was making some kind of point. *A haunted pile of rocks*, Terrence's character had called it, and it fit.

Carlo approached me somberly, wringing his hands, and apologized again, before heading to inspect the long extension cords snaking from the lighting setup to the castle door. He muttered under his breath about the wiring in the castle being a disaster.

I never even fully understood why we needed lights for outdoor shoots—something to do with backlighting or shadows—but apparently, we couldn't do without them, and Carlo worked fast to clear the broken light and haul in a new one.

We had to do far more takes than we should have, after that, and I knew it was hardly my best performance.

When we finally wrapped, I was still rattled. Not only that, my neck was sore, my lips were chafed, and my ego was critically wounded.

Everything about the shoot struck me as a bad omen.

And I never, ever wanted to kiss Terrence Leopold again.

CHAPTER 11

After I'd changed into comfortable clothes and scraped the last of the makeup off of my face, I went in search of my aunt's bedroom. I hadn't seen her since her tantrum in the kitchen two days ago, and I didn't know if she'd gone on her trip already or if her reclusiveness had led her to hide away. It was hard to imagine her behind the wheel of a car. It seemed too modern, and she struck me as much a part of the castle as the suit of armor and the waterlogged cherubs.

And the ghosts.

She belonged to it; she belonged to a different time.

So I went to see for myself if she was still lurking about.

I had a better understanding of the layout of the castle by now, and went through the first floor room by room. The sky was pitch black outside, and the west side of the castle didn't even have functioning electricity, so I stumbled through the gallery. It seemed longer than I remembered. I would have touched one of the walls to help me feel my way forward, but I was scared of spiders.

I managed, though. I also inspected the library in the south wing and a ramshackle music room in the east wing. The walls here were covered in beautiful, faded red and green frescoes framed by ornamental molding, and the floor was mosaic tile instead of terra-cotta. Entire segments of the mosaics had been removed, revealing powdery white plaster beneath, and the dust in the air was so thick that I sneezed.

After passing through the dining room, I found myself back at the northeast tower and bumped into one of the production assistants, Roberto.

"Do you know where Gabriella Conti's bedroom is?" I asked, sweetly. I could spend all day trying to find it. Luckily, he knew. It turned out the entire top floor of the northeast tower, right above the room where I stayed, was dedicated to her bedroom suite.

By the time I finished climbing the steep, spiral stone stairs, I was out of breath. It seemed terribly inconvenient to have to climb those stairs every day, but at least it explained her slim figure.

I opened the stairwell door and stepped into darkness. I groped along the plaster wall until I found a switch panel with a knob. I turned it, and several chandeliers blazed to life. I would have knocked if I'd realized there was no hallway of any kind; I'd stepped right into a remarkable, enormous round room, with a massive four-poster canopy bed, a tufted chaise lounge, a dressmaker's dummy, several huge overlapping oriental rugs, and racks upon racks of clothes skirting the perimeter. The walls were hung with paintings, but they were colorful and abstract, nothing at all like the dark old-fashioned oil works I'd seen elsewhere in the castle. The overall effect was fabulously bohemian and eccentric. It couldn't have been anyone's room but hers.

She was nowhere in sight. I frowned. She was an odd one, but the fact that she'd sneaked off for her vacation without saying a word to me stung a little.

I should have left, but I didn't. Instead, I walked over to inspect the racks of clothes, which were stuffed to bursting. I pawed through them, admiring the rich colors and couture styles. There were psychedelic Pucci prints and Simonetta evening gowns, as well as sheath dresses that I wondered if she'd sewn herself. Under one rack, I found several dusty pieces of leather luggage. Of course, she could have had other suitcases, but it struck me that the room didn't bear any of the usual signs of packing. No clothes seemed to be missing, and there were no empty hangers askew. Some sewing patterns and a copy of

Italian *Vogue* were strewn on a wooden marble-topped vanity, where I also found her makeup kit. That was strange. I couldn't imagine her leaving it behind.

Perhaps she hadn't left, and I'd just missed her. She could be in the great hall, getting a late dinner. I did a final sweep of the room, in case there was a hidden door or something like that, but there wasn't—just the plastered-over stone of the tower walls.

As I stepped around to the other side of her bed, I tripped over something low to the ground and cried out. My toe throbbed. I looked down and saw that it had been an antique wooden cradle, with faded red, green, and gold paint.

The sight of it gave me the chills. The cradle certainly looked like it could be a few hundred years old, and Gabriella had said the nursery that the ghost haunted had been in this tower. What on earth would have possessed her to turn it into her bedroom?

Of course, the cradle could have been Gabriella's. She and her husband had been childless, but perhaps they'd once had other plans. The thought made me sad for her, and I pitied her all over again, for being alone for so many years.

The room was colder than the rest of the castle, and I rubbed my arms. Suddenly it felt a bit creepy rather than arty and offbeat. The dressmaker's dummy cast a human-like shadow on the wall, and I headed straight for the stairs.

I was relieved to return to the great hall, which still had a handful of cast and crew hanging about, laughing over paper cups of wine. I was grateful for the presence of other people. I spied Richard and Lucrezia in conversation and went over and tapped Richard's shoulder.

"Do you know if my aunt went to the resort already? I never got a chance to speak to her after her little episode the other day."

Richard, usually serious, looked particularly somber, and even Lucrezia looked perturbed, as if I'd interrupted an important conversation. "Yeah, she did. She split."

I thought of the pile of suitcases in her room, the makeup askew on her vanity. "How do you know?"

He shrugged. "After I spoke with her, she said she was leaving right away. I thought you knew. Roberto can get the number for you, if you want to call her." He turned back to Lucrezia, his shoulder blocking me from their orbit, and I took the hint and retreated. I wondered what Lucrezia would want with Richard; he didn't exactly seem like her type. But maybe they were talking about the movie.

I located Roberto and got the number Richard promised. It was for a beach resort in Santa Marinella, only about an hour away. I went to find the phone I remembered seeing in the kitchen, and spun the numbers around with shaking fingers. I didn't know why I was uneasy. Most likely, she'd be there, just like Richard said she was. There was no real reason she shouldn't be.

But something didn't feel right.

A female hotel clerk answered promptly. "*Pronto.*"

"Hello. Is this Le Naiadi?" I asked, in Italian.

"*Si.*"

"I'm hoping to speak with one of your guests. Gabriella Conti."

"I'm happy to take a message for you," she replied. Her voice was bright and crisp, too cheerful for the late hour.

"Can you connect me to her room? It's urgent."

The phone went silent. Then I heard mumbled Italian in the background, the woman speaking to someone else at the desk. "Hello?"

"I'm sorry, but Signora Conti hasn't checked in yet. I can pass along a message when she arrives."

The receiver turned to lead in my hand. "Thank you." I dropped it into the cradle, too hard, and the resulting clang made me jump. I sunk into a chair.

I knew in my gut that something was very, very wrong.

Richard and Lucrezia were still deep in conversation when I returned to the great hall. Lucrezia pouted. She'd abandoned her paper cup and drank straight from a wine bottle, which had stained her full mouth red. It made me think, fleetingly, of the scene where the witch drank Bianca's blood to complete her transition back to her corporeal form. Carlo had set up some extra lights in the room, since the existing fixtures weren't very powerful, and Richard stood in front of a bright, harsh beam that reflected off of his coke-bottle glasses and turned his doughy face even paler. The effect was a little frightening.

"He could find more money, if he thought it was important," she said, as I neared.

"But it's not important. You getting to go dancing at Bricktop's in the evenings is not a priority, Lucrezia."

"What's the matter?" I tried to sound casual, but I was shaking. Richard, I'd decided, had lied to me. It was the only explanation. He'd said my aunt had readily agreed to his request and left to pack right away, but I no longer believed it. The abandoned espresso cup, the untouched suitcases in her room, and the information from the hotel clerk told quite a different story.

My aunt either left the castle in a great hurry—or she had never left at all. I couldn't ignore the zapping of my nerves, and the mounting suspicion that something bad had happened to her. Maybe it had just been a terrible disagreement of some kind, and she'd stormed off somewhere, but if that had been the case, surely someone would have noticed the commotion. Whatever had occurred, I was starting to think Richard knew more than he was letting on.

I walked over to the craft services table and poured myself a paper cup of the wine. I drank it in a single gulp and then poured another. It was smooth and light and went down easy. The buzz of alcohol in my blood calmed the trembling of my hands. Some of the crew were still chatting and drinking nearby, and the hum of conversation reverberated strangely in the enormous space. The two camera operators, the grip, and the director of photography had squeezed together on the fringe-bottomed sofa, and it dipped under their weight.

"Lucrezia wants us to film all of the interior shots at Cinecittà. I told her we can't afford it. Not only would we need more money for the sets, it would extend production, which means we'd have to pay all the actors more. Terrence already cost a fortune. It would sink the picture."

"No one would mind the extra time if we were in Rome."

"It's not about *minding*, it's about *salaries*, Lucrezia."

Lucrezia sighed dramatically and swigged from her bottle. Somehow she made even that look chic. I swallowed my own wine greedily, and my limbs and tongue loosened. I took a deep breath and launched in.

"My aunt is not at the beach resort, Richard." I ran my tongue over my front teeth, already furred with Chianti. "You were the last person to see her. I want to know exactly what happened."

Richard ran a hand through his brown bob and tugged some of the strands in exasperation. He stared at the ceiling and groaned. "I just can't, with the two of you. Anyone else have a fucking complaint they want to throw at me right now?"

I drained the paper cup and crumpled it in my fist. "She's *missing*. This is serious. Tell me what you said to her."

Lucrezia let the bottle of wine dangle from her hand and looked curiously at me, then at Richard. "I don't understand. What happened to your aunt?" She slurred her words a little, and her eyes drooped attractively.

"She was refusing to leave the castle during the production, and then she said she wanted to cancel the whole thing. But Richard somehow magically changed her mind. Except that he didn't, because she never checked into the beach resort they booked for her. She's just *gone*. Something happened, and I want him to tell me the truth."

I hadn't meant to shout, but I'd picked up steam somewhere in the middle of my little speech. My cheeks were hot, and the balled-up paper cup was clutched tightly in my fist. The group on the sofa stopped their conversation to stare at me.

Richard heaved a sigh. But I had his attention. His ice-blue eyes and thick glasses glinted in my direction.

"Look, I already told you everything. She said she was leaving. So what if she's not at the beach resort? She probably just went somewhere else. She could have gone anywhere."

I studied him, and he didn't avert his gaze. He had spoken passionately and sincerely. He was a terrific liar, if he was lying, I'd give him that much.

"Who left the kitchen first, you or her?"

At the very least, I could establish a timeline of events. Perhaps someone else had seen her leave. Richard furrowed his brow, as if trying to remember. "I did. She was still standing at the window when I left."

I tossed the balled-up cup onto the table. Lucrezia watched its arc and then opened her sleepy eyes wider. "I don't like this. We should be in *Rome*. It doesn't feel right. This whole place. Can't you feel it?" She placed a silky hand on my arm. She looked afraid. "It's not because I want to go *dancing*, Richard. Something is wrong here. I'm with Silvia on this." She came closer and tucked her arm around mine.

"Thank you, Lucrezia." I was starting to feel a little drunk. "I want to find out what happened to her, Richard. You find out where she went." I jabbed my finger in his direction. Then Lucrezia steered me out of the room.

"Never underestimate the power of a dramatic exit," she whispered, as we neared the staircase to our rooms. "It will be all right, Silvia. We'll find out where she is. I'm sure she's okay." She patted my hand as if I were a child. I didn't mind being coddled by her; she was soft and beautiful and smelled like gardenias. Anyone would like it.

"You're so nice. And you're so talented. You were wonderful yesterday."

"I didn't know you'd seen." She smiled at the compliment.

"Terrence said I looked like a dying fish in my scene today. I'm worried I'm going to ruin everything."

She stopped short. "Never let a man make you doubt yourself, Silvia. Okay? Now come on. You have an early call time tomorrow."

I let her lead me upstairs. I thought longingly of my bed. It had been an emotionally exhausting day.

Suddenly, a cry tore through the air, and Lucrezia tightened her grip on my arm, startled. We both stared at each other, wide-eyed.

A woman moaned, long and distraught. It was coming from the bedroom across from Lucrezia's. Terrence's room.

"Come on. Let's go help." I tugged Lucrezia along with me, and we burst the door open.

At first, I didn't understand what I was seeing. A tangle of limbs, a woman wailing as if in pain.

And then I saw Terrence's bare, sweaty chest, chiseled and covered in dark hair, and the woman bent over on her hands and knees in front of him. He was thrusting into her so fast and hard her whole body was shaking, and I understood she wasn't crying out in agony but ecstasy. He looked up and locked eyes with me, then grinned and continued his attack. Lucrezia erupted into a fit of giggles and dragged me out of the bedroom.

In the hall, she doubled over laughing. "Your face, Silvia! Oh, that was too good."

"Oh my God."

"Don't look so horrified. I don't think he minded the interruption at all."

The screaming continued, if anything, louder than before, until it crescendoed in one final howl, a male voice blending in with the female.

"Was she actually enjoying it, do you think?" Lucrezia whispered, her eyes full of mischief.

"No. Faking for sure."

"Hmm. It makes one curious." Lucrezia tapped her chin with a polished nail. I raised my eyebrows. "Oh, don't look so shocked. I didn't say I was going to go to bed with him, just that I was *wondering* about it. Look, I'm not a good girl, Silvia. And if you're going to be bad, why not go all out?"

I was still recovering from my mortification, but I managed a chuckle. "Fair enough."

She shrugged. "I like to have fun. But I value my friendships above everything. That's one thing you should know about me." She hooked her arm in mine again. "Let's go tuck you in."

The door to Terrence's room creaked open, and he emerged in nothing but a robe. He looked relaxed and satisfied, and completely unabashed. He'd lit a cigarette and took a long drag as he eyed us with evident amusement. "Did you ladies enjoy the show?"

Even from three feet away, he reeked of whiskey. "Not particularly." I crossed my arms. "Your acting partner was terrible."

"We thought the poor girl was being tortured to death," Lucrezia added.

"She'll recover, I think. Lovely thing from craft services. That could have been you, you know, if you'd ever brought me the sandwich I asked for." He winked at me and walked closer. I made a face. The impact of his handsomeness had started to lose its effect on me. Seeing him at first was sort of like when you walk out into a startlingly bright day, blinded and blinking, but then your eyes adjust. Now the sight of him only reminded me of his callousness.

"I'll stick to acting, thanks. And tell her she should stick to sandwiches, if she knows what's good for her."

He exhaled a puff of smoke and a trace of laughter.

"You know, next to each other like this, you could be sisters." He leaned toward me, so that I could feel his hot whiskey breath on my ear. "There's always a prettier sister, though, isn't there?"

He eyed Lucrezia appreciatively so that neither of us would misunderstand whom he meant. I backed away. I didn't know what he was after, putting me down like this, but I refused to let it impact me. If this was how things would be between us, I'd have to prepare for it so that his needling wouldn't hurt my performances.

"No. There isn't," Lucrezia snapped, and fixed him with a scathing glare. We both turned on our heels, and Lucrezia came into my room with me. I guess she'd meant it literally when she said she wanted to tuck me in. She sat on the end of my bed. "What an absolute pig. You don't have a cigarette, by chance?"

I shook my head. "I don't smoke much."

Lucrezia clapped her hands together. "I knew it. You are a good girl. You know, I feel it is my duty to corrupt you."

I turned to the corner and stripped before tugging my nightgown over my head. People in show business weren't modest about that sort of thing. Then I crawled under the covers and faced Lucrezia straight-on.

"I'm not a good girl, believe me." I had no intention of telling her or anyone about Lulu, because once a secret like that got out, everyone would know. Single mothers were scorned by society; even with movie people, it was looked down upon. Sleeping around was one thing, but getting into trouble was quite another. Her father and I hadn't used protection because he hadn't wanted to and because, of course, he'd promised to marry me. I was barely seventeen when I took up with him— he was twenty-four—and we couldn't get a license without my mother's consent, which she staunchly refused to give. The relationship flamed out within a few months; his drinking drowned the charisma that had first pulled me in. I left.

I hadn't known I was pregnant at the time. When I found out, he'd already left Los Angeles to go on tour with his band, and the thought of tracking him down in some scummy motel room to beg for money he didn't have—well. It seemed better to say nothing at all. It was my mother who came to my rescue, who moved to Los Angeles and promised to care for her grandbaby, who painstakingly helped me pick up the pieces of my broken life.

Not that I regretted Lulu for a single instant. My love for her was the best and purest part of me.

Lucrezia must have read something in my face, because she stood. "I don't suppose we are quite drunk enough to tell each other all about our conquests. But maybe next time." She smiled indulgently at me. "Sleep well, Silvia. Tomorrow, we'll look for your aunt, okay?"

Then she got up, light as a cat on her feet, and slipped out of my room.

I closed my eyes. Even though my mind was full of my aunt, spinning with all the things that might have happened to her, it didn't take long to drift off. The last image in my mind before I did was of Terrence Leopold smoking in his robe in the hallway, his eyes amused and cruel.

Chapter 12

I was trapped. The maze of the town had penned me in, the *vicoli* narrowing around me. The footsteps of my pursuer clapped the stone, not far behind me now, not hurried. There was no need, because the steep little passageway I'd turned into went nowhere. Before me was a dingy alley with empty vegetable crates, a string of laundry, a bag of garbage, and an unyielding wall of stone. A dead end.

I rattled the handle of a faded green door, pounded on the wood, but to no avail. I knew the person following me wanted to kill me. I didn't know why. But someone had hooked an arm around my neck, covered my mouth to muffle my scream, before I broke free. Soon, I'd know who it was.

I kicked the door, bruising my toe. My jagged breaths and those footsteps, drawing closer, were the only noise.

And then I woke up. The sheets were tangled around me, hot and damp. It had been a nightmare. Thank God. My mouth tasted like sand, and I shakily poured a glass of water from the pitcher beside my bed and gulped it down. It had seemed so real.

By the time I'd readied myself to go downstairs, the details had grown fainter, but the sense of foreboding remained.

My poor sleep must have shown in my face, because Aurelia clucked over me in the hair and makeup chair. She rubbed something underneath my eyes. My head ached.

The awful dream had only strengthened my conviction that my aunt must be found. My subconscious was clearly trying to tell me something. I summoned Roberto and told him to please pass along the message that I thought we should delay filming until more inquiries had been made about Gabriella, and in no time at all, Paul and Richard appeared.

"Before you even ask, I already phoned the beach resort again. She's still not there," Richard said. He glared at me. "But we're not delaying. There's no room in the schedule."

I jutted my chin out, meeting his scowl with my own. Paul's face was neutral, appraising. "I can't just go and do my scene like nothing is wrong. She's my family. I think we should call the police."

My worry had increased. And there was no one else, besides me, who would care to look for her. She'd offered to take me in when I had nothing and had given me hope that Lulu and I wouldn't have to be alone in the world, after my mother passed. I owed this to her. And to Lulu.

"The police? Don't you think you're being a bit dramatic?"

"I'm an actress," I snapped. "But no, I'm not."

Paul wore brown corduroys and a white T-shirt that revealed his strong arms. I'd never seen him in a T-shirt before, and the effect was a bit intimidating. I supposed the fixer of a production had to be fit, like a nightclub bouncer. It gave the impression that if you didn't comply with his instructions, you could get kicked off the picture. That handsome, friendly veneer just helped ensure you'd go quietly. Richard was stocky and, in flared checkered pants, considerably less intimidating, but still plenty unpleasant.

"Look. This isn't really my area, but I'm going to say it anyway. You're an unknown actress. You've only filmed one scene. From a budget standpoint, if we had to recast you, we could take the hit. The more scenes you film, the harder that gets. You understand?" Richard adjusted his giant glasses, and his enlarged blue stare made me feel like a bug under a magnifying glass.

I gripped the makeup chair with slippery palms, and the moist castle air turned my sweat cold. "Is that a threat?"

He shrugged. "Not a threat. Just a reality. It doesn't help that Terrence doesn't like you."

"Has Mr. Meyerson said anything about recasting me?" My voice reached a slightly hysterical pitch. Paul looked sorry for me, and I resented that even more than Richard's warning.

"He hasn't. I don't think it's even crossed his mind," Paul said, using a placating spooked-horse voice on me. I glowered at him. "Richard is going to look into this business about your aunt, urgently. I promise you."

"Sure. I already said I would."

"I understand you're worried about her. And if you're not up for acting today, I'll go talk to Mr. Meyerson, and we can change the setup for one of Lucrezia's scenes."

"Like hell we will. That will mess up the whole schedule. It will take them hours to do another setup." Richard's voice grew wheezy. He was acting exceedingly put-upon and teetering on the brink of being truly angry.

I squared my shoulders and took a deep breath. "No. I can do it. Just promise me you'll find out where she is."

I hated going along with it, but Richard's cold, heartless logic had made its desired impact. Nothing had changed about how desperately I needed this job. And I didn't actually *know* my aunt was in trouble. I just felt it in my gut. What other explanation made sense? She could have had some sort of accident. I remembered the maze from my dream; maybe she had gone into town and tripped down a staircase. Or perhaps she *had* tried to go to the beach resort, and taken a train, but gotten terribly lost, or mugged, or—it was no use guessing. The point was, there was a good chance something was really wrong, and it was heartless to just do nothing.

Richard was tense and fidgety, like he'd had too much caffeine. He didn't relax after my concession; he just nodded to acknowledge it. "I'll work on it. It's going to end up being a whole lot of nothing, you know." He strode off, slapping his hands against the sides of his legs.

Paul studied me with concern, as if I were a car he were inspecting for damage—probably because he wanted to make sure I wouldn't risk the schedule again. "I'll see you out there, okay?"

He lit a cigarette. In contrast to Richard, whom I could already tell was the tightly wound type, Paul seemed unflappable. I watched him go, and saw that he stopped to speak to Sarah and Mrs. Leskowitz. The three of them laughed over something. He was charming, I'd give him that. Good-looking, too. Not like Terrence, whose handsomeness dazzled you; whose perfectly coiffed hair and too-white teeth gave him an air of unreality. Paul was less polished, more rough-hewn. I didn't know why I was noticing, or why it irritated me the way Sarah's dark eyes lingered on his over their shared joke. He wasn't mean like Terrence, but for some reason, he still made me uneasy. I couldn't relax around him.

Once my makeup was finished, I headed to the lowest tier of the garden, where we'd be filming the scene I'd first auditioned. Mrs. Leskowitz had dressed me today in a checkered pink-and-white dress with a bow at the waist; it was light and fresh and summery, and I didn't give a damn what Terrence thought of it. I looked pretty and feminine, perfect for Bianca in this moment, still naïve and carefree.

Claude and his set designers had done a number on the garden. They'd somehow made its wildness even spookier—adding extra vines draping over the statue of the nymph Daphne, weeding the base so that we could see her marble feet turning to tree roots. They'd placed several taxidermic crows on the garden wall nearby, and I startled as one of them took flight. Apparently a real one had momentarily paused to join its dead cousins.

Terrence was late again, and I could sense Mr. Meyerson's mounting annoyance as we waited. He looked tired. Every other time I'd seen him, he'd been immaculately dressed, but today his slacks were creased, and a few strands of his Brylcreemed hair curled at odd angles. Roberto brought him his coffee with milk instead of black, and he dumped it out in front of him into the garden dirt, his eyes challenging. Mr. Meyerson spoke accented Italian to the non-American members of the crew, which was most of them, and he swore at him in Italian now. The profanity shocked me. Roberto was smart enough not to say anything, and jumped backward before scurrying away to get a fresh cup. Mr. Meyerson had only ever been kind and patient toward me, and his petulance surprised me.

"Claude, we are going to do the statue shots, since Terrence is delayed," Mr. Meyerson said after twenty minutes of waiting.

Claude and one of his set designers readied the plaster replica of the statue of Daphne, where she was smiling instead of looking afraid. As he worked, the wind fluttered his paisley scarf, even brighter than the one I'd seen him wear before.

Mr. Meyerson examined the replica with a critical eye. "The placement of the vine there doesn't quite match."

Claude adjusted the vine the tiniest degree. "There. Is that better?"

Mr. Meyerson stepped back. "Yes. So much better." Mr. Meyerson replied to Claude with an exaggerated lisp. Claude didn't lisp, but I'd heard that he was a homophile, and it seemed that Mr. Meyerson was mocking him for it. A flush crept up Claude's neck. One of the camera operators chuckled. Claude seemed too upset to say anything and walked out of the shot with his face toward the ground, his hands stuffed deep in his pockets. I didn't know him well, but my heart broke to see his mortification, and I wished I could offer him some sort of solace.

Paul beat me to it. He was by his side in a moment. I couldn't hear what he was saying, but I could imagine him using the same calming tone he'd used on me that morning.

The camera operators changed positions to do the close-up shots of both statues, the real and the fake. Terrence arrived just as they were finishing, looking completely unrepentant about his tardiness. He came to stand next to me, and my mind filled with the image of him naked on the bed, stomach slick with sweat as he pounded away at his latest conquest. I could barely meet his eyes.

"Sorry. I was up late last night." He winked at me.

Based on Mr. Meyerson's mood that morning, I expected him to give him hell, but he just frowned and called out, "Let's get to work."

Terrence, to my relief, behaved all through rehearsal. I thought I'd done quite well. But before the first take, he looked at me and sighed. "Look, Herman, I'm still really struggling with the casting here. She just doesn't *look* like Bianca to me."

Terrence kept his tone calm and reasonable, as if he merely wanted Mr. Meyerson's insight to help his performance. It was more insidious than criticizing me again directly, and he smirked at me. My insides boiled.

"How do you imagine Bianca?" Mr. Meyerson sounded genuinely curious, and suddenly I couldn't catch my breath. Richard had said they could afford to recast me at this stage, and Mr. Meyerson surely knew it, too. Was he considering it?

"More like Lucrezia."

My pulse ticked in the hollow of my throat. It would be easy to make that call; since she was already in the picture, they'd hardly lose any time. Lucrezia could even play both parts, since Bianca was meant to be the descendant of the witch's cousin. Mr. Meyerson looked thoughtful. He took Terrence by the arm and led him toward me.

"In the story, the witch represents our carnal desires. She is female sexual power, manifested. So she must be an incredible beauty, ethereal, unattainable. Bianca is uncorrupted. We want her to be more—accessible." He waved a hand over me as he spoke. "They are each other's counterparts. The witch is what Bianca could become, the temptation she must vanquish. Does that make sense?"

Terrence's lip curled. "So the witch is sort of like the prettier sister?"

Mr. Meyerson nodded. "Something like that."

I took a deep breath and went to stare at the lake. The sky was a vivid blue today, the sun blazing, but the turquoise water was opaque, seeming to swallow its light. I didn't really care that Lucrezia was more beautiful than me, but hearing her complimented so repeatedly, when I had yet to earn any sort of praise, hurt. This was my first starring role, and I'd been doing my best, but no one had acknowledged my efforts. Instead,

I was constantly on the defense, having to prove I deserved to be there. It was emotionally draining. The water before me was calm, but inside I struggled to contain my waves of feelings.

I placed my hands on the low stone wall and tilted my face toward the sun. But almost immediately, I withdrew them; I'd touched something slick and wet. Some sort of garden slime. I looked down and screamed.

My hand was red with blood.

I kept screaming, completely overcome. There was a large ugly stain at the edge of the wall, about the size of a salad plate. Or a head.

Blood had seeped into the gray rocks, turning them maroon, and some of the lower rocks were smeared, as well. It looked— well, it looked just like someone's skull had been bashed against the stone.

I stepped abruptly back, tripping over a root and landing hard on my rear. It knocked the wind out of me, and only then did my shrieking stop.

Mr. Meyerson hurried over to help me up. "What's wrong?" His accent always sounded thicker when he was expressing emotion. I couldn't speak, and got shakily to my feet. The fall had hurt, and I could feel a bruise blossoming.

Paul strode over. "Look. There's blood on the wall. Quite a lot of it."

"Claude, was this you?" Mr. Meyerson's words were short and clipped. I let myself relax a fraction. Perhaps it had been part of the set decoration. They would be using fake blood when Terrence's character cut himself on a bramble and dripped onto the witch's altar. And in plenty of other scenes, too. I'd heard there'd been a debate over whether to shoot the movie in black-and-white, but they'd decided on color, and they planned to take full advantage of it, painting every scene with lurid, symbolic shades, especially red. I studied my hand, and the crimson blemish across my palm, dotted now with pieces of gravel from my tumble. It didn't look like fake movie blood.

"No. It wasn't us." Claude spoke quietly, his words flat.

Terrence approached and stood next to Paul. Paul was a couple inches taller and a little leaner, and even beside Terrence, he still looked like a Spaghetti Western movie star. And he looked at Terrence like a gunslinger intent on a duel. I supposed he had minded his lateness more than Mr. Meyerson.

"It could have been an animal. A hawk could have gotten a squirrel." Terrence sounded entirely uninterested—bored, even. "Come on. We're wasting time."

Paul snorted, probably at Terrence's hypocrisy, and muttered something under his breath.

"I don't think it was a squirrel." My voice cracked. Paul scrutinized the stain and then me. He furrowed his brow. "What if it was Gabriella? Something could have happened to her." The shock had started to fade, replaced with a rising panic. I already knew Gabriella liked her coffee with *grappa*; maybe she'd gotten drunk and had a terrible fall? But no, that wouldn't do, because where was *she*?

I sucked in a breath and peered over the edge of the wall, half-expecting to see her corpse floating below, ugly and distorted. But the lake stretched out before us and without a single ripple, its cloudy water hiding its secrets.

Maybe it was the menacing setting that made my mind take a dark turn, but a more horrible theory began to take shape. If it had been an accident, her body wouldn't have disappeared, which left only a grislier alternative: that someone had killed her and hidden the evidence of their crime. It would have been all too easy to fill her pockets with stones before tipping her over. Or perhaps they had dragged her down to a boat first and then deposited her in deeper waters. I knew the blood was hardly proof, but I sensed in my bones that she was out there somewhere. That she was gone.

I put a hand over my mouth, resisting the urge to scream again. Now that the idea had presented itself, it struck me as the only logical explanation. True, I didn't know who would do such a thing, or why. But Gabriella was passionate and didn't mince words, so I supposed she could have insulted the wrong person. Or someone in town could have had a grudge against her; after all, the card players had made it clear she wasn't exactly popular.

Maybe Gabriella had been right when she called the castle cursed.

"What a load of rubbish." Terrence's nonchalance had turned to anger. "Come on, she's holding things up here."

He sounded personally affronted and seemed agitated. I wondered why. He'd sure been awfully quick to offer the theory about the squirrel, and his behavior struck me as a bit odd. "You know the saying, 'The lady doth protest too much'?"

"Excuse me?"

"It's Shakespeare. *Hamlet*. Heard of it?"

"Of course I know bloody *Hamlet*. I played it at the Globe. What exactly are you accusing me of?"

"You tell me."

The truth was, I didn't know what I was accusing him of, but his behavior rankled. He huffed. I was too preoccupied to care about his indignation. Mr. Meyerson placed a hand on my forearm. His earlier churlishness had vanished. "I want to find her too, my dear. We will do everything we can. I'll have Roberto ring the police now."

I exhaled. "Thank you."

Roberto, as if on cue, bobbed down the steep stone garden steps, with Richard beside him. Richard assessed our concerned huddle and frowned.

"Am I interrupting, or is this a good time?" he called out. He strode toward us along a gravel path at the base of the stairs, his gait slightly duck-footed. He could see for himself that we weren't filming.

"What is it?" Mr. Meyerson was attentive and concerned. "What did you learn?"

"It was a whole lot of nothing, just like I said. Her car is gone."

CHAPTER 13

Somehow, I managed to muddle through the scene after Richard's announcement, but I wouldn't be winning any awards for that performance. It was mortifying—both my acting and the way I'd behaved over the blood on the wall. If her car was gone, she'd obviously driven *somewhere*, and I felt like a fool. Now the rest of the cast and crew would think I was a drama queen. Probably Terrence was right, and it had been a squirrel or something. This castle had me spooked, and I wasn't acting rationally.

After we wrapped, I headed straight to town. As soon as I reached the cypress-lined path and passed through the arch into the piazza, my breathing grew easier. It was a beautiful evening, warm and breezy, and the town's quiet seemed peaceful today rather than ominous.

Lulu shrieked with delight when she saw me and handed me a petunia that looked like it came from someone's flower box. My mother gave a little head waggle as if to say *what can you do?*

"Thank you, darling, it's lovely. What a lovely purple flower."

"Geen." She pointed insistently at it, her voice rising and her eyes big.

"Yes, it's green too, on the stem. That's right. How nice of you to give it to Mommy, thank you."

"Welcome!" She gave me a hug, and I clung to her, as if I could absorb every molecule of her love, until she got bored and squirmed away.

"How was her day today?" My mother looked pale, her eyes deeper in their sockets than when I'd seen her last. "Why isn't she still with Signora Ricci? You shouldn't watch her alone. It's too much." I took my mother's dry hand in mine and led her to the chair.

"It's only been five minutes. We already ate dinner with them all. She didn't nap well today, so I took her up. I thought she might want to turn in a little early."

"I'm sorry I wasn't here sooner." My voice caught. The guilt of all the time I'd spent away pressed down upon me. I stroked Lulu's forehead, and she let out a big yawn.

"Don't ever apologize for that, Silvia. You're doing what you have to do. Just like I did."

She stuck her chin out, challenging me with her gaze. I'd never thought about it that way, but I supposed she was right. She'd had to raise me herself after my father died. Even then, I'd known she was doing the best she could. I could only hope Lulu would understand that when she was older.

I snuggled up with her in the bed and read her stories until she dozed off. My mother lay down on the other side of her. She'd changed into her nightgown. "I might turn in early, too. You should go back. See your castmates, do the politics thing. This is your big break. Don't mess it up because of me."

I studied her, trying to assess if she meant it or was just playing the martyr. Either way, I wasn't going to take her up on it. "I'd rather stay here tonight. I might not get another chance for a while. Besides, it was an awful day. I could use some time away."

"What happened?" She rolled over on her side to face me. We were both stage-whispering the conversation across Lulu's sleeping form. She had a stuffed bunny tucked under her arm.

"My scene today was horrible. Gabriella disappeared so suddenly, without saying goodbye, and I'd thought something had happened to her—"

My mother rolled back over to face the other way. "I don't care to discuss her, Silvia." Her voice had turned hard. "I don't want to hear you speak her name."

I groaned. I had hoped that being so physically near to her sister would at the very least make my mother more receptive to talking about her. But she was intractable. I hated that I couldn't even tell her about my day, especially when I really needed support. "Fine. I'm going out to grab a bite; I didn't eat yet," I snapped. I knew that I shouldn't get angry at her, when we didn't know how much time she had left, but she tested my patience.

My frustration only increased as I headed down the fluorescent-lit staircase and out into the night. It had grown darker, but the lanterns along the walls cast haloes of yellow light. My feet slapped the cobblestones as I sought out the square with the tiny café I'd seen when I first arrived in town. I smelled garlic and onions simmering as I passed people's houses, and my mouth watered.

The lone table out front was vacant this evening, the card players probably home eating dinner with their families. My stomach growled riotously, which did nothing to help my mood. A blue and red tin sign affixed to the side of the door advertised LIMONAPPIA, a type of Italian cola, and another above it read PERONI, BIRRA SUPERIORE D'ITALIA.

Inside, the café was smoky and brightly lit, with a few tables covered in red-and-white-checkered cloths, and slightly grubby tile floors. There was a long wooden bar, something I'd noticed in the cafés in Rome, too, where patrons drank their coffee standing up.

There were a few people at it now. None of them were women; I couldn't remember ever seeing a woman in the café. It didn't shock me that the town was old-fashioned that way, but it did make me feel slightly unwelcome as I peeked inside. I saw a man with a checkered sport coat and a newspaper protruding visibly from his front pocket, an older white-haired man with slightly stained shirtsleeves—and Paul.

It was unmistakably him, elbows on the bar, smoking a cigarette. He wore a lightweight khaki jacket over his white T-shirt, and he was drinking an espresso, just like an Italian. The tiny cup looked slightly ridiculous in his hand, and it was evident he didn't quite know how to hold it.

I decided to sneak off and find food elsewhere, but just then he turned, his brown eyes locking on mine. The sharp hunger in my stomach was suddenly dulled by anxiety. I didn't want to see anyone just then who had witnessed my meltdown over the blood and the ensuing disaster of my performance. But he waved me over, and there was nothing to do but oblige.

"You looked deep in thought over there. I hope I'm not disturbing you." Paul cocked a lopsided smile, as if he didn't really believe his presence would disturb anyone. His seemingly unshakable confidence irked me, especially right then, when I was feeling raw and vulnerable.

"I was just wondering if a person can actually die from embarrassment." I propped my elbows on the bar next to his, and he chuckled. I waved down the barista and pointed at a savory pastry in the glass case, which was stuffed with some kind of green vegetable, and he delivered it to me on a porcelain plate. I also got a half carafe of red table wine and tipped a measure into a little stemless glass. It tasted earthy and rough. Paul accepted some, too.

"You shouldn't be embarrassed."

I raised my eyebrows. I scarfed down the pastry in a few hungry bites and finished the glass of wine. Afterward, I felt a little calmer. "You don't have to lie. I know how bad I was today."

I gave Paul credit for not immediately denying it. He pulled on his cigarette, drawing the moment out before he replied. "Are you familiar with method acting, Silvia?"

"Of course." I bristled. I was a trained professional, after all. I'd been in a prestigious acting workshop in Los Angeles.

"See, this is what I'm talking about." He chuckled to himself. "You're insulted, and you think I'm a bit of a heel. I can see it on your face plain as day."

I let out a shocked laugh. "Sorry." I already knew, of course, that my face betrayed my emotions more than I would like.

"Don't be." He stubbed out his cigarette in an ashtray. "You can use that, you know? That's all I'm saying."

I stared at the crumbs on my plate, my cheeks warm. I'd expected him to try and assuage my ego. Instead, he'd given me advice. Even as irritated as I was, I could see he had a point. If I could do a better job of emotionally inhabiting my character, of really becoming her, the right expressions would come easily. I'd been so distracted over my aunt that I hadn't been putting in the proper work.

"Anyway, you'll get another chance at the scene. The film from today was ruined." Paul sounded grim.

"What?"

"The camera operator says he has no idea how it happened. But it's not usable." Paul shrugged. My chest tightened. Richard had said it would be easy to recast me at this stage. Even though I was glad to have another shot at the garden scene, I also knew that my position would become more secure the more I filmed. After the light nearly falling on me, and now this . . . I couldn't help but wonder if whatever happened to the film hadn't been an accident. It crossed my mind that someone could be sabotaging me to get me off the picture. I didn't remember seeing anyone near the light when it fell, but I'd been too alarmed and shaken to pay close attention.

I breathed faster and dug my fingers into my palms. I debated asking Paul his opinion, but I knew I'd come across as irrational, especially after the unnecessary fuss I'd kicked up over the blood on the wall. I'd already made enough of an ass of myself for the day.

Paul clanked his espresso cup down and asked for our checks. I should have been relieved—I'd wanted to be alone, after all— but for some reason, I was disappointed. He paid for both of us, and I didn't protest. It was probably production funds, anyway. He turned toward me. "Do you have anywhere you need to be right now?"

"Why?" I thought of my mother, fuming alone in the *pensione*. I knew I should go back, but I was still angry at her. The idea of spending a little more time with Paul suddenly appealed to me. Between his company and hers at that moment, it wasn't a tough decision.

"I have a surprise for you."

This piqued my curiosity. My mother had probably fallen asleep by now, anyway.

"I suppose."

"Come on." I followed him back into the street. "There's a little movie theater up this way where we've been screening the dailies."

"This town has a movie theater?" It seemed impossible that somewhere so quiet and removed from the world could have something so noisy and bright and modern.

"Sure. Mussolini had to distribute his propaganda, you know? You'd be amazed at the number of movie theaters in Italy. The Italians love their cinema."

His comment about propaganda made me think fleetingly of Gabriella, and wonder for the umpteenth time just where she had got off to. I was as frustrated with her as I was with my mother. I'd risked my job because of her lack of consideration. Whatever my mother thought, she and her sister were very alike in some ways. They could both be incredibly selfish.

"But how can we watch the dailies from today if the film was destroyed?"

"We can't. I actually have something else in mind."

The theater was minuscule—just a marquee on an old stucco building. In the lobby, Paul clasped hands with one of the employees and went over some instructions before leading me into the theater's single screening room. It was actually quite lovely, with high painted plaster ceilings and cushy red seats. Paul explained that they had arranged to use the theater at set times every day. We settled in, and I found I was actually a bit nervous. Being alone here with Paul almost felt like a date. Not that I *wanted* to be on a date with Paul, even if he was handsome. I could never trust the movie fixer, who would put the success of the production above everything else. Even now, that's what he was doing—fixing me, so I wouldn't mess up any more scenes. His knees bumped the seat in front of him, and his arms spilled out over the armrests; he couldn't help it. His skin grazed mine, and I moved my hand to my lap.

"I got the reels for some of my favorite horror movies. We were using them for creative inspiration. But I thought you might like to see some of the female lead performances. It's always helpful to study the greats."

"Oh. Thank you." Excitement coursed through me. The truth was that I hadn't seen much in the genre. It would help me get in the right mindset.

"It might take a few minutes for them to get everything set up." Paul moved the arm that had been grazing mine and stretched it behind my chair. He'd only been doing it to get it out of the way, but it seemed even more physical than the touching, almost like he'd draped it around my shoulders. "Were you in town visiting your mom?" He asked the question casually. It was an invitation to share something personal, but gently made. I appreciated the tact, especially when he didn't even know she was sick.

"Yes." I paused for a moment and stared at my hands. I didn't know if I wanted to talk about her illness with him, but I hadn't been able to talk about it with anyone else. The pressure of it all had been mounting inside of me for so long. "She's not well. It's cancer. Chronic lymphocytic leukemia." I enunciated the three words carefully, the three words that had become imprinted on my heart. Everyone knew cancer was a death sentence. The new chemotherapy drugs approved in recent years by the FDA weren't worth considering, the doctor told us—their side effects were horrible, and they likely wouldn't help in her case. Instead, he prescribed "watchful waiting"—essentially, doing nothing but waiting for her to worsen and then die. "The doctor said she might have a few more good years. It's the reason we came to Italy. She was born here and said she wanted to die here. It took all our savings."

"God, I'm so sorry." His eyes searched mine. Then he groaned and put a hand over his eyes. "I was such a jerk when we first met. Can you forgive me?"

I pressed my palms into the plush red fabric, as if it would help me release my surge of emotion. "It's okay. Thanks for listening. It feels good to talk about it."

I wasn't exactly sure why I'd opened up to him; he was just the kind of person you couldn't help telling things to. He had probably heard all kinds of secrets in his career. I didn't regret it, though. I felt lighter.

"It's hell, going through something like that." He shook his head. I started. It sounded like he was speaking from experience.

"Do you—have you lost someone? You don't have to say."

"It's all right. My dad died of a heart attack when I was ten. He was my hero. He was in the movie business, too—one of the first sound engineers for talking pictures." His eyes crinkled fondly at some private memory. "I was the oldest of four, so it fell to me to help keep the other kids in line."

"I can see that about you." I smiled at him. It struck me how similar our childhoods had been, losing our fathers young. I felt sudden kinship toward him. I hadn't expected that.

"Yes. I chose the right profession." He laughed and plucked a cigarette from his pack. "Although I'd love to direct someday."

Just then, the lights dimmed, and the screen before us flickered to life.

The first clip we saw was one I didn't recognize: Barbara Steele in a film called *Black Sunday*. Paul leaned over and whispered in my ear; his breath was warm and smoky. "We took a lot of inspiration from this first scene." Barbara Steele's vampire-witch character was being executed, surrounded by men in black hoods. She gave an impassioned speech, much like Lucrezia's, and a spiked metal mask was hammered into her flesh.

She was incredible.

We cycled through a dozen more examples. Jane Asher in *The Masque of the Red Death*. Hazel Court in *The Curse of Frankenstein*. Janette Scott in *The Old Dark House*. Candace Hilligoss in *Carnival of Souls*. Julie Harris in *The Haunting*. I learned something from each performance, hoarding every bit of knowledge like a pearl I'd discovered.

Finally, the lights went back up. Paul looked as reverent as if we were in church.

We stared at the screen in silence for a minute after it had gone blank, still absorbing the impact of what we'd seen. It had been a physical assault on my senses, leaving my head ringing and my bones vibrating.

I understood now what Paul hoped we could accomplish.

And I knew I'd never, ever be capable. The women I'd just watched were icons—beautiful, emotive, inspired. It was absurd to think I could ever be in their league.

I replayed snippets over in my mind, especially Julie Harris's speech where she declared she never wanted to leave Hill House. She was dreamy and fragile and passionate and strange, and her words left me chilled.

We headed back to the cobblestone street, walking slowly, both quiet, the way people are when they've witnessed something moving and are lost in their own thoughts. I wondered if Paul had come to the same conclusion as I had.

"I'm hopeless, aren't I?" I hadn't even meant to say the words out loud, but in the silent night, they hung in the air, undisturbed by even the wind.

"Why would you think that?" Paul looked sideways at me, puzzled.

"I'll never be as good as them."

I steered us back toward my *pensione*. Most of the windows around us were black, but here and there, one would still be lit, a rectangle of yellow spilling onto the stone. A donkey brayed plaintively somewhere in the distance. We reached my building, and I turned to face him as we lingered outside the door. I wanted to see his expression when he offered me false assurances, but it was too dark to make it out clearly.

He paused before answering. "Silvia, when Herman was talking today about you being more 'accessible'—"

I huffed. "I don't want to hear it. I'm neither talented nor beautiful enough for this role. I get it."

"Hear me out." The tip of Paul's cigarette glowed orange. "It's not about your looks. It's your expressiveness. An audience will see you as a real person. They'll care what happens to you.

Only the best actresses have that quality, Silvia. When you first auditioned, every one of us in that room saw it. We all knew we were in the presence of a star."

The night, already quiet, grew flat and still. It paused. Paul ground his cigarette beneath his shoe.

"That's probably the nicest thing someone has ever said to me." My voice was hoarse. It was true. No one had ever paid me a compliment like that before. Until now, I'd been so focused on getting parts, on scraping by, that I hadn't spared much thought for greatness. Every actress has that dream somewhere in the back of her mind, that maybe she'll be the lucky one who makes it big, but for some reason I'd never allowed myself to believe it could be possible. Even when I'd landed this part, I knew the production budget was slim, and I didn't expect this movie would be a box office smash. But now I saw the glimmer of possibility. His words lifted my spirits so much that I felt like I might drift away into the night.

Instead, I stepped forward and kissed him.

I placed a hand on the back of his neck and pressed my body into his. His mouth was rough and warm, and I felt the muscles beneath his shirt tighten. My blood raced in a way it hadn't in a long time, and I pressed against him harder.

He kissed me back at first, fierce and short, but then he pushed me away and stepped back. "No. I'm sorry." He was breathing hard.

"What?"

He looked like he was trembling. "It wouldn't be right. Because of my position." He ran a hand through his hair. I stared at him, trying to make out his face, not comprehending. Was he trying to be noble? I didn't buy it. Men were never that noble.

I was utterly humiliated. I wished I could evaporate into the darkness. Of all the blows to my ego from that day, this one struck the hardest. Any of the women we'd just watched on screen, standing before him now, would have been irresistible. But he'd had no trouble resisting me.

Some star.

I couldn't find my voice to speak a single word, so instead, I turned and opened the door, hoping he wouldn't see how much he'd upset me.

"Silvia, wait, let me explain—"

But I didn't hear the rest. The wooden door thudded shut behind me, muffling his excuse.

I'd been right about him from the first. He was just a fixer. He probably hadn't meant a word he'd said to me. He didn't actually care.

When I entered the bedroom, my mother's breathing was deep and even. Lulu lay horizontally across the bed, her legs sprawled out and her arms by her head, the safe, secure sleep of childhood. I scooted her over gently, and she nuzzled into my chest.

I stared at the ceiling and held a breath, as if I could bottle my feelings inside along with the air. I hadn't even thought I'd liked Paul, but it hadn't just been gratitude that prompted me to kiss him. In that moment, I'd been overcome with a powerful attraction. I'd wanted him. This evening, I'd thought I'd seen a different side of him, and it had changed my feelings instantly and dramatically.

But I'd been wrong.

And I wondered for the second time that day whether a person could actually die of embarrassment.

CHAPTER 14

Across the bridge, the door to the castle compound hung partway open, revealing a gash of darkness. It was still hours before dawn, but after tossing and turning in the bed at the *pensione*, I'd given up on sleeping. A cloud drifted over the moon, plunging me momentarily into blackness, and I crossed toward the castle carefully, scraping my palm along the stone wall of the bridge.

Inside the courtyard, a shadow lurched, and I froze, imagining for a moment the attacker from my dream lying in wait. My heart and my breathing both sped up, and my muscles tensed. Then a cat slunk forward, and I relaxed, scolding myself for being silly. But I was still slightly wary as I climbed the final flight of stairs. Luckily, I found the tower door unlocked. I'd expected to have to rouse someone, or else steal back to the *pensione*, so I was grateful, if a little surprised. The massive wooden door groaned open, and I slipped inside.

No one seemed to be awake. It was strange, when I was so used to seeing the castle bustling with activity, but it was quiet. And dark. The only light came from the moonlight spilling through the windows.

I rubbed my arms. Outside it had been warm and humid, the early morning fog coalescing over the cobblestones. As usual, it was cooler inside. I was glad it was an uncomplicated journey back to my room—just straight across the great hall from the northwest tower to the northeast. I wouldn't have relished the idea of having to wander through the maze of big empty rooms.

In the great hall, racks of costumes hulked, casting unsettling shadows. The suit of armor seemed to be watching me through the black slit in its helmet. I could almost believe someone was really inside. I could just make out a glowering face in an oil painting near the armor, perhaps of the armor's original owner, and it felt like he was staring at me, the whites of his eyes almost glowing in the dark.

My spine tingled. This place was creepy enough in the daytime, and right now I was feeling legitimately spooked.

I had an early call time today, and wouldn't have been able to see Lulu before she woke up in any case, so I'd decided to come back and work on my lines. Seeing the performances last night had motivated me to do a better job getting into character. I was beginning to regret my plan. I stumbled along until I found the door to the stairs in the northeast tower, cold stone spiraling up into blackness. I had no desire to break my neck, and I turned the knob for light. My fingers sparked with a little zing of electricity.

The wash of yellow didn't dispel my fear as much as I'd thought. The bulbs in the sconces were weak, and painted the stone stairs in shadows.

I ran my fingers along the wall to keep steady. I watched my feet as I climbed, one step and then the next, my eyes itching from tiredness.

Halfway up, I heard a cry.

I was so intent on my task that the noise startled me, nearly causing me to lose my balance. I stopped, my heart thudding and my hands clammy. Then I forced myself to climb faster. It had sounded like a woman in distress.

The sound continued louder than before, a keening wail that made the hairs on my arms stand on end. The woman sounded like she was in agony. I emerged onto the second floor, where the bedrooms were, but the cry was coming from above.

From my aunt's bedroom. Which was also the ancient nursery.

I hadn't forgotten her ghost story. Another wail echoed, and this time it seemed to come from everywhere, as if it were within the walls themselves. It was high, anguished, and unnatural.

Supernatural.

I shook my head. That was nonsense. I didn't believe in ghosts.

I went back to the staircase and climbed to the third floor. I'd see for myself who was up there. The thought crossed my mind that perhaps Terrence had decided to bed one of his conquests upstairs, only the crying I'd heard couldn't be mistaken for anything like pleasure. I'd made that mistake once, but not again.

Whoever I'd heard was in despair. On that front, I had no doubts.

I opened the stairwell door and stepped into my aunt's bedroom. I could make it out quite clearly in the moonlight, thanks to the number of windows.

It was empty.

And yet, the air was disturbed. I couldn't explain how I knew exactly, but the room lacked that quality one expected from abandoned places—the stillness, the mustiness that comes from dust settling. I had the sensation that someone had just been here.

My eyes swept the room, examining it for changes. The bed looked the same, perfectly made. The dressmaker's dummy was still there, eerie in the moon shadow. I walked toward my aunt's vanity, still strewn with her makeup. The items looked like they had been rifled through. I couldn't form a clear picture in my mind of how they had looked before, but I was certain someone had touched them.

Even though I wasn't superstitious, I was starting to get scared. I knew I should just go back downstairs—the sensible part of me wanted to get out as quickly as possible—but curiosity won out. I continued circling the room. As I neared the bed, I heard an odd creaking that made me pause. I looked down and saw the cradle, gently rocking.

I screamed.

I hadn't meant to, but I was legitimately afraid now. There was no draft—no earthly reason at all for that cradle to have been moving.

I clamped a hand over my mouth and ran toward the door to

the staircase. I didn't bother with the light knob this time and rushed down, twisting my ankle slightly on the last step.

When I emerged into the hallway, several doors opened, tousled heads popping out to stare at me. I was breathing hard.

"What was all that bloody noise?" Terrence strode out, his dressing robe gaping open to reveal his chest. He turned the knob on the wall, and the sconces blazed to life. Lucrezia emerged from another door, and Mr. Meyerson came from a third, wearing striped silk pajamas, his silver hair disheveled. He looked distinctly annoyed.

"That's what I was trying to find out." I breathed a sigh of relief. At least I wasn't the only one who'd heard her. "There was a woman crying, so I rushed upstairs—"

"No, I heard a scream." Terrence crossed his arms. "You screamed. Again. You know, it won't help you become a 'scream queen' if the cameras aren't rolling."

I was shaking. My arms were still covered in goosebumps. My thoughts remained upstairs, focused on the cradle, and the woman I'd heard. Could it have been a ghost? I'd never believed in that sort of thing, but I'd never given it much thought. My mother had raised me Catholic and I believed in God, and life after death, but the Bible didn't have much to say about ghosts besides the Holy Spirit. In California, the climate didn't seem right for ghosts, with its square modern buildings and palm trees and sunshine. But here . . . it wasn't such a stretch to think that perhaps there was a spirit roaming the nursery. Serena, my aunt had said her name was. Normally, her suicide would have been a mortal sin, but she'd only done it so her son wouldn't have to die alone. Maybe she was wandering purgatory, here on earth.

"I didn't mean to. But before that, you didn't hear a woman wailing?"

Terrence stared at me. "I only heard you. Why don't you tell us what the hell is going on so we can get back to bed."

Three pairs of eyes blinked at me, their attention absolute. And my focus shifted away from the nursery, back to the here and now. There was no way to explain that wasn't mortifying. So I settled on the truth.

"I thought I heard a ghost." I was still trembling slightly. I knew after my scene with the blood, and now this, I would become a subject of ridicule. But I had no energy left to spare on embarrassment just then; I'd expended it all when Paul rejected me. My ego had already shriveled down to nothing.

"I would say you're taking getting in character a bit too far, only your performances would suggest otherwise." Terrence adjusted the belt of his robe, and the open flap revealing his chest grew wider. Lucrezia watched this with interest. "I'm going back to bed."

His barb barely even pricked. I was finally growing numb to Terrence's insults, just as I'd grown numb to his beauty. But his comment about getting in character took me a moment to process. I knew that in my scene tomorrow, Bianca was visited by the ghost of the witch in her dreams, and I hadn't put together the connection. It was a rather strange coincidence, but it would make my job a lot easier. I'd hardly even have to pretend to be Bianca, when I was being haunted, too.

Even her inheritance of an ancient castle didn't feel so far-fetched anymore. With my aunt away, I did feel a sense of responsibility for the castle, a protectiveness.

I frowned. The similarities with Bianca were greater than I'd realized. It should have encouraged me, but it unnerved me.

Lucrezia, bless her, came and hooked her arm in mine and patted my hand. "I don't blame you. This castle seems full of *fantasmi.* I can barely sleep a wink here."

Mr. Meyerson's annoyance disappeared, replaced instead by keen interest. He had hoped being in the castle would help us identify with our characters, after all. It would appear his plan was working. Too well.

"Let us go find some espresso, and you can tell me about it. I want to hear every detail." His eyes gleamed. I was relieved he wasn't angry at me, but I was surprised by the intensity of his interest. But then, creative people were often like that when they got excited about something. I would know. "I'll just go and change."

"I'll meet you in the kitchen."

Lucrezia kept her arm hooked in mine. "I'm not going to be able to fall back asleep now. I'll come, too. I love a good ghost story."

She wore a lacy negligee that revealed her décolletage. She must have been freezing. She saw me staring. "I'll get dressed first, don't worry. I wouldn't want your eyes to pop out of your head." She winked at me and sashayed back to her room.

She was quick—quicker than Mr. Meyerson—emerging only a couple of minutes later looking like she'd walked straight out of a fashion catalog, in a short tangerine dress with a Peter Pan collar. We descended the stairs together and crossed the great hall, now showing signs of life. Aurelia was there, readying her makeup station, and Sarah was ironing one of the costumes.

"You're lucky Mr. Meyerson likes you so much," Lucrezia whispered. There was no need, since he was still upstairs, but I understood her desire to be discreet. "When I auditioned for the witch, he flicked rubber bands at my head. Can you believe that?"

"What? You're joking."

"No. I lost my temper and yelled at him. And that's the reason I got the part, if you can believe it. He went, 'There. That's the sort of anger I want to see.'"

I shook my head. It was becoming clear that Mr. Meyerson was a bit of a bully—but an entirely different sort than Terrence, who was blunt and cruel. Instead, he was puerile, like a child who gets pleasure in doing the thing you've asked him not to, just to get a rise out of you. I'd already witnessed that he was prone to tantrums and determined to do things his own way. As the mother to a toddler, I knew how to handle that sort of behavior. Perhaps that was why I got along with him better than most.

By the time Mr. Meyerson joined us in the kitchen, the sun had risen, painting the sky orange. He looked immaculate again in perfectly ironed trousers and slicked-back silver hair: every bit the mature man he was not.

But Lucrezia was right. For whatever reason, he did seem

to have a soft spot for me. He smiled indulgently at me when I handed him his espresso cup.

"Now." He steepled his fingers. "Let's go to the beginning. Tell me everything, in as much detail as you can."

I sipped my hot, bitter drink and let it settle on my tongue before swallowing. Lucrezia yawned elegantly. And I told him, pushing aside my concerns about sounding foolish. He encouraged me to continue throughout my tale, and never once betrayed any sort of judgment or scorn. He was rapt.

"This is marvelous. I want you to use this today, Silvia. And you too, Lucrezia." He slapped the table. "When we start to confuse what is real and what is not—that is when we are close to greatness. That blurred line is where the true artist lives." He reached over and squeezed my hand.

His grip was dry and firm. After a moment, I took my hand back and sipped my espresso to hide my expression. I hadn't expected him to believe me, but I also didn't deserve his praise. I hadn't begun to confuse myself with Bianca, and I wasn't hearing ghosts because I was so deeply embedded in the character's psyche.

A woman had been crying in the nursery. I couldn't explain it, but I was sure of it. I knew what I'd heard.

Mr. Meyerson was right about one thing, though: I could use it in my scene today.

Whether Paul had meant what he'd said last night or not, he'd reminded me of what was possible. If I did my very best on this movie, I had a real chance to become a star.

It would mean I could give Lulu the life I wanted for her. It would mean that even when my mother was gone, I wouldn't have to fear the social workers with their clipboards and black suits and pursed lips coming to take her from me. I'd be able to provide for her.

It was time for me to stop squandering that chance.

Today, I had to redeem myself.

CHAPTER 15

It seemed fitting that in my first scene with Lucrezia, I'd be half-naked. I supposed that was overstating things a bit. The nightgown went down to my knees, and was a virginal white, but it was low-cut and clingy and half-sheer, leaving very little to the imagination. Mrs. Leskowitz explained that I was supposed to look pure and tantalizing at once, a woman at war with her own desire.

Even though I hadn't slept, I was sheer adrenaline. Every nerve was alive, every muscle zinging.

We were shooting on the second floor today, which I hadn't really explored, in a large bedroom suite. It was the only bedroom I'd seen not located in one of the towers. I guessed no one had been put up here because of the decision to use it as a shooting location. The green velvet canopy on the bed appeared to have been chewed by mice along the bottom, and I spied some droppings in one of the corners. I was glad they'd changed the sheets for me.

We spent about half an hour filming the beginning of the scene, where I was thrashing about in bed, deep in a nightmare. The success of it rode entirely on my expressions. I barely had to act. I knew all about nightmares, from my childhood of loneliness and sleepwalking, and my fear from hearing the ghost only hours before still coursed through me. I tossed and turned, contorting my features into expressions of terror. We took multiple takes just because Mr. Meyerson wanted a lot of options here and said this bit might get used in the trailer.

Mr. Meyerson clapped his hands together once after the final take. "Yes. That was very good, Silvia. Well done."

The setup had to be adjusted for the next shot, where I would rise from bed and confront the witch for the first time. I went to chat with Lucrezia while they changed the lights and camera positions. She wore a long, voluptuous red dress—similar in spirit to the medieval outfit from her first scene, but sleeker and more modern.

"You look wonderful."

"Mrs. Leskowitz said I was supposed to look like sex on a platter. Those were her exact words." She adjusted the tie on the capelet that accompanied her dress.

I laughed. "She did a good job."

I was nervous and excited, but mostly excited. I'd already performed so poorly the day before that the possibility of failure didn't scare me as much anymore. I'd already been through it and survived.

When Terrence appeared to watch our take, his handsome mouth arranged in a smirk, it didn't even faze me.

Mr. Meyerson finally declared, "Action." I was as ready as I'd ever be.

I rose slowly from the bed at the exact moment Lucrezia stepped forward, as if a magnetic attraction pulled us toward each other.

"Who's there?" I stared straight at her, but pretended to be blinded by darkness. Lucrezia stepped closer, slowly, until she was inches from me, but still my character couldn't see her.

My character's ignorance of what was right in front of her made the scene suspenseful, and as I looked right past the witch, I harnessed both my fear from when I'd heard the wailing last night, and the lust that had coursed through me when I'd pressed my body against Paul's. The witch, Mr. Meyerson had explained, was sexuality: men were terrified of its power, wielded by a woman who knew how. My character was scared of what her own impulses might make her do.

And then the witch reached out to caress my face with long, red-lacquered nails.

I screamed and cupped my cheek.

"Cut!" Mr. Meyerson clapped his hands together again. "That was sublime. We got it in one take."

I smiled and glanced toward Paul. He had bruised my pride, and I couldn't help but wonder what he thought. He was staring right at me, his eyes dark and focused, his Adam's apple bobbing.

"Paul!" Mr. Meyerson sounded annoyed. Apparently, Paul had forgotten himself.

"Sorry. Check the gate," he said to the camera operator. His voice was gruff. "Calling makeup."

Aurelia bustled over to add streaks of red blood where Lucrezia had caressed me.

In the next shot, Lucrezia would lunge at me to attack, and then my character would emerge from her nightmare. When she looked in the mirror, she'd see very faint scratches left by the witch's touch.

Mr. Meyerson called "action," and Lucrezia lunged. I lurched back, and the motion revealed a rip in the nightgown I hadn't noticed before, exposing a slice of my thigh. The material was flimsy, and I'd probably just twisted the wrong way.

"Cut!" Mr. Meyerson jumped out of his chair. "Get Mrs. Leskowitz here *now*." His whole face quivered with fury. It exploded so suddenly that it startled me.

"Calling wardrobe!"

Mrs. Leskowitz and Sarah arrived within moments, needles at the ready. Sarah approached and stitched up the gash, without me even needing to get undressed.

"There." She bit off the thread. It had only taken a few minutes, but Mr. Meyerson still looked irate.

"Look. It's not flat. You can see it bunching near the stitching." He came over to me and yanked the dress. I tried to hold still and not react, but it made me uncomfortable, as if I were merely a prop. "It will ruin the continuity of the scene."

"I can steam it in ten minutes; you won't be able to see a thing." Sarah's soft, high voice went softer and higher than usual. Her eyes were wide and frightened. Mrs. Leskowitz looked sourly at Mr. Meyerson, her arms crossed.

"Fine. Everyone take ten." For a minute, no one moved. No one wanted to attract the attention of our mercurial director. But then one of the camera operators rose, scratched his belly, and disappeared in the direction of the marble stairs leading down to the great hall. Others started stirring, as well. Sarah and Mrs. Leskowitz flanked me, ready to escort me to their station, and Mr. Meyerson watched them, still looking thunderous. "When you're finished, I want you both off the picture."

Everyone who had been moving stopped.

Mrs. Leskowitz lifted her chin. Her gray corkscrew curls bounced. "You can't do that. You need us." Her gaze was steely.

"I can get new wardrobe people here from Cinecittà tomorrow. I want you both gone by morning. After you fix Silvia's dress, I don't want you to so much as touch another costume."

He crossed his arms loosely, a posture of casual disdain.

I gasped.

"*Madonna,*" Lucrezia swore. "It wasn't their fault. These things happen. Don't take it out on them," she said. I should have echoed her, but the words got stuck in my throat. I was too scared to say anything lest I incur his wrath, too.

He ignored her. I could tell by the way he squared his shoulders and the pulsing muscle in his neck that he wouldn't change his mind. He seemed obstinate that way. When he made a decision, even if it was a bad one, he stuck to it.

"By morning," he said again, and spun nimbly on his heel, his shoes clicking on the tile as he headed toward the stairs.

Sarah's pretty dark eyes filled with tears, and she wiped a paisley sleeve across her cheek. "Bastard."

Mrs. Leskowitz patted her back. "He's not worth crying over. The pig." She turned to me, thread between her teeth, and inspected Sarah's handiwork. "I'm doing this for you, dear, not him, but I'll be damned if I'm steaming it, too. After this, we're through here." Her fingers traced the seam. "What the—"

She studied the bottom of the dress. I turned to watch and saw as she lifted up a fold of fabric at the back.

"It's torn in three other places. No, not torn. Someone cut this. Slashed it."

"What? Why would someone do that?"

She didn't answer. She didn't have to. I knew the answer as soon as I'd asked the question. My suspicion had been right: someone was sabotaging me. Maybe it was a mean-spirited prank. But after the light and the destroyed film, I didn't think so. I wouldn't put it past either Terrence or Richard, and the thought frightened me. In my insubstantial nightgown, I trembled.

"You have to tell Mr. Meyerson." His ire was unwarranted no matter what caused the cuts, but I hoped the new information might help him see reason.

"You think he'll believe us?" She quickly sewed up the tears, looking grim. She was right, of course. He'd only think they were making up a story to save their positions.

She took Sarah by the hand and pulled her away, back toward their station, I presumed. As rattled as I was by Mrs. Leskowitz's discovery, I was also terribly sorry for her and Sarah, both of whom I liked and respected. To see them treated like that disgusted me.

Lucrezia, for her part, resumed cursing loudly in Italian. "*Che cazzo!* Paul. Go after him. Do something about this," she spat, pointing one of her blood-red nails at him, as if she meant to scratch him, too.

He had his hands stuffed in his pockets and his jaw ticked. Normally he looked loose and calm, and I'd never seen him like this before. He was angry. Furious, even. His brown eyes, normally warm and appraising, were molten.

"Don't do anything foolish." I could tell in this state, he was liable to get himself kicked off the picture, too. I couldn't meet his eyes when I addressed him; I was still embarrassed from the previous night.

"You think that was their fault?" Paul's voice was dangerously soft.

"No. That's not what I meant at all." My cheeks burned. Most of the crew had dispersed for bathroom and coffee breaks, but the camera operator lingered somewhat near, so I stepped closer and lowered my voice. "I just mean it seems like no one is safe from him, that's all. I was trying to tell you to be careful." How lucky I'd been that Mr. Meyerson hadn't turned on me when I'd awoken him last night. He hadn't slept well because of me; maybe his mood today was my fault. I felt instantly guilty.

Paul snorted. "You don't see the pattern in who he targets? Claude, Sarah, Janine?" Janine—I realized I'd never known Mrs. Leskowitz's first name. I processed his words, trying to understand the link.

Lucrezia joined me, and her proximity made me stand a little taller. She made me stronger and better—a fabulous quality in an acting partner, an even better one in a friend. "Ah. I see." She nodded, her face solemn.

"You do?" I turned toward her, my brow furrowed. I put a hand over my mouth as I understood. "Oh."

"He's a bigot." Paul smacked his pack of Lucky Strikes against his palm and retrieved a cigarette. His movements were tight and jerky as he lit up.

I'd been so naïve. I should have seen it. So many people were still so small-minded. "There's nothing you can do. We just have to keep our heads down and carry on, I suppose. Risking your own neck won't do any good."

Paul sucked his cigarette and said nothing, but he looked disappointed. Not at the situation—with me. I had the distinct impression that I'd let him down.

"Only one way to find out." His outrage had distilled into cool-headed purpose. He was almost relaxed as he strode toward the stairs, and he didn't hurry. Lucrezia and I followed him to the great hall. Even though Paul had turned me down, I didn't want him to get fired. In fact, the prospect of not seeing him again made me anxious and slightly nauseated.

"Herman!" Paul looked just like the cowboy hero calling out the villain for a duel. Broad-chested, blond, a little weathered, cigarette brandished like a gun.

Mr. Meyerson was at the craft services table, pouring a cup of coffee.

"What is it?" Herman's hard German consonants clicked like his shoes as he turned. His voice was mild.

"If they're off the picture, so am I." He took a languid puff. He didn't say anything else. No pleas, no explanations as to why Herman should want them all to stay. Just one economical sentence that spoke volumes.

Mrs. Leskowitz and Sarah emerged from their racks of costumes to watch.

Herman paused. I could see the calculation in his eyes as he decided which course to take. Finally, he threw up a hand in mock surrender and chuckled a little, as if this were all a great joke. "Goodness, Paul. Let's leave the dramatics to the actors, shall we?" He sipped his coffee. "You must allow me the occasional moment of frustration. Of course nobody is off the picture. I want everyone back in their places in three minutes."

Sarah and Mrs. Leskowitz didn't celebrate. Mrs. Leskowitz glowered at him as he walked back toward the stairs. I wondered if perhaps they would leave anyway, after enduring that kind of treatment. But I knew how excited they'd been about their work. As far as I was concerned, they were both geniuses. Finally, Mrs. Leskowitz stepped forward to take my arm. "Take your nightgown off; I'll fix it up a little nicer."

She nodded once at Paul as we headed toward her station.

Relief swooped through my belly. That she and Sarah would be staying, of course, but also for Paul. My eyes swept over every tanned and chiseled inch of him, beholding him with awe.

I'd been wrong about him. Utterly, completely wrong. Paul Rudderman wasn't the fixer of the picture. He actually cared.

To my great astonishment, Paul Rudderman had turned out to be the only noble man in Hollywood.

Chapter 16

I stood by the narrow window in my room and stared at the stars. They were bright tonight. I wondered if Paul was looking at them, too. I wondered if he was as disgusted with me as I was.

I'd been completely and mortifyingly wrong about him. He had shown moral courage today. I hadn't.

I could blame my finances, of course, a justification I'd used to excuse so much already. My aunt's disappearance, for instance. The moment Richard had offered a semblance of an explanation, I'd taken it. I hadn't wanted to look closer, hadn't wanted to risk my role and my paycheck.

The lake shone blackly under the moon, and if I listened hard enough, I could almost imagine I heard its lapping at the stone wall of the garden. Serena was down there, somewhere, if my aunt's story was to be believed, her bones nestled into the muddy bottom or else dissolved to nothing. Another woman with flexible morals, an adulteress, who in the end had made a terrible choice.

But it wasn't Serena's sightless eyes that flashed into my mind just then. I was suddenly assaulted by a vision of my aunt, sinking into the lake's depths. I imagined her choking on the thick water, her lungs burning, clawing for the surface, and my own breathing grew uneven as I eagerly pulled in air. Or perhaps she'd gone silently, already unconscious as blood swirled from a head wound and diffused into nothing. Her corpse could be settled into the sludge next to Serena's remains, her elegant, arresting face bloated beyond recognition. I shook my head, trying to clear it from my mind. Had my instinct been right, and she was out there in the lake with Serena? Or had she found her way to the beach resort? I couldn't picture her basking on a striped lounge chair, jammed elbow to elbow with the other tourists.

The lake pulled at me, and I sensed that it held answers. This place was getting under my skin; Mr. Meyerson had been right about that much. The movie seemed all too believable now, or perhaps it was my own life that had become unreal.

I didn't know how long I stood there, but finally I went to bed. I tossed and turned, and thrashed about in the bedclothes, just as Bianca had in the scene that morning.

Finally, I drifted off into a fitful slumber.

The castle's ghosts haunted my dreams.

The shock of icy water woke me. My feet were frigid and numb. I blinked, disoriented, but I couldn't see anything at first. I'd been dreaming of the lake, of ghostly fingers pulling me down beneath the inky surface, and I knew I must have been having a nightmare. I was still in its grip, that was all, and I waited for the sensation to fade, and to find myself in the warm, soft bedding in the castle.

But it didn't. I was so, so cold, and the bottom of my nightgown was wet and heavy, and something was sucking me down, trying to swallow me.

I stepped forward, and sharp stones cut the bottoms of my feet. I shivered. I blinked again, and the world tilted. I no longer looked inward, but outward, my nightmare evaporating. Above, I could see the sky painted with glittering stars.

I was standing in the lake. Not in a dream—in reality.

I tried to scramble to the shore but tripped, falling forward, soaking my arms and torso. Rocks sliced my palms. Sobbing and confused, I flailed, half-swimming, half-crawling, until I emerged onto a tiny rocky beach.

I looked around, and dark shapes took form in the starlight. A long, steep staircase rose in front of me like a row of teeth, and scraggly branches cast shadows against stone walls. I was at the base of the garden. The stairs reached all the way to the lake itself, and nearby I could make out a rotted pier and an ancient rowboat with a single oar bobbing.

I clamped a hand over my mouth to stop from screaming. I must have sleepwalked, something I hadn't done in years. Fully awake now, I started climbing wildly, wanting to get away from the lake as quickly as possible, and my nightgown clung to my calves. My skin was ice, and my feet slipped on the stone steps. I crawled on my hands and knees like an animal, my heart thudding against my ribs and tears salting my tongue.

Finally, I reached the terrace at the base of the castle, my whole body shaking. I looked back, once, horrified that I'd gone down the stairs while asleep. I could have broken my neck. The castle door still hung open, and I hurried inside, but the chill didn't abate, nor did my fear. I was desperate to get warm and dry, but I couldn't bear the thought of being alone in my bedroom in the northeast tower. I no longer had any trouble believing that the castle was haunted. And I had the disturbing idea that a ghost had lured me to the lake tonight.

So I went instead to the southwest tower. I took the path through the dining room and the library to avoid the long unlit gallery, but the pitiful, buzzing electricity didn't make me less scared. It only magnified the rooms' emptiness.

The second floor of each tower sported a set of bedrooms, and I had a decent sense by now of who slept where. Or at least, I'd taken note of this information for one person in particular. I climbed a spiral staircase identical to the one in my tower. Upstairs, the hallway sconces had been left on, and the doors still had pieces of paper taped to them with the names of their occupants, from when we received our room assignments.

I found the one I was looking for and spun the knob.

Paul was on his back, sprawled out, one arm above his head. It was the untroubled sleep of a man with a clear conscience. Nothing like how I slept.

I closed the door behind me, and he stirred, sitting up slowly and rubbing an eye. He'd left the lamp on, and a book lay open on his nightstand. When he saw me, he froze, his whole body so still that I could see the rising and falling of his chest. His Adam's apple bobbed, as it had earlier today after he watched my performance. He stared at me, at my now-translucent nightgown, transfixed.

We both knew why I'd come. I tugged up the sodden material, unhurriedly, lifting it up and over my head. I stood naked before him, damp from the lake, my nipples as cold as the rest of me. My olive skin glistened in the weak light.

I was nervous he would reject me again. Honorable Paul. Handsome and caring and nothing like the men I'd known before. I wanted comfort right now, a warm body to take my mind away from death and ghosts. But I also wanted *him*, the longing so strong I was drowning in it.

For a horrible moment, he lay motionless, still just watching me, and I was sure he would ask me to leave. To tell me that my presence was inappropriate.

But then he stood and crossed toward me in two long strides. He grabbed the back of my head, twisting his fingers in my hair, and kissed me—softly at first, then more deeply. His other hand cupped my breast, his thumb rubbing my nipple, then trailing down my belly and between my legs. I moaned into his mouth. It had been so long since I'd been touched.

I could hardly believe this was really happening; it felt like it might also be a figment of a dream. But he was real. The fine stubble of his face against mine, the shivers of pleasure now traveling through me as he explored me, were very much of this world.

I broke away for a moment to catch my breath. "I thought you said it wouldn't be right. Because of your position." I couldn't help needling him, just a little. His hand was still between my legs, his finger circling, and he stopped. His brown eyes bore into me.

"I try to be a good guy, Silvia. But Jesus, I'm not a saint." His voice was rough. He removed his hand and ran it through his tousled blond hair. "Do you want me to stop?"

"No. Don't stop." My mouth went dry. "I was just teasing."

"Are you sure?" He still looked concerned.

"Do you want me to beg?"

Now his face broke out into a roguish smile. My heart kicked in response. "I wouldn't mind it."

I reached forward and caressed his stomach and pulled his T-shirt over his head. He wore only briefs on the bottom, and I pulled them down, releasing him. He kicked them away. He was magnificent—strong and unselfconscious as he pressed up against me, pulling my legs up and around him before depositing me on his bed.

"God, you have no idea how much I've wanted this. When I first saw you audition, I wanted to throw you down and have you right there."

"Did you? I thought you didn't even like me."

He paused for a moment to locate a condom in his dresser drawer, and I helped him put it on. He kissed my breasts, my neck, and his hand found its way between my legs again, his fingers exquisitely gentle. I trembled, but I was no longer cold.

"I'm a professional. I was trying to keep a professional distance."

I wanted him so much I was overcome. "Is this a professional distance?" I wrapped a leg around his back and guided him inside me. Paul went still. His whole body was long and hard.

He whispered in my ear, "I thought you were going to beg?"

He kissed me again, and I gasped. I squirmed beneath him, rocking my hips into his, desperate for more, and he pinned me down, one hand on my hip, the other holding my hands over my head.

"Please. Please, Paul."

He released me and thrust into me, agonizingly slowly.

"Oh, God." I grabbed him and pressed up to meet him, urging him faster. He pinned me again. "Please."

He obliged, driving into me faster, and I moaned as the pressure built. Finally, I cried out as my body convulsed in ecstasy. Every nerve sang.

"I'm not finished with you yet." He kept going, harder than before, my whole body shuddering with so much pleasure that I didn't think I could handle any more. But I came again, and this time, he followed. Our bodies were slick with sweat, our limbs tangled together, our breathing heavy.

He rolled off me and propped up on an elbow to look at me.

"What do you think? One more take, just to be sure?" He didn't crack a smile and used his most serious directorial voice.

I burst out laughing. "You're insatiable." I was still catching my breath, and the laughter pinched my side.

"Just very thorough."

"A true artist."

He gave me a half-smile, his eyes suddenly far away. "No. That would be you. You were incredible today. I couldn't take my eyes off you."

I felt sated, and relaxed, and deeply grateful for the compliment. I hadn't done much in the film until now that was worthy of praise.

"Thank you. You were wonderful today, too. With Mr. Meyerson. I—had misjudged you. I'm sorry for that."

"Well, you made it up to me." The corner of his mouth tilted upward. He pulled a cigarette out of his pack. "Do you mind?"

"No. I'll have one, too."

"I thought you didn't smoke."

"Not usually." He flicked his lighter in front of the tip of my cigarette, and I inhaled. I didn't enjoy it the way some people did, but it felt like the right moment for it. The smoke made me a little light-headed.

"So." He took a long drag. "Are you going to explain why you were dripping all over my floor when you showed up? I meant to ask about it, but I got a bit distracted."

I took a short, careful puff before answering. "I used to get these night terrors, when I was younger. They started after my father died. With sleepwalking. I hadn't had one in ages, but tonight I woke up standing in the lake."

His mischievous smirk vanished, replaced by worry.

"My God." He looked me over carefully, as if assessing me for any harm, his eyes lingering on my body. "Are you okay?"

I shrugged. "It was frightening. This sounds odd, but I feel like my subconscious was trying to tell me something. About my aunt. Her disappearance still seems so strange to me. Something doesn't feel right."

He nodded. "It doesn't sound odd. I get it." He pulled me closer to him, and I lay my head in the crook of his arm. "So we'll find her. I'll help." He made it sound so simple. *We'll find her.* But I believed him. Suddenly, the pressure in my chest eased. Paul was so capable and determined; with his assistance, the idea of discovering what happened to her no longer seemed so daunting.

"You will?"

"Look, I don't want to get ahead of myself here, but—I think I'd do just about anything for you."

A warm feeling spread under my breastbone. No man had ever said something like that to me before, much less meant it. "Anything?" I raised my eyebrows.

"Now who's insatiable?" But the laughter disappeared, replaced by calm focus. He took my cigarette and placed it in the ashtray with his own. Then he rolled on top of me, and soon the last traces of my nightmare were entirely forgotten, the ghosts banished.

The only screams echoing through the castle that night were my own.

CHAPTER 17

Paul's arm was draped over my torso, and I shifted under its weight, deeply satisfied and more rested than I should have been, given how little we'd actually slept. The bright morning light filtered through the small window onto the bed, and it felt like we were floating in a pool of sunshine. Paul's hair shone golden, and I watched him sleep peacefully for a while, so happy I thought I might burst.

Finally his eyelashes fluttered, and a smile crept across his face as he pulled me closer.

Then he bolted upright. "Shit, what time is it?"

I yawned and watched in amusement as a naked Paul leapt across the room in search of his wristwatch. Regrettably, he pulled on a pair of jeans with remarkable speed, hopping as he stuffed his long legs into denim. The T-shirt came next, his taut stomach still evident beneath it. Actually, he looked nearly as sensational as he did undressed.

"Do you really have to go?" Today was Saturday, and Terrence would be filming scenes with an actor named Mario Spinelli, who had arrived the day before and would be playing the comic Italian guide. I had one scene but not until later, so I wasn't in any hurry. "You could be a little late." I stretched out across his bed, still stark naked, and Paul's eyes followed my movement with careful attention.

He shook his head, his brown eyes mournful, and I admired the line of his square jaw, his lean muscles. "I can't be late. It's my job to stop other people from being late." He leaned over and kissed me deeply, a kiss that traveled through me, firing up all the nerves and synapses that had been so recently pushed to the limit of pleasure.

"Stay right there. Just like that. I'll be back as soon as I can."

He gave me one longing parting look, and was gone.

I rolled over, lazy and relaxed, and reluctantly climbed out of bed. My nightgown, when I located it, was still damp with lake water. I turned to his dresser; I doubted he'd mind me borrowing a robe.

His drawers were impressively tidy. It didn't surprise me. He'd said he was the oldest of four, and must have had to grow up fast when his father died. I wondered if his mother had been anything like mine in those first days of grieving: absent-minded, staring into the distance at odd moments, leaving laundry to pile up. I'd learned a great deal of self-sufficiency in those months. Eventually, she'd shaken off her stupor and thrown herself into work and mothering with renewed zeal, as if she were making a point. It had worn her ragged. I wished I'd had the wisdom then that I had now and had shown more appreciation.

I fingered the carefully folded shirts and pants, but didn't find anything approximating a robe. I guessed Paul wasn't the robe sort. On top of the dresser were a small jar with loose change and a neat stack of papers that a glance revealed to be the contract he'd shown my aunt. I rifled through—it wasn't personal, after all—and saw that it was unsigned, likely a copy. I frowned, thinking again on my failure to press for answers. Today perhaps I'd ask around in town and see if the locals could tell me anything about Gabriella. They had to know more than I did. Surely she'd come to town at least occasionally for provisions. If she had gone somewhere, maybe they'd have some clue.

As appealing as it was to just stay in Paul's room and wait for him to come back during a break, I had things to do. With no other choice, I put my nightgown on again and peeked my head out of his room. I padded down the empty hallway and then the stairs, barefoot, the soles of my feet still cut and raw. The castle's labyrinthine layout meant that the second floor of this tower didn't connect to mine—each tower was cut off from the rest of the castle. It was probably useful protection when you were under siege, but it wasn't the most helpful when you were trying to sneak back to your room without being seen.

I considered my options. I could take the route that went through the library and dining room, which would be less crowded but where my exploits would be more obvious to anyone I did see. I didn't relish the awkward questions. Or I could go through the gallery and then the great hall, where I might get overlooked in the general hubbub.

I chose the latter, and luckily, everyone was so busy with their own preparations that no one paid me much attention as I skirted the perimeter. If anyone asked, I planned to say I'd just come to get coffee without getting dressed first. An odd thing to do, undoubtedly. I kept my eyes to the ground, not wanting to catch any knowing looks in my direction.

I made it all the way to the base of the stairs to the northeast tower before Lucrezia bombarded me. She, of course, was perfectly dressed, her makeup precise and her hair smooth. I must have looked frightful. Her eyes widened in delight. She handed me a cup of coffee and laughed.

"Oh, this will be good. Spill."

I had no desire to spill anything, least of all in so public a place. "Come upstairs with me. I want to get changed."

"Not to be indelicate, but you really should. You look just like you rolled out of someone else's bed, which I'm guessing you have, and I want to hear absolutely everything."

She followed me to my room and waited patiently while I made myself presentable. I didn't really want to tell her about Paul. I supposed friends shared that kind of information with each other, but I wasn't used to it. My last close friend had been in high school, but we'd drifted apart when I moved to LA, and then she abandoned me altogether when I got pregnant. I'd been friendly with some other models and actresses, but I hadn't really had time to keep up a new friendship, not after Lulu.

"It's still so early. I'm not sure I'm ready to talk about it yet." I brushed my hair while she perched on the end of my bed. She rolled her eyes.

"Oh, come on, don't leave me in suspense. At least tell me if it was Paul. The way he was *looking* at you yesterday."

I couldn't suppress a smile.

"I knew it!" She snapped her fingers. "How was it?"

I blushed. Lucrezia clapped her hands. "That good? Well, at least one of us is getting pleasured. It's been *weeks*." She flopped backward onto my bed.

I laughed. "What torture."

"Easy for you to tease me when you're standing there looking smug and satisfied."

I surveyed my reflection in the small mirror above my dresser. She wasn't wrong. My skin glowed, and my eyes were bright.

"You have a day off soon. Maybe you can go visit—Massimo, was it?"

"Oh, Massimo. Lovely boy, but not worth going all the way to Rome for." She flicked a nonexistent piece of lint off her dress.

"Well, I have to head off." I hovered awkwardly near the door. "I'm going to see my mother in town, but I'll see you for our scene later."

Lucrezia rose and pouted a little. "You're so mysterious, Silvia. So full of secrets. I'll get them out of you one of these days." She winked at me and left.

As I walked to town, I pondered her words. I'd always considered myself forthright. No one had called me secretive before, and it wounded, though I doubt she'd meant it to. But I supposed outspokenness wasn't quite the same thing as letting your guard down. No one at the castle knew about Lulu, and having kept one secret like that, it wasn't so hard to keep others.

My mother was sitting quietly in a chair in front of the *pensione* when I arrived, watching several girls play hopscotch in the street. Signora Ricci wasn't there, but an older girl held Lulu's hand, and Lulu jumped up and down as she watched the game.

"Mommy!" She broke out into a huge smile, and my heart

was so full of love it hurt. "I'm jumping!" She bounced up and down energetically. "Like a bunny!"

Lulu had loved bunnies ever since I'd read her *The Tale of Peter Rabbit*. Her little red jumper had a white rabbit sewn on the front.

"Very good, darling. What lovely jumping."

My mother shifted as if preparing to stand, and I shooed her back down. "Don't get up." Her mouth was tight. We hadn't spoken since our tiff the other night, and I could tell she was expecting an apology. *I* was the one who deserved one, but she wasn't reasonable that way. She never apologized. She looked so fragile today, her eyelet dress looser on her frame than I remembered it, the bones in her face sharper. It stilled my tongue. Our arguments often devolved into a stalemate like this, me with hot anger festering, her silent with cold disapproval.

The town's usual morning fog had burned away, and I played with Lulu for hours in the hot July sun, jumping and skipping up and down the *vicoli,* which were steep enough to tire out an adult but apparently not a determined two-year-old. The flower boxes in front of the windows were full of sickly looking flowers, wilting from the heat. Sweat trickled down my back, and Lulu screeched with pleasure as I chased her, then burst into fits of giggles when I caught her and tickled her belly.

I rated it unlikely that anyone from the production would spot us, but kept to smaller side streets just in case. If we did run into someone, I would say she was my sister, a well-worn lie that it always gutted me to use. *So full of secrets*, Lucrezia had said. Maybe I was more like my mother than I'd realized.

As I walked with Lulu back to the *pensione* for lunchtime, though, I had the uneasy feeling that we were being watched. I turned back to look up the *vicolo,* and a line of sun-bleached white laundry swayed in the still air. An orange cat stared at me from beside a flowerpot, grumpy and sunbaked, before turning its attention to the air behind me. Its fur bristled, and it hissed. My nightmare came to me then, of being trapped in the maze of the town as an attacker chased me, and the back of my neck prickled. We moved faster after that, even though I was tired. The oppressive heat had made me light-headed, and as we walked I sought any scrap of shade I could to try to escape it—and I felt somehow safer in the shadows. I couldn't shake the feeling that someone was following us, spying, and I turned to look behind us every third step. Once, a pair of pants drying swung on its string a little too quickly, as if someone had just jostled it—but no one was there. I squeezed Lulu's hand a bit too hard, and she yelped. Then she melted down into a full-blown tantrum, more from tiredness than anything else, and I picked her up to soothe her and kiss her cheeks.

I exhaled in relief when I finally caught sight of the *pensione*'s sun-kissed stone, and handed Lulu off to Signora Ricci. The *pensione* exuded a sense of homeyness and security, and I instantly felt calmer. I wished my mother a terse farewell.

I had given myself a little extra time so that I could make some inquiries in town about my aunt. I passed through the piazza with the café and the empty fountain, and was encouraged to see the three men from my first visit at their usual table, playing a lively game of *scopa*. They drank red table wine from little glasses, and one of them motioned to the waiter to bring another carafe. The café was playing some sort of Italian pop music today, a jarring contrast to the typical quiet. I wondered fleetingly if Italians had discovered rock and roll yet, but the idea of the Beatles or the Rolling Stones blasting in this lonely outpost was so incongruous as to be absurd.

One of the three men was bald as a monk, and was jabbing his friend amiably about his "capture" of one of the cards. I couldn't remember all the rules of *scopa* that my mother had taught me, but it looked like fun. He sucked his lips as I approached as if to say, "Here's trouble."

"I'm sorry to bother you all again. I'm not sure if you remember me. I'm Silvia Whitford. We weren't properly introduced before."

I spoke in Italian, of course, and held out a hand, my heart hammering. If anyone in town could tell me about Gabriella, it had to be these three. They sat in the café so often that there was probably little they didn't see or hear.

The bald man paused for an agonizing moment before taking my hand. His neighbor had big gray eyebrows and a nearly equal amount of hair growing out of his ears. The third man had an impressive round belly and a leathered face. They told me their names, but we were only exchanging them out of a ritual of courtesy, and I forgot them almost the instant they uttered them.

"I'm starring in the picture being filmed up at the castle. Also, I'm the niece of Gabriella Conti."

All the men sat up straighter, and there was a round of general exclamation and cigarette waving. "Her niece? But she hasn't any family in the world."

I shifted uncomfortably. No one had offered me a chair. "I grew up in America. She and my mother haven't spoken since the war."

At this, the men nodded sagely. The war had torn apart plenty of families. "Are you famous?" the bushy-eyebrow man asked. He studied me.

"Not yet." I smiled apologetically.

"You do look just like her. Funny we didn't see it before." The round-belly man had a wheezy voice, and his watery eyes were amused and alert.

My heart gave a little pang. I'd known I resembled her, but hearing him confirm it made it realer, somehow. I may not have known her well, but we were bonded by blood. "The reason I'm intruding is that my aunt drove off somewhere before filming started, and none of us know where. I'm trying to contact her. I thought perhaps someone in town would have an idea as to where she might have got off to."

At this, all three men burst out laughing. The one with the round belly held his stomach. He answered me first.

"Sweetheart, Signora Conti hasn't left this town in years. She doesn't own a car. She doesn't even know how to drive."

CHAPTER 18

I was hopping mad by the time I got back to the castle. I didn't even notice the climb. Pure fury drove me up that hill, and I wouldn't have been surprised to see steam trailing behind me.

Richard had lied to me.

And I wanted to know why.

Alarm bells rang distantly in some corner of my mind, whatever part houses fear, but my anger muffled them. I knew that Richard had been the last person to see my aunt before she disappeared, that he could be dangerous, but just then I didn't care.

It didn't take long to find him. I knew that they had set up some office space in the library near the southeast tower, because we'd all seen Richard and Paul and Mr. Meyerson in and out of it at various points. I figured he might be there, and I barged right in. Sure enough, I found him hunched over a ledger book behind a makeshift card table.

The library itself was rather astounding: walls of dark wooden shelves stretched up toward a distant ceiling, and an enormous crystal chandelier missing half its strings hovered rather precariously above. There were a few moldering books, and the ceiling featured gilded octagonal coffers and rosettes against a blue background. An enormous old mirror leaned against one wall, its glass shattered within the frame into long, sharp shards, silvery and mottled.

There was no furniture aside from what the production team

had brought in, although there was a set of elaborately designed silver fireplace tools beside a monumental white marble hearth.

But I had little attention for anything besides the unpleasant man before me. He certainly didn't look like a villain, with his bland, roundish pale face framed by his dark shaggy bob and sideburns, and those awful coke-bottle glasses.

"What the hell did you do to my aunt?" My voice barreled out, echoing in the quiet room. Richard glanced up and rolled his eyes.

"Not this again." He took off his glasses and pinched the bridge of his nose.

"She didn't drive anywhere. She didn't own a car." My voice was too high and too loud, but even so, I could barely hear myself over the ringing in my ears.

Richard just shrugged. "So she took the train."

"No, she *didn't*. She's a recluse. She never leaves. That's what all the townspeople say."

"Oh, if the townspeople all say so." He sighed and leaned back in his sad little folding chair. "Look, when we discussed transportation to the beach resort, she said she would handle it herself. I figured she'd drive. We went over all the cars parked at the castle and identified each and every fucking one—which was a job, and took a while, not that you thanked us—and none of them were hers. So I figured it was gone. Okay? Jesus Christ, you're acting like you think I killed her or something." He dropped his pen on top of his ledger book and lit up a cigarette.

"I *do* think something could have happened to her. Why aren't you taking this seriously?" My whole body was shaking.

"Right. The blood." He let out a stream of smoke in the direction of the rosettes. He snapped his fingers. "Hey, I know. Maybe the ghost did it." He smirked.

I seethed. It didn't surprise me he'd heard about the ghost incident. People talked, after all, movie people even more than most. I couldn't explain what I'd heard the other night, but I knew it had nothing to do with what had happened to my aunt. Gabriella had said she'd made her peace with the ghost long ago.

One thing was clear, at least: she hadn't driven off for a mysterious holiday.

If she'd never left the castle . . . well, it wasn't such a leap to think something horrible had occurred.

And if it had, I was convinced nothing supernatural had bashed her head against that stone wall. It had been a person of flesh and blood.

"You know what I think? I think maybe you know exactly where she is."

Richard leapt up and fixed me with a freezing stare, his blue eyes sharp and cold. I took a careful step back, those alarm bells ringing a little louder now. But then he seemed to gain control of himself and sat back down.

"Look, I think you're just overwrought. Don't beat yourself up, it happens a lot when they cast amateurs for big parts. It's too much stress."

"I'm not an *amateur.* You aren't listening."

He continued, not acknowledging my comment. "I'll check with Paul if we can move things around so you can have an extra day off tomorrow. I'm sure he'll be all too happy to help." That smirk was back, and my cheeks, already flushed with anger, grew even hotter. Either Lucrezia had talked, or my little jaunt in my nightgown that morning hadn't exactly gone unnoticed.

"You're useless. I'm going to find out what happened, you know."

"Okay, Nancy Drew. Keep me posted." He picked up his pen again, still pinching his cigarette with his other hand, and returned to whatever tedious task he'd been focused on.

I wheeled around, my heart like thunder in my chest, and headed to the one place that might give me answers.

The scene of the crime.

The gardens were abandoned, thankfully, so there was no one to see as I crept down the steps, teetering on each lip of stone and trying not to look down. I kept thinking about how I had done this *asleep* and then also wondering about my aunt's descent, why she'd gone to the gardens, when, and with whom.

The last tier looked just as it had when we'd filmed, scraggly but beautiful, overrun with untamed shrubs but also salvias and geraniums and bright pink bougainvillea. Wisteria vines thicker than my wrist strangled an old rotted wooden trellis. Rosemary spilled over from the tier above, and the lemon trees were heavy with fruit. The air was tangy and fragrant, and bees hummed between the plants, blissfully unaware of the violence that had happened here.

I walked to the wall, the spot I remembered near the statue of the terrified nymph. The blood was still there, the ugly maroon staining the garden indelibly. This time, I allowed myself to look closer. It had dried, of course, the color now browner than before. Despite what I'd said to Richard, I wasn't really *sure* it was hers, but seeing it again almost persuaded me. It was hard to imagine an animal leaving that particular smear pattern.

I looked over the wall to the turquoise lake lapping below, as if it could give me answers. Could Gabriella be down there, somewhere? Eerie as the lake was, it was also lovely in the bright afternoon, still as glass and surrounded by the carpet of rich green trees. Its beauty belied its danger. I shuddered, remembering the icy shock of water from my living nightmare.

To the left, I spied the tiny rock beach and the tumbledown pier. If the worst had truly happened, and she was dead, it occurred to me that more evidence might be there. Even if the blood was unrelated, she could have gone for a swim and drowned. Maybe her body had washed ashore.

I hated going back there. I had no desire to revisit that terrifying moment. Still, adrenaline from my fight with Richard coursed through me and propelled me onward, down the final set of stairs, until I stood just where I had when I'd been drenched with lake water in the moonlight.

The beach looked different in the day. The sun beat down, the rowboat gently lolled, and flowers from above scented the air. It was almost peaceful. The small gray rocks looked harmless, not like the instruments of torture designed to mangle bare feet.

The stretch of shore was teensy, easily crossed in a few strides, and I stood at the lake edge and evaluated the pier. Half of the boards had fallen away, but the rowboat was close, the water to reach it only shin-high. It was possible it held clues, but I couldn't persuade myself to inspect it. Adrenaline only carried you so far, and the idea of wading into the freezing lake made my chest tight with fear.

I turned instead to the beach itself. I crouched down and perused the small jagged rocks, turning over one and then another, tossing a few in retribution for the pain they'd caused me. And then I paused, my eyes raking over the pebbles. *There.* Red dribbles of blood on a small patch of the beach.

I knew all too well, though, that I'd cut my own feet here the night before. It was impossible to tell if the blood was hers or mine.

I stood, my legs stiff. Besides the rocks, there wasn't much else to see. Near the base of the stairs was a pile of what appeared to be garbage, and I moved closer until I identified it as a dirty old tarp and some rope, perhaps for covering the rowboat in winter.

And then I saw the blood. Not just flecks—a lot of blood. A wide, long trail leading to the pile, as if someone had been dragged. My own blood rushed through me in nervous anticipation.

Maybe someone had planned to row her out to deeper waters and discovered the pathetic little boat wasn't up to the task. Maybe, instead, they'd left her here. I pulled the tarp aside, steeling myself to face the corpse I expected to find.

I exhaled in relief when I saw it wasn't there. There were only a few empty brown bottles—and a shoe.

My breaths grew shallow as I moved closer still and bent down to examine it.

It wasn't just any shoe. It was a woman's leopard-print flat, with a small square heel.

My aunt's shoe.

*   *   *

My heart beat in time with my steps as I climbed back toward the castle. A single phrase repeated in my mind, keeping rhythm.

I have to call the police.

Before, her murder had been theoretical, but the day's events had changed all that. There was no reason for that amount of blood to be on the beach. The set decorators wouldn't have come down here, and it was far too much to have been an animal.

I was frightened. Someone in the castle had killed her. I had no doubt that her body had been hidden on that beach. Maybe the murderer had needed more time to fully dispose of it. It was probably at the bottom of the lake now.

It was a hot, still day, but I trembled as I neared the tower door. My aunt was a stranger to everyone, even me, really, so if her killer had been someone in the castle—which seemed likely—the motive couldn't have been personal. Her disappearance had been so sudden, right after she had threatened to stop filming from proceeding. Had someone been so desperate for this movie to move forward that they had gotten rid of her? It was hard to fathom that anyone would murder for that.

But then, people had killed for less.

I have to call the police.

I repeated the phrase in my head like a mantra as I entered the castle and walked to the kitchen. I wouldn't allow myself to meet anyone's eyes, knowing that I'd look furtive and guilty. I forced myself to walk slowly, to relax my limbs. I wanted to attract as little attention as possible. I took a deep breath and wished I were braver.

Once I called the police, everything would change. I pictured interviews, searches, dogs, and a boat dragging the lake. For a while at least, the picture would come to a grinding halt. Depending on what they discovered, it might be over for good.

I was risking my big break and my livelihood, but I couldn't ignore what I'd learned. Paul had shown moral courage and reminded me of what it meant to do the right thing. Now it was my turn.

I have to call the police.

The kitchen was blessedly empty, though there was detritus from the craft services ladies: some empty aluminum containers from their restaurant in town, a well-used cutting board. They could reappear at any moment, and I placed the phone firmly beside my ear. Because of my mother's illness, I had taken particular care to research the emergency phone numbers in Italy, and I didn't hesitate as I dialed.

A woman answered, her words calm and practiced. "What is your emergency?"

I swallowed, but my voice when I answered her was steady and sure. "Hello. I'd like to report a murder."

CHAPTER 19

The town of Castello del Lago, I was unsurprised to learn, did not have a police station.

So I was connected to the *carabinieri* in a neighboring town, and the officer who finally answered my call (after five rings) had a deep, businesslike voice. I pictured a beefy, hard-boiled man at a desk, black hair slicked back, cigarette and espresso on hand.

"Captain Bruno."

"Hello. I'm calling to report a murder," I said again, in Italian, the words tumbling out even easier this time, ringing with certainty.

"Are you currently in any danger?" The man spoke quickly and urgently.

"No. But my aunt, Gabriella Conti, is gone." I was pleased with how calm and reasonable I sounded, but I pressed the phone so hard against my ear it hurt. The pressure kept me grounded.

"Okay. Where's the body located? Where are you now?"

"I'm in Castello del Lago. We're filming a horror movie at the castle. I don't know where her body is, I don't know what happened to her, but there's a lot of blood—"

"Slow down." His words turned sharp, almost angry. "You said this was a murder."

"Yes. No one has seen her since Monday. And like I said, there's a lot of blood—" My voice rose in pitch, and even I could hear that I sounded desperate, hysterical.

"This sounds like a missing person's case, not a murder." His baritone crackled through the phone. "You should come to the station so we can take your statement, okay? Do you have a pen?"

I didn't waste my breath arguing with him. Instead, I jotted down the directions to the station, squeezing the pen so tightly the tip bit into the scrap of paper. Once we had a proper conversation in person, I'd make him understand. "I'll be there soon."

No one in the castle had taken me seriously, but they would.

I'd feel safer, too, once the police were here. The moment the light had come crashing down beside me, sharp glass littering the terrace, appeared in my mind. I already knew Terrence and Richard believed I was miscast and hurting the picture. If someone had killed Gabriella for threatening the movie, who was to say they wouldn't do the same to me?

Paul's car keys, I remembered, were kept on top of his dresser near the loose change. He was busy on set, and I figured he wouldn't object too much to me borrowing his car, not when it was for a good cause. So only ten minutes later, I seated myself in the red Fiat and carefully reversed out of the drive.

The journey to the neighboring town was harrowing. I wasn't a great driver to begin with, but the roads were appalling, and the hilly terrain full of stomach-dropping twists and slopes. The town itself did allow cars, and I was momentarily relieved when I reached it, thinking the worst was behind me. But then I had to navigate through a warren of streets better suited to donkeys than vehicles. I was sure on several occasions I would scrape the doors, but somehow I eked my way through. By the time I found one of the few slightly wider streets and parked, I was shaking hard, and I sat behind the wheel for several minutes to collect myself before I emerged.

The directions the officer had given me had gotten me to the town all right, but the station house itself was another matter. I wandered around the tangle of streets until I was certain I'd gone in a circle. Even though it was another hill town, the character was entirely different from Castello del Lago. This town felt *alive*. A woman in a stylish green-and-white-striped dress emerged from the *panetteria* with loaves of sweet-smelling bread peeking out of her shopping bag. A couple on a Vespa whizzed by, laughing, the young woman clinging tightly to her boyfriend's middle. There were young people here, I realized. In Castello del Lago, the only children I'd seen were Signora Ricci's, and I hadn't seen a single person my age who actually lived in the town.

Finally, a passerby was able to show me the way to the police station, a small, single-story building of terra-cotta brick with a wooden double doorway framed by imposing marble. I stepped inside and found myself in a tiny waiting room featuring terrazzo floors, three empty modern chairs, and a single officer stationed behind a tall desk. After I explained my business, he led me down a hallway to a larger office, this one with multiple desks and a handful of officers. A few were in loud, jovial conversation. I coughed from the haze of cigarette smoke.

The waiting room officer introduced me to Captain Bruno, whom I'd spoken to on the phone. He was in his forties and thinner than I'd pictured, but more intimidating, thanks to his smart black and red uniform. All of the other officers eyed me with interest—a bit too much interest, and I shifted uncomfortably.

"American, eh?" Captain Bruno asked me, after I sat. It came out sounding like an accusation.

"Yes. My mother is Italian. I guess my accent gave me away."

"Hmm." He searched through his files for specific forms, and I spent at least ten minutes answering routine questions—my full name, nationality, place of residence, purpose for being in Italy, that sort of thing. He scribbled down my responses a bit haphazardly and paused often to continue whatever conversation he'd been having. Finally, he returned to the topic of my aunt, but it was evident that he found my presence irritating, as if I were disturbing him. He had a list of questions for this part, too, and he began without enthusiasm.

"Was your aunt of sound mind, Miss Whitford?"

I paused, momentarily unsure how to answer. She was eccentric, and a recluse, but she wasn't a danger to herself, which was probably what he was asking. Someone else had been a danger to *her*. "Yes."

"And what gives you cause to believe she is missing?" He scratched his arm.

"Bruno, your wife called, and I told her you were busy talking to a beautiful American woman," one of the officers hollered from across the room. "I told her not to worry, she is the only woman who would have a man as ugly as you."

I frowned. The other men burst into laughter. I chose to ignore them and answer the question. The sooner I got through this report, the better. I pushed my tongue into the roof of my mouth, thinking. I was determined to choose my words carefully. "She is renting out her castle for a movie production, and she had a reservation at Le Naiadi in Santa Marinella. But she told me she didn't plan to go—in fact, she hasn't left Castello del Lago in years—and she never showed up at the hotel."

"I see. Does your aunt have friends or other family she may have gone to visit?"

I thought fleetingly of my mother, alone at the *pensione*. "No. No one. Well, no family; I don't know for sure about friends."

"Hmm. And how old is your aunt? Is she able-bodied?" He sighed, clearly bored of the exercise, and lit a fresh cigarette.

It occurred to me I didn't actually know how old Gabriella was, only that she was my mother's older sister. "Um, she's in her forties, and yes, she's able-bodied."

"I see. And she was planning to go on holiday?" This question hadn't been on the form, and he looked coolly at me. I didn't like the direction things were going.

"Well, yes, technically, but I think something bad happened to her. There was blood on the garden wall, and on the beach, and I found her shoe there." My voice sounded shrill, my words feeble, and I took a deep breath to calm myself. Finding the shoe together with the blood had seemed like such a major discovery. But I supposed it was possible the shoe was a coincidence. Anyone could lose a shoe on a rocky shore, after all. Still, it didn't explain the blood. I hoped he would see that.

"Blood? Can you describe this in more detail?"

I let out my breath in a whoosh. Now we were back on track. "There was a lot smeared on the beach, in a wide trail. And a big red stain on the garden wall. At first we thought it was the set department—it's a horror movie, as I mentioned—but it wasn't them."

I'd meant this to prove that I'd already ruled out outside possibilities, but the officer snorted.

"I see." He looked back to his form and droned on. "Did your aunt have any enemies? Anyone you know of who wished her harm?"

I crossed my legs, attempting to get comfortable in the torturous chair, and one of the other officers whistled. I ignored him and continued. "She said she didn't want the filming to proceed. She disappeared right after that." I decided not to mention Richard's assertion that she had changed her mind.

"How many people are at the castle, would you say?"

"A couple dozen, I guess."

"And no one saw harm befall her?" His eyes were sharper now, studying me, the pen limp in his hand.

I tensed. When he put it like that, it sounded unlikely that her murder would have gone unnoticed. It must have happened in the dead of night.

"Not to my knowledge." I gritted my teeth.

"And once again, she had no specific enemies, that you knew of?"

"Well, I thought figuring that part out was your job," I snapped. "You aren't listening to me. She's a recluse who can't drive, and there's blood, *real* blood, all over her beach." I pounded the table with my fist, and his face turned blank, vacated of any minor interest he'd had in my story.

My damn mouth had run away with me again.

The officer coughed, and when he spoke again, his tone was blunt. "Look, Miss Whitford, your aunt was an able-bodied adult, of sound mind, with preexisting plans to travel. Right now, she is not a missing person. But if she doesn't return when her holiday was scheduled to end, you can come back, okay?"

He shuffled the papers on the desk in front of him. The officer who'd teased him about being ugly had been listening to our exchange and called out, "Yes, come back any time, beauty!"

My cheeks flamed. "But she's not traveling. She could be dead. Something's happened to her. You're wasting time."

Captain Bruno's annoyance gave way to contempt. He stood up. He was taller than I realized, and seeing his sharp uniform in all its glory reminded me that the *carabinieri* were technically part of the military. I was in a foreign country where I didn't fully understand how things worked, and I instantly regretted my outburst. Insulting a figure of authority hadn't been particularly wise, and I grew a bit nervous. He was old enough to have been in the war, and I wondered if he was a fascist like my aunt. He could have fought for Mussolini. In fact, I rated it likely.

"We have other missing person cases in this region. Missing children. We can't go chasing after every lady who changes the details of her holiday plans."

He gestured toward the door. I was stunned, slack-jawed, and I couldn't move. I considered refusing, but I could tell it would be useless. They wouldn't help me. Finally, I rose and walked slowly out of the station with my head held high.

Outside on the cobblestone street, I paused, momentarily overwhelmed by my failure. This outcome had never occurred to me. I figured after getting up the courage to call and go to the station, the rest would have come easily. I'd expected a smartly dressed officer to speed right down, car lights flashing, and grill Richard until he cracked.

I had no idea what I was supposed to do now.

CHAPTER 20

The drive back was just as bone-rattling as the way there, and my thoughts careened along with the car. No matter what the police said, the more I thought about it, the more convinced I was that my aunt was dead and her murderer was in the castle. To me, it was the most logical conclusion when you considered the new evidence. There had been a struggle in the garden before my aunt's body was taken to the beach and dragged under the tarp. Then most likely the killer had come back later to dispose of her, maybe putting her in the rowboat and ferrying her to deeper water. I considered going back and kicking up another fuss over the shoe and making everyone else listen.

But the indifference of the police gave me pause. It was possible the cast and crew would react just as they had. The only person who would know for sure I was right would be the killer.

I could go back to Rome and take my mother and Lulu far away from here. But I was still broke, and if I quit a picture I'd already started, I'd never get another acting job in this town. Besides, I'd never learn what happened to Gabriella. She'd never find justice, or peace, and despite my mother's protestations I knew part of her had come to Italy seeking closure. Otherwise, why had she saved my aunt's letter?

The only solution that presented itself was one that terrified me: continue on the picture as if nothing were wrong, and investigate her disappearance myself.

I parked Paul's car, astonished that it, and I, had survived the journey. My nerves were fried, and I probably looked like a mess. I'd spent the morning chasing a toddler up and down the *vicoli* and the afternoon on my own personal Italian roller-coaster ride. When I emerged into the great hall, Paul crossed over toward me in long purposeful strides, looking confused and concerned.

"Silvia, I've been calling you for the last five minutes. You're due on set." His eyes raked over me, and my heart stopped.

"*Shit.*"

I had completely lost track of time. After my discovery, my scene had been the last thing on my mind. I'd thought by now the police would be on their way.

But they weren't.

"Is everything okay?" His gaze was protective, proprietary even. But beneath his worry, there was irritation, too. I hadn't even been to hair and makeup yet, which would take a while.

"No. Everything is not all right."

I closed my eyes, attempting to calm myself. Acting right now seemed wrong, impossible. There was a murderer among us.

I hesitated. Paul's eyes darted back and forth. I pictured taking my family back to Rome, finding a waitressing job, and scraping by. My mother growing sicker and more bitter.

No—difficult as it was, the best option was still the one I'd decided on in the car.

There was another reason I wanted to stay, of course, one I could barely admit: I wanted to be a star. Paul had made me believe it was possible, and deep down I knew at least part of my motivation was selfish. I brushed the thought away. I'd gone to the police, hadn't I? I'd been willing to risk all that. I'd done my part.

"I'll go to Aurelia right now. I'm so sorry."

"Silvia . . ." He crossed those strong bronze arms over his chest, the arms that not long ago had been pinning me down beneath him.

"I'll tell you everything after the scene."

I hurried over to Mrs. Leskowitz's station, then Aurelia's. I was embarrassed that I'd held everyone up; it made me look unprofessional. An *amateur,* Richard had called me, and it still rankled. But it wasn't wounded pride making my heart pound. It was the fact that I didn't know who in the castle might be dangerous. Still, I stayed seated. Desperation was a powerful motivator. So was ambition.

"Stop frowning," Aurelia said, while she sponged foundation over my face. I obliged, but it wasn't easy.

My scene today was another one with Bernard, where Bianca tries to seduce him after the witch infiltrates her mind. He turns her down, shaking her and snapping her out of her reverie, saving her from the witch's possession. It would be another kissing scene.

By the time I finally arrived on set, Terrence was furious.

Mrs. Leskowitz had dressed me in a sheer red negligee, even more scandalous than the one I'd worn yesterday in the nightmare scene. I was keenly aware that despite the pasties she'd put over my nipples and the nude underwear I wore, my body was on near full display. Terrence made no effort to conceal his appraisal of my figure, and nothing he saw removed the nasty sneer from his face.

Mr. Meyerson was also clearly displeased, his mouth tight. But he didn't yell at me.

"We're going to have to skip rehearsal," he said, the closest he'd ever come to censuring me.

We got right to work.

The only way to make up for my lateness was to be terrific.

I was usually pretty good under strain, fortunately. And once again, it wasn't hard to get in character. After my night with Paul, I could still practically feel his touch on my skin, my hair, between my legs.

"Bernard." I stretched out a hand and caressed Terrence's face, just as Lucrezia had done to me in our last scene, when the witch came to Bianca in a nightmare. "I want you to take me, Bernard. I've wanted this since the moment I saw you."

I pretended it was Paul I was seducing instead of Terrence,

that I was running my hands down his chest. I pressed myself against Terrence and kissed him, ignoring his rigid lips and the whiskey on his breath. I put aside the questions crowding my mind about who might have murdered my aunt. I couldn't allow myself to dwell on the possibility that I was acting alongside a killer. In my mind, it was Paul I was kissing. My blood raced again, and I must have been doing my work a little too well, because after the second take, the sneer finally disappeared from Terrence's face.

"You know, we really should have rehearsed this scene more beforehand. Privately," he said, his words slurring the tiniest degree. He winked at me. "You're really not doing bad at all, but I could have warmed you up a bit."

"You're a pig, Terrence."

"Have it your way."

My hair had gotten mussed, and Aurelia came over to douse me with hair spray, which made my eyes water. I blinked the chemicals away and looked toward Paul. I hoped he didn't think I'd been taking advantage of him by my lateness. His gaze locked on mine, but he didn't even smile. Suddenly it felt like I'd swallowed ice. Perhaps he merely wanted to maintain a professional distance while we were in public.

Or maybe he was angry with me. Given all that had happened, it shouldn't have been anywhere close to my chief concern at the moment, but the heart isn't rational that way. I cared a lot about what Paul might be thinking.

"You know, Herman, I'm struggling a little with Bernard's decision here. What kind of man turns down a half-naked woman who throws herself at you?" Terrence took in another eyeful of me. His words pricked my mind. Was that the only reason Paul had gone to bed with me? I had done just what Bianca was doing, only Paul hadn't resisted, as Bernard did.

"There's no love scene in this movie. I really feel like it needs one," Terrence continued.

I turned again toward Paul, but he was still impassive. Wait—there. Something had flashed in his eyes when he looked at Terrence. I couldn't make sense of it. His blond hair was still adorably rumpled after our exertions the night before, since he hadn't had time to shower. I wished I could go to him and wrap my arms around his waist, but I didn't want to make him even angrier.

"That's the point. Bernard doesn't want the witch, he wants virginal Bianca. Her purity must be preserved for the story to make sense," Herman replied, his clipped vowels revealing his impatience.

"Poor blighter. No sense at all, really."

We did one more take, and in this one, Terrence turned up the heat—really sinking into our kiss, letting his hands wander a little bit. I had become completely inured to his perfect, sculptural handsomeness, and in the moments where I had to look at him—which was all of them except for the kissing—it took the full depth of my talent to pretend I wanted him.

We finished up the scene pretty quickly—by being *on*, I'd helped us make up for some of the lost time. I flicked my eyes over at Paul so often, I'm sure everyone noticed, but I couldn't help it. He kept avoiding my gaze.

After we wrapped, I could hardly stand it anymore, and I approached him tentatively. Once I explained Richard's deceit about the car, my discovery on the beach, and the police, I was sure he'd understand.

"Paul—" I was only ten feet away, but he didn't acknowledge me. He was chatting with the camera operator about something, but I knew he'd heard me, because his eyes blazed. And then to my dismay, he turned and walked away. I was dumbfounded and hurt.

Instead of going to wardrobe, I went straight to his room, still wearing the red negligee. He wouldn't be able to avoid me there. Maybe he didn't want to fight with me in front of everyone. I paced the tiny quarters, my blood whooshing in my ears, panicking.

His door creaked open only a few minutes later, the raw emotion on his face no longer hidden. He was furious.

When he saw me, he stopped short. His jaw ticked.

"I came to apologize for being late. Please don't be mad at me. I can't stand it."

Paul laughed, dry and humorless. "You think I'm mad at you for being late?"

I frowned, bemused. "Aren't you?"

"I'm mad at myself." He stripped off his khaki jacket and threw it on the bed. "I knew better than to get involved with someone I work with."

The ice was back, whole buckets of it filling my stomach. My heart beat in my throat. The idea of a murderer in the castle had scared me, but the idea of losing Paul's affection terrified me to my core. When I fell for someone, I fell hard.

"I'm not normally late. It had nothing to do with—last night." I hated how pathetic I sounded. But now that I'd experienced what it felt like to have Paul, I couldn't lose him. I took a step back to make room as he approached me, bumping up against his dresser.

"If I'm with you, I can't do my job, Silvia. I just had to watch you in the arms of another man for two hours, and I couldn't fucking bear it." He slammed his hand against the wall, shaking a little dark oil painting of a man holding a sword. The agony on his face made my spirits soar.

He wasn't angry at me. He was just jealous. Relief flooded me. *Jealous* I could work with.

It all made sense now, and in his shoes, I would have behaved the same way. If I'd had to watch for hours while he seduced, say, Lucrezia for the cameras, I'd be ready to boil over, too.

The air between us was charged. I pushed myself up onto the dresser behind me and slowly pulled my red negligee up to my hips. Paul went perfectly still, but beneath his white T-shirt, he was breathing hard.

"Terrence is a swine, Paul. I endured that scene by thinking about you."

Paul reached me in a single stride, and his fingers were firm and sure as he yanked my panties down to my knees. I nudged open the drawer beneath me to locate a condom and then deftly unbelted his pants. There was no gentle exploring this time, no tender kissing before he entered me. He shuddered as he shoved himself deep inside me, his face pure rapture.

I barely noticed the cold wall against my back, the hard dresser beneath me, knocking against the plaster. I was too full of Paul, too high on the thrill of being the center of his attention for that moment.

CHAPTER 21

Paul smoked languidly, exhaling toward the ceiling, and I lay on my stomach, tracing my fingers along his belly.

We'd ended up in bed somewhere along the way, and the intensity of my attraction for him and my growing feelings overwhelmed me. It was different from the utter devotion inspired by Lulu, but still astoundingly powerful. It wouldn't be hard to love a man like Paul. A summer thunderstorm had rolled in while we made love, quick and clamorous, and water pooled beneath his window. The castle wasn't particularly weatherproof, it seemed, which explained the mildewy smell.

I'd just filled him in on the events of the day, and he'd listened with careful attention. He hadn't judged me or made me feel foolish. I couldn't name the last man who'd made me feel like my perspective was valued.

"So you think someone killed her because she would have stopped us filming at the castle?" Paul looked thoughtful.

"I can't think of any other reason. And the timing seems suspicious."

He stroked my hair. His hand spanned my whole skull, and his touch was featherlight. "It's weird, I agree. Something's definitely not right about the whole thing."

I was grateful he didn't disparage my theory. If he had doubted me too, after Richard and then the police officer, I might have questioned whether I was overreacting. I couldn't tell if he was entirely convinced she'd been killed, but he seemed genuinely open to considering my view of events.

"It just seems so extreme. Couldn't they just have picked another castle?"

Paul let out another billow of smoke. "No. Getting her to pay us back wouldn't have been easy. And Richard did look into a few other castles we were interested in, but they were too expensive or not available. We might have been able to figure something out, but the setback would have been costly. It definitely could have ended the picture, if she'd pulled the plug."

Outside, the sky was still gray from the late afternoon storm, which had lightened to a steady drizzle. Paul looked beautiful in the half-light. When I switched on the lamp beside the bed, it gave me a little shock; I'd been zapped by fixtures semi-regularly, thanks to the castle's faulty wiring. Paul sat up, stretching, and his body cast a long shadow on the wall.

"Did anyone even know about her decision, besides Richard and Roberto?" I asked the question almost offhandedly, but I was keenly aware of the accusation behind my words. I didn't know much about Paul's relationship with Richard. I'd been puzzling over this question, because if Richard was the only senior member of the crew who knew about Gabriella's threat, it made him the most obvious suspect.

Paul shook his head. "No. Roberto told a bunch of us. Terrence had just arrived, and Roberto came bounding out looking like a kicked puppy, and said that Richard had to come quick because Gabriella wasn't going to let us shoot at the castle. I was there, and so were Herman, Lucrezia, and Terrence."

My fingers had been circling his belly button, and I stopped. "Oh." I still thought Richard was the most likely suspect, although I didn't say so. Terrence was a possible candidate, too, although I had a harder time believing someone as famous as he was would go to such lengths to see this movie succeed.

"Should I go grab us some food? I don't know about you, but I'm starving. Worked up an appetite, I guess." He draped an arm across me and pulled me close to him, nuzzling my neck.

"I have to go anyway. My mother is probably expecting me."

We lay there for a moment, warm skin to warm skin, smelling of salt and sex.

"I wouldn't want her to be disappointed. But God, I can't seem to get enough of you." He kissed me, and his words caused a surge of joy.

Still, duty made me climb out of bed and don my red negligee. I groaned. "I never returned this. You don't have a robe or anything, do you?" I was already pretty sure he didn't, from my snooping, but maybe I'd missed it.

Paul shrugged. "Sorry. But I can go ask Mrs. Leskowitz for your clothes."

"That would be worse. Then everyone would know for sure that we're sleeping together."

He reclined, one hand behind his head, his arm making a neat triangle. The sheet covered only his lower half, and I admired the rest of him, his chest muscled but not excessively so, just enough that you could see the outlines of everything. *You couldn't pinch an inch,* my mother would say of a figure like that. I sensed she would approve of him. He displayed *la bella figura* quite admirably. "Would that be so bad?"

"Oh, I don't care. I thought you did. Professional distance and all that." It was true. I certainly wasn't a good girl, whatever Lucrezia initially thought, and I wasn't worried about pretending I was. Besides, I was proud of being with Paul.

He laughed, flashing those white square teeth. "I think we're well past that, don't you?"

I smiled. "So you don't mind, then? If everyone knows we're—together?" I hesitated before saying the last word. After all, we hadn't declared anything. We were screwing, that was all. But I hoped he wanted more than that.

"I want to shout it from the rooftops. And I'm sorry about before. The whole Terrence business."

It took every ounce of willpower I had not to return to bed. I was utterly infatuated. "It's okay. And don't worry about the clothes. I'll grab them myself on my way out."

Before I could change my mind, I slipped out into the hallway.

The route back to the great hall took me through the gallery, and the windows here, too, bore signs of leaking. My exposed skin—which, in the red negligee, was nearly all of it—prickled in the dank air. I had to strain to see, since there were no lights here, and rain clouds obscured the sun.

I was glad to reach the costume station in the great hall. Mrs. Leskowitz wasn't around, but Sarah was there, ironing, and she hid a giggle behind her hand when she saw me.

"Sorry I'm late. Bad habit today."

"Don't worry about it. Shame to waste an outfit like that." She giggled again, and I replied with a sly grin.

If I'd had my own dressing room, I could have kept my personal affairs a little more private, and most stars would complain about not having one. Terrence certainly had, until they'd found a space for him. But I'd never had one before anyway, so it wasn't a luxury I'd grown used to. I didn't mind changing in the curtained area they'd set up.

I emerged in my own clothes, glad to be covered up again.

For her part, Sarah was wearing a floral blouse with long, wide sleeves, a thick headband, and long earrings. The effect was trendy and bohemian. Given her profession, it made sense she had terrific personal style. I hadn't really spoken to her since her almost-firing, and I was deeply ashamed of my behavior.

"Sarah, I just wanted to apologize. I should have stood up for you, when Mr. Meyerson . . ." I trailed off uncomfortably.

Sarah's smile disappeared. She kept her face neutral while she ironed sharp pleats into a gray pant leg, but I thought I detected a flash of something in her eyes. Anger, maybe. Finally, she put the pants aside and stared right at me. I'd expected her to accept my apology and for us to move on.

As the silence continued, and sweet Sarah's eyes hardened, I saw that it was selfish of me. I'd just wanted her to assuage my guilt. I hadn't really acknowledged my role in what had happened. My complicity.

"I was wrong. I was in a position to do something, and I didn't."

She turned away from me, grabbing another pair of pants for

the ironing board. She attacked them energetically. Finally, she spoke. "Next time."

It took me a moment to comprehend what she meant. *Next time.* Mr. Meyerson wouldn't be the only one to treat her that way. I'd even witnessed disrespect toward her from a couple members of the crew. Whether on behalf of her or someone else, I had to do the right thing next time. Because there would always be a next time, and confronting that reality—one that she lived with every day—made my heart break.

"Next time," I agreed.

It reminded me that there was one more right thing I could do right now, for my aunt. I waited a minute, as if studying the costumes.

"Sarah, can I ask you something? Can you remember the last time you saw Gabriella? Before she—left." I kept my tone casual. There was no need to raise the alarm about her disappearance all over again, not yet.

The iron steamed, and the line of her jaw relaxed. Her eyes were mildly curious.

"Monday morning, I think. I was here getting your dress ready for your first scene on Tuesday, the champagne one." She flicked her eyes over to the racks where it hung, limply elegant, like a lady reclining after a long night out with too much drink. She beamed at it, proud of her handiwork. "I tailored that one myself, you know."

"It's the prettiest dress I've ever worn. You're very talented." I meant it.

She nodded, acknowledging the compliment. "I remember your aunt crossing toward the kitchen. I noticed because I liked her outfit. A belted peach sheath dress. It suited her."

"What about later?"

She shook her head. "I wasn't paying close attention. We were so busy."

"That's all right. Thanks."

I sighed. Her answer didn't surprise me. No one seemed to have seen Gabriella after that morning.

It was like she'd disappeared into thin air.

CHAPTER 22

I hadn't told Paul the entire reason I had to trade his bed for the plain, wrought-iron contraption with the lumpy mattress at the *pensione.* Of course I hadn't. I was desperate to see Lulu, for one, and she was a topic I didn't feel anywhere near ready to broach with him. And then there was the urgent conversation I needed to have with my mother.

It was time for us to talk about her sister. We had to. Something was really, truly wrong, and I needed her to hear it.

I didn't have an umbrella, but it wasn't raining much as I made my way through the town. Rivulets of water ran down the steep stairs and alleys, and created giant puddles in the main piazza, so by the time I reached the *pensione,* my sandals were soaked and mud flecked the backs of my bare legs. At least the air was fresher than in the moldering castle.

I arrived in time for dinner with the Riccis, and my stomach grumbled. Paul wasn't the only one who had worked up an appetite. A wriggling Lulu was positioned on my mother's lap, and I picked her up and squeezed her, then kissed her chubby cheeks.

"I hope I'm not intruding." The wide, wooden table in the dining room groaned with food.

"Don't be silly. There's plenty. It's for Rita's birthday," Signora Ricci said. She was wide-hipped and had a broad, friendly face, and her short, black bob was streaked with gray. Her husband was jolly, sturdy, and sun-beaten.

Rita, I knew, was her eldest, a buck-toothed, wryly funny girl of newly minted thirteen.

"Happy birthday, Rita. That's a lovely dress."

She beamed at me. "Thanks, Silvia. Lulu was pretty good today. She only bit me twice."

"Oh, no. I'm sorry about that. We've been working on it."

Rita shrugged. "Kids bite. I know I did. I don't anymore, though. Here, you can sit by me." She patted the chair beside her.

I joined them at the table, and we feasted on *cacio e pepe* and *saltimbocca* and stewed eggplant, and even my mother, wan and quiet, managed to eat more than her usual few mouthfuls.

I ended up in a lively conversation with Signora Ricci about the town.

"None of the young people stay, anymore. They all are going to Rome, and Florence, and Milan," she said, a little sadly. "It's mostly just the old-timers left, still nursing their resentments against each other from the war."

This comment interested me, as it brought to mind the ill feeling between my aunt and my mother. I wondered how common their situation was. "What type of resentments?"

Signora Ricci shrugged. "It's hard to know where to begin. There was civil war in Italy when we switched sides. Some people had sons who ended up fighting alongside the Germans, some had sons fighting against them."

I sipped my wine, embarrassed by how little about Italy's history I knew. It seemed my ignorance about my mother's history and that of her home country went hand in hand. Signora Ricci continued: "I have a good example. We just got a new priest in town. A truly holy man. During the war, he helped protect Jews from being sent to the camps. But the priest we had before him, he helped support the ratlines, and aided Nazi war criminals escaping to Rome and then South America. For years, many of us here felt we couldn't even turn to God with our troubles."

I digested this information along with the heavy food. I remembered the shuttered church on one of my first visits, the empty shrine. Perhaps that had been before the new priest arrived. What she'd said also explained the strange tension in the

town, and the eerie quiet. I pictured the hatred festering between the villagers over the years, cloaking the town like the
morning fog.

When we retired upstairs, my mother remained taciturn, and
I figured I was still being punished for the last time I'd tried to
bring up her sister. Which meant I had little to lose by trying
again.

Lulu climbed onto the bed and began jumping energetically,
still excited from the big feast.

"No, *piccola*. That's enough," my mother said, sternly. Lulu
started crying big crocodile tears, and I picked her up, then
whirled her around in a circle until her tears turned to peals of
laughter. We collapsed on the bed, dizzy.

"You shouldn't spoil her. She needs discipline," my mother
said.

"She's two." I took a deep breath. This wasn't the fight I had
come here to pick, and I needed to conserve my energy. I decided
to launch right in, before I lost my nerve. "Your sister is missing.
I think something happened to her."

My mother's face grew pinched. "I told you I don't want to
talk about her."

"Too bad." I exhaled slowly, as if I could release the frustration that had been building inside me for so long. "No one has
seen her since Monday. There was blood in the garden and on
the beach that led to one of her shoes. She might be dead. I
know you've spent my entire life hating her, but I can't believe if
she's dead you won't care at all."

My mother turned away from me, her slim body shaking.
"I *don't* care. For me, she died a long time ago." She spoke in
short, restrained sentences, and her lack of feeling turned my
blood cold. "Besides, she's probably just being dramatic. She'll
turn up. Now let's get Lulu ready for bed."

When she turned back around, her eyes were dry, her lips
firm. I wanted to scream. Even my own mother wasn't taking
me seriously, and it was starting to feel like I was losing it. There
was real evidence of a crime, and no one seemed to appreciate
the urgency or the danger. *Was* I making too much of things?

I shook my head. I knew I wasn't.

We scrubbed Lulu's hands and face in the washbasin and changed her into a frilly nightdress, speaking to her but not each other. After she drifted off, my fingers tangled in her hair, my mother spoke again.

"I've been thinking that Lulu and I should move to the castle."

I sat upright, jostling the bed, and winced. Luckily, Lulu stayed asleep. *"What?"* She'd been so opposed to it before that the reversal in her opinion stunned me.

"Signora Ricci said her daughter, Rita, could come with us. She's mad about cinema. The movie is all anyone in town will talk about. It would be fun for me to see you working. And we'd get to spend more time with you."

"But—" I sputtered. I didn't understand. She'd wanted absolutely nothing to do with her sister, and even though Gabriella wasn't there, I was astonished she'd be willing to stay in her home.

"Lulu is getting old enough to understand, you know. You can't tell people she's your sister forever."

Her accusation burrowed itself into my chest, prickly and painful. I despised the lie. And she was right; Lulu understood so much now, and it confused her when people didn't refer to me as her mother. Back in Los Angeles, she'd revealed the truth on several occasions to casual acquaintances—the lady at the diner, an irritating neighbor—simply by calling out to me. "I'm not planning to pretend forever. It's not about that. I don't want the men I work with to think they can get in my pants because I have a kid."

My mother snorted. "Too late."

"Excuse me?"

"Oh, don't pretend with me. You smell like sex, and you were smiling like a fool all through dinner. I think you just don't want your new boyfriend finding out about her. That's what I think."

I got off the bed, too angry to worry about jostling Lulu this time. My mother knew exactly how to wound a person. Her perceptiveness was typical, and I should have prepared myself for it. And I understood, now, why she wanted to come to the castle. I'd let someone else into my affections, and she was protective and jealous, as usual. She wanted me all to herself.

Her insinuation that I was ashamed of Lulu and cared more about my relationship with Paul was way off base.

"That's not it at all. You couldn't possibly understand how judgmental people are. How cruel they can be." I covered my mouth. Just imagining how Terrence would react, what Mr. Meyerson would think when he found out that the actress playing his virginal ingenue had a child out of wedlock, made me panicky. I'd had to endure so much already. Bringing Lulu to the castle would undoubtedly make things worse, possibly much worse.

My mother got up, too, and glared at me from the other side of the bed. The square room suddenly felt too small. It was spare, furnished with only a wrought-iron bed, a battered old wardrobe, a weak lamp, and a washbasin, but even so, there wasn't enough space to also contain our mutual fury. I opened the window, letting in a gentle breeze that smelled of rain, and it fluttered the white organdy curtains.

"You think I don't understand?" Her face was drawn. "I understand better than anyone, Silvia."

"You couldn't possibly. Not unless you've been in my shoes."

The silence that followed lasted a long time. I listened to the crickets chirping outside the window and watched Lulu's chest rise and fall, counting her breaths. My mother gripped the iron spindles of the footboard with white knuckles. "I have been in your shoes."

I stared at her, stunned. "I don't understand."

My mother's eyes were sorrowful. "There's something I've wanted to tell you for a long time, *mi amore*. Your father and I weren't married until after the war."

The night around me paused. I no longer heard the crickets, or the wind; the only noise I perceived was that sentence echoing in my mind.

My mother struggled to continue. "I wrote to your father to tell him about you, as soon as I knew, and he submitted an application to the army to marry me. While I waited for him—well. Italy was not a kind place for unwed mothers. A boy I grew up with cut off my hair to shame me. There would have been little hope for us, if your father had not come back. I was a single mother with no money."

"You mean you and Daddy—it was just a fling?" I'd always believed they'd fallen in love at first sight, and that they'd gotten married after two short weeks because they'd known they had to spend the rest of their lives together. The romantic tale of their union meant a lot to me, especially after my father died. It mattered to me that my parents had loved each other, truly and deeply. Now it turned out it may have been honor that brought my father back for my mother rather than passion.

"The story we told you was mostly true. We did fall for one another. We just didn't get married. But I believed—and I believe still—that even if you hadn't come along, he would have come back for me."

I didn't know whether she was telling the truth or whether she was just trying to make me feel better. But I could trust my own recollections, and I could remember flashes of my parents together, the serene, companionable banter, the friendly affection. Whatever had led to their marriage, they'd been happy. I breathed out, my surprise at the news giving way to sympathy for my mother.

"I'm sorry. What you went through must have been awful." My mind spun. She looked as breakable as porcelain in her nightclothes, with her sharp bones and pale skin and gray-blond hair in a braid, but I knew that despite appearances, my mother was made of strong stuff. I'd never guessed how strong.

It made sense that they hadn't gotten married before my father's regiment moved on, and it should have occurred to me to question it before. "So Daddy returned to marry you after the war."

He would have had to, before we could travel to join him in America. She was hardly alone; thousands of women traveled to the U.S. after the war to reunite with their husbands. Operation War Bride, they'd called it. But I'd never known about the discrimination she'd had to endure before then.

My mother stared at a point above my head, and I realized she wasn't looking outward, but inward. "He did." Her voice was a whisper. "Your father was a very good man. He had his faults, but he loved you so much. Just like I do." She skirted the bed now and touched my cheek with papery fingers.

I swallowed. "Why didn't you tell me before?"

That part I didn't understand. She'd been so disappointed in me when I'd fallen pregnant. True, she'd never wavered in her support, but she could have commiserated. She shrugged, defeatedly. "I meant to."

"It's okay. I'm glad you told me now."

"Forget I asked about the castle. It's not important. Let's get some sleep, hmm?"

I nodded, but while she crawled beneath the covers, I rose and stood by the window, studying the dark street below.

I needed time to process what I'd learned, to pick apart her words once more.

I was a bastard from the war. A love child, whose birth had secured me and my mother a new country to call home. It was an entirely new identity, thrust upon me.

There was one thing I knew for sure, just as I had on another night, after a different fight in a different hotel room.

There was more she could have told me.

CHAPTER 23

There was no such thing as weekends when you were shooting a picture, but that didn't matter to Lucrezia. After we wrapped on Sunday, she decided to throw a party.

"If we can't go to the Piper Club, we'll have the Piper Club here," she declared, and she enlisted the gaffer, Carlo, to turn the dusty dining room into a *discoteca*.

It was more successful than I expected. He got flashing strobe lights set up, and Lucrezia hauled out a record player and speakers that she'd brought with her in her mountains of luggage. The Piper Club, Lucrezia told me, was the hottest club in Rome, only just opened that February, and located in an abandoned cinema. The cavernous dining room of a ramshackle medieval castle would do quite nicely as a replacement, she said.

And she was right. The whole cast and crew assembled to drink sidecars and gimlets, mixed efficiently by Paul, as well as generous pours from jugs of Italian table wine. A haze of cigarette smoke blanketed the room. Lucrezia had records, too, beat music that got everyone dancing and laughing. It had been the longest week of my life, but I couldn't entirely relax, not knowing what I knew.

"Dance with me?" Paul abandoned his post by the gin and cognac, the bottles hulking on the long ornate table in the darkened room, then shining like fine crystal when the lights hit them. I let him wrap his arms around me, his hands warm against the base of my spine. We moved well together, having already begun to become acquainted with each other's rhythms, and I could sense myself becoming caught up in music and motion and Paul.

"Let's take a break," I said, after the song ended. Paul was wildly distracting, but I didn't want to leave the party just yet.

"Sure. I better get back to mixing drinks, anyway. The crew is getting restless."

He wasn't wrong. People had begun to help themselves, and I watched Carlo appropriate an entire jug of wine and take it to the other side of the room. He'd earned it, in my view.

Paul, it surprised me not at all, made a natural bartender. He was quick and focused, and I admired his forearms as he poured and mixed. His job as assistant director made him responsible for the health and safety of the cast and crew, and he took it seriously. I understood now that he truly felt responsible for all of us. He wouldn't get in the way of anyone's good time—in fact, he'd facilitate it—but he was in a position to keep an eye on things, and cut anyone off who needed cutting off.

Mr. Meyerson was more like the displeased chaperone at a school dance, glowering in the corner, arms crossed.

I helped myself to several swallows of wine and felt the tension in my body loosening. Lucrezia arrived beside me at the end of the gothic dining table, breathless and laughing after dancing with the grip.

"So you and Paul," she said, and a strobe light hit her face. Even on beautiful Lucrezia, the effect was slightly frightening. "All out in the open then, hmm? Everyone's talking, you know."

This didn't surprise me in the least. I'd expected it. "Let them talk."

Lucrezia was the type, I guessed, who didn't mind being gossiped about—relished it, even. I hadn't been in Italy long enough to know anything about the Italian society rags, but I could easily picture the *paparazzi* snapping Lucrezia's photo outside a nightclub, arm in arm with a dashing American movie star.

She clasped my hand and whispered in my ear in an intimate purr. "And that's not all they're talking about. Your fight with Richard, too. How perfectly morbid."

Her tone was impressed, congratulatory, even. Within a week, I'd bedded the assistant director and accused the production manager of murder; from an outside perspective, I could see how it might look like I was *trying* to be the talk of the picture. But I wasn't. I merely followed my passions wherever they led me. I'd certainly changed Lucrezia's initial impression of me, anyway, and I wasn't sorry for it.

I was a bit surprised Richard had told people about our altercation. But then, I may have raised my voice. People could have simply overheard.

The wine had rushed to my head by then, and I decided to confide in Lucrezia. I wanted a friend. The idea that she had been involved in my aunt's death struck me as unlikely, and her ear for gossip could prove valuable.

"I meant what I told him. I think someone murdered my aunt. Someone in this room." The wine had dulled my fear for a moment, but it returned now. I gazed forlornly at my empty cup before discarding it.

Lucrezia's hand tightened on mine. I could still make out her figure in the dark, in a classic black cocktail dress to her knees, with a low V-cut and black bow cinching her waist. Her black hair glistened in the lights. She looked spectacular.

"You really think so? You weren't just putting Richard on? He'd deserve it if you were; I wouldn't judge you. Slimy little worm."

"I wasn't putting him on."

She turned toward me, the lights flashing on her face once again, and her dark eyes were wide, her full pink lips arranged in a semicircle of amazement.

"How awful. It's just like a real *giallo*. Here, we need more drinks." She pulled me toward the middle of the table, until we were right beside Paul. "We need gimlets, urgently," she declared, and Paul reached for the gin, his movements practiced and sure. He watched me as he mixed, not even glancing at Lucrezia, and brushed his fingers softly against mine when he handed me my cup. My mouth went dry, and I sipped the gimlet, letting the citrus and juniper berries coalesce on my tongue.

"I was on a detective picture last year, you know. The key to solving a murder is *motive*." Lucrezia tapped her chin with a lacquered nail. "If you like, I can help."

I could easily picture Lucrezia in some lurid police mystery, maybe as the love interest whose life is threatened, or perhaps the secretary to some gruff private eye.

"Oh?"

She shrugged an elegant shoulder. "Sure. Who are the most likely suspects?" She looked around the room, where people danced or chatted or, in the case of a local girl and one of the production assistants, kissed furiously in a dark corner.

"Everyone who knew about my aunt threatening to back out of the contract. So Richard, Mr. Meyerson, Terrence, and Roberto. Us too, I suppose, although it's probably safe to exclude ourselves." I glanced at Paul, and though he was still busy bartending, I could tell he was listening.

"No, we shouldn't." She shook her head. "We must be fair and thorough. But we can start with them. Shall we each pick a target?"

She sounded excited. This was only a diversion to her, but I didn't mind too much. At least she was offering to help.

"A target?"

"To spy on. And discover motive. I'll take Terrence. I know how to get him talking." She flounced her hair and smoothed her dress.

"I'll bet you do." I rolled my eyes, but she wouldn't see in the dark. She'd been looking for an excuse to sleep with him, and now she had one.

"What about you? I mean, you have Paul well covered, obviously." I blushed furiously, grateful no one could see. "Maybe you should take Mr. Meyerson, since he likes you so much." She reached over and touched Paul's shoulder. "Paul, Richard might talk to you. A fellow man's man and all that."

Paul passed some drinks across the table to the production assistant and his new friend, who had emerged from their corner and were grinning sheepishly. I was close enough to make out his expression, which was perfectly neutral. He'd be deadly at poker. "Sure. I can grab a drink with Richard. Find out more about him. We're friendly. But I think you're barking up the wrong tree. He's a decent guy."

I snorted. "Agree to disagree."

"Oh, not a lovers' quarrel already?" Lucrezia's laugh was delicate and high, like the clink of china. "Well, I'll leave you two to sort it out. I have to get to work."

And she left us, those remarkable legs carrying her across the room to where Terrence was in conversation with his young woman from craft services. Lucrezia was shameless, cutting right in and apparently asking Terrence for a dance, because I watched her drag him to the middle of the room, leaving her poor rival with her head spinning. I felt a little sorry for her. Especially because Terrence and Lucrezia, on the surface at least, were such a natural pair—so beautiful, it almost hurt to look at them. And Lucrezia could dance like no woman I'd ever seen. The way she moved was hypnotizing.

Terrence was a rather easy mark, because after two songs, Lucrezia led him by the hand out of the room. I caught a glimpse of his face, as they passed near us in the dark on the way out the door, and he wore a smug grin, as if this development were somehow of his doing.

I thought Lucrezia's plan was reasonably sound. What did I know about police work? Being on a detective movie made her better qualified than I was. I didn't doubt she'd ferret out the specifics of Terrence's financial woes, or whatever other reason he might have had for getting my aunt out of the way. At first, I'd had a hard time believing someone so famous could be a heartless criminal, but now I'd warmed to the idea. He was entitled enough and cruel enough. After Richard, he struck me as a strong possibility.

Despite Lucrezia's assignment for me, in that moment, striking up a conversation with Mr. Meyerson sounded about as appealing as jumping in the lake. Now that I knew his true colors, I struggled to maintain my composure around him. I also had no idea how to begin.

"Why would Mr. Meyerson desperately need this picture to

succeed, do you think?" I asked Paul, still idly sipping my gimlet. My brain had started to fog.

"I think he might have put some of his own money in. He's got some points on the back end." I nodded. It made sense Mr. Meyerson would have negotiated a deal that entitled him to a percentage of the profits. Paul leaned over, his lips by my ear, his breath hot on my neck. "Does that mean your homework assignment is done, now? Can we get out of here?"

"I thought you'd never ask."

"Let's go. They can mix their own drinks."

The room was warm from all the dancing, so we went out to the terrace to enjoy the breeze. He had tucked a bottle of wine under his arm, and we perched on the stone steps down to the garden and took turns swigging from the bottle. The wind was tinged with lemons.

"Have I mentioned lately just how much I like you?" Paul slurred a little. I'd never seen him tipsy before. He was always so in control.

"It's been hours. Just what do you like about me, Paul Rudderman?" I'd meant it jokingly, but halfway through the question, the lightness left my tone. I actually wanted to know. I mean, I knew why most men liked me, but I didn't know why *Paul* liked me, exactly. I didn't think it was just my looks, but I wasn't sure.

He assessed me, his brown eyes taking on that same serious, thoughtful expression they'd had when he'd first visited the castle, and I asked him to help me get a screen test. "You say just what you think. There are no games with you. I know where I stand. I like that. I can just—be, you know? It's nice being around you. Comfortable." He hung his arm around my shoulders.

"I'm—comfortable? That's why you want to be with me?" I pouted teasingly at him.

"That's not all of it. You care about your family. Your mom. What you're doing for your aunt, it's really noble."

I nestled closer, feeling his body heat against my back. "You're comfortable, too. Like a chair." I leaned back into him, and he laughed. I loved making him laugh, and how easy it was. Paul's default mood was relaxed and happy.

"Are you close with your siblings?" I asked. His comment about family had made me curious.

"Very. My sister Louisa just had a baby girl. Her second. I'm going to fly back to LA in a few months to meet her."

My thoughts turned to Lucy, and I didn't feel quite as drunk, suddenly. I pictured her asleep with her little bunny, and my love for her consumed me. I took another swig of the wine.

"Are you good with kids?" I forced myself to sound only half interested, like our whole future together didn't hang on his answer.

"I'm the world's best uncle. I'd love to have a few of my own. Someday. Not anytime soon." He laughed again, but I didn't join him. I knew I should tell him about Lulu, but I couldn't bring myself to do it. Instead, I kissed him.

"You should know, I'm not that noble, Paul," I said. He was the noble one.

He stroked my arm, then casually ran a hand across my breasts. I gasped, and blood rushed to the point between my legs. I didn't resist as he helped me up from the step and led me off of the terrace and to his room. Didn't resist as he unzipped my little cocktail dress and slid it off me so that it pooled at my feet. Nor as he kissed me, thoroughly, from my lips down to my breasts, then lower still.

I didn't resist at all.

CHAPTER 24

The opportunity to snoop on Mr. Meyerson presented itself on Tuesday, two days later. My call time wasn't until late morning, and I meant to savor it. I emerged from my room feeling fresh and summery in a yellow cotton dress, not minding at all the narrow corridor lined with bedrooms and its dark abandoned air. After all, I was headed to town for a dose of Lulu and sunshine.

I walked toward the stairs, across a faded oriental runner that traversed the tile, which was worn down to a dull shine. I passed Mr. Meyerson's room and noticed that the door hung open, almost in invitation.

I paused.

I peeked into the room beyond, the bed made with careful precision, a gleaming leather suitcase balanced on a chair.

Even though Paul had supplied a possible motive for Mr. Meyerson, it wasn't *evidence*, and I wouldn't get the police to come without something more definitive.

I still didn't really suspect him, but I was nosy. And he wouldn't be on break for hours. Everyone was busy downstairs. There didn't seem to be much harm in lingering for a few minutes.

I reached out a hand, tentatively, and pushed the door open wider. It creaked. I held my breath, looking up and down the corridor, before stepping over the threshold.

The room smelled of aftershave and hair cream, a distinctly

masculine odor that reminded me of my father, who'd also been a fastidious man. He'd insisted on hospital corners on the beds and that every article of clothing be neatly ironed, even his underwear. The army did that sort of thing to people.

There were no picture frames—no Mrs. Meyerson, not even a spoiled beloved niece or nephew. Lucrezia had told me he was a bachelor, and the bare dresser top confirmed it. It fit my picture of him: opinionated, set in his ways, egotistical, a little lonely. There are jolly bachelors out there, of course, but he wasn't one of them.

Perhaps it was hypocritical of me to assume there was no one in his life, since I didn't have a photo of Lulu displayed. I did have a wallet-sized one I kept in a drawer, though.

Out of idle curiosity, I tried Mr. Meyerson's top dresser drawer. It was all socks, all folded in straight little rows.

And one thing more.

A pistol. Wood grip, long thin barrel with a suppressor screwed on. I knew diddly squat about guns, but P38 was engraved onto the side.

I carefully closed the drawer, my pulse jumping.

It didn't necessarily mean anything. After all, a lot of people had guns. My father had had one much like this, a souvenir from the war that he'd claimed he'd taken from a Nazi prisoner. But the surprise of finding it there, and the casual violence of its arrangement—the sleek gray metal nestled against ribbed cotton—rattled me.

"What are you doing?"

I spun around. Herman Meyerson hovered in the doorway, and my heart leaped into my throat.

My mind went perfectly blank. Mr. Meyerson's expression of mild alarm turned indignant. I couldn't think of a single thing to say. I just stood there like a fool for what might have been a second or a minute, his question filling the air.

I couldn't breathe. In that terrible moment, I knew that there was no possible explanation he would believe. I'd ruined the one chance I had to give Lulu the life she deserved, probably my only chance.

Mr. Meyerson took a step forward. He was a bigger man than I'd realized, now that I saw him in the confines of his tiny quarters. Heftier. His eyes, I noticed, were blue-green, reminding me of the lake. Their depths were just as unreadable.

He took another step and stopped, an arm's length away. The movement broke my trance, and I cleared my throat. I found my voice.

"I'm so sorry. I wasn't paying attention. I meant to go into Lucrezia's room to get something for her."

I couldn't believe how careless I'd been, and for no good reason. I hadn't even learned anything particularly useful—nothing that tied him to my aunt's murder. He had a gun, but there was no reason to believe my aunt had been shot.

His eyes remained inscrutable. Surely he recognized the flimsiness of the lie.

"Don't look so startled. I don't bite." The tension in my chest eased a fraction. "Mistakes happen, after all. Take a seat, Silvia, if you can spare a minute."

It was a command, not a request. But he didn't seem angry anymore, and I could hardly believe my luck. Still, I wasn't out of the woods yet. There was a hard spindle-backed chair in the corner, and I moved the luggage off of it to sit, reluctantly. Mr. Meyerson hitched up his slacks as he took a place on the end of his bed, across from me. I was grateful for the distance between us. Even though he'd never tried anything with me, being alone with him in his bedroom made me profoundly uncomfortable.

"I was mugged, about two years ago. In Trastevere. The man beat me, badly, and even after I recovered, I was shaken. That's when I got the gun."

I nodded. So he had seen me looking in his drawer. He'd arrived so quietly, I hadn't been sure. "You don't have to explain. I didn't mean to intrude." Another lie, because of course I had. That's exactly what I'd meant to do.

"I don't mind. I have nothing to hide. There's not room to hide anything here, anyway." He smirked and spread his hands wide to acknowledge the spareness and smallness of the space. "Were you headed to town, to see your mother?"

The abrupt change in topics disoriented me. I was still in shock that Mr. Meyerson had so easily accepted my excuse.

"Yes."

"We don't often have time for personal conversation, do we? But I have a short break, now. The wiring here is a problem, as you know, and one of the lights malfunctioned, again. They're fixing it. I just want to get to know you a bit better."

He crossed his legs, and something about the posture made him more human, somehow. It was true that I'd kept my distance, particularly after the incident with Sarah and Mrs. Leskowitz. I knew it was in my best interest to be friendly, but it was difficult when I'd lost all respect for him. Given the circumstances, though, I hardly had a choice.

"I'm taking her for a little walk, if she's up for it. She's not well."

"I'm sorry to hear that. She's Italian, yes?"

His face betrayed nothing except polite curiosity. It was strange, to be making small talk after being caught rifling through his drawers. "Yes. It's her first time back. Since the war. That's when she met my father. He was a soldier."

"Ah. That sort of thing happened a fair bit, didn't it?" His tone sharpened slightly, or perhaps I just imagined it. He was Swiss-German, and Switzerland had never been invaded, but perhaps he'd been sympathetic toward his Nazi neighbors. Maybe he disapproved of the American G.I.

"I guess so."

"And what about you? Have you been to Italy before?"

I shook my head. "No. Never. Well, except being born here, I suppose." I felt blood rush to my cheeks. I hadn't meant to share so much.

Mr. Meyerson raised his eyebrows, connecting the dots. "I see." He recrossed his legs. "I would have thought you both would have come to visit your aunt. You've been so worried about her, I assumed you were quite close."

Sweat dampened my forehead. It was warm, and his questions made me nervous. No one in the castle had asked about my relationship with my aunt before, and only Paul knew its nature. It wasn't easy to explain.

"I met her only recently. She and my mother are what you'd call estranged, I guess."

"Every family has its dramas. I sincerely hope she contacts you soon, to put your mind at ease. I do wonder where she could have got off to." Mr. Meyerson spoke the last part as if to himself. I appreciated his concern; he was one of the only people who had taken her disappearance seriously. Yet part of me wondered if his questions meant that he somehow guessed why I'd been in his room. Unlikely, or he would have been outraged. I squirmed in my chair. It really was quite uncomfortable.

"I'm not so sure she went anywhere." I paused briefly before deciding I should risk sharing my suspicions with him. "I found more blood on the beach. And it turns out she didn't have a car."

He listened with interest, and his forehead creased. "How distressing. I'll tell Richard to look into it again more thoroughly." I barely managed to suppress an eye roll. Richard certainly wouldn't be any help. But then, neither would the police.

Mr. Meyerson consulted his wristwatch. "I'm sorry, Silvia, but I have to get back to set. We can talk again later."

He stood, and I did the same. "I trust you'll pay more attention next time when going into people's rooms, hmm?" He said it mildly enough, but he'd made his point. He'd let me off the hook this time, and whether he believed me or not, I didn't know. But I might not get away with crossing the line on a second occasion.

"Yes, of course. I'm sorry again."

I exited the room as quickly as decorum permitted, relieved to find myself in the corridor once more. I exhaled, then took in a deep lungful of air. The interaction had drained me.

We walked to the great hall together in awkward silence, leaving me time to digest our talk.

And what I'd found.

Having a gun for personal protection wasn't so hard to believe.

But it was the silencer, cylindrical and bulky, that made something itch in the back of my mind.

If the gun were for self-defense, what could he possibly need the silencer for?

"Goodbye, Silvia. I enjoyed our little chat. I'll see you for your scene with Lucrezia later."

I nodded and forced a smile, but it strained my cheeks.

Maybe Lucrezia had the right idea about how to do police work after all.

But it wasn't a game, like she thought. It was deadly serious.

Lucrezia found me the moment I returned to the castle, my scare from the morning diminished after an hour with Lulu, leaving behind only a feeling of mild unease. She accompanied me to wardrobe, and then hair and makeup, and pulled up a chair as Aurelia began her ministrations.

"I slept with Terrence," she whispered, her eyes shining with mischief. "After the party, and last night, too."

"I had a feeling." I glanced up at Aurelia, but her face was carefully blank. She was probably used to this sort of thing, if she'd been in the business long.

"I only did it in the name of research, of course." She flipped a strand of shiny black hair over her shoulder. Her lips were pink and glossy today. My next scene was with Terrence, so she wasn't in any rush.

"And?"

She sighed elaborately. "It was terribly disappointing. I gave him a second chance, just to be sure, but"—she shrugged and looked to the ceiling, as if examining the frescoed angels—"the problem with men that handsome is that they've never had to *try*. He was only interested in his own pleasure."

I laughed. This evaluation of Terrence's abilities surprised me not at all. I didn't agree with her that this failing applied to all handsome men, though. Paul was arguably as handsome as Terrence, after all. "I hope you're not planning to give him a third chance."

"I haven't decided. They do say third time's a charm, don't

they?" She smiled slyly. "Oh, but that's not the most interesting bit." Now she did flick her eyes toward Aurelia, who was putting her finishing touches on my look: rose, glossy lips, much like Lucrezia's; darkened dramatic brows; a sweet little updo that helped show off a strand of pearls and the low back to a pink cocktail dress.

"All finished," she said, perhaps sensing that Lucrezia had something private to share.

She did. She steered me slowly toward set, her voice hushed, as she continued. "I learned a good deal. When Terrence has been drinking, you can't get him to shut up, really."

"Isn't he always drinking?"

"Well, when he's been drinking more than usual, I suppose. But anyway, he's in debt up to his eyeballs, because of all the alimony, but that we pretty much knew. What we didn't know is that he has a financial interest in the picture. Points on the back end. They would never have been able to afford a star like him otherwise."

It made sense, but even so, it irked me. I expected him to have a higher salary than me, since he was the bigger star, but points on the back end could be phenomenally lucrative, if the picture did well. I was getting paid more than I had been as a sassy secretary, certainly, but my offer wasn't as substantial as it could have been given the size of my role. I knew I was lucky to get the part at all, and that it could be a launching pad to bigger and better things, but even so, the vastness of the discrepancy nettled me.

"Mr. Meyerson has points, too." It seemed everyone was incentivized for the picture to do well. "And he keeps a gun with a silencer in his sock drawer."

"You went into his room?" Lucrezia eyed me with something like awe. "Silvia, you continue to surprise me."

"We don't really have anything on Richard, though." He was still the person I suspected most. Paul had followed through on the plan and gotten drinks with him last night, and when he stumbled into my room, he was drunk and affectionate. We hadn't slept together—he was too drunk for that, or maybe I was too sober in comparison—but he'd complimented me in great detail, my talent, my beauty, my goodness. I'd let him. It was such a pleasant contrast to Lulu's father. When he drank, he got mean.

After he'd finished rhapsodizing, he'd told me that Richard was a decent guy. He repeated it several times. He had nothing to hide, he insisted.

But maybe that didn't matter. I already knew he had a temper. I remembered too clearly the moment I'd provoked him, the chilliness of his gaze. Maybe Gabriella had pushed him too far.

"Oh, well. He's a bastard, and that might be reason enough." Lucrezia laughed. We had reached the set, which was in the dining room that had so recently been a disco. "Break a leg, darling." She kissed each of my cheeks and left me.

My anxiety increased as I went to take my place in front of the camera. Paul was there, thank goodness, his eyes warm and admiring. But so was Terrence, who greeted me with an unpleasant smile, and Mr. Meyerson, whose blue-green eyes had gone flat and still. Even Richard had emerged from the library for some reason, and hovered ominously on the periphery, watching.

Richard. Terrence. Mr. Meyerson.

The killer could be any one of them.

CHAPTER 25

I struggled with the scene. Anyone would, I think, knowing what I knew. Before, I'd had my suspicions, but now I'd confirmed that my colleagues had motive for murder.

Richard, with his cold eyes and hot temper. Terrence, with his ex-wives and debts and utter self-absorption. Mr. Meyerson, with his puerile bullying and his gun.

Meanwhile, Bianca and Bernard were supposed to be having a romantic dinner together. It was a scene that took place before their first kiss, when they were still getting to know each other, and was full of flirting and innuendo.

"Do you spend a lot of time wandering through women's gardens?" I asked coyly, toying with the peas on my plate. The food was cold and unappetizing, and I was glad I didn't have to actually eat any of it. Mr. Meyerson didn't want to take extra time monitoring and replenishing the portion in front of me between takes to maintain continuity.

"Whenever the opportunity presents itself." Terrence clinked his silverware, a wicked smile revealing a slice of his too-white teeth. His eyes were empty. Like him. All those years watching him on screen, and somehow I'd never noticed. I suppressed a shudder and smiled invitingly instead.

"Cut." Mr. Meyerson stalked over. "Silvia, you're flirting with him, not inviting him to bed. Bianca would not be so seductive. She is still an innocent." *Unlike you*, was the implication behind his feedback. By now, everyone knew about Paul.

His tone no longer held the soft friendliness I'd grown accustomed to from him. It was our third take, and he was getting frustrated with me.

He must have minded my intrusion more than he'd let on. Or maybe he just minded my sleeping with the assistant director.

"I'll tone it down." I didn't like to do it. My version of Bianca wasn't a simple ingenue. She was a woman in control of her charms, and she was using them to her full advantage. She was desperate to leave the castle, and she wasn't going to let this handsome American get away.

It was the version of Bianca I'd auditioned, and the woman who came through so clearly in Mr. Meyerson's script. But apparently, his vision had changed.

"I thought we got it, that time," Paul volunteered. "Besides, Richard says we're running behind schedule."

Richard scowled at me. He and Paul had been having an animated conversation between takes, and it wasn't hard to overhear. I knew it was Terrence's consistent lateness that had caused the issue, but Richard seemed determined to place the blame on my shoulders.

An amateur.

I was intent on proving him wrong. Not just for my own pride. After what happened to my aunt, I didn't want anyone thinking I was also putting the picture at risk. Making errors could also be dangerous.

"One more take," Mr. Meyerson insisted. "You are a wide-eyed ingenue, not a temptress, understood?"

I was hardly in a position to argue. I closed my eyes, trying to calm down. If I felt frightened, I'd look frightened. I had to be brave.

I had to remember a time when I was young and naïve, like the Bianca Mr. Meyerson wanted. Before I'd met Lulu's father, before I'd become a model who had been groped by photographers and casting directors.

I opened my eyes, and in the next take, I was childlike, looking at Terrence as if he were a sweet puppy I'd discovered. It was dull and sexless. Mr. Meyerson approved.

Somehow, I endured the rest of the day and pushed my fear down deep.

After we wrapped, I hurried toward my room, wanting to be alone with my thoughts. As I approached, I noticed the door was ajar. I was almost certain I'd closed it. I nudged it open with my shoe, and the stink of cigarettes assaulted my nostrils. I frowned. I'd spent the prior night in Paul's room, so it wasn't because of him. I breathed shakily as I turned on the lights, but at a glance, nothing appeared out of place. I couldn't even feign moral outrage if someone had snooped, since I'd done the same thing to Mr. Meyerson.

I stepped forward toward my bed, and something squished under my shoe. I looked down and screamed in horror.

A dead mouse lay limp and bloody on the tile, its guts strewn beside it.

I screamed again, and Lucrezia burst in, looking alarmed. "What's that godawful racket? Are you all right?"

My fear from the day resurfaced in full force, and sobs wracked my body. I looked in the mirror, and my skin was mottled and blotchy.

"Did Paul dump you? I'll smack him." Her neon-pink painted nails protruded from her hands like claws, her long ladylike fingers tense. The red nails from our scene had been fakes, and her actual nails, I'd noticed, changed color every couple of days. She must have been a genius at painting them herself.

"No. Paul and I are fine." I wiped away my tears.

Lucrezia noticed the mouse and wrinkled her elegant nose. "Ugh. One of the castle cats left you a present, I see."

"I'm not so sure." I stared at the little corpse, its beady eyes empty and shining. "I think someone might have left it here. As a warning."

After my bad day on set, maybe the mouse was a message. I swallowed hard. I explained to Lucrezia about the slashed nightgown, too. Could the culprit have been the same person who killed Gabriella? If they thought I was threatening the movie, just as my aunt had, then these weren't mere pranks. The knowledge was a crushing weight, squeezing the air out of my lungs.

Lucrezia looked truly concerned, but I couldn't tell if she believed me.

I kicked off my shoes and sat on my bed, hugging my knees to my chest. Lucrezia curled up on the end.

Paul entered a moment later and stopped short when he saw the mouse. Then his eyes went to mine. "Is everything okay? Silvia, have you been crying?" He poked his head into the hallway and closed the door before lowering his voice. "Herman's blind, Silvia. You were brilliant. Don't let that old square get under your skin."

He sidestepped the mouse and leaned over to kiss my cheek, his lips soft.

"She thinks someone's going to off her if she messes up a line." Lucrezia picked at the skin beside her nail.

I heaved a breath and didn't deny it. I told him quickly what I believed the mouse meant, and he gallantly found a rag and disposed of it. Then he came to sit beside me, precariously angled on the edge of the mattress. There wasn't room for all of us. "I'm sorry you're so worried." This was code for, *I think you're being dramatic, but I'm not dumb enough to say so.*

"Cheer up, Silvia. It might not have been them. It could have been one of us, and we wouldn't off you."

"Thanks, Lucrezia, I feel so much better."

"I'm serious." She had kicked off her shoes, and her bare feet were tucked under her. She tapped her fingers against a shiny, smooth leg. "We have to examine ourselves. Fair's fair."

Paul and I just stared at her. I should have realized she'd jump at the opportunity to look into my aunt's death. She adored gossip, and I'd given her an excuse to stick her nose everywhere that it didn't belong.

"Fine, I'll start. I want to be famous." She shook her shiny mane and combed her fingers through it. "I mean it. World-famous. I called the *paparazzi* myself when I went on my date with Roy Samuels. There was a small item about it in *Lo Specchio. Oggi,* too. This is the first film I've been in that will be distributed in America as well as Italy. If my tits make it past the censors, I'll be unforgettable. Maybe even if they don't. So there you go."

None of this shocked me, but Lucrezia's expression was vulnerable. It hadn't been easy for her to admit this about herself. Still, I didn't believe for a second she would have resorted to violence to get what she wanted.

"Someone else go," she demanded, and I detected slight color in her cheeks.

I had no desire to share, even if her own confession made me feel obligated. "I didn't do it. Why would I be looking into what happened if I had?"

"To distract attention from yourself, of course. Do you mind if I smoke? I'm feeling a little jittery." She didn't wait for my reply before lighting up, and her face relaxed as she inhaled. Not many women in Italy smoked, I'd noticed, and seeing her smoke with abandon was almost like witnessing an act of transgression. There was something illicit about it. In Italy, only fast women smoked, modern women, and Lucrezia was both of those things.

I hugged my knees tighter. I was feeling a bit shaky myself. "Fine. I needed the paycheck. Really needed it. So that's my motive." I felt as exposed as I had when I wore the red negligee. Lucrezia inhabited a world of expensive clothes and glamorous nightclubs, and it embarrassed me to reveal how beyond me all that was. It wasn't even the whole story, of course—there was a Lulu-shaped hole right through the middle of it. And Lucrezia sensed I was holding something back.

"That's not all, though, is it?" She peered at me from beneath her thick dark lashes, blinking prettily. My breath hitched. Could she have seen me and Lulu together in town? I didn't think she'd reveal me in front of Paul, but you never knew. "The truth is, you might not even remember what you did."

I furrowed my brow, not understanding.

And then, suddenly, I did.

I'd confided in her about my sleepwalking incident, and she was suggesting that I could have killed my aunt while I was unconscious. The idea was completely preposterous. "Oh, come on," I scoffed.

"I agree, it's a bit far-fetched, but we have to consider all the angles." She shifted her position, straightening her legs on the bed so that her feet were near mine. Her toenails matched her fingernails. "Okay, Paul, your turn."

Paul stood and leaned casually against the plaster wall. He stuffed his hands in his pockets. His face was strained, as if he were thinking hard. "The picture could be good for my career, I guess. I don't know. I don't like this." He looked distinctly uncomfortable. Noble Paul couldn't even imagine a reason for doing something so horrific.

"It could be good for *all* our careers. Come on, I'm sure you can do better than that," Lucrezia said, her gorgeous face blurred by a haze of smoke.

"I don't think I can." He ran a hand over his jaw. "I guess I didn't have a motive. I'm sorry." He did look sorry. I could tell he'd really struggled to think of something. He was fair-minded that way.

"Oh, it's all right. It wasn't us, anyway. I just thought we should be thorough, to do it properly." Lucrezia waved her cigarette, and I winced as she littered ash onto my comforter. "And what about little Ricardo?"

"You mean Roberto?" I asked.

"Whatever. He could be a sex maniac or something, for all we know."

The idea of sweet, nervous Roberto as a sex maniac made me laugh. I was relieved to shift the conversation away from ourselves, and we spent a few minutes debating whether the jumpy production assistant could actually be a devious killer.

Lucrezia finally stretched luxuriously and excused herself, and Paul took her place on the bed. I was sick of talking, and luckily, what he had in mind didn't require it.

Later, as I lay in his arms, warm and comforted, Lucrezia's words resurfaced in my mind.

During my night terror, I'd made it all the way to the lake without knowing. It was the rush of cold water that woke me, and I shivered, remembering it, reliving the terror of dislocation.

But what if I hadn't gone into the lake? Would I have awoken somewhere else, or made it back to my room? Was it possible

I'd been out of my bed on another night? There was no way to know.

In the dark castle bedroom, lit only by the chilly moonlight, her suggestion no longer seemed so preposterous.

I was beginning to thoroughly regret asking for her help.

CHAPTER 26

Filming the next day went, if anything, even worse. I played the part just as Mr. Meyerson told me to, but then Terrence compared me to a dead fish again. There was no pleasing either of them, and I was discouraged to see Bianca being reduced to a limp archetype. I reassured myself that a lot of personality could be added when we did the sound syncing, and hopefully Mr. Meyerson would see the light before then.

At least we managed to wrap before sunset, which meant I'd have time to see Lulu before she went to bed. But as soon as I reached the castle door, Lucrezia joined me, linking her arm in mine as if we were two schoolgirls.

"Are you going to town? I'll join you. I could use some fresh air. You don't mind, do you?"

"Of course not." My voice was too bright, and my lungs suddenly seemed to hold less oxygen. I minded a lot.

But there was nothing to do except let her accompany me. I walked slowly, hoping to come up with an excuse to get rid of her before we reached the *pensione*. We meandered toward the cypress-lined path, talking about nothing, but my mind was racing. The evening was warm, and the birds sang in the trees, but I felt cold.

"I wouldn't mind meeting your mother. I would have thought you'd have asked her up to the castle, by now. Or does Richard not allow it?"

I felt almost feverish now, the sultry summer air assaulting my chilled skin. This is exactly what I was worried might happen. She couldn't meet my mother, because she couldn't meet Lulu. I wasn't ready for that.

"My mother thought it would be too hectic at the castle. She likes the quiet."

"Well, this town is quiet, all right."

We walked down a *vicolo* I hadn't paid much attention to before, even though I'd probably been down all of them by now. Up ahead was a *macelleria*, with strings of sausages and garlic hanging in the window, as well as a leg of what looked like wild boar, the fur still on. I paused to peer inside, giving myself a moment to collect my thoughts.

"I'd love for you to meet her, only I'd want to warn her, first. She's a bit sensitive about her appearance these days. Is that okay?"

I held my breath. She looked in the window of the butcher's shop, too, and pulled a pair of large black sunglasses out of her purse and arranged them on her face. She was looking at her own reflection—not at the body parts dangling from the ceiling beyond. A pig's head grinned at us from the window display. I felt faintly nauseous.

"Of course. I just had a little idea that it might be helpful. It's so hard to be objective about one's own mother."

"What's that supposed to mean?"

"Don't be sore. It's just that on my last picture, the detectives said that it's usually family who are responsible." She said this in an offhanded way, as if that would blunt its impropriety.

"She's a sick woman, Lucrezia. This isn't funny."

Even behind her bug-eye glasses, her face was beautiful and solemn.

"I never said it was funny." She took her glasses back off, apparently changing her mind about them. Her eyes were tragic.

I was annoyed. I knew she didn't really mean anything by it, but she'd gotten my hackles up.

"This isn't a movie, Lucrezia, this is real life."

My irritation was turning to real anger, and I glared at the pig instead of at her. It glared back, its eyes black and beady. She was way out of bounds, but at the same time, her words snaked their way into my brain. I rubbed my arms, the chill deepening.

She took a lipstick from her bag and began applying it. "Please don't be upset at me. I know you don't like prying. You like to keep your little secrets." She put her lipstick away. "I better stop here and buy something, after looking in the window so long. Just think about what I said, hmm?" She pulled the glass door, and the smell inside—blood and death—made me gag. I watched as she disappeared into the store, every sleek, tan inch of her.

How dare she. I seethed as I continued down the alley, my pulse pounding in my ears. I knew she wasn't one to hold back her opinions, but attempting to interrogate my mother was outrageous.

I calmed down a bit by the time I reached the piazza and its decaying fountain. Lucrezia had only done exactly what she'd promised she would: investigate. She wasn't trying to be cruel, she was just being herself. And her forthrightness was part of what had appealed to me, when I'd first met her. It was something we had in common.

Maybe I'd gotten so upset because there was some logic to what she'd said. My mother had never hidden the fact that she despised my aunt, after all.

I remembered the police officer's deep voice crackling through the phone. *Does your aunt have any enemies?*

Absurd. I shook my head. My mother was probably too weak to even climb to the castle by herself, much less engage in a violent struggle. And she was my *mother.* Yes, she could be stubborn—intractable, really—but she loved me and Lulu with her whole heart. She was a good person, and I would never, ever believe she was capable of something like that.

Lucrezia probably didn't really think so, either. More likely, she just wanted an excuse to peek into my life. She had probably wondered about my trips to town, my sick mother. She knew I had a secret; she just didn't know what.

By the time I reached the *pensione*, I'd almost managed to put Lucrezia's probing out of my mind. The tan stone was clean and sturdy, and the flowers in the window boxes were a cheerful white.

Signora Ricci appeared at the door, her wide face flushed and her hair askew. "Thank goodness you're here. There's been an accident."

For a moment, I just stared dumbly at her, unable to move. Flour dusted her apron and several strands of her short black hair. The usual smile straining her wide cheeks was absent, replaced by grave worry.

"Oh, no."

I rushed inside behind her, her hips swaying as she clambered up the stairs. The fluorescent light flickered. My whole body was numb with panic, my legs propelled forward by some miracle of adrenaline. *No, no, no. Not Lulu. Please let her be okay.*

"She just had a little fall. But she hit her head. She's upstairs in bed resting." She spoke over her shoulder. We reached the landing, and a sob bobbed in my throat as she opened the door.

My mother reclined against the pillows, the floral chenille bedspread tucked tightly around her. A ghastly bruise decorated her left temple. Relief flooded me that it was her and not Lulu, and then I immediately felt guilty.

"Mama, what happened?" I sat on the edge of the bed and grabbed her hand. Her eyes were glassy. "Has a doctor been called already?"

She smoothed the comforter with her other hand. "There's no need to make such a fuss. I'm fine."

"You are not fine."

"I haven't called yet; it only just happened," Signora Ricci said, from the doorway. "Rita is watching Lulu," she added, preempting my next question.

I opened my purse to retrieve the health card I'd purchased at the travel agency, and the little booklet with the doctors affiliated with the *Roue Blanche Internationelle Sanitaire Touristique.* I'd been concerned about my mother having access to adequate medical care in Italy, but she hadn't been. She'd only waved me away and said, *I'm dying, what difference does it make?* Still, I'd done my research and knew that in theory, it was six dollars for a home visit. Only, I'd expected that we would be in Rome, and I had a sinking feeling that the doctors in the booklet might not come all the way to Castello de Lago, especially at dinner-time.

"My neighbor's brother-in-law is the town doctor. Should I call him?" Signora Ricci wrung her hands. She was an efficient, capable woman, and I was so grateful for her in that moment I couldn't find my voice. I nodded instead and put the card and booklet away.

"I don't need a doctor. It's just a little bump." My mother frowned, mulish as ever.

It wasn't. It looked awful, raw and red. "How did it happen?"

She tilted her head back onto the pillows and closed her eyes. "I just got a little dizzy. Lost my balance taking my shoes off. It could happen to anyone."

I pursed my lips and didn't reply.

The doctor arrived only ten minutes later with his black medical bag and *tsk*ed his tongue when he saw the injury. I explained, quickly, about the cancer, and his plain oval face was serious as he listened.

"Did you lose consciousness at all, Signora Whitford?" He took her bony wrist in his hand, counting the beats of her pulse.

"No. I just bumped my head on that knobby thing on the footboard. It's nothing."

He examined the footboard, his black bushy eyebrows crouching together, then turned back to her. "Please follow my finger with your eyes." He moved his pointer back and forth in front of her face. "Good. Very good. There's no concussion, but you'll have a nasty bruise for a couple of weeks."

My mother made a noise with her lips, her disdain evident. "I already knew that." Her tone was sharp. The doctor cleared his throat uncomfortably, and I winced.

"Thank you so much for your time, Doctor Alessi. And for coming so quickly."

"Of course." He gave my mother a tight parting smile as he donned his hat, and gently pulled me aside, onto the landing. I knew what was coming before he said it. It didn't make it any easier to hear. "She shouldn't be left alone. She needs someone to help her."

I swallowed. He was right. Only I didn't know how I'd be able to care for her properly and still do my job. It had been hard enough to arrange that with Lulu, and now I had both of them to worry about. "Of course. Thank you." My voice was faint. I paid him his fee, counting out the lira notes carefully. With the *pensione,* and the extra money to watch Lulu, I was spending money more quickly than was comfortable. I snapped my purse closed forcefully, overcome with a flash of anger at Terrence and his points.

After the doctor left, I returned to sit beside my mother, steeling my courage for what I must do.

"You should come to the castle. You and Lulu. I was wrong not to let you."

It would mean I'd get a little more time with her. I'd allowed myself to think we still had years left together, but the truth was neither of us really knew how long we had. And though I'd still be working, at least I could *be* there if something happened. Rita would come during the day, and though I knew a thirteen-year-old girl was hardly enough help for both my mother and Lulu, I didn't know what else to do.

A poor solution, but I was out of ideas.

Lulu's arrival would cause quite a commotion, of course. I could try to pretend she was my sister, but that lie only worked for people we saw for a few minutes in passing, now that Lulu was talking. I had to hope it was too late for them to decide to replace me.

My mother held a cold washcloth to her head and frowned. "No. I changed my mind. I like it here."

I groaned in frustration and covered my face with my hands. It was just like her. She knew the reason I wanted her to come, and wanted to prove her independence.

"I thought you said you wanted to see me at work? It's quite exciting up there, you know." It took enormous effort to persuade her to do something that neither of us wanted. But I knew it was necessary.

"I like my privacy."

I took a deep breath and stared at the cross hanging on the wall over the bed while I calmed myself. It was Signora Ricci's, not ours. My mother had rosary beads she used to worry, and a small statue of Saint Catherine of Siena she had kept on a shelf, but I hadn't seen either since we'd arrived in Italy. Which was a bit strange.

"Is it because you're worried . . . *she* might show up again?" I asked. It had confused me that my mother had been willing to come to the castle at all, before, for this reason. I drummed my fingers nervously against my leg. Lucrezia had made me think about things that I really didn't want to think about. I studied her, waiting for her to recoil at the mention of her sister.

If she believed Gabriella was alive and well, and abhorred the idea of ever seeing her again, why would she have taken that risk?

"Yes. Yes, that's the reason." She sounded tired, and not particularly convincing. She looked out the window, at a bird hopping on the windowsill, instead of at me. Her eyes were unfocused. "She came back, you know, after your grandparents died. Just for a little while. I never told you the story."

I went still. She knew very well that she'd never told me the story. I strained my ears, almost afraid to breathe in case I missed a single word.

"Your grandparents were farmers. We had a good farm, and a beautiful stone house on the top of a hill that we shared with my aunt and uncle and cousins. It broke our hearts when Gabriella left us, and when the Americans came in 1943, I thought she might return. Her boyfriend had gone back to Germany. She didn't, though, not yet. I don't know how she kept herself."

One hand squeezed the washcloth at her temple, and the other ran over the flowers on the chenille comforter, trembling slightly. "My father was a very brave man, Silvia. You should know that about him. He was sympathetic to the Resistance, and we let many of the partisans hide in our fields. It seemed like there were always young men sleeping in the barn. My cousins were gone by then, and the boys we sheltered helped with the work when they could." She smiled a little at the memory, and her fingers shook as she continued smoothing the blanket, pointlessly.

"But the summer of 1944 was very bad for the people here. Italy had surrendered to the Allies, and the Germans were retreating. They were angry. They felt betrayed. They massacred civilians in some of the towns. Reprisals, they said." She swallowed. "There were a couple of Nazis stationed near our farm. They would come and steal our food. And one day . . . one day, they came into the house. My aunt and uncle were out doing chores, and they found only me and my parents. They demanded that I come to the fields with them."

I pinched my fingers. After years of craving this story, I wasn't sure I wanted to hear any more.

"My parents refused. They stood up to them, and one of the Nazis shot them. They died right there in the kitchen. They murdered them in front of me." She paused, too upset to continue. She closed her eyes, retreating deep inside herself. Her voice, when she spoke again, was a whisper. "And then they took me to the bean field. But one of the boys in the Resistance, Nico, he saw what was happening, and he saved me. He killed my captors." She took a deep breath, choked with emotion. A tear slipped down her papery cheek. "My parents died to stop the Nazis from taking me; meanwhile, Gabriella had given herself over willingly. It sickened me. She arrived at the farm a month later, contrite and in mourning, but she wasn't truly sorry. She didn't stay long before going back to her rich *fascisti* friends." She spat out the final words, her face twisted with rage. I closed my eyes, attempting to still the flurry of my thoughts, my throat sore from my own repressed tears. I couldn't imagine surviving such a tragedy. I'd known that the war had been painful for my mother, but I'd always been so focused on ferreting out the details of her past, I'd never really paused to consider why she hadn't wanted to share it. Now I knew, and I was ashamed for my insensitivity.

My mother clutched the comforter, her fingers claw-like, and turned her gaze from the window to me, her blue eyes probing. "Do you think, Silvia, that some things are unforgivable?"

The ache of sorrow bloomed behind my breastbone. I shouldn't have been shocked by her question, now that I better understood the depth of her anger at my aunt and its justification, but I was. A breeze whipped the organdy curtain, and I looked at it rather than her while I considered.

"I don't know." My mother had raised me to be a good Catholic girl, although admittedly, there were a few parts of the Bible I'd paid less attention to than others. Still, any Christian knew that forgiveness was a key tenet of the faith. *And forgive us our trespasses, as we forgive those who trespass against us.* I may not have been to Mass in a little while, but the *Our Father* prayer would be etched on my brain until I died.

But if I'd been in my mother's shoes, I didn't know if I'd be able to find it in my heart to forgive my aunt, either.

My mother stared into the distance, her thoughts far away. She placed the washcloth on the nightstand and settled deeper into the bed. "I'd like to rest, now."

"Of course. I'll just take Lulu for a little walk."

I knew I should press her about going to the castle, but I didn't have the heart, after she'd opened up to me. I also knew there'd be no arguing with her once her mind was made up.

I went downstairs to relieve Rita and took Lulu outside with the idea that we might walk to the café for gelato. The sun was just starting to dip in the sky, and my thoughts swirled. Only Lulu's tiny hand in mine kept them from spinning out of control.

My inquiry into Gabriella's disappearance had seemed like the noble thing to do. But I'd never given proper consideration to my mother's perspective. I'd brushed Gabriella's past aside so easily, and I'd even allowed myself to like her. My mother had seen it as a betrayal, and she was right. It had been.

I felt awful.

Still, whatever Gabriella's own sins, it didn't change the fact that something had happened to her. And the possibilities were more intricate than I had ever anticipated.

Terrence. Mr. Meyerson. Richard. Lucrezia. Me.
My mother.
All of us could have wanted Gabriella dead.
And the more I picked it apart, the more I worried that maybe
I wouldn't like what I found.

The café shone in the dark, and Lulu and I lingered in the
warm pool of light it cast on the cobblestones, our fingers sticky.
Her cheeks were covered with chocolate, and I clucked over her
as I wiped them with a napkin. In Rome, people would have
been out promenading after dinner, smoking and talking, but I
knew better than to expect that here. The piazza was deserted,
and the only soul to see us was the man behind the bar in the
café, wiping down glasses with credible disinterest. Yet I had
that same sensation again, as if someone were watching us.
I tugged Lulu's hand until we were out of the halogen glow,
tucked safely into the shadows.

A loud creak above made my heart leap. I peered up and
could just make out a drooping shutter, the likely culprit, but
still it was as if cold fingers had trailed along my spine. After my
mother's story, my imagination was running wild, and I dwelled
on the people who had lived here during the war, the people
who had died here.

Most likely, there was no one lurking in the black alleys,
stalking us as we made our way back to the *pensione*. It was
only that the town was full of ghosts.

CHAPTER 27

I met Lucrezia's gaze bravely. We were shooting one of the principal scenes of the movie, where the witch tells Bianca her sad story in an attempt to engender her sympathy. We had just finished rehearsal, and my body buzzed with excitement. Lucrezia had been wonderful, and I could tell the scene had the potential to be powerful.

Lucrezia had apologized profusely after our altercation, and I'd chosen to let it go. The conversation with my mother had made me more willing to move past it. Maybe some things were unforgivable, but Lucrezia's transgression wasn't on that list.

We were filming in the second-floor bedroom suite again, and she stood before me, her hand outstretched, as if she meant to touch me. But unlike in the scene where she'd caressed Bianca and left behind blood on her face, my character was no longer afraid.

Lucrezia cried real tears before she began, just two, each streaming silkily down her sculpted cheeks. "I had only ever used my magic to help the villagers. I gave them herbs to cure sickness, spells to ward off evil. For my troubles, I was burned alive." Lucrezia's expression was heartbroken, her voice choked with emotion.

"But why, if you only ever did good?" I challenged her. Whatever the witch had once been, she was no longer. She tormented Bianca in her nightmares. She had even possessed her once, in the scene when she attempted to seduce Bernard. Every night, the witch's nocturnal visits drained more of her life force, and the witch grew stronger. But Bianca had started resisting the witch's intrusions into her mind, delaying her return to corporeal form. The witch still needed Bianca; she needed Bianca to let her in.

"Your ancestor, and my second cousin, Lord Baldini, wished to marry me. When I refused him, he leveled charges of witch-craft," she said. "On the day of my death, I swore my revenge on his descendants." Her eyes blazed, as if shining with the fire that had consumed her.

I found I couldn't make myself utter the revised line Mr. Meyerson had written into the script. "But you became the monster he said you were. I have no sympathy for you," I was supposed to say.

But how could the heroine *not* sympathize with the witch, when the injustice of her death had been so evocatively described? My expression contorted into one not of scorn, but pity.

"I'm sorry for what happened to you. But *I* have not wronged you," I said instead.

"Cut!" Mr. Meyerson stalked over, his jaw screwed tight. "What was that?"

I heaved a breath, summoning my courage. I hadn't dared to question his direction ever since he'd caught me in his drawer. Lucrezia watched with interest. "I liked it," she volunteered. "Bianca should be conflicted. It's more interesting."

I nodded, grateful she had articulated exactly what I'd been thinking. "Yes. It doesn't feel like Bianca should have such an unequivocal view of right and wrong. I think she's morally con-fused. Part of her is tempted by the witch."

It made more sense to me. If the witch represented carnal sin—well, Bianca had flirted shamelessly with Bernard. She wasn't pure as the driven snow, despite Mr. Meyerson's attempts to sanitize her.

"It might be more suspenseful," Paul put in. "If the audience isn't sure whether Bianca will resist the witch."

But Mr. Meyerson only glowered. I recognized, too late, that we'd taken the wrong approach. When someone pushed him on something, he only dug his heels in even more. We should have used gentler, more subversive tactics. "Do it again. With the right line, this time."

The grueling filming schedule had been hard on all of us, including him. His eyes were bloodshot, and it looked like he hadn't shaved in a couple of days. Only his gray suit was still neat and pressed. His exhaustion hadn't done anything to improve his moods.

I clenched my fists. Lucrezia rolled her eyes behind Mr. Meyerson's back. I knew the line could always be changed in syncing, but even so, it pained me to say it. At least my expressions could contain more nuance.

We did a few more takes, and I threaded the needle as best I could, trying to find a happy medium between his way and mine.

Finally, we broke for the crew to do another setup. Days on set sometimes stretched as long as sixteen hours, and it would be another late night. I was getting thoroughly sick of the gloomy castle. I couldn't wait for the day when my mother, Lulu, and I could go back to Rome together, and I pictured us all in some charming flat with a view of ancient ruins, a cat curled on the balcony. I'd still have the sound syncing work to do at Cinecittà, and after my next paycheck I'd have enough money saved for us to get by. This image of our sweet Italian life was what I'd dreamed of even before we arrived, on the endless TWA flight that took us halfway around the world.

Only now, a fourth person had crept into the picture: a man casting a long shadow in the setting sun as he smoked beside the cat and the flower boxes, foot perched on the balcony rail, my arm around his waist.

Soon, it could all be true.

"Silvia." Paul's voice sent a shiver of pleasure up my spine. He crept up behind me while we waited for Carlo to finish with the lights. "We'll talk sense into him before syncing starts." He'd said this to me before—multiple times, in fact. Both of us needed to believe it. Paul wasn't happy with Herman's vision, either. But he said we had enough good footage that it could all still be put right, with the syncing and the edit.

"I hope so." I turned around to face him. Only Paul's tremendous stamina had held up against our rigorous schedule. Everyone else was weary, but if anything, he seemed more energized than ever. His eyes were bright, and I could tell it would take some time after we wrapped for him to come off the high of the work, to disentangle his thoughts from the movie.

I knew that I had to tell Paul about Lulu soon. Before we returned to Rome, certainly. Somehow, the moment never seemed to present itself.

Now certainly wasn't the time. In the next scene, Bianca would have a nightmare of Bernard holding her under in the bathtub, sent by the witch to make her distrust him and open herself up to the witch instead. We had to get it in a single take, since hair and makeup would take too long to redo after I got wet, and I was nervous about getting it right. Mr. Meyerson approached us, still looking peeved.

"There's no time to clear the set. We are too behind schedule as it is."

"What?" I'd be naked, aside from pasties and nude underwear. "But you said—"

"We'll start rehearsal in five."

He strode away to consult with the director of photography about something, not waiting for my reply.

"I'll clear it anyway. I don't care what he said." Paul wore his fiercest expression, his still brown eyes fixed on Herman's retreating back. Anger radiated off of him.

"No. It's okay. I can handle it." Whoever had tried to scare me off the picture hadn't attempted anything since the mouse. The absence of incidents unsettled me, too. The anticipation of what might happen, and not knowing when it would come, was almost worse. I still feared doing anything that might hold things up, and I'd already expended my bravery for the day when I'd pushed Mr. Meyerson on the line. "I promise. It's no big deal." I squeezed his hand and turned away so he wouldn't be able to tell that I was lying.

* * *

My whole body shook as I cowered, next to naked, in the cold water. The bath had probably been warm at first, but it hadn't lasted. The camera operators, production assistants, grip, Carlo—everyone was getting quite the eyeful. Mrs. Leskowitz and Sarah were the only crew members who were women.

I tried my hardest not to care, but I was uncomfortable, exhausted, and vulnerable. I wanted the day to end.

Worst of all, Terrence stood right behind me. He placed his hands on my shoulders.

"Neck massage while we wait, love?" He slurred and, as usual, smelled of whiskey.

"Get your hands off me." I couldn't see him, but could easily picture his leer.

Mr. Meyerson called "action," and I relaxed in the clawfoot tub, pretending I was warm and soothed instead of freezing and embarrassed.

Terrence put his hands on me again, and I thrashed as he pushed me under the surface.

I twisted and kicked. I didn't have to act. He was strong, and when I pushed against him, ready to come up for air, his fingers only dug in deeper. I looked up at him through the water, and his handsome features were strange and distorted, but I could just make out his malicious smile.

I wrapped my hands around one of his wrists to pry it off me, but he still held fast. How long did he mean to keep me down? Confusion gave way to real alarm. I'd been under a long time, and my lungs burned. Was he trying to kill me? Would I die, right now, cameras rolling? I recalled the sensation of waking up in the frigid lake. My real-life nightmare had given Mr. Meyerson the idea for this scene, of Bianca's dream of a nearly fatal submersion. It would be ironic if this killed me when the lake had not. Or perhaps Serena had a hand in this, somehow, and was claiming me after she'd failed before.

I clawed at his arms and fought him with all my strength. I gulped down water. Spots danced beneath my eyelids.

I couldn't believe this was really happening—that I'd be

murdered on a movie set, in what would probably be deemed a tragic accident. Lulu would be motherless because of Terrence's cruelty. Maybe he didn't understand the danger I was in, or maybe he didn't care.

I didn't have any strength left, and sank deeper into the tub, my thoughts growing blurry and slipping away. And then, finally, his grip slackened. With a final burst of adrenaline, I managed to push myself to the surface and emerged choking and terrified. The movie lights blinded me.

Paul rushed over with my robe and helped me out of the tub. "What the hell was that, Terrence?"

I coughed a few more times, my airway clearing. I clutched the robe and pulled it tighter around myself. Paul shoved Terrence, his hand fisted, as if he meant to hit him. He was breathing hard.

Terrence stepped back and brushed himself off. "I just wanted it to look real," he drawled, unconcerned. "She's all right, isn't she?" He smirked at me. Mr. Meyerson joined us. His eyes glittered.

"That, Silvia, is the scene that will make you famous."

It scared me how far Terrence had gone. The morning after he almost drowned me, as I crept through the dark in search of the tiny, tiled washroom with the yellowing porcelain toilet, I was wide awake and vigilant. I knew Terrence also had an early call time, and I didn't relish the prospect of bumping into him. Paul would have interfered on set sooner, but Richard had distracted him with a question before he understood what was happening. I knew Terrence enjoyed torturing me, but I understood now he wasn't only a mean drunk—he was a dangerous one.

I just wasn't sure *how* dangerous.

I stopped abruptly as my fingers met something wet and sticky. I pulled them back from the plaster, my heart pounding so hard my ribs ached. I turned the knob for the lights, and then I saw it: big block letters painted onto the wall, each several inches high.

In blood.

I cried out as I read the message, my own blood going cold. YOUR SECRET ISN'T SAFE.

I put a hand over my mouth to muffle a scream. I'd forgotten the blood on my fingers, and I screamed again at the realization I'd smeared the congealed liquid onto my cheek.

Paul tumbled out of my room seconds later, shirtless, his hair askew. "What is it? What's wrong?" He stopped, his eyes going wide. "Is that blood? Are you all right?"

He was looking at me, not the wall, but he saw it soon enough. His strong, square jaw opened in amazement.

Now that he was here, I calmed down a fraction, enough to take in more of the details before me. There was a small console table beneath the writing, which supported a bronze statuette of a Greek god holding a spear. An old, bleak oil painting of a dour-looking man in Renaissance dress, which had once hung above, had been impaled upon it, adding to the violence of the scene.

A few more doors opened, and soon Lucrezia, Mr. Meyerson, and Terrence joined us, all wearing similar moues of displeasure. Until they noticed what we were staring at.

"Good God. Is this some kind of joke?" Terrence looked bleary-eyed, and his words were garbled. He was still drunk from the night before. His drinking had only gotten worse as the days got longer, and the amounts I'd seen him consume were staggering. Most men would die after imbibing as much as he did. It took a lot of practice, and a lot of abuse to one's liver, to manage that volume.

Lucrezia had never gotten around to giving him that third chance. She looked at him now as if she'd just tasted something sour.

"Whose secret?" she asked, yawning. "Nobody has any secrets around here. Everyone gossips too much."

Her eyes met mine for a moment and then flicked guiltily away. We were both probably recalling the times that she had tried to ferret out secrets of mine and failed. I felt suddenly sick. This display was theatrical enough to have been her. But I didn't know why she'd try to pull something like that on me. It was mean, and whatever else she was, she wasn't mean.

At least, I hadn't thought so.

Paul took my hand, and I realized I was trembling.

Mr. Meyerson was still looking at the message in shock, his face white as a sheet, his eyes even more bloodshot than they'd been yesterday. He looked frightened. "Whoever did this will be punished." His voice was deep and severe.

"I still don't understand. Who's the message *for*?" Lucrezia yawned again and stretched. "You'd think they'd have been a little clearer."

I stared at the blood, garish and bright red, shining in the light of the sconces. Movie blood, at least, almost certainly.

YOUR SECRET ISN'T SAFE.

As I read the words a fourth time, I finally grasped their meaning. My breath hitched as fear overcame me.

Lulu.

CHAPTER 28

Your secret isn't safe.

I have to reach Lulu.

Those two phrases were a drumbeat in my mind as my legs hammered the stone. I sprinted through the castle courtyard and didn't even slow as I crossed over the ravine, ignoring the low sides of the bridge and the bottomless drop into darkness. I was barefoot, but I barely noticed the pebbles when I reached the path beyond, or the cool morning air whipping through my thin nightdress.

The tunnel of cypresses was longer than I remembered it, the tall, tapered sentinels seeming to close in around me as I passed between them.

I finally reached the tiny piazza with the *bar-tabacchi*, where a couple of lanterns glowed weakly in the hazy morning fog. The doors and windows of the buildings were all shut tight. The air was clammy and close. I didn't think about which direction to go, I just *ran* down the nearest *vicolo*, one so narrow I actually scraped my arm along its side in the dark. The arches above reminded me of ribs, caging me in.

My path was steep, and I tripped, scraping my hand, feeling the sting of blood. I got up and ran on, my lungs burning now. I didn't stop to consider who might have left the message, or why: I thought only of getting to Lulu.

Your secret isn't safe.

I traveled down another *vicolo*, the one with the *macelleria*, and the dark outlines of suspended animal parts made me shudder.

At last, I reached the *pensione,* the white flowers in the window boxes uncannily vivid in the predawn light.

I didn't have the key.

I bit back a cry. It had been foolish to forget it, but I hadn't paused to prepare. I had only one goal: to save my daughter from peril. I approached the door and pressed the buzzer, not caring about the hour, needing only to get inside as quickly as possible.

I waited. And waited. I buzzed again, banged on the door, and shouted with whatever air was left in my lungs.

Finally, a very irritated Signora Ricci appeared, slippers on her feet and curlers in her hair.

"I'm sorry. It's an emergency," I said, and pushed past her. I caught a glimpse of her stunned, offended expression before I climbed the stairs. I didn't have time to feel sorry.

I burst through the door to the room my mother and Lulu shared, terrified of what I might find.

My mother and Lulu were both prostrate on the bed, my mother's skin waxy in the dark. Lulu's little head was on her pillow, her dark curls spilling across the cotton. They'd grown thicker, these past weeks. She was perfectly still, her hand clenched beside her cheek, her frilly white nightgown reminding me of a burial shroud.

I crept up beside her and watched for her breath, for the movement of her eyes beneath their lids as they followed the movements of her dreams.

I couldn't discern either.

I bit hard into my hand as a sob wracked my whole body, and then I scooped her into my arms. Her body was soft and warm. And limp.

But then a wail pierced the night, and it took me several heartbeats before I recognized it not as mine, but hers.

"Oh, thank God. Thank God, baby." I kissed her head, which smelled of lavender. Lulu rubbed her eyes, and tears spilled out. Her lip wobbled. I squeezed her so tight that she cried harder.

Beside her, my mother sat up slowly. "What's going on? What's happened?" Her voice betrayed no hint of grogginess; it was clear and sharp. "Silvia, why did you wake her?"

Lulu had stopped crying and clung to me like a little monkey, her hands tight around my neck, pulling strands of my hair.

"We have to go. Right now. Change quickly. We can send for the rest of your things later."

My mother's spine straightened, and she swung her legs over the side of the bed. "Not until you tell me what's going on."

It was so like her to always demand answers, to always want to remain in control. "For once, can you just listen?" I was hysterical. "Please."

Shockingly, my mother didn't argue. She got dressed, quietly, while I continued to cry and stroke Lulu's hair. "I'm so sorry, baby. Mommy's here now."

"Mommy, why you crying?" Lulu asked, still rubbing her eyes. She was talking so well lately. Just in the last week or so, she'd started stringing together sentences of four or five words.

"Mommy was a little scared, sweetie. But everything will be okay." I managed to get myself under control, not wanting to alarm Lulu further. "We're going to go for a little walk and watch the sunrise. Doesn't that sound lovely?"

I carried her down the stairs, gingerly, and thankfully, Signora Ricci seemed to have gone back to bed. As we emerged onto the cobblestone street, I breathed in big gusts of air.

I had Lulu. She was safe.

"We're going to go on an adventure, pumpkin. We're going to see a great big castle. Like in the fairy tales." My voice was shaky. Lulu just lolled her sleepy head on my shoulder.

My mother emerged behind me and touched my elbow. She didn't ask questions, but I knew they were coming.

The Riccis kept their donkey, Ruffina, in a basement stall at night, accessible from a street-level door. I didn't know much about donkeys, but I knew my mother probably couldn't handle the walk to the castle. I set Lulu down for a moment and she clutched my mother's leg while I coaxed Ruffina out to the street. Luckily, the saddle wasn't too complicated to put on, and Ruffina held still patiently as I hoisted my mother onto her back.

We started off, creeping carefully through the hushed town, the clopping of Ruffina's hooves echoing in the silence. In these last weeks, I'd discovered that the place contained some charm, but in the empty streets before sunrise, I wondered if maybe I'd imagined it. It was as if the town had lured us in before revealing the full extent of its sinister nature.

The sky lightened from black to cobalt as we climbed, but the sun wouldn't rise for another hour or so. We walked slowly, and my arms ached from carrying Lulu, but I was so comforted by the warm weight of her that I didn't consider putting her down again.

Finally, my mother spoke. "Why are we going to the castle?" Her slim, pale figure looked ghostlike in the dark. She clutched Ruffina's reins tightly.

"Someone left a threatening message. It's possible it was about Lulu." I explained about the wall, and the warning in blood that had been scrawled there. She listened without interrupting, which was unlike her.

"But you don't know for sure the message was meant for you?" She didn't ask in her usual brusque, opinionated way, but more delicately. I think she appreciated just how upset I was and had chosen to be tactful. So I answered in kind.

"I don't. But it could have been. And if it was, I don't want her out of my sight." I hadn't spared much thought for what else it could have meant, but now I considered.

Anyone could have had a secret. But there'd been incidents directed at me before, and I'd been the one prying into Gabriella's death. And I'd questioned Bianca's line, yesterday; maybe someone didn't appreciate me holding things up. Of course, Lucrezia and Paul had questioned it, too.

I ruled out Mr. Meyerson, because his shock at the message had been utterly real. Richard might have done it, but it hardly seemed like his style.

The person who came most immediately to mind was Lucrezia. The choice of words, and the dramatic method, all fit. I just didn't know *why*.

"It's for the best. I think the time is right, now," my mother said, but so softly I wasn't sure I was meant to hear. I opened my mouth to ask her to explain what it was the right time for, but decided to let it go.

Finally, we reached the cypresses, which watched us with sightless branches. The donkey stopped abruptly, snorting and braying, the high-pitched noise making it sound as if she were in pain. She backed up slowly, as if afraid, and flattened her ears against her head.

"You don't like the castle, old girl, do you?" I rubbed her nose. I balanced Lulu on one hip before helping my mother off Ruffina's back, and then tied her to a black iron hitching ring on the stone archway. I'd send a production assistant down soon to return her.

The three of us crossed the bridge, and I squeezed Lulu tighter, not allowing myself to look over the sides at the vertiginous drop.

I had half a mind to just take her and my mother back to Rome. If someone had meant to do Lulu harm, I wouldn't stay for anything. But now that I'd had time to settle down, I was more convinced that the writing was someone's idea of a prank. It didn't strike me as the handiwork of the killer, or even whoever had been sabotaging me; the previous incidents had been sly and subtle, nothing like this. Most likely, it was Lucrezia's attempt to find out what I was hiding.

Well, it had worked. I wasn't hiding Lulu anymore.

I breathed easier once we reached the courtyard. A pair of yellow eyes flashed at us: one of the cats. "If you close the gate to the bridge, this might be a good play space for her," I said. It was large and flat and completely bare. There were the stairs to the front door, but Lulu was good at climbing as long as you held her hand. "There's another staircase in the great hall, but you'll be able to avoid the stairs in the towers, since there are doors. I'll ask the production assistants to hide the suits of armor. And you'll have to keep her well away from the armory, of course." My mind raced as I considered all the preparations that would need to be made to make the castle suitable for Lulu.

"We'll be fine. And Rita will come every day. We won't be alone."

I turned to face her. Her eyes were wide as she craned her neck, taking in the grand scope of the building before her. I'd forgotten that she'd never seen it before, up close. Her expression was one of anguish.

Thinking of Gabriella, most likely. It occurred to me now that entering her sister's home might be emotional for her.

As we climbed the stairs to the door, I hesitated. Maybe bringing Lulu here was a mistake. Perhaps she'd still be safer in the *pensione*, out of sight.

I shook my head, dispelling the idea. If it had been a prank, the author had probably meant to threaten the fact that Lulu was a secret, not Lulu herself.

And I wouldn't be intimidated. I'd reveal the secret to everyone myself; I wouldn't let someone lord that power over me. And I meant to confront Lucrezia and discover if it was her.

The large front door groaned open. The massive vestibule beyond wasn't lit, and I fumbled on the wall for the knob. The chandelier flared, revealing one of the more impressive rooms of the castle, a showcase for the few visitors who ever dared to come. There were elaborately carved, throne-like chairs against the wall, and a half-dozen large oil paintings that were less dour than most I'd seen in the castle. These were mostly of landscapes and Greek myths.

My mother took it all in, her face contorted as if she were in pain.

"Are you all right?"

She nodded, but I knew she wasn't.

Maybe she was thinking of our shabby little bungalow, the long hours she'd droned away typing in an office. Meanwhile, Gabriella had been living here.

I wanted to prod her further about their relationship. In this setting, I thought perhaps she'd finally open up. But just then, Paul burst through the door, his face flooded with relief at the sight of me.

"Thank God, Silvia. When you ran out of here like that . . ." He ran a hand through his already tousled hair. "I've been worried sick."

He noticed my mother, and Lulu, and I studied his reaction, the subtle furrowing of his brow.

I stood up straighter and adjusted a curl that had fallen in front of Lulu's face.

"Paul, I'd like to introduce you to my daughter. Lulu."

CHAPTER 29

Paul stared at my precious little girl with an unreadable expression. My mother evaluated Paul with open curiosity. Critical as she could be, she appeared somewhat approving. Paul did cut an impressive figure.

"You have a kid?" Paul stuffed his hands in his pockets.

"I'm going to go look around the rest of the castle," my mother said. Such courtesy was unusual for her; I'd expected her to grill Paul. But I was grateful for the privacy.

As soon as she left, I answered. "Her father's not in the picture. At all." Lulu had fallen asleep in my arms on the walk, and I kept my tone hushed.

"I can't believe you didn't tell me." Paul wasn't angry, exactly, but he was clearly experiencing a strong emotion. For a moment, I thought I'd detected a flash of something like jealousy.

"I'm telling you now."

I knew it would be difficult to have this conversation with him, but I'd always pictured him responding perfectly: wrapping me in his arms and telling me that it didn't matter, that he'd love her just like his own. Paul had been so completely ideal, until that moment, that I couldn't quite believe he wasn't reacting the way I wanted him to.

"I—it's not what I pictured for us." He ran a hand over his jaw, and his words pelted my heart like stones.

I closed my eyes, trying to understand. Maybe I shouldn't have been so shocked. Paul was kind of proper, in a way. He liked things organized, and he was a planner—when it came to his work, certainly, but his personal life, too. He would expect it to unroll according to his own specific vision, and in the right order. Marriage, house, and then babies. His own.

I'd managed to have a few dates, after Lulu's father—an actor I'd worked with who'd met me at a smoky bar where we drank dry martinis and ate salty olives, the leather banquette sticky against my legs. I'd seen him twice, and made excuses about being busy to avoid seeing him a third time. It never crossed my mind to tell him about Lulu. And then there'd been a casting director who—well. It certainly couldn't be described as a date. After that, I didn't see anyone, and did my best to fend off the advances of other predatory men. So Paul didn't appreciate, I thought, just how significant it was for me to tell him about her at all. To be with him at all.

"How did it happen?" His voice was thick.

I raised my eyebrows. "Babies are all usually made pretty much the same way, I expect."

"Come on, you know that's not what I meant."

I didn't like talking about Lulu's father. I never wanted to see or think about him ever again. But I forced myself to explain. "I fell in love with the wrong guy. He was a bum. And violent. He doesn't even know about her, and I plan to keep it that way."

Paul's eyes flashed at the word *violent*, and he stepped closer to me, as if he could protect me from events that had already transpired. "If I ever meet him, I'll—"

"You won't. He's out of my life." He had never come looking for me, thank God, after I'd left him. He was a good enough guitar player—barely—to be able to woo other girls who were as impressionable as I'd once been, I supposed, so he hadn't bothered to try and win me back. I paused, readying myself to ask the question I dreaded. Paul and I had only just gotten together, after all. We hadn't declared anything or made any promises. No one would blame him for making a clean break.

Yet my parents had only had a couple of weeks together. Sometimes that was enough. I knew how I felt about him, and knew that if our roles had been reversed, I'd still want to be with him. I chewed my lip. "Does this change things between us?"

He didn't respond right away. He stuffed his hands deeper in his pockets and kept his eyes fixed on the floor. My stomach roiled.

"It doesn't change how I feel about you. But I need some time to wrap my head around all this."

Something sharp stuck in my windpipe, just as it had when I'd first met him and he'd fired me from *Five Days in Roma*. I swallowed around it. Just then, Lulu shifted and lifted her darling head. "Who dat, Mommy?" she asked, blinking her big brown eyes. She looked like me, thankfully. Not him. It shouldn't have mattered, but I was glad not to have to be reminded of him.

"That's Mommy's friend Paul." The words scratched my throat.

Paul softened at the sight of her sweet little face. His eyes locked on hers, as if he'd never met anyone as wondrous as a child before. "Nice to meet you, Lulu."

I looked away. I couldn't bear the idea that Paul, whom I'd thought to be so noble, might reject my beloved Lulu. Might turn us down, not interested in the package deal. Tears threatened, and I knew I had to excuse myself before they surfaced.

I felt utterly betrayed by him.

"I'm just going to go put her back to bed."

I walked around him, leaving as wide a berth as I could in the vestibule, as if he were radioactive.

He didn't come after me.

I steeled myself and swallowed down my tears. I didn't want Lulu to worry. She nuzzled her little face into my neck, and I kissed the top of her head.

My mother was waiting politely in the great hall. The production assistant, Roberto, was there, too, preparing for the day, and he promised to return Ruffina for me. My mother followed me without comment as I headed toward the stairs to the northeast tower.

When we reached the hallway, I saw that someone had

scrubbed the writing off the wall, leaving behind a large patch of red on the plaster.

Inside my tiny bedroom, I laid Lulu gently down and tucked the covers around her. She slipped her thumb into her mouth, a habit she'd turned to less frequently, lately, but the disruption of the surprise move from the *pensione* must have made her want comfort. It made my heart ache. My mother arranged herself beside her.

"I'll stay here with her. You go get ready."

I nodded. I was overdue at hair and makeup. "I'll call for Rita, as soon as she wakes up. And I need to apologize to Signora Ricci for waking her."

"We'll be fine. Go."

So I went.

As I exited the stairs, I ran into Lucrezia, herself fresh from Aurelia's station. Her black hair was in dark, smooth curls that tumbled past her shoulders, and her lips were painted a violent shade of crimson. She wore another stunning red dress, this one more ethereal than the last, more reminiscent of the first one she wore, when she was burned at the stake. Ruffled layers met at her ankles, and a deep V neckline nearly reached the cinched waist.

She smiled at me, but I didn't smile back.

"Was it you? The message?" I was past niceties. Lucrezia's beautiful face transformed into an aspect of offended astonishment. It was convincing, but then, she was a terrific actress.

"How could you think such a thing?"

She sounded genuinely hurt, but I persevered. It had to have been her. "I have a daughter. I was never married to her father. So there's my big secret. Now you know. You can't threaten me with it anymore."

She blinked her thick dark eyelashes, and a touch of color rose in her cheeks. "I'm sure your daughter is lovely. I'd love to meet her. And I would never threaten you."

"But you're always prying." I sounded petulant, rather than righteous and indignant. I was desperate for it to be her.

She considered this. "Maybe so. Only because I wanted to

know you better. And you wouldn't let me in. I don't have many close female friends, you know." Her tone was regretful. "Why would I do such a horrible thing?" She shook her head, as if such an act were beyond comprehension.

I felt faint, my legs unsteady beneath me. I didn't really know why she would. But if it hadn't been Lucrezia, if it hadn't been a prank . . . no, it had to be. "Maybe you're jealous, I don't know. Afraid I'll steal your limelight."

Lucrezia only looked sad. "I always thought there was enough—what is this word? Limelight?—for both of us." She grasped my hand with her soft and supple one. "You are my friend, Silvia, and you've had a shock. So I will forget this unkindness." Her eyes flashed. "But you must learn to trust your friends if you wish to keep them."

Then she sashayed away from me, her flowy dress giving the impression that she was floating.

Guilt sliced into me, but only for a moment. Because she was wrong. I couldn't trust her, or Paul.

All I needed were Lulu and my mother. It was us against the world, just like before.

I hadn't predicted the impact of Lulu's charm. When I'd pictured bringing her to the castle, I'd only ever thought about the judgment and scorn that would be heaped upon me.

But everyone adored Lulu. Of course they did. How could they not? She was the sweetest little girl in the world. Aurelia chucked her chin and called her *piccola*; Lucrezia—while careful not to address me directly, after our fight—positively gushed over her; and even Mr. Meyerson took a moment to bounce her on his knee, his eyes surprisingly fond. I hated to let him, and the sight of them together made me queasy. But at least he wasn't complaining about her presence in the castle.

In fact, no one complained. Several people were even sympathetic, now that they understood the message had likely been directed at me. And while I'm sure people whispered to each other about who the father was, and what had happened, no one actually asked me about it directly.

It had gone over far better than I ever could have anticipated.

And Lulu adored the castle. She had been too cooped up in the *pensione*, without many places to play besides the narrow streets of the town, and she approached the castle like one giant playground. One of the castle cats had recently given birth in the storage room off the kitchen in an old vegetable crate, and Lulu had spent the morning playing with her tiny kittens. She was in heaven.

I came to check on her again during one of my breaks that day, while they changed the setups, and found her in the sewing room with Sarah and Mrs. Leskowitz, buried in a pile of sequined cloth. They'd moved the sewing room from the armory for the scene today, and it was in an empty room near the library in the southeast tower. This room had polished herringbone brick floors instead of terra-cotta tile, and the walls sported faded, chipped frescoes depicting a countryside scene with dancing, diaphanously clad women. The overall effect was one of waning splendor. Maybe the wives of Renaissance lords had once used this room for their sewing, too.

"Where Lulu go? Is she hiding?" she asked me, and then ripped the cloth off her head and said "boo" before collapsing in peals of giggles.

"We've been playing this game for about fifteen minutes," Sarah told me, laughter in her eyes. "She never tires of it."

Lulu put the cloth over her head again, still laughing. "Oh, no, I lost Lulu! Have you seen her?" I asked, and she burst out in screams of laughter as I pulled the cloth off her head.

Rita stood nearby, hounding Mrs. Leskowitz. "Who's the most famous person you've dressed?" she demanded, in Italian. "Is it true Terrence Leopold has four ex-wives?"

Mrs. Leskowitz looked completely at a loss.

"Rita, I think Mrs. Leskowitz and Sarah have work to do," I chided, gently. "And I'm not sure they speak Italian."

Her eyes were big as saucers. It made sense she was a little starstruck, and I thought of Gabriella, growing up in a small town and eager for a brush with fame. And I remembered Signora Ricci's comment, about how all the young people left as soon as they got a chance. I had a feeling Rita would be one of them. "I've never been inside here before. Your aunt doesn't like anyone coming here."

"So I've heard."

"They said she went crazy after she lost her child."

I choked on my spit as I swallowed. "What?"

Rita nodded sagely and sucked on her prominent teeth. "That's why she's so bitter. Or was. Do you really think she's been murdered?" Rita was blunt and socially unaware, but I usually found her forwardness a bit funny. Now, though, I frowned. She sounded morbidly fascinated, as if this were merely a topic to entertain. Perhaps, in town, it was. It surprised me a little that she'd heard about my theory, but someone from the movie had probably mentioned it in the café. A village this small didn't have many secrets.

Secrets. Just thinking the word stole my breath. "Where's my mother?" I asked, rather than replying to her question. The information about my aunt's loss saddened me, and I thought again of that empty cradle.

I saw her ghost story, too, in a whole new light. She'd said Serena had killed herself and her son to protect him from a crueler death at the hands of her husband. I didn't know the nature of Gabriella's loss, but her sympathy with the ghost made even more sense to me, now.

I made my peace with the ghost long ago.

Maybe the ghost had felt sorry for Gabriella, too.

"Oh, she went to set," Rita said, pulling me from my reverie. "She said she wanted to watch your next scene. I'm going to take Lulu over to watch, too, if that's okay."

"Sure, that's fine." My heart increased its tempo. The idea of performing for my mother made me nervous. I turned to Sarah. "Is Lulu bothering you? Rita can take her somewhere else."

"Not in the least. She's a breath of fresh air in this old place."

I smiled. Every mother likes to hear her child complimented, and I was bursting with pride at how the cast and crew had welcomed her.

It made me feel a little foolish for dreading this scenario so much. But I had cause to worry. Many people had been far less kind, when they'd learned the truth, and it had made me protective.

It was best to keep one's guard up, I'd learned. Maybe Lucrezia was right. I didn't let people in easily, but her cruel joke just proved that I had good reason.

I sneaked away while Lulu was hiding under the cloth again, so that she wouldn't make a scene over a short goodbye. In the scene we were shooting in the armory, Bianca and Bernard met with a local priest to enlist his help in banishing the witch's evil spirit from the castle.

The armory was located off the northwest tower, near the entrance to the castle and the foyer, and they'd chosen it for this scene so that the characters could evaluate which holy weapons might aid them against evil.

On the way, I bumped into Richard. I would have avoided him if I could, but I spotted him too late, and it wouldn't have made sense to turn around. He must have been in the library and chosen the same route as me, through the gallery. It wasn't my favorite room. The air in here was even fustier than in the rest of the castle, and a massive crack on one wall reminded me of a giant spider. The few remaining hanging oil portraits were all of somber-looking men, perhaps the ancestors of Gabriella's husband. They'd been dead hundreds of years, yet their gazes were oddly alive, their eyes following me as I walked.

I gave Richard as much space as I could, but he ignored it and came closer. Like almost everyone lately, he looked like hell. His bob had gotten shaggier, and his round face looked swollen, as if from lack of sleep. He fixed me with that magnified ice-blue stare, and I shuddered.

"I heard about, you know, the writing. I suppose you're going to blame me for that, too?" He spoke gruffly, but beneath that, he sounded almost wounded. I hadn't thought Richard had cared at all about my accusations before. He'd been so derisive.

"No. I don't think it was you, actually."

"*Actually.* Gee, thanks." We walked in silence for a minute. Richard looked sideways at me. "The message might not have been for you, you know."

I sighed. "I know."

"Glad you're on time today. We are two days behind schedule. When your aunt comes back, we'll probably have to offer her more money."

I frowned at the mention of my aunt. He was just needling me. I decided not to bite.

"Didn't the contract give you any leeway?" I would have assumed they'd given themselves some kind of buffer. Not that it mattered, because she wasn't coming back. But it interested me that he was making a point of acting like she was, and I wanted to test him.

He only laughed, meanly. "The contract." He paused for effect, as if he had something important to say, and leveled a cool stare at me. "Didn't your boyfriend tell you? He messed up. She never actually signed it."

CHAPTER 30

My stomach churned. Richard appraised me, a sneer on his lips. His frigid blue eyes bored into me.

"You're lying." I clung to that possibility. I didn't trust Richard, after all. And surely Paul would have told me. I could picture him so clearly, leaning against the wall of my bedroom after Lucrezia and I had exposed our own flaws, struggling to think of a motive for himself.

If Richard were telling the truth, he'd had one. Because if my aunt hadn't signed the contract and then the picture had fallen apart, it would have been his fault. Conscientious, diligent Paul would have been responsible.

If he'd admitted it, I would have thought nothing of it. But for some reason, he hadn't.

"Ask him yourself, sweetheart."

We reached the armory, and Paul was there already, in discussion with Mr. Meyerson about the setup. The room, strangely, was one of the only ones in the castle that hadn't been picked bare. A dozen suits of armor stood sentry, their backs to the walls, and the plaster was decorated not with paintings but with spears and shields and swords. Claude's team had set up an ornate table in the center of the room on which the characters could evaluate their arsenal.

Paul flinched when he saw me enter, but then he crossed toward me straightaway.

"Can we talk somewhere privately?" He sounded like he was

in physical pain, and his eyes were a bit wild. My heart pounded so hard in my chest, it hurt. I nodded curtly, once, and followed him to a little annex off of the armory, a rounded wall of mullioned windows overlooking the gardens and the lake. The room was musty, and the blue-green water seemed to surround us. I suddenly found it difficult to breathe.

"Look, about before. I'm sorry. It doesn't matter to me, that you have a daughter. I was just upset that you hadn't told me about it. I know it hasn't been that long, between us, but I just felt—I thought things were getting serious." He ran a hand through his hair and stared at me with a tortured expression, his eyes still darting around in their sockets. "When you ran out of here after we all saw the message, I was scared, Silvia. Really scared. And then, meeting Lulu—it just surprised me. I'm not always good with surprises. I handled it poorly."

Fifteen minutes ago, it would have been everything I wanted to hear. I still did want to hear it. I allowed his apology to sink in and touch my heart. But it was no longer enough. I couldn't help hearing the hypocrisy ringing in every syllable, much as I wished to ignore it.

The unsigned contract I'd happened upon on his dresser hadn't been a copy.

He'd expected me to reveal my whole past to him; meanwhile, he hadn't bothered to tell me a vital piece of information about my aunt's disappearance. He knew I'd been investigating it, and the contract issue made my theory about her even more likely.

So why hadn't he said anything? Unless . . . I closed my eyes, forcing myself to finish the thought.

Unless he had something to hide.

I felt ill. I was suffocating in this airless room. Looking outside only made it worse, the panes of glass revealing only a stretch of sickening turquoise.

I didn't know exactly what I was suspecting him of, and I could barely make myself articulate my fears. What I did know was that my judgment when it came to men, in the past, had been flawed. Since Lulu's father, I no longer allowed myself to completely trust it. But I thought Paul had been different. Everything about being with him was nothing like anything I'd experienced before. I'd thought maybe I'd finally caught a break.

But I could have been wrong.

"Paul, when we came to visit Gabriella together. Did she ever sign the contract?"

"What?" He was taken aback by the sudden change in topic. His mouth dropped open slightly, his forehead crinkled. Then he sighed. "No. I messed up. She told me she did, and I never actually checked. But—why? What does that have to do with anything?"

I stared at him in astonishment. Did he really not understand the significance of that omission? He wore an expression of sweet puzzlement. It was so authentic. If it *weren't* real, well, Paul was the best damned actor of any of us.

"Because someone killed her, Paul. And without a signed contract, she really could have ended the picture if she chose." I spoke slowly and carefully, enunciating every word. I drew in the room's stale air, attempting to slow my racing pulse.

He shrugged. "I guess I didn't think it really mattered. I mean, we'd paid her, the contracts are just a formality. They don't have any teeth. We'd never actually take the time to go to court. If someone wants to be uncooperative the contract wouldn't make much of a difference."

He was so matter-of-fact, still wearing an expression of polite bemusement.

I desperately wanted to believe him.

"I'm sorry I didn't mention it, okay? It should have occurred to me. I guess I was a little embarrassed. I don't like making mistakes."

"I know." I sucked in the stuffy air, attempting to fill my lungs. Paul liked predictability and valued competence. Gabriella's erratic behavior would have been anathema to him.

I tried to picture it, my darling Paul committing a heinous crime. He was passionate, there was no denying that. Passionate about his work, a passionate lover. And someone with that kind of energy driving them—well, it wasn't impossible it could be twisted in the wrong direction.

I'd seen with Lulu's father how that could happen. Except with him, that undercurrent of cruelty had always been there, worming its way to the surface every time he drank. His honeyed words would sour with every sip of beer, becoming barbed remarks, then outright insults. And a few times, when he was so drunk he couldn't see straight, he'd hit me.

Paul wasn't cruel. I couldn't believe it of him. I didn't. I was disgusted with myself for even considering it. I knew Paul, knew his heart, and he was not capable of such an act.

Gabriella's disappearance, the castle, the movie, all of it had made me paranoid.

Still, it didn't change the fact that Paul had lied to me. By omission, yes, but a lie all the same. His jealous streak, his first reaction to meeting Lulu, and now the unsigned contract all showed me that he wasn't as perfect as I'd hoped. If it were only my heart on the line, if I were the only one bearing the risk, I wouldn't have cared.

But it wasn't just about me. And the idea of him letting down my sweet Lulu was more than I could bear. The walls to my heart that had been lowered for him went back up, strong as the castle's.

"I can't do this anymore, Paul. I'm sorry." The words hurt my throat. The time I'd spent with him these last two weeks had made me sublimely happy. Looking after Lulu and my mother could be exhausting, and it had been such a relief to have someone caring for me for a change. I'd very nearly fallen in love with him. Even now, looking into his heartbroken brown eyes, something inside me cracked.

"Why?"

I shook my head. "Let's not do this, okay?"

"Are you really breaking up with me because I didn't tell you about some stupid paperwork? Is there a single goddamn person you'll let yourself trust, Silvia?" he yelled, running a hand over his anguished face.

At the word *trust,* I recoiled. Lucrezia had said something similar. I knew that he had a point, and that I had trouble letting people in, but I had good reason. I'd learned the hard way. I hugged my ribs.

"I'll see you in there." I turned to go.

"Is this really it?" His back was to the windows, and the lake framed him. He appeared golden and beautiful, in sharp relief to the sickly color of the lake behind him. I didn't want it to end, but I knew, too, that he was right. I didn't trust him anymore, not completely.

"I'm really sorry."

"Wait, Silvia—"

But I didn't hear the rest.

A breakup didn't stop Paul from wrangling everyone into place on time. Usually, though, he was unflappable and authoritative. Today, his energy level was noticeably low. My gut twisted with guilt, but I didn't allow myself to question my decision. I wouldn't be strong enough to withstand my own interrogation.

The actor playing the priest was a short man with a short black beard covering a long, equine jaw. He was noticeably starstruck by Terrence, which made me feel a sort of pitying kinship toward him. I'd been like him, in the beginning. Terrence treated him as he might a bothersome fly, mostly ignoring him or swatting him away with pointed comments.

Once we were rolling, though, the actor was a complete professional, adopting the calm, patient mien of a man of God. He wore a full black cassock and a large gold crucifix. The ridiculous thought crossed my mind, for a moment, that if he were a real priest, he could take confession of everyone here.

He might learn quite a lot.

"Once the witch takes corporeal form, she can be destroyed," he said. "You must burn her again, to banish her wretched soul from the earth forever."

"But isn't it dangerous, to allow her to come back to life? What about Bianca?" Bernard demanded, placing a territorial hand on my shoulder.

The priest nodded gravely. "The witch gaining such strength will drain Bianca greatly. She will be close to death." He steepled his fingers, and I jumped back, clinging to Bernard and burying my face in his shirt. At least I didn't have to look at Paul in that moment. But I could feel his gaze on me, all the same, tickling my skin.

"No. We must find another way," Bernard said, and stroked my hair.

"There is no other way. The witch will continue to steal Bianca's life force, no matter what we do. This is the only way to stop her." He ran his hands over the assorted weapons on the table and paused on a crossbow. "Use fire arrows. After Bianca falls asleep tonight, the witch will enter her dreams a final time. And then she will reappear in the flesh, ready to take her vengeance on the village. You must be ready."

Bernard nodded that fine cleft chin. "I will be."

"Bianca, you must also prepare yourself, my child."

I clasped Bernard's hand. Mr. Meyerson had instructed me to act sweet and afraid, overwhelmed by what I must face. But I allowed Bianca to be a little braver, her chin high as she met the priest's gaze.

"What must I do?"

"The witch will plead with you for sympathy. You must harden your heart against her. There is a connection between you, a strong one, and you must not let her in at all. Do you understand? You cannot." His voice rang out, and he pounded the table.

"What would happen?" Bernard demanded. It had been my line, originally, but Mr. Meyerson had given it to Bernard, preferring that his character take charge. As the man, it was his duty to protect Bianca, he explained. So even though my character had the most at stake, I was mostly a bystander while the two of them planned how to take down the witch.

"If Bianca allows it, the witch could maintain a foothold in this world. Even if you succeed in killing her."

"Like a possession?" Bernard put his arm around me, as if determined no one should possess Bianca but him.

"Not quite. But a glimmer of her spirit will remain behind, in Bianca's mind. Bianca won't ever be the same."

Bernard tightened his grasp, his fingers digging into my flesh. I acknowledged the pain, letting it show on my face. Because it hurt to shut people out, as I knew all too well. Ending things with Paul had been utterly devastating, and Bianca would struggle to cut ties with the witch.

But then I looked inward, picturing the fortress I'd hid my heart behind, the only barrier that could save me. That could save Bianca.

My eyes blazed with righteous conviction as I replied, "I won't let her in, Father. I have no compassion for the witch."

"Cut." Mr. Meyerson sounded pleased. I exhaled in relief, and pried Terrence's hand off of me.

I couldn't help stealing a glance at Paul. The raw heartache I saw there stole my breath. I almost caved right then, and it took every ounce of my strength not to run into his arms.

He strode over to me, not caring that people were around, and took my hands in his. "Tell me what I can do to make it right." His voice was a low growl. Then he leaned in and whispered, his breath hot against my neck. "Do you remember when I told you that I'd do anything for you?"

I swallowed. I remembered. We were in bed, after the first time we'd slept together, and he'd been almost too beautiful to look at. I could still almost feel the warmth of his strong chest as I'd curled against him, the slickness of our skin.

I knew Paul well enough now that I could read the full range of his expressions, and I recognized his admiration for my performance, his anger at how I'd wounded him, and his lust, all mingled together. He'd said after my first audition that he'd wanted to have me right there, and I knew he wanted it now, too. For a moment, I allowed myself to imagine it, our bodies thrashing as we purged the fight from our system, until both of us found a different kind of release.

But he'd taught me just how powerful desire could be, and I couldn't allow myself to be pulled under. A person could drown in it.

My aunt, for example. She'd been so overcome that she'd abandoned her family.

I would never make that same mistake. He'd lied to me, and I wouldn't let anyone into my heart who might hurt me and Lulu. It was as simple as that.

"There's nothing you can do."

His jaw ticked, and he was breathing hard as he struggled to contain his emotions. I couldn't stand it. I shifted my eyes away from his face, toward the suits of armor.

Unbreakable. Unyielding. If only I were as strong. I closed my eyes. For Lulu, I had to try.

CHAPTER 31

By the time I finally stumbled into my room that night, my whole body ached. My feet, my calves, my throat, my heart.

I found Lulu still awake, despite the hour, tucked against my mother while she read her stories. The sight of them both together filled me with so much love that, for some reason, I burst into tears.

My mother looked up, startled, and Lulu tilted her little head. "You get a booboo, Mommy?"

"Yes, sweet one. Mommy got a booboo." I placed a hand over my chest.

"She's wired because she's excited about being in the castle. And we both saw you perform today. She loved it." My mother glowed with pride. I'd seen her there, of course, and was relieved that she'd come on a good day. Mr. Meyerson hadn't picked on me for once. Maybe he'd been sensitive to her presence. "Does this mean he ended things, then?" She studied my tears. Of course she'd guessed their source accurately. They were for Paul.

I myself hadn't even realized it until she'd said something. But I still cared deeply for him, and still craved his touch like a drug. And yet I believed I'd done the right thing.

"No. I did. It wasn't about her, actually. It was something else." I sat on the bed and hugged Lulu. I wouldn't let any man into her life unless I was utterly convinced of his absolute goodness. Lulu was excited, bouncing up and down. Her curls had gotten thicker and longer, and I encountered several knots as I ran my fingers through them. "Can Mommy comb your hair, angel?"

"Okay!" She scrambled over to sit on my lap, and I scooted back deeper into the bed.

My mother handed me a comb. "I'm sorry to hear it."

"You are?" My mother never liked the idea of me dating. After I left Lulu's father, she'd actively discouraged it, and had given me the cold shoulder for a week after my two dates with the actor. I hadn't mentioned them to her, but she'd smelled the smoke on my clothes when I came home, heard my martini-slurred words, and she'd known. "You always said that I couldn't trust my own judgment, when it came to men." She'd had a point. Lulu's father had proven that. It was another reason I'd felt justified in my decision to break things off with Paul. I truly didn't know whether I was capable of assessing his character correctly. It had felt different, it was true. Lulu's father had put me down, and made me so desperate to please him, I'd overlooked his awfulness. I'd had to beg for scraps of his affection. I'd known it wasn't healthy, but I hadn't been able to help myself. But Paul made me feel good. He'd made me feel adored, and valued, and being near him had lit me up inside.

"I can't keep you all to myself forever. Especially now that—" She cleared her throat. I squeezed her hand.

"Hey. Yes, you can. You and Lulu are all that matter."

But she shook her head. "No. You're young, Silvia. You have to have a life. I've been selfish."

I attacked Lulu's hair with the comb, my emotions swirling. I couldn't believe she was reversing course so drastically after always despairing over my taste in men. "But how do I know if I can trust him? You know I haven't always made good decisions."

I'd wanted to let others into our little bubble, but when I'd tried before, it had ended badly. My mother had disliked Lulu's father from the beginning and been beside herself when I'd moved into his apartment in Los Angeles. Right now, following my undependable instincts could be dangerous.

"You haven't. But you've learned from that, I think." She

spoke quietly. I could hardly believe my ears. I'd wanted her to make me feel better and tell me I'd done the right thing. Now I felt more confused than ever. I sniffled through a fresh wave of tears.

The comb snagged on a particularly nasty tangle, and Lulu yelped. Then she began bawling. I hadn't really hurt her; mostly, she was just overtired. But I put the comb aside and gathered her up. She put her arms around my neck and cried into my shoulder.

"You hurt me, Mommy." She hiccupped between her sobs.

"Mommy is so, so sorry, baby. It was an accident. I didn't mean to."

"I have a booboo."

"I know. I feel so bad." I kissed her head.

My mother watched the exchange, riveted, and for some reason, she chuckled.

"What's funny?"

"I just wish it were always so simple."

"What?"

She didn't reply, but after a moment's reflection, I understood what she meant. Apologizing. Forgiving. She must be thinking of my aunt.

It also made me think about my scene tomorrow. We still had a few more days of work, afterward, for pickup shots and a few reshoots, including the garden scene, since the film had been destroyed. But the plot would come to its dramatic conclusion the next day. Bianca would confront the witch, and drive her out of both the castle and her mind. She would deny the witch's apology, and offer her no succor. Then she and Bernard would have a white wedding.

All wrapped up neatly with a bow. Utterly boring and predictable.

Paul and I had discussed the scene together a couple of times. It didn't sit right with either of us. The message it sent—that the witch was evil, that her sins were unforgivable, that sex was bad—felt outdated. Almost twee.

Lulu settled down, and after a few minutes, she finally

drifted off. My mother got under the covers beside her. I was still clothed and wide awake.

I needed to *think*. To process what had happened between me and Paul, to figure out how to approach my work in the morning. And then there'd been the message on the wall, which I still believed had been a prank by Lucrezia, but she'd been so convincing in her denial that a shadow of doubt had been cast.

There was no room for my thoughts in the minuscule bedroom.

"I'm going to get a snack. I didn't really eat dinner." I needed to walk somewhere to let my mind churn.

"All right."

I wasn't actually hungry, so instead, I went outside to the terrace to get some fresh air. The night was cool, and in the light of the half-moon, I could make out the contours of the gardens below. Branches stretched upward like claws, and the shrubs hulked together in a black formless mass. I couldn't see the lake, aside from the pale yellow reflection of the moon on its surface, one bright spot in the dark. But I knew the water was there because of the vast expanse of nothingness beyond the gardens, a blank void.

I stared into it, as if I could fill it with the eddy of my thoughts.

"I hope I'm not disturbing you."

I jumped. Mr. Meyerson came to stand beside me and leaned over, resting his elbows on the stone wall. He wore a red dressing robe, thick and expensive-looking, a shock of color in the colorless surroundings.

"No. I was just thinking about the scene tomorrow."

He lit a cigarette. I'd never noticed him smoking before, but maybe he was an occasional smoker, like me. He'd seemed stressed lately, and it probably helped with his nerves. The scent was rough and heady and unrecognizable, some foreign brand.

"Me, too. I won't be able to sleep tonight. So I figured, why try?"

We stared at the indiscernible lake before us, each lost in our separate reveries. His presence did bother me, but of course I couldn't say so.

"Your daughter is lovely, by the way. A smart girl. Advanced for her age." I smiled. I never failed to appreciate compliments about Lulu, even from someone like Mr. Meyerson. "Good genes, on your side, at least. Who is the father?"

He asked the question so casually, and I watched the tip of his cigarette bob in front of his face. I bristled. I'd hoped I'd make it to the end of the picture without anyone prying.

"He was a musician in Los Angeles. He died in a car accident." A lie, of course. I didn't mention anything about marriage, but a death always made people assume you were widowed. He could easily discover that I hadn't been, since I worked for him and my paperwork listed me as unmarried.

"Good family?" I glanced over. I couldn't make out his expression clearly. His questions unsettled me. It didn't feel like just friendly banter.

The truth was, I didn't know much about his family, but I doubted anyone would describe them that way. Did being from a good family mean that they were nice, respectable people, or that they had good genes, like me? Whatever the hell having good genes meant. Probably something racial and offensive. Mr. Meyerson didn't know a damned thing about my heritage, aside from being Italian on one side, but maybe he approved of Italians. I didn't want to inquire, because his answer was sure to make me say something to him that could get me in trouble.

In any case, Lulu's father was not from a good family. His mother was dead, and his father was a mean, grizzled old thing whom I'd met only once. "I guess."

"Good. That's good." He spoke as if to himself. "So. What is troubling you about the scene? Shall we discuss it?"

I was grateful for the change in subject. "Yes. I'm just wondering how much Bianca should struggle, I guess."

"Ah. An excellent question." He turned to face me, so abruptly that I stumbled back. "It should be a physical thing, when she drives out the witch. You'll be lashed to the bed, and we must see your body contort and writhe. It will be almost sexual."

I cringed. I'd meant how much Bianca should struggle emotionally, not physically, but I didn't bother to correct him. He continued.

"Imagine that doorway there is the one to the bedroom. You'll be almost done fighting, too tired to go on, and she will appear. Right there. And your head will snap up from the pillows when she speaks to you."

He turned his attention back toward the lake, but I continued staring at the door to the northeast tower, leading to the storage room with the vegetable crates. It hung open, and weak light filtered out.

We stood in silence, and I sensed the air between us shift. Some intangible force made goosebumps prickle my arms, and Mr. Meyerson's posture grew rigid.

"Was it you? The message?" Mr. Meyerson asked the question calmly enough, but menace lurked beneath his words.

"What?" The abrupt change in topic disoriented me. And he'd seen me run out of the castle and must know the message had been meant for me. But it seemed like he was accusing me of *writing* it, which didn't make any sense.

"Do you know?" On the edge of my vision, I saw him reach into the pocket of his robe.

"Know what?" My blood pounded in my ears. Something was very wrong. His voice was flat, and strange.

Your secret isn't safe.

I hadn't spent much time considering who else in the castle might have a secret to hide. I recognized now how shortsighted I'd been. Had it been meant for Mr. Meyerson? Why would he think I knew something about it?

Was his secret dangerous?

I was afraid to face him, and kept my eyes fixed on the tower. As I looked, a figure in white appeared, almost glowing in the night.

I gasped. My first thought was that I was seeing Serena's ghost. Something about the silhouette was almost unearthly.

It was probably just tiredness. I rubbed my eyes, and sparks danced beneath my fists.

When I opened them again, the figure was still there, unnaturally still. Watching. And then she emerged onto the terrace, her figure ethereal and her movements slow.

Mr. Meyerson must have sensed something, and he spun around. His body went rigid with shock.

The ghost floated closer, and closer, until I could see that it was not a ghost, but a woman.

She wore a blindingly white caftan that billowed about her legs. She was only feet in front of us now, a single dramatic eyebrow arched as she appraised Mr. Meyerson coolly. Then, to my shock, she came to stand between us, her body close in front of mine, as if shielding me from him.

"Gabriella." Mr. Meyerson clutched his robe tighter around himself. He spoke her name softly and intimately, like someone who knew her well. Like a lover might.

"Herman. I think it is time we had a little talk."

CHAPTER 32

It was a shame there weren't cameras rolling, because if they'd been there to capture the astonishment and alarm on my face, it would have been the performance of my career.

"Has he hurt you? Are you well?" Gabriella demanded, and I'd forgotten just how husky her voice was, how imperious her tone.

"I'm fine." I didn't understand what was happening, or why Mr. Meyerson should hurt me, but I thought of his gun, and the way he'd reached his hand into the pocket of his robe a moment ago. My heart stumbled in my chest. My ears rang.

Mr. Meyerson dropped his cigarette and ground it beneath a leather slipper. "So it is you. I thought it might be." When he spoke in Italian, his accent grew thicker, and his tone harder. "She looks just like you."

"You've gotten old."

So they did know each other. Not only that, Mr. Meyerson must have recognized my resemblance to her the first time he saw me. Maybe it had something to do with why he'd cast me so quickly, and why he'd chosen Gabriella's castle.

The tension between them grew thicker, and I held my breath, as if a single sound might provoke them. I couldn't see Gabriella's expression, but Herman's was determined and a little sad, as if he had an unpleasant task before him.

"I don't understand. I thought you were dead," I told her. My tongue was sluggish, and I struggled to form the words. I swallowed, and the motion was painful, straining my throat. I was confused and scared. Whatever was going on, it was clear something was terribly, terribly wrong. I sensed the danger, crackling in the air, waiting to strike.

"Silvia, I want you to go inside. Herman, she doesn't know anything." Something like fear crept into her voice, and that startled me, because I hadn't imagined her as afraid of anything. I didn't argue. I stepped carefully backward.

"Maybe she does, maybe she doesn't. I can't take that chance." Mr. Meyerson spoke slowly and resignedly. His broad, pale forehead crinkled; his red robe stood out like a gash in the night.

I was stiff with shock. My mind wouldn't work properly, and neither would my feet. I knew that I should probably run, but the situation didn't quite seem real. Would he actually harm me? It was difficult to process. My legs shook, and I could only manage a single additional step.

I forced myself to consider everything I'd heard, to pull myself out of my stupor. How did they know each other? In the kitchen, when Gabriella had looked out at the drive and panicked, was it because she'd seen him?

"You should have left, Herman. When you saw my message. I warned you."

Her posture was tense and angry. *Her message.* Suddenly, sharp understanding cut through the fog in my brain. The blood on the wall hadn't been meant for me. It wasn't about Lulu.

It had been for him.

"And done what? What kind of life would I have had? I would have to sacrifice everything I've worked for." His jowl quivered, and a drop of spittle landed on my arm.

"You can go to Argentina. Leave now, Herman, I'm begging you."

At the mention of Argentina, something snapped into place. I'd seen headlines here and there, of Nazis who had fled justice, or adopted new identities, and been discovered. Many had gone to South America. I gagged, and my throat and stomach turned cold, as if I'd swallowed the freezing water of the lake.

If that were his secret, and Gabriella knew it—that he was not Herman Meyerson from Switzerland, but someone else— she would have been a threat to him. And if he thought I knew, too . . .

My breathing grew fast and ragged, as I gulped air like someone who'd been drowning. Mr. Meyerson—although that was almost certainly not his real name—watched me, and I think he sensed that I was beginning to understand.

"No. I'm sorry. There's no other way." He reached into his pocket so quickly, I nearly missed it. I blinked, and found myself staring at the long, thin barrel of his gun, the metal flashing in the moonlight. Somewhere in the distance, a dog howled, and a scream rose up in my own throat.

"Herman, think. You won't get away with it. You'll be caught."

The gun wavered in the air, and he looked over his shoulder at the inky lake. "Everyone will think she went away. Like you."

My blood rushed through my veins. He meant to kill us and dump our bodies. The idea of the icy dark water enveloping my corpse as I sank into that fathomless depth filled me with a cold terror unlike any I'd ever known. It would mean abandoning my mother to die alone. It would mean never holding my darling Lulu again.

Suddenly, I was no longer numb. Remembering Lulu awoke all of my senses in an instant. I could see the outlines in the garden better now that my eyes had adjusted, and smell the fragrant blossoms, and hear the wind rustling in the branches and the distant lapping of the lake. I could taste the faint tang of coppery blood on my tongue, from biting my cheek. I could feel the sheer horror of this moment in every part of my body. My muscles cramped as my calves flexed, preparing to run.

"I didn't want it to come to this. She is as magnificent as you once were."

I gasped, the noise disappearing into the soft breeze. He'd seen her perform. All at once, I understood how they must know each other: he'd been her lover when she starred in the Mussolini propaganda film. Maybe he'd been the director. He was the man she'd fallen so deeply in love with that she'd be-trayed her family.

Gabriella swore under her breath. "She's your daughter, Her-man."

Her declaration took a moment to sink in, and I thought it must be a lie to buy us time. Surely he wouldn't believe it. My father was an American G.I.

But Mr. Meyerson wore a look of surprised understanding. My body went numb.

I didn't want it to be true. It couldn't possibly be true. My father had been Roy Whitford, a brave veteran, a car salesman, affectionate and flawed and devoted. And my mother would have had nothing to do with someone like Herman. It didn't add up.

And then a howl erupted from somewhere deep inside, stran-gled and agonized, as I understood.

The story my mother had told, of Gabriella returning after their parents' death, appeared crisply in my mind as if it were a memory. I pictured her dressed in black, walking along a dusty road.

A baby in her arms.

Horror and disgust overcame me as I locked eyes with the man before me. My father.

I shook my head, my body wracked with sobs, as I grappled with the truth. My whole life had been a lie.

It made sense of so many things.

The years of secrets, my mother's unwillingness to see Gabri-ella again, her insistence that she needed me right now . . . I saw all of it with new eyes.

The woman who had raised me was not my biological mother. She was my aunt.

"You were pregnant?" The gun went slack in Mr. Meyerson's hand.

"Yes. I gave her to my sister to raise. It was the greatest mis-take of my life." Bitterness infused every syllable. My mind reeled. She regretted it, but still, she had given me up. Even now, in this moment, it hurt to hear.

He lowered his gun.

"Go now, Silvia," Gabriella said, and I didn't wait. Maybe he wouldn't hurt me, now that he knew the truth, but I couldn't take that chance.

The terrace behind me felt too open, and lanterns on the castle walls cast haloes of light. So by sheer instinct, I sprinted instead toward the stairs to the garden, into the dark. Gabriella ran, too, and Mr. Meyerson—or whoever he was—didn't chase us.

I quickly realized my mistake. In the garden, we were trapped. If he came after us, he wouldn't have to hurry.

Shit. I had no choice but to stay the course. I went all the way down to the lowest level, going as quickly as I could without falling, my heart in my throat.

I turned into the garden itself, which I knew to be the wildest and most overgrown tier. Because I'd spent so much time shooting here, I knew my way around it a little better. Even so, bushes scraped my legs, and branches reached out to grab me. I paused to catch my breath beside a large hedge, and Gabriella reached out to clasp my hand. She put a finger to her lips, and together we crouched down. My breathing slowed a fraction. Maybe he couldn't find us here, if we stayed still. In the Stygian grounds, we might appear like just another shrub.

We waited. Questions swirled, but I didn't dare speak.

Her hand was soft and dry in mine. My mother's hand.

No. I banished the thought. Elena Whitford was my mother in every way that counted. Still, as I listened to the quiet whistle of Gabriella's breathing, I sensed the connection between us. And her love for me.

I began to think Herman had given up on chasing us, and was almost tempted to stand and stretch. The muscles in my legs ached.

But then I saw a flashlight, slicing through the dark, and I froze, my calves burning. Gabriella tightened her grasp. Mr. Meyerson paused, only ten feet from us, and called out into the night.

"I wondered if our paths would ever cross again, Gabriella. I knew you would happily destroy me if you could."

Whatever relationship they'd had must have ended very badly. Had she known that Herman had assumed a new identity? If the truth came out, his career in Hollywood would be over, at the very least. And if he had been more than a propaganda director and committed any atrocities, he could have been evading prison or worse. I flinched, remembering how he had balanced Lulu on his knee.

My legs trembled beneath me, but I didn't dare move an inch. If Gabriella had known he was still in Italy, her well-equipped armory made slightly more sense.

"When I saw Silvia audition, I realized how badly I wanted closure. To make sure that chapter from my past stayed buried. The chance to see you again was irresistible. I'm only sorry that Silvia had to come into this." The beam of light cut through the bushes and bounced against the wall only feet from my head.

And then the light hit me, flashing right in my eyes. I was blinded. Beside me, Gabriella stood, pulling me up with her. We were caught.

CHAPTER 33

A sob escaped my throat as I thought of Lulu, asleep upstairs. I would die soon and leave her behind, and it felt like my chest was being ripped in two.

Mr. Meyerson appraised me and shook his head. "Silvia, I'm truly sorry. Know that your daughter will be well cared for." He added, in wonder, "My granddaughter."

"No." The word erupted from me as a wail, long and keening. I doubled over, afraid I might be sick. I couldn't die and let Lulu fall into the hands of this monster. It flashed before my eyes in an instant, Mr. Meyerson swooping in to console my mother and Lulu over my disappearance, and taking Lulu under his wing when my mother passed. Who knew what awful things he might teach her. Who knew if she'd be safe from physical harm. I couldn't bear to contemplate it. I had to act.

But it was Gabriella who lunged forward first. His flashlight clattered to the ground, temporarily plunging us into black, and I heard a muffled *bang* as the gun fired. Even with the silencer suppressing the noise, it still reverberated through my skull.

The gravel crunched, and I could hear both of them breathing heavily. Then it sounded again, and this time it was followed by a loud thud as a body hit the ground.

It happened in the space of a few heartbeats. The moon emerged from behind a cloud, seeming somehow brighter than before, and I waited for it to reveal Gabriella's corpse, and for another bullet to whiz in my direction. I braced myself for the pain.

But the figure standing before me was Gabriella. I stared in confusion, expecting her to collapse at any moment, but she remained straight and still. I stepped forward to find Mr. Meyerson on his back, blood seeping into the pebbles near his head.

Gabriella bowed her head over his prostrate form. "I've killed him." She was matter-of-fact, as if making a casual observation. I gawped at her. It had been sheer luck that she'd triumphed in the struggle. A wave of fear rolled off my body, leaving behind exhaustion and heartache.

"You saved us."

She shrugged. But when I moved closer, I saw that she was trembling.

I glanced at Mr. Meyerson, his sightless eyes and his mouth sagging open, part of his cheek raw and exposed where the bullet had sliced through, and then looked away. This wasn't a movie set, and he wasn't an actor wearing convincing makeup. This was really happening. It seemed as though I were observing everything from the outside, from some future time when I could look back with cool detachment. It was too much for me to absorb.

Mr. Meyerson had been the mentor who'd given me my big break. Then his bigotry had caused me to lose all respect for him. Now my feelings went through another evolution, as I confronted the full scope of his awfulness: he was a Nazi who would murder his own daughter to save his reputation.

And he was dead.

There was no getting around that. I didn't experience any sadness, only shock. He may have been my father by blood, but I'd never known him as one.

"When I saw him arrive, I knew I would be in danger. I always worried he might come find me one day." She rubbed an eye, and I was astounded to see that she was crying. "I was young, Silvia. And I was in love, at first."

Tears coursed down my own cheeks. I'd learned the hard way how passion could make you lose all reason, when I'd fallen for Lulu's father. I knew how it clouded your judgment.

"Where have you been all this time?"

The blood, the shoe, the unpacked suitcases—none of it made sense.

"It's a medieval castle. There are many places to hide," she said, dryly. "There's a concealed staircase off of my bedroom, built by my husband's ancestors. It has stairs down to the cellar. I tried to make my disappearance appear suspicious so the police would come, and maybe Herman would get spooked and scurry off."

I shook my head in amazement. My crusade had been a fool's errand. I understood now, too, that the woman I'd heard wailing hadn't been Serena. It had been her. She'd been in her own bedroom that night, and I'd heard her crying. There'd never been a ghost.

"I knew he would guess we were related. The resemblance is too great. He worried from the beginning that I'd told you, I think. I shouldn't have provoked him with that message," she spat, shaking her head. "I just wanted him to leave." She stared hard at me, as if trying to read my expression in the moonlight. "I've been looking out for you. I tried to get you to leave, too, to keep you safe. I destroyed the film one day. Your costume."

"The light? The mouse? That was all you?"

"I don't know what you mean."

"Never mind." The light must have been a freak accident, and a cat had probably been responsible for the mouse, like Lucrezia said.

"When I saw him follow you tonight, I suspected the worst. I knew I had to stop him."

"What do we do now?"

There was no reason anyone else should come to the gardens in the middle of the night, but our inaction made me nervous.

Gabriella didn't seem to sense the urgency. She gazed at the lake. "He must disappear."

A shiver ran down my spine. Her meaning was perfectly clear, but I couldn't quite believe what she was suggesting. After all, we'd done nothing wrong. "Shouldn't we just call the police?"

She laughed humorlessly. "It doesn't matter that it was self-defense. We will both be suspects for murder. Italian justice is not fast. And the *carabinieri* are not known for being clever."

A chill coursed through me. I thought she must be overreacting. Surely if we explained who he was, and that he'd tried to kill us, they'd understand. There was no need for dissembling.

What she was describing was a crime. Concealing a body.

"They don't like Americans," she continued. "And you may have noticed, but I don't have many friends. Maybe they will be reasonable, but maybe not. I think not." Her voice faltered. I closed my eyes. I remembered my time in the station all too well, the lecherous stares and rudeness. What she was saying struck a chord.

I couldn't risk prison, not when I had Lulu to think about.

"Trust me, Silvia, this is simpler. We will call the papers tomorrow. Before, I didn't have enough proof for them to run a story, but if he suddenly disappears . . . everyone will wonder why. And they'll look at his past. They'll think he fled."

"But what if he's found?"

"Suicide." She nodded, once, decisively.

My head grew light. I wished this were one of my nightmares, and that I'd wake up in my soft bed with Lulu snuggled against me. Maybe my mother—my real mother, who had raised me—had been right to keep my history from me. I wanted to be Silvia Whitford from San Diego, daughter of Roy and Elena Whitford.

I didn't want to be the girl who'd just watched her mother kill her father in front of her.

I closed my eyes, quaking, and Gabriella came and placed a hand gently on my arm. "You don't have to. It is too much to ask. I will call the *carabinieri*. I won't mention you were here." She sounded sad. Without a witness to verify she acted in self-defense, she'd be under even more suspicion. But if I did explain my role, she was right; we'd both be at risk.

"No." I heaved a breath. "He should disappear."

Gabriella didn't hesitate. She gathered heavy stones to fill the pockets of his robe, wiped clean the gun, and placed it in his hand. Her movements were quick and sure, and her white caftan clung to her figure, vivid as the moon. I only watched at first, still doubting my decision, but when the time came, I helped her drag his limp body to the wall. She hitched her hands under his armpits, and I grabbed his feet, still clad in his leather slippers, his legs swaying as we carried him. I gagged.

Together we hoisted him up and over the stone, and I held my breath as we let go. My arms were abruptly loose and weightless, and his robe fluttered as he fell. He hit the water without a splash, with hardly a ripple, before the lake swallowed him.

I looked over the edge, nauseated, as we waited. He didn't resurface.

"Oh my God. What have we done?"

I turned and vomited into a rose bush, and afterward, the taste of bile lingered. I wiped my chin.

"No more than we had to do."

As despicable as Mr. Meyerson was, I was profoundly disturbed. Not long ago, he'd been alive, smoking a cigarette. He'd had a cold, lonely burial, with no prayers uttered over him, no mourners.

As I stared over the edge of the wall at the still water, I searched my heart. I didn't know if I'd ever be able to come to terms with his crimes. I only knew that in that moment, as I watched the spot where he'd gone under, I couldn't summon any pity.

CHAPTER 34

I sat up all night in the kitchen with Gabriella, drinking espresso until I was jittery. She'd changed from her white caftan, which had been sprinkled with blood, into a mustard-yellow sheath dress. We didn't talk much. As many questions as I still had for her, I couldn't find the words. We sipped and stared into the air and thought about what we'd done.

The sky began to lighten the tiniest degree, indigo shifting to cobalt.

"Did you really love him, once?" I asked, my tongue gummy.

"I thought I did. I was empty-headed and naïve. But I began to see what he was, and then when I found out I was pregnant, I knew I had to get you away from him. I was determined he should never know about you. I couldn't bear the idea of him raising you and poisoning your mind."

She closed her eyes and placed a hand over her forehead, as if she could block out the pain of the memory. The explanation was so familiar to me that it stole my breath. It was exactly how I felt about Lulu's father. We'd both found ourselves drawn to violent men.

"Is that why? Why you gave me up?" I hated the hopeful lilt in my voice, how desperately I wanted it to be true.

"Part of the reason. I wish I could say it was the only reason."

I nodded and sipped my espresso, wishing it could wash away the taste of disappointment. I'd half expected it, but it still hurt to hear.

"You were the sweetest baby. You were almost a year old when I gave you to Elena, and it hurt more than anything in the world. You'll be twenty-two this fall, you know. September seventeenth. I light a candle for you every year."

I hadn't thought about this yet, that I was older than I'd always believed.

Her voice cracked. "I didn't tell you who I was, right away, when you showed up, because I wanted to get to know you a bit first. Before you judged me for what I'd done."

She studied me with those remarkable eyes, and the raw emotion there stirred my pity. She wanted so desperately to be forgiven. Telling me she had been a fascist right off the bat, I guessed, had been a test of sorts, to see how much I might be willing to absolve. I clasped her hand. "I think I understand. I know it couldn't have been easy."

It was the best I could offer. She looked relieved.

"I always dreaded that someday he might find out about you. When I saw him appear on the driveway, I could hardly believe it. It was everything I'd feared. I hated him, by the end of our time together. I've had many years to grow ashamed of it."

She shook her head.

"I haven't had good judgment about men either." It was the closest I could come to pardoning her for her role in it. And if she hadn't made such a mistake, I wouldn't be here.

"I knew if he saw me, I'd be in danger. And I knew he'd ask about you. Hiding was the only thing I could think of. But I was always looking for you, and listening for you, to make sure you were safe and well. But tonight, I looked out the window of my room and saw you alone together, and I panicked. I didn't have a plan, but in case he meant you harm, I knew I had to try and protect you."

Suddenly I was trembling, and the little espresso cup clanked the saucer as I shakily put it down. Despite the hot drink, I was cold all over. I was lucky to be alive.

"And you did. Thank you."

Gabriella nodded once, her lips—for once bare, her lipstick long since worn off—pressed firmly together. "I could do no less."

We parted to get ready for what was sure to be a difficult day. I showered long before anyone else awoke, scrubbing every inch of my skin raw. Afterward, the smell of death and gun smoke still filled my nostrils.

The minutes until dawn ticked by impossibly slowly, and I both longed for it and feared it. Surely everyone would be able to see my guilt written on my face. They'd know that Gabriella wasn't telling them the truth.

As soon as orange streaked the sky, Gabriella and I went to the great hall, where she waited like a queen holding court for everyone to assemble. She received many startled looks as people began to trickle in, but she said nothing to anyone. She sat regally on the fringe-bottomed sofa by the fireplace with her head held high. I stood near her, stiff as one of the suits of armor.

When Paul arrived and saw her, he stopped short and swore under his breath. Guilt sliced into me as I remembered how abominably I'd treated him.

"It's you."

"Yes. I have an announcement, if you will have everyone gather." She was direct and demanding, and Paul didn't hesitate to comply. It was only then, once everyone was in the great hall, that Paul noticed Mr. Meyerson's absence. I saw his brow furrow as he craned his neck.

"All right. Everyone is here." Gabriella clapped her hands together once and scanned the crowd. My mother and Lulu were not present, and I guessed my mother had heard of Gabriella's reappearance and stayed away. "The man you knew as Herman Meyerson is, in fact, a man called Herman Günther, who was an official in the Reich Ministry of Propaganda. I knew him during the war. He encountered me when I returned from my holiday last night and fled. He will not return." She sat back down on the chair and lit up a cigarette, coolly, as if she'd just announced a change in the shooting schedule. Everyone watched her in stunned silence.

"Is this some kind of joke?" Richard stepped forward, his thumb tucked into the waist of his checkered pants.

"No."

"Jesus." He rubbed a hand across his cheek. "I better go make some calls."

Paul looked shaken. After a minute, he used his megaphone to announce that shooting was paused until further notice, and everyone slowly dispersed, the rush of whispers whipping about the room like wind. I could see the confusion and concern on everyone's faces and heard snatches of their conversation. *Is the picture finished? Will we still get paid for this week? A Nazi, can you believe it?*

No one seemed to doubt the story, but I was sick with dread. I didn't know what would happen next. Maybe his body would reemerge and the police would be called. They'd find the stones in his pockets, the bullet in his head, and what would they think? Would they believe it was suicide? Maybe the *paparazzi* would come sniffing, an outcome that was just as worrisome. They would be relentless.

We'd left Mr. Meyerson's things in his room untouched. It was better that way. Maybe people would wonder why he hadn't taken anything, but if his body were discovered and his things had been disturbed, it would be even more suspicious.

Paul needled his way through the crowd to find me, and I grew even more ashamed. I'd been uncompromising and distrustful, just like my mother. Now that I struggled under the weight of my own secret, I saw clearly just how unfair I'd been.

"I'm so sorry, Paul. I was awful. I feel like such an idiot."

My relationship with Paul should have seemed like such a small thing right now, compared with the enormity of what had happened the night before. But it didn't. I needed him more than ever. His eyes locked on mine, but he didn't reply. I felt my cheeks turning red.

"You're right, I do have a hard time trusting people. I don't expect you to forgive me." I bit my lip, holding back tears.

Then, suddenly, he wrapped a hand around my back and pulled me against him, so that his face was inches away. "I have a really good idea of how you can make it up to me." He brushed his lips softly against mine, and then kissed me more deeply, stealing my breath.

It felt wrong. As much as I cared about him, my guilt weighed on me and wedged itself between us. He moved his mouth to my ear. "No more secrets. Let's promise each other, okay?"

His words snaked their way around my heart, squeezing it in my chest. My mouth tasted bitter from the soured espresso and the lie I was about to tell. I swallowed it down. If I told Paul what had happened last night, I didn't know how he'd react. But I knew, too, that I couldn't bear to keep the truth to myself forever. I'd seen what that had done to my mother, how closed off it had made her.

I heaved a breath. "I want that, too. But there is something else that I'm not sure I'm ready to talk about yet. I promise to tell you everything soon."

It was the best I could offer right now, and I hoped it was enough. Paul stepped back to appraise me, a little surprised but taking it in stride. "Okay. I'm a patient guy."

"I love you." I stood on my tiptoes and kissed him once more. "Whatever comes next, I want you to know that." A smile spread across his face, and seeing his uncomplicated happiness made me ache. He might feel differently if he knew about last night. "Don't say anything back. Not yet. Not until I tell you everything, okay?" I wanted it to be real. And while I didn't feel remorse over what I'd done, I knew it might be too much for him to look past. He had a strict moral code, and I'd certainly violated it.

"Is it something about this Herman business?" His expression turned grave.

"It might be."

"I wish I could say I didn't believe it of him. But it makes a certain kind of sense. What a . . ." He clenched his fist and shook his head.

"I know." I squeezed his hand. "Look, I have to go. My mother hasn't seen her sister in twenty years. I think it might be time."

Gabriella accompanied me on the search to find my mother. We located her and Lulu playing in the first tier of the garden, and my heart pounded as we descended the flight of stone steps. The garden wall was too high for Lulu to climb, but her being here still made me nervous. The dizzying height made the setting feel dangerous, and I didn't like her being so close to the scene of last night's events. Her sweetness shouldn't be tainted by the garden's aura of violence.

"Where's Rita?" I asked as we approached.

"She had to come late today." My mother had her back to me and was crouched down beside Lulu, who was watching the salvia in front of her, transfixed. I knew Rita was just a girl, but I still experienced a twinge of annoyance.

"She didn't say anything to me."

"Look, Mommy, a butterfly!" Lulu ran over and hugged my knees. Then she looked up curiously at Gabriella and ducked her head behind my legs as shyness overcame her.

My mother turned. At the sight of Gabriella, the blood drained from her face. The two women stared at each other, and I thought of my father's old expression about me and my mother. *Fire and ice.* My mother's expression was chilling, and Gabriella's eyes blazed with anger.

"Did she tell you?" my mother asked, the same question she'd put to me in the hotel room in Rome, only this time, I knew what she really meant.

"Yes."

Her shoulders sagged, and her body went limp and defeated.

"I only told her that I was her mother by birth. Not about how you took her from me," Gabriella said, her rich voice sharp, like a razor blunted by velvet. My heart stuttered, and my mother went even paler. It couldn't be true. "I regretted giving you up almost right away. You must understand, I had no way to support you and with a child, no way to make a good marriage. My aunt and uncle had lost their sons, and I knew they could help Elena. It seemed like the right thing to do." Gabriella pinched her lips together and pinned me with her dark eyes, as if imploring me to understand. My throat constricted, and I swallowed painfully. "But then I did make a good marriage, an illustrious marriage, and I wanted you back. I could have raised you like a

little princess. But your mother stopped returning my letters."
She spat out the words. "I should have come to America to find
you. But I was scared you would reject me." Her expressive eyes
welled with tears. I'd never had a chance to know my biological
mother, who was elegant, dramatic, and brave. Who'd killed a
man to save my life.

Lulu tucked her face between my knees, peeking at Gabriella
through the gap. She stayed silent, aware that something serious
was happening. I exhaled deeply, as if it could dispel my grief. I
was emotionally exhausted and sick to my stomach. Despite my
tense relationship with the mother who raised me, I loved her. I
could hardly bear to contemplate the level of betrayal Gabriella
had described. "Is that true?"

My mother wore an anguished expression, her lips twisted in
apparent pain. "She couldn't have any more children. She only
wanted you back when it was convenient for her," she told me,
a sob breaking through. "Children are not toys you can put
aside when you tire of them, Gabriella. And you didn't know
the first thing about loyalty. About commitment. You expected
me to just send her back. A four-year-old with no memory of
you. Roy had pretended she was his, and mine, to make her
an American. A selfless man, who loved her by then like his
own. You weren't thinking of her, you were thinking of yourself. Like always."

Lulu started crying at the sight of my mother's tears, and I
picked her up and made shushing noises. My mind spun with
everything I'd learned. My emotions were so knotted and tangled that I didn't quite know how to feel. My mother did have a
point. And if it had been Lulu, I would have moved heaven and
earth to get her back.

"Silvia, I always meant to tell you. But then I got sick, and
I—I was afraid. I didn't want to lose you."

I closed my eyes and let the breeze tickle my face. I mourned
the years my mother's secret had come between us, and the
years I'd never known her sister. Her hatred of Gabriella had
haunted us for my whole life. I should have been resentful that

she'd hidden the truth for so long, but I was tired of anger. That was what had gotten us here. Blaming my mother now would only perpetuate the cycle.

I could make a different choice.

"Oh, Mama. You could never lose me." I leaned over and kissed her dry cheek.

"Do you forgive me, then?" She dabbed her eyes with a handkerchief, and Lulu snuffled in response. Her words from the *pensione* after her fall appeared in my mind, as if they'd floated there on the wind. When she'd asked if some things were unforgivable, she hadn't been thinking of Gabriella. She'd been thinking of herself.

"Yes." I'd learned from my mother what it did to a person to hold onto a grudge, and as I spoke the words, I felt lighter.

Gabriella lit a cigarette and gazed at the lake, bilious aquamarine trapped in its perfect circle. "You're right, Elena. I was selfish and vain. A little fool." She exhaled loudly. "I've had many years to reflect on my failings. Many lonely years. I've had to live with the fact that I traded my only child for this corrupted stack of stones." She gestured toward the castle. It hovered above us menacingly.

Beside me, my mother softened the tiniest degree, her scrunched face turning smooth. Lulu rubbed a fist into her eye and settled her head against my chest, her tears gone.

"There's much to discuss. So many years to catch up on." Her fingers shook as she pulled another drag. "I can make us espresso."

I remembered the moment Gabriella had made me the same offer, after I'd learned of her politics, and I saw my mother wrestle with her response, as I had. Maybe there was too much bitter history between them to overcome, too much anger.

And maybe not.

I did know that my mother had carried the weight of her fury with her a long time, and that I hoped she could find a way to free herself of it.

My mother closed her eyes, looking inward. "I'd prefer coffee."

Gabriella chuckled. "Okay. Coffee then."

I clasped my mother's delicate hand, supporting her on the uneven gravel, and we all walked toward the castle together.

I stood sentinel outside the door to the kitchen. I'd excused myself after Gabriella had made coffee for my mother and a *caffè corretto* for herself. There were some things, I sensed, that they needed to say without me there. So I waited, straining to hear, then chastising myself for snooping. Occasionally I heard shouting. Once, I heard my mother's shocked laughter.

My mother rarely laughed. A lump formed in my throat.

"What's going on in there?" Lucrezia asked, a cigarette perched between her elegant fingers. "They're out of coffee at the craft services table. Is it safe to enter?" Her tone was guarded.

"Not really, no." I explained quickly what was happening, and her eyes widened. "Lucrezia, look—I just want to apologize. You were right, about everything you said."

Lucrezia may have had her flaws, but then we all did. She was a good person, and she'd proven herself to be a good—and very patient—friend. She paused, her face grave, and then broke into a smile. "If you can sneak in there soon and get me some coffee, we'll call it even, okay?" She winked. I laughed, and promised I would whenever it was a good moment.

A minute after she bustled off, Paul appeared, perhaps with similar caffeine-fueled motives. I gathered my courage. If my mother and Gabriella were brave enough to face each other after all these years, I could at least tell Paul the truth.

"Hey." He stopped in front of me, his errand apparently forgotten. "You all right?"

I shook my head, and my story came tumbling out along with my tears, about my biological parents, and the meeting happening at that moment between Gabriella and Elena.

And finally, about what had happened to Herman. I refused to think of him as my father. Elena and Roy were my parents, and the circumstances of my birth didn't change that.

He stared at me intently while I spoke, his brown eyes searching mine. When I finished, he pulled a cigarette out of his pack and left it unlit between his fingers. His gaze shifted to a spot above my head, and he was silent for a long time.

"Your father. He was your father."

"I suppose."

"And he's dead. And you—" He couldn't finish the sentence. His tan complexion had turned pale. He attempted to light his cigarette, and the lighter sparked four times, five, before he could manage it.

"Look, I understand if you don't want to be with me anymore." I swallowed hard, my throat raw.

But then he hugged me, his strong arms locking me in place against his chest.

"There's nothing that would make me not want to be with you. Do you hear me?"

I sagged against him in relief. "But what I did . . ." I couldn't finish. I knew Paul, and I worried he'd see me differently, now, and that the knowledge of what had happened last night would come between us, slowly pushing us apart.

He stroked my hair, and his body pressed to mine was warm and solid.

"I'm just glad you're okay, Silvia. I love you. Nothing matters more than that."

CHAPTER 35

The landlady twisted her key in the cheerful green door, her wide hips jostling from the movement.

"After you," she said, and when I stepped in, the smell of lemony soap assaulted me, transporting me across the years to the bungalow where I'd grown up. My mother's kitchen had always smelled of lemons. I stepped carefully down the hallway, afraid the sensation would disappear. Even Lulu, who'd been growing into quite the chatterbox, was quiet, her big brown eyes wide with wonder.

The space itself was everything I could have hoped for: it was sunny, with terra-cotta tile floors and a balcony from which you could just glimpse the dome of St. Peter's. I actually laughed when I saw a cat curled up against the black wrought iron.

"Shoo. I'm sorry, he's just a neighborhood cat. They're like pigeons around here." The landlady sounded apologetic.

"It's fine. He can stay."

I investigated the sweet little kitchen with mosaic tiles above the stove, and my mother ruffled the checkered curtains by the window.

"What do you think?" my mother asked. She was keeping her tone carefully neutral, but her eyes were hopeful.

"I think it feels like home."

She broke into a smile. She'd grown wearier, even just this last week since we'd been back in Rome, and it gratified me to see her happy. I wanted to give her every comfort I was able, for as long as we had left together.

Even though she was growing physically weaker, she was calmer and more at peace than I'd ever seen her. We were closer than ever, too. Now that she was unburdened of her great secret, it was like the floodgates to her soul had opened. We had stayed up late the other night talking and laughing, reliving fond memories. She'd talked about my father—Roy, the only father that counted—sharing stories I'd never heard before. It was as if keeping one secret had made her keep so many more, but now they were all coming tumbling out.

We'd asked Gabriella to come and visit us at the hotel where we were staying, but she'd made an excuse. It was agoraphobia, I think, and I had to admit it was hard to picture her in the crowds of Rome, away from her castle, which provided her with a suitable dramatic backdrop. Now that I was in her life, I think she hated the castle a little less, since it no longer served as a reminder of what she'd lost. We had agreed to go visit her there this weekend. She and my mother were still hardly the best of friends, and their conversations over the phone were awkward and painful, but both were still willing to make an effort. I hoped things might become less strained between them.

Paul popped his head into the apartment just as I was about to go peek into the bedrooms. I'd asked him to come, to get his opinion.

"Am I too late?"

"No. We're still poking around."

I frowned as I walked through the bedrooms. There were three, but I'd been told there were only two. We needed two so my mother could finally have her own, and sleep in peace. Lulu had a habit of kicking. But three bedrooms would stretch the budget too far.

"Excuse me, ma'am, I think there's been a mistake. The listing said two bedrooms. You've shown us the wrong apartment." I couldn't conceal my disappointment. The place was perfect, and I'd fallen for it.

She smiled at me. "We'll look at the two-bedroom next. I wanted you to see this one first."

"I can't afford three bedrooms," I said woefully, switching to English for Paul's benefit.

He approached me then, smelling of soap and cotton, his shirt soft against my cheek as he pulled me into an embrace. My whole body glowed with love. When I was with him, it felt like everything in the world was going to turn out okay. He also felt like home.

"I asked her to show you this one. *We* can afford it."

He clasped my hands in his, and I gasped in surprise. Lulu crawled over and hugged his leg. "Leg ride! Leg ride!" she insisted, and Paul laughed and obliged by holding her hands and lifting her into the air with his foot. Her peals of giggles, and Paul's suggestion, filled me with so much joy I couldn't speak for a moment.

"Are you sure?"

"Never been surer about anything in my life." He grinned at me, that same toothy, square-jawed smile that had first won me over. It still caused a swoop in my belly.

"Okay. Let's do it."

We signed the paperwork on the spot. I could hardly believe it was real. I was giddy, and Lulu must have picked up on my mood, because she started running through all the rooms and singing.

After we got through the last page, Paul checked his watch. "We're due at the studio soon. I'll drive you over."

A wave of gratitude overcame me. I had a home, security, love. And the end of the movie was in spitting distance, promising to launch a new era for my career.

Heart pounding, I squeezed into Paul's little red car with my mother and Lulu, and we all headed to Cinecittà to finish filming the movie.

The soundstage at Cinecittà Studios looked so much like the castle that I shuddered as I approached. A week away in the yellow Roman sunshine, and I'd almost forgotten its sense of claustrophobia, its moldering dampness. But here were the plaster walls, draped for this scene excessively with spiderwebs, an antique four-poster bed with a ratty green velvet canopy, a severe wooden door.

Except when I looked up, the walls ended abruptly, and the distant ceiling was not the castle's, but equipped with the industrial beams and lights of a modern movie studio. My breathing grew easier as I approached the bed and climbed in, preparing for the scene where the priest and Bernard would attempt to banish the witch. The actor playing the priest already stood beside the bed, as did Terrence, wearing his usual sneer.

"Remember, when the witch approaches, we must see your attitude transform slowly—from fear and revulsion to pity. We must recognize the exact moment Bianca lets the witch in." Paul squeezed my hand, and then kissed it. It had taken a short while to sort everything out after Mr. Günther's disappearance. But he'd persuaded the producer to let him finish directing the picture. It hadn't taken much convincing; he was the obvious choice. Securing additional financing to finish shooting at Cinecittà rather than the castle and to get Terrence for a few more days had been slightly more complicated, but it had come out all right in the end. The press around Mr. Günther's past, far from ruining the picture, had only helped our cause. The scandal and the real-life mystery had created intrigue that aided our publicity efforts. And now that Paul was in charge of the final cut, audiences would be able to watch without giving Mr. Günther credit for the result.

Terrence and Lucrezia had helped with publicity, too, by getting photographed kissing outside of the Piper Club a few days before. Lucrezia was ecstatic to be in all the gossip columns. We'd become even closer friends after our fight and Herman's disappearance. The drama had bonded us, like fellow survivors of a disaster.

She was thrilled we were finishing the picture in Rome, of course. Gabriella had declined Paul's offer for more money to finish shooting at the castle. We were over schedule, and she had no obligation to accept. I knew her real reason. She didn't want anyone around, in case the lake should choose to divulge its most recent secret. So far, though, Mr. Günther had stayed hidden. When I thought of the sickly, sinister water that had claimed him, I sensed he would remain so.

Before he departed to stand behind the camera, Paul leaned over to whisper in my ear. "Everything that happened—use it." He smiled at me, knowing and a little sad.

I settled myself into the covers, my throat constricting. I allowed the terror of my confrontation with Mr. Günther to wash over me, as I waited for Lucrezia to appear with bated breath.

It would not be the ending Mr. Günther envisioned. In Paul's version, a fragment of the witch's spirit would remain within Bianca. The final scene, now, wouldn't be her white wedding with Bernard. It would be them on their honeymoon, Bianca walking toward Bernard in his lounge chair wearing a racy red bikini, looking confident and sensuous. Bernard would watch her approach with a glimmer of fear in his eyes, his smile slightly off-kilter.

A better ending, one that revealed the true reason men found the witch frightening. She represented the impure woman, one whom they couldn't control.

My mother, Gabriella, me—she was all of us. She was real.

Paul's version would embrace her rather than reject her, forcing audiences to confront their own discomfort with her. It was an ending that stuck with you, like a thorn in your side. It made the movie memorable, and elevated it beyond cheap thrills.

And I was determined to do it justice. After all, I understood it all too well.

I'd been having nightmares every night since Mr. Günther's death, visions of his bloody face and sightless eyes, of dark waters that sucked you down. But I couldn't change the past, even if I wished to. What was done was done.

It was the same for Gabriella, and my mother. They couldn't erase the years of estrangement, or undo the choices they'd made.

The door creaked open, and Lucrezia stepped through, beautiful and sad, her eyes pleading. I allowed my expression to evolve as Paul had instructed, from terror to gradual acceptance.

Because in the end, none of us can vanquish our sin.

We can only learn to live with it.

CHAPTER 36

I stepped out of the red convertible onto the sidewalk in front of the Hotel Excelsior. The premiere of *The Revenge of the Lake Witch* had been at Fiamma Cinema just down the street, but stars, Lucrezia had told me, laughing, didn't walk.

And we were stars. I'd barely allowed myself to hope for such a thing, but by now, Lucrezia wasn't the only one being photographed for *Lo Specchio*. The press had taken an interest in me, as well. And the film, which I'd just seen in its entirety for the first time, was wonderful. It had been strange watching myself on screen, and slightly surreal. The movie clearly riveted the audience, who gasped and screamed in all the right places. It seemed destined to be a hit.

I wore a sleeveless, form-fitting pink-sequined evening dress, and necks of passersby craned to watch me. Paul squeezed my hand in his, and he stared at me, too, looking dazzled. In a tuxedo, he was pretty dazzling himself, his windblown blond hair spilling over his forehead, his white smile creasing his tan cheeks.

The street buzzed with Romans out on their *passeggiata* and tired but smartly dressed American tourists with cameras dangling by their sides. The air smelled of car exhaust and cigarettes. Bright neon lights advertised the famous cafés, the same ones where I'd been unable to land a job. Well, my days of waiting tables were over, and of playing sassy secretaries, too. I could hardly believe it.

I remembered so clearly the first time I'd seen the *paparazzi* outside the Hotel Excelsior, when I'd just arrived to the city, scared and broke. Now I was headed inside to the tony Caffè Doney for an exclusive after-party. I blinked as a camera bulb flashed in my eyes.

Tonight, the *paparazzi* were here for me.

ACKNOWLEDGMENTS

As an aspiring author, I always loved reading the acknowledgment sections of books I admired. When we first start out as writers, it's often a solitary endeavor, and I read the names of all the people being thanked covetously.

I'm happy to say that I've found my people. First, I'm so grateful to my agent, Danielle Egan-Miller, whose name I first discovered in an acknowledgments section and decided to query. She plucked me out of the slush pile, decided to give me a chance, and then proceeded to make a lifelong dream come true. Your guidance has made my work incalculably better. To her and the entire Brown & Miller team (special shoutout to Eleanor Roth Imbody): thank you.

To the Kensington publishing team: thank you for seeing something in my work and for bringing my books to life. I'm so fortunate they found a home here. To my editor, John Scognamiglio: I'm so appreciative of your brilliant feedback.

To my writing group, which has existed in various incarnations, and with various levels of attention paid to actual writing, over the years: you're the best. You've become some of my closest friends and none of this would be nearly as much fun without you. Thanks to Carolyn Kylstra for first inviting me into the fold way back in 2011, and to Hannah Howard, Jess Manners, Yelena Schuster, Desiree Byker Abiri, and Simon Morris, for your advice and encouragement. Extra-special thanks to Kate Fridkis Berring, my closest critique partner and writing partner in crime, for being there to commiserate or cheer for all the ups and downs of this roller coaster. This never would have happened without you.

As the wife of a teacher, I'd be remiss not to thank some of the educators who influenced me over the years: Sharon Stout, Patricia Fels, David Maisel, Cynthia Huntington, Ernest Hebert, Thomas O'Malley, Roger Ulrich, and Jeremy Rutter.

To my sister, Emily: not many writers can boast having a sibling who is a bona fide librarian, and I'm so lucky to have you. To my parents, thank you for being entertained rather than alarmed by the scary stories I told as a little kid, even when all the characters died. Your steadfast belief in me over the years has given me the confidence to keep going. How wonderful to be born into a family that loves books. We may not choose our family, but if we could, I'd choose you every time. To my in-laws, Ann and Brian, thank you for your unwavering support (and all the childcare help!).

Steve: you've probably read this book more times than anyone, and it is so much better because of you. You, Walden, and Cecilia are my world and I love you all more than words can express.

THE WOMAN IN THE CASTELLO

ABOUT THIS GUIDE

The suggested questions are included to enhance your group's reading of Kelsey James's *The Woman in the Castello*!

7. Silvia has cut Lulu's father out of her life and relates to Gabriella falling for the wrong man—to a degree. Do you empathize with Gabriella at all?

8. Silvia tells Elena: "I'll always put you first, Mama. You and Lulu." In what ways does she have to sacrifice for her family? Do her personal desires and her duty ever come into conflict, and how does she handle it? How do we see this play out in her romantic relationship in the book?

9. Silvia says that we can't vanquish our sin, but can only learn to live with it. The "right" choice isn't always obvious for the characters in this book, and Gabriella, Elena, and Silvia all harbor regrets. Are there any decisions they made that you would have made differently? Have you ever found yourself in a situation where you struggled to know what to do?

10. Elena wonders if some things are unforgivable. What do you think? Did any of the characters behave in a way that you wouldn't have been able to forgive?

Discussion Questions

1. Gabriella became an actress because she wanted to be famous, while Silvia became one to support her family. How else are these characters different? In what ways are they alike?

2. Silvia is desperate for money when she first arrives at Castello del Lago and trapped by her circumstances. How might that have contributed to her perception of the town and castle? Has your emotional state ever influenced how you feel about a place?

3. Did the political polarization Silvia observed in Italy feel relatable to you? How did politics impact Silvia's family? How do they impact your own?

4. Silvia tells us: "Until now, I'd been so focused on getting parts, on scraping by, that I hadn't spared much thought for greatness." How do her feelings about fame evolve over the course of the book?

5. Herman wants Bianca's character to remain pure and virginal. Silvia, who is an unwed mother, wants Bianca to be tempted by the witch, and by her desires. Why do you think Silvia feels that way? Which version of Bianca do you like better?

6. Elements from *The Revenge of the Lake Witch* begin to seep into Silvia's reality—and vice versa. For example, Bianca is haunted by the ghost of the witch, just as Silvia seems to be haunted by the ghost from Gabriella's story. What did you think of these parallels? How did they impact your understanding of the characters and story? Were there any ways in which you found this book relatable to your own life?